The Scientific Romances of
J.-H. Rosny Aîné

THE GIVREUSE ENIGMA
And Other Stories

also by Brian Stableford:
The Empire of the Necromancers: 1. The Shadow of Frankenstein.
2. Frankenstein and the Vampire Countess
Sherlock Holmes and the Vampires of Eternity
The Stones of Camelot
The Wayward Muse

also translated and introduced by Brian Stableford:
Sâr Dubnotal vs. Jack the Ripper
News from the Moon – The Germans on Venus (*anthologies*)
by Félix Bodin: The Novel of the Future
by André Caroff: The Terror of Madame Atomos
by Charles Derennes: The People of the Pole
by Henri Duvernois: The Man Who Found Himself
by Paul Féval: Anne of the Isles – The Black Coats: 'Salem Street;
The Invisible Weapon; The Parisian Jungle; The Companions of the
Treasure; Heart of Steel – John Devil – Knightshade – Revenants –
Vampire City – The Vampire Countess – The Wandering Jew's
Daughter
by Paul Féval, fils: Felifax, the Tiger-Man
by Octave Joncquel & Théo Varlet: The Martian Epic
by Jean de La Hire: The Nyctalope vs. Lucifer – The Nyctalope on
Mars – Enter the Nyctalope
by Georges Le Faure & Henri de Graffigny: The Extraordinary Adventures of a Russian Scientist Across the Solar System (2 vols.)
by Gustave Le Rouge: The Vampires of Mars
by Jules Lermina: Panic in Paris – Mysteryville
by Marie Nizet: Captain Vampire
by Henri de Parville: An Inhabitant of the Planet Mars
by Gaston de Pawlowski: Journey to the Land of the 4th Dimension
by P.-A. Ponson du Terrail: The Vampire and the Devil's Son
by Maurice Renard: Doctor Lerne – A Man Among the Microbes –
The Blue Peril – The Doctored Man – The Master of Light
by Albert Robida: The Clock of the Centuries – The Adventures of
Saturnin Farandoul
by J.-H. Rosny Aîné: The Navigators of Space – The World of the
Variants – The Mysterious Force – Vamireh – The Givreuse Enigma
by Kurt Steiner: Ortog
by Villiers de l'Isle-Adam: The Scaffold – The Vampire Soul

The Scientific Romances of
J.-H. Rosny Aîné

THE GIVREUSE ENIGMA
And Other Stories

translated, annotated and introduced by
Brian Stableford

A Black Coat Press Book

Acknowledgements: I should like to thank John J. Pierce for providing valuable research materials and offering advice and support. Many of the copies of Rosny's works and critical articles related to his work were borrowed from the London Library. Also thanks to Paul Wessels for his generous and extensive help in the final preparation of this text.

Visit our website at www.blackcoatpress.com

Table of Contents

Introduction

This is the fifth volume of a six-volume collection of stories by J.-H. Rosny *Aîné* ("the Elder"), which includes all of his scientific romances, plus a number of other stories that have some relevance to his work in that genre.[1]

The contents of the six volumes are:

Volume 1. THE NAVIGATORS OF SPACE AND OTHER ALIEN ENCOUNTERS: The Xipehuz, The Skeptical Legend, Another World, The Death of the Earth, The Navigators of Space, The Astronauts.

Volume 2. THE WORLD OF THE VARIANTS AND OTHER STRANGE LANDS: Nymphaeum, The Depths of Kyamo, The Wonderful Cave Country, The Voyage, The Great Enigma, The Treasure in the Snow, The Boar Men, In the World of the Variants.

Volume 3. THE MYSTERIOUS FORCE AND OTHER ANOMALOUS PHENOMENA: The Cataclysm, The Mysterious Force, Hareton Ironcastle's Amazing Adventure.

Volume 4. VAMIREH AND OTHER PREHISTORIC FANTASIES: Vamireh, Eyrimah, Nomaï.

Volume 5. THE GIVREUSE ENIGMA AND OTHER STORIES: Mary's Garden, The Givreuse Enigma, Adventure in the Wild.

Volume 6. THE YOUNG VAMPIRE AND OTHER CAUTIONARY TALES: The Witch, The Young Vampire, The Supernatural Assassin, Companions of the Universe.

The first volume of the series includes a long general introduction to Rosny's life and works, which there is no need to

---

[1] *Le Félin géant* (*The Giant Cat* a.k.a. *Quest of the Dawn Man*) and *Helgvor du fleuve bleu* (*Helgvor of the Blue River*) will be reprinted in their original English translations in a seventh volume.

repeat here; the following introduction will therefore be limited to a brief account of the stories included in this volume, which will be supplemented by a more detailed commentary contained in an afterword.

The three stories collected in this volume are not thematically connected, as the stories in each of the first four volumes were, and there is a sense in which this volume merely picks up oddments that continue or digress from the themes established in the first three of those volumes. "Le Jardin de Mary" (here translated as "Mary's Garden") was presumably published in a periodical before being reprinted in the Plon collection *Resurrection* (1895), but I have been unable to trace or date its original publication. It is, however, undoubtedly an early work—a product of the same "passion for science" that produced "La Légende sceptique" (1889; tr. in vol. 1 as "The Skeptical Legend").

One of the projects that Rosny recalled working on during his first year in Paris, 1885, was entitled *Le Livre étoilé* [The Starry Book], and that title was included in a list of books that Albert Savine apparently planned to publish, before changing his mind; one is tempted to wonder whether "Le Jardin de Mary" might not be a fragment escaped from that book, but there is no way to know. If it is, the novel in question might well have been akin to Camille Flammarion's *Stella* (1877), which describes the education of a female visionary in the science of astronomy. The materialist Rosny would inevitably have avoided the naked mysticism of the latter novel's ending in favor of the subtler quality of the terminus described here. Mary's final assertion presumably refers to Rosny's notion of "planetary physiology," as expressed in "La Légende sceptique," rather than to Flammarion's notion of cosmic palingenesis, introduced in *Lumen* (1867-69 in periodicals; 1872 in *Récits de l'infini*; expanded for separate publication in 1887) and popularized in *Rêves étoilé* (1888) and *Uranie* (1889). Even if Rosny's story is not directly derived from the ill-fated *Livre étoilé*, it presumably sprang from the same

8

source of inspiration, and represents Rosny's most straightforward literary extrapolation of his enduring fascination with the starry sky.

The publication of *L'Enigme de Givreuse* (here translated as "The Givreuse Enigma") by Ernest Flammarion—Camille's brother—in 1917 was probably also belated. After Plon's publication of the book version of *La Force mystérieuse* (1914; tr. in vol. 3 as "The Mysterious Force"), which had appeared as a serial in 1913, Rosny had not succeeded in publishing any new books for an interval of three years, presumably because of the effects of the Great War. He began publishing again in 1917 when Flammarion issued a novel directly concerned with the war, which might be regarded as a propaganda piece, *Perdus?* [Doomed?], quickly following it up with *L'Enigme de Givreuse*, which also contains a morale-boosting episode in which a French inventor develops a new weapon and deploys it heroically in an attack on a German submarine. That episode is entirely gratuitous, however, and was probably inserted into a pre-existing manuscript in order to make the novel publishable in war-time.

If one ignores the gratuitous insertion, the content and form of *L'Enigme de Givreuse* strongly suggest that it must have been started as an exercise in the subgenre of "scientific marvel fiction" identified by Maurice Renard, who had tried hard in the years before the war to persuade Rosny that he was a significant pioneer of that kind of fiction, and to persuade Rosny to write more of it; *L'Enigme de Givreuse* was probably the third result of that persuasion, after "La Mort de la Terre" (1910; tr. in vol. 1 as "The Death of the Earth") and *La Force mystérieuse*, and might have been started, if not actually completed, in the latter months of 1914, when the early events described in the story are set. It is the most theoretically-adventurous of Rosny's scientific marvel stories, although the author evidently became more interested, while in the process of writing it, in the unusual existential predicament thrust upon its protagonist.

La Sauvage aventure, published by Albin Michel in 1935, was the final version of Rosny's most oft-repeated plot formula—featuring the abduction of a woman by a human of a different race, occasioning a pursuit by her own people—which he had first employed in "Nymphée" (1893; tr. in vol. 2 as "Nymphaeum") and repeated many times over in stories translated in the earlier volumes of this series. Here the story is presented as a straightforward exercise in pulp fiction, probably in response to the fact that Rosny's final prehistoric romance *Helgvor du fleuve bleu* (1930; tr. as "Helgvor of the Blue River") had been translated in the US pulp magazine *Argosy*. It may well have been written in a hurry, based for convenience on the near-identical plot of "Les Hommes-Sangliers" (1929; tr. in vol. 2 as "The Boar Men"), but substituting a different conclusion a little more suited to pulp romance.

If *La Sauvage aventure* was an attempt to get back into the US pulp market, however, it failed, and the novel remained untranslated until now. Some bibliographical lists give the date of its original publication as 1932, but I have been unable to trace any serial version issued in that year. It is perhaps the least satisfactory of all Rosny's exotic adventure stories, if only because everything in it is second-hand, giving it the appearance of an exercise in self-plagiarism, but its inclusion here rounds out that aspect of his work and serves to re-emphasize the mysterious force that drew him back to the formula so insistently.

The version of "Le Jardin de Mary" that I used for translation is the one contained in the 1975 Marabout omnibus of Rosny's speculative fiction, *Récits de science-fiction*. The versions of the other two texts that I used were the first editions in volume form.

Brian Stableford

MARY'S GARDEN

As Mary approached death she entered into a lucid delirium, in which she became a child again, with all sorts of old beliefs that had vanished over time. Then she said to the man who loved her: "Let's go see the garden in which I shall dwell."

The man who loved her knew perfectly well that she was talking about the firmament, and burst into tears. But Mary insisted so strongly that the doctor thought it best that she go to see the sky that was causing him such grief.

The little rooftop observatory where Mary had studied the stars was warmed up, and the dying woman was taken to it. The glass walls were so transparent that one might think that one was in the open air, and Mary propped herself up on her elbow to study her garden.

The air was marvelous; the delightful infinity was full of little points of light. The Milky Way displayed its fine gauze, sown with constellations. The quaternaries of Sagitta were hanging low in the west, ready to set. Cygnus traced its cross against the milky background, and Cassiopeia its Y. Perseus gathered his stars, Auriga his pentagon, in which the superb diamond of Capricorn threw forth its fire. Very low, in the south-south-east Monoceros was extended, a white asterism between Procyon, the Gemini and the dazzling Orion.[2]

---

[2] Rosny gives most of these constellations their common names rather than Latin names, but many of those common names do not translate directly into English, so I have used the Latin names, many of which are familiar to lovers of horoscopes. The reference to "the diamond" of Capricorn is puzzling, as that constellation has no very bright stars; Rosny's other works often refer to "the diamond of Cygnus" (Deneb)

Nothing was moving. The Earth's heat was radiating away, and an intense frost made the snow on the roof glitter. Mary's eyes shone very brightly; a little blue scarf rendered her angelic face even whiter. She smiled at her beautiful garden and put her hands together, then continued her voyage.

She had moved out of the Milky Way; she wandered among the blue surfaces. She travelled through the stars of the hyperborean regions. Ursa Major and Ursa Minor dragged their tails there, Draco uncoiling between them and lifted its head toward Hercules; the ravishing Vega, the blue pupil of the north, palpitated over Lyra.

"Dear, dear Vega!" sighed Mary.

She remained magnetized for a few moments by the star, as it sent the long threads of its radiance into redoubtable spaces—and, in the night full of peace, her sweet reverie and her dying enthusiasm seemed to loom over the white roofs, the square and the trees like a blessing.

She idled slowly as she descended westwards. From the scattered stars of Delphinus she passed the pale constellation of Equuleus, and from Aquarius she climbed back toward the zenith via the superb Pegasus, whose immense square dominated the corner of Pisces.

Then she paused briefly. In the pure blue, the marvelous Mira Ceti shone, at the apogee of its magnificence. Mary sang "Twinkle, twinkle, little star" in a voice so weak that the man who loved her had to hide his face; then she went up to the zenith again, via Aries and Triangulum, and reached Andromeda and Perseus, in a swarm of stars, and finally the great region of fire. The primaries accumulated, their red and white light overlapping. The red eye of Taurus, Aldebaran, trembled gently against the golden background of five tertiaries. The splendid belt stars[3] stood out in the center of Orion, whose

---

and it is possible that this passage was slightly muddled in the publication process.

[3] Rosny refers to Orion's belt stars as the "Trois-Rois" [Three Kings]; although that designation is not common in French, it

giant rectangle extended, brightened by Betelgeuse and the double star Rigel. Then, in profusion, Procyon, Pollux, Castor and Capella opened their radiant corollas on the dark beach, amid the bright stream of their constellations.

Then, paler still, Mary felt her enthusiasm mount, an enthusiasm of light, of the divine palpitation of infinity. It was as if she were giving way beneath the immeasurable weight of the stars, while her bosom caused the blonde lace of her corsage to tremble gently.

"Look," she murmured. "My brightest flower is about to rise!"

She pointed to the south-east. Lepus had leapt. A gleam fringed the line of the horizon. Two quaternaries were positioned on the edge of the Milky Way, and Sirius emerged. Shivering, Mary watched it climbing the blue slope for some time. Sirius! The finest of the gems of space, white with a bluish tint, which takes 14 years to send us a little sapphire quiver!

"How beautiful it is!" said Mary, taking my hand. "I'd like to go while gazing at it, with your head against mine."

I put my head next to hers, and I heard something terrible coming, which comes to the Earth incessantly. But she murmured: "All that is so far away, you see, and yet so close that we can see it with our feeble eyes. That's why, my dear friend, my dear lover, it's necessary to believe that nothing is foreign to us. *There are no other worlds*; all of this is in contact. If one is so afraid to leave, it's because any parting is sad, and this is the greatest of all departures. But you will come; nothing is more certain."

She continued wandering, with a profound gentleness, and I felt that I was becoming a child again, in spite of the *something* that was still drawing nearer.

"Give me a kiss," she said.

---

had been used—adapted from its German/Dutch equivalents— by Alphonse Daudet in *Lettres de Mon Moulin* (1866).

I gave her a kiss, with all my heart, and then she murmured, in a breath: "Au revoir!"

She had gone, and I was dreaming through my sobbing, that *all of this* was indeed *in contact*, and that I really was much closer to Sirius, much closer to the most distant nebula, than to the child that I loved.

THE GIVREUSE ENIGMA

Part One

One evening in the first half of September 1914, four stretcher-bearers were crossing the heath of the Loup Rouge. Darkness was falling, formidable and terrific. Between the sky and the ground it was Hell; a furnace of sulfur and blood was disclosed in the clouds. Man-made thunder growled beyond the hills, shaking the trees to their roots and the rocks to their depths. The stretcher-bearers were coming back from the field-hospital and returning to the killing-ground. One of them mopped his brow and murmured: "They've all been picked up."

"We've advanced again," replied his companion.

There was horror on the heath. The blood formed pools, coagulating amid the grass. Cadavers were extended, peaceful and sinister. Suddenly, a hand was raised beneath a tree-stump and a feeble plaint was heard.

"One that wasn't noticed!" said the one who had spoken last. He went to the stump.

A soldier was looking round, dazedly. He was a tall man, whose face was scarcely muddied by the shell-fire. His hair was reminiscent of the color of ripe oats and his moustache that of spelt straw; he had large jade-colored eyes, feminine cheeks and a high forehead sharply angled at the temples. Black blood was drying on his skull.

"It's all right," said the stretcher-bearer, "someone's here."

The man did not reply. His eyes were misted; he seemed to be about to fall asleep.

"Not a good sign," the stretcher-bearer went on. "Hey, Charlet, are we taking him?"

Charlet, however, was going toward a tall clump of bracken, attracted by some clue. "Another!" he muttered. He had perceived the other one at the same time as the man discovered by his comrade, through a gap in the bracken. The dusk had scarcely begun to gather; the air was diaphanous.

Charlet looked at the two wounded men and remarked: "One might think that they were related." Then, with increasing astonishment, he added: "It's quite extraordinary. They must be twins! Come on then, Henriquet!"

A red-haired stretcher-bearer came over to the two wounded men in his turn and declared, with conviction: "They're twins, and no mistake!"

The second wounded man reproduced the features of the first identically; he too had clotted blood in his hair. His jade-colored eyes were misted by a dream, and one might have thought that he was about to fall asleep.

"That's rare!" Charlet observed.

"Right! What about their identity tags? Let's see: Givreuse, Edouard-Henri-Pierre. And the other?"

"I can't find anything—his tag's been removed."

"That's okay," said Henriquet. "We'll find out later. Time's pressing—let's not dawdle. It seems to me that they ought to be kept together."

Henriquet and Charlet loaded the man from the tree-stump on to their stretcher, while the other two loaded up the man from the bracken. There was no indication that the wounded men were conscious of what was happening.

The little company left the heath and went through the grounds of Grantaigle. The château's two towers were visible, one of them collapsed. A chapel raised its thin steeple in front of a copper and aquamarine cloud. A look-out post was dangling from the crumbling, smoking walls. A flock of crows fled over blue beeches while flames scaled the debris. One of the stretcher-bearers, who was an educated man, murmured: "One would think we were in the times of Philippe-Auguste."

They went past the château; the field-hospital—a large shed and some huts—appeared at the far end of a field, on the edge of a small village. Plaints rose up, punctuated with a wild clamor, and the scent of rotting flesh spread around, mingled with less precise odors.

On the threshold of the first hut, a medical orderly barred the way. "Full up! The hut's bursting. Over there, look—the sixth should still have space…"

At the "sixth" a corpulent doctor was washing his hands in a bowl. Large folds of flesh hung down from his slack jaws. "It'll be the death of us!" he cried, on seeing the new arrivals.

"It's one case," Alexandre observed, softly. "Twins, Major."

"What do you want me to…?"

"All the same, it's rare that one sees the like on a battlefield."

The major turned his surly gaze to the two soldiers, distractedly at first, and then more attentively. "They're as similar as two of the 69th's shells!" he muttered. "Where did you pick them up?"

"On the heath, near the Château de Grantaigle."

"I didn't know…"

"Thirty paces apart…"

The major leaned over each of the men in turn. "There's a difference, though. One's face seems slightly...very slightly…longer than the other's."

"Do you think so?" said Charlet.

A tall, slender woman approached, like an oread in her white uniform. She studied the two wounded men with an alarm that gradually became intense. "One would think that they had *the same wound* on their heads," she said, uncertainly.

The doctor parted the blood-matted hair as best he could, and became pensive. "It's fantastic! One would think that two identical pieces of shrapnel had struck in the same place."

There was a pause. The major seemed ill-at-ease. The stretcher-bearers looked at one another vaguely and the woman put her hands together in a mechanical gesture.

"No, it's not natural!" sighed the stretcher-bearer named Alexandre, finally.

"Everything's natural!" said the doctor, impatiently. "Let's go—we have to get them inside."

There were only two free beds, one near the entrance and the other at the far end of the hut. The wounded men were undressed, without either of them emerging from their semi-lethargy.

"He's also got a wounded tibia," remarked the woman who resembled an oread. She was standing beside the one who had been installed near the door; she was washing his face gently.

At the back of the room, Major Herbelle was examining the second casualty. The skull fracture was quite serious. A bullet had broken the tibia, seven or eight centimeters below the knee. "This torpor," Herbelle soliloquized, "doesn't seem to be a consequence of the wounds. It's true, though, that an explosion…the war will produce a great many nervous disorders…" He gave orders for the wounds to be bandaged, and headed for the other. "Nothing other than the skull fracture?" he asked.

"A bullet's gone through the left tibia," replied an aide.

"The left tibia!" cried Herbelle, in consternation.

"Yes, six or seven centimeters below the knee."

"That's impossible!"

"Why?" asked the young man, involuntarily.

"Because the other also has a tibia split by a bullet, and…" The major's eyes expressed a sort of religious horror. Leaning over the soldier, he groaned: "It's *the same* wound…*the same*…"

"Just like the skull," sighed the nurse.

The man and the woman dared not look at one another. The prodigy was manifest. It filled Herbelle with repugnance and caused the tall nurse to bow her head.

"We're dreaming!" whispered the doctor, his mouth marking his rebellion.

"We're dealing with a higher reality!" affirmed the woman.

"If they would just wake up," said the major, naively, "we could find out..."

"Their identity-papers!"

"Of course!"

Three minutes later, Herbelle held two sets of identity-papers, which resembled all military identity-papers, but which nevertheless filled the hearts of the woman and the two men with a kind of fear. *They were absolutely identical.* Each of them referred to Edouard-Henri-Pierre de Givreuse, born at Avranches on March 17, 1889. Each of them recorded a height of 1.74 meters, and advertized the nth company of the nth infantry division.

"It's the same identification!" Herbelle concluded.

"But no authority would have consented to give two identical sets of identity-papers to different individuals!" observed the young man.

"Unless the authority was deceived, at least," retorted the major, in a voice impregnated with a strange bitterness. He leafed through the papers feverishly, searching for some difference, but found none. On the contrary; a small ink-stain was identically reproduced in both documents. But what can it mean?" Herbelle moaned, putting his fists to his temples. "Of what supernatural trickery are we victims?"

"So you admit that it's supernatural?" said the nurse.

"Oh! No, I don't admit anything...I don't know anything...I must be hypnotized."

The young man scrutinized the documents in his turn. "The paper's well-worn," he murmured. "The sheets are scarcely holding together."

"Ah!" exclaimed the major. "Does one appear to be older than the other?"

"My word, no. They're equally fragile."

"If they were false, at least—that would be a relief..."

"Aren't there any men from the same regiment here?" asked the nurse.

"Not in this hut—but surely in one of the others…"

At that moment the wounded man opened his eyes. He looked at the people standing next to his bed in puzzlement, then voiced the plaint of all men in pain: "I'm thirsty!"

The nurse lifted his head and helped him to drink. He swallowed greedily at first, then with a weary slowness. Little by little his gaze cleared. "Am I wounded?" he asked.

The major and the nurse looked at him in bewilderment. "Yes you're wounded."

"Ah!" He seemed thoughtful. At intervals, his lips trembled and his eyelids fluttered slightly. Eventually, he whispered: "I remember…I fell in the forest…"

"On the heath!" the doctor corrected.

"The heath? No—in the forest, near the edge. We were beating a retreat. A shell-burst struck me in the head…but I carried on going…I think I dragged myself…and then…" A deep crease formed between his eyelids. "Then…let's see… where did I get to? I don't know any more…" His voice weakened; his eyes clouded over again.

"Your name is Pierre de Givreuse," said the doctor, hastily. "You were born in Avranches in 1889?"

"That's right. My name is Pierre de Givreuse."

At the far end of the hut, the aide was making signs. "Do you have a brother?"

The pale face showed surprise. "A brother? Me?"

"Yes—a brother who looks like you."

"I'm an only son." He released a long sigh. His eyelids fluttered, then closed.

"It's terrifying!" said Herbelle, passing his hand over his forehead.

"It's not terrifying," replied the nurse, making the sign of the cross. "It's a higher reality…"

The major had just caught sight of the aide's signs. He hurried to the far end of the hut. The other Givreuse still had his eyes open, but they were already misting over.

"Is your name Pierre de Givreuse?" exclaimed Herbelle.

The question appeared to revive the wounded man slightly. "Yes," he replied, "Pierre de Givreuse."

"Born in Avranches in 1889."

"Yes."

"Do you have a brother?"

The wounded man appeared to make a considerable effort to think; in a drowsy voice he muttered: "I have no brother...no brother!" His eyelids were closing.

"Try to remember!" Herbelle demanded—but Givreuse made no reply.

An hour later, Herbelle brought two slightly-wounded soldiers from the nth regiment to the bedside of the first Givreuse. "Do you know this man?" he asked.

"He's only in my company!" one of the men replied. "He's a pal—a good bloke. His name's Givreuse."

The major turned to the other soldier. "What about you?"

"No mistake, sir, that's for sure. He's not in my company, but I know him well—I've hung out with him."

"But there's another Givreuse in the same company?"

"Another?" exclaimed the first infantryman. "Well, he's invisible then—I've never seen him."

"Nor me!"

"You've never heard mention of a second Givreuse who resembles this one?"

"No, never."

Herbelle shook his head sadly, then said: "Follow me."

He led the men to the second Givreuse. "Look!"

They stood there open-mouthed. "You could knock me down with a feather!" muttered the man from the same company as Givreuse. "It's the same man. A double!"

"A double!" repeated the other.

Herbelle said nothing.

The two soldiers murmured "Oh!" and "Well!" repeatedly; then the first declared; "It's too much for me...but perhaps he's in another regiment."

Herbelle had them taken back to their hut. Something re-doubtable had been added to the universe, and the doctor stood still for a long time, paralyzed by the dream, enveloped by a strange shadow in which there was a glimmer of the Abyss.

II.

They remained unconscious for 60 hours. They were transported to Gavres, to a hospital where their presence pro-duced a strange emotion, which bordered on fear in a few of the women. For various reasons, Major Formental did not in-stall them in the same room. Their case interested and shocked him. This was a duplicate man. In the magnificent and horrible mystery of life, he saw a definite end—death without after-math—but he was nevertheless religious at heart. By contrast, the head nurse, Louise de Bréhannes, had an indomitable and immutable faith stripped bare of mysticism.

On the Tuesday morning, Louise de Bréhannes and For-mental met up at the bedside of one of the two Givreuses. They had called him Givreuse I in order to distinguish him from the other, who had become Givreuse II. The soldier re-mained motionless, unconscious to human presence, voices and light. His sleep was profound; he was breathing regularly and effortlessly; the rhythmic movement of his breast was visible.

"Temperature 37.1," said Louise de Bréhannes, "pulse 75."

"I don't understand," said Formental, pensively. "Such an abnormal torpor shouldn't be accompanied by so normal a state."

"It's simply a good sign," affirmed Louise de Bréhannes. "The true cure of rest..." She wore an austere smile. A tall woman with flinty eyes, a jutting nose and shiny lips, she had a tyrannical manner.

Two young nurses were standing a short distance away. They were anxious. One of them murmured: "Long sleep often follows reincarnation..." Her name was Diane Montmaure; she was an occultist in whom shreds of evangelism persisted.

Formental heard her, and replied: "If Herbelle's report is accurate—and the official documents support it—this is almost the opposite of a reincarnation..."

The occultist looked at the doctor. It was impossible to say exactly whether her hair was chestnut-colored or dark blonde; the play of light and shadow made the two shades alternate in their predominance.

Formental smiled wanly. "Thus far, the adventure surpasses both the classic supernatural and the classic natural."

"What do you mean by the classic supernatural?" asked Louise, rudely.

"I mean all catalogued religious and mystical facts, Madame."

Madame de Bréhannes started laughing silently. "What! On the contrary—the *Menechmes*... Sosie... We're dealing with the most classical natural and supernatural..."[4]

"I don't think so. Don't forget that the two men don't know one another at all, and that the soldiers of the nth regiment have only ever known one Givreuse—and yet, each of the Givreuses claims to have been born in Avranches in 1889, and their individual identity-papers are as identical as they are. Finally, that they have *absolutely identical wounds*."

---

[4] *The Menechmes*, or *The Twins*, is a comedy by Plautus, which served as the model for a play of the same title by Jean-François Regnard. Sosie is the valet of the eponymous protagonist of *Amphitryon*, another play by Plautus, whose plot was similarly recycled by Molière; the name became synonymous with that of a double because Sosie's features are duplicated in the play by Mercury in the course of carrying out a mission on Jupiter's behalf.

"Might not one be the other's *double*?" suggested Diane Montmaure, timidly.

"A double is, by definition, a sort of shadow. Here we have two bodies of the same kind."

"They're both extremely light," the other young woman put in. "The weight of a child!"

This remark made an impact on Formental. "They must be weighed," said Louise de Bréhannes. Formental gave the order. The trolleys that transited wounded men to the operating theater came to fetch the two Givreuses. They were weighed.

"37 kilos 200...37 kilos 215 grams," announced an aide named Charles.

"That's practically the same weight...and that is indeed an abnormal density—half of the expected density," said Formental feverishly. "Measure them, Charles."

Charles went to fetch a horizontal apparatus of American design, on which the two wounded men were extended in turn. "Slightly less than 1.74 meters," Charles pronounced.

Formental checked it carefully. "Yes, about two millimeters less. Let's check the other..."

"Almost exactly 1.74 meters," Charles soon replied. "A trifle more—one millimeter."

"The identity-papers register 1.74 meters. The slightest difference of position would be enough to explain the difference. They definitely have the same stature and the same weight...abnormal. The logic of the mystery—*the logic of the absurd*—is confirmed. And they're still asleep!"

"Because they haven't entirely quit the other world," murmured Diane Montmaure.

No one replied. Even Louise de Bréhannes was in a sort of trance, in which terrestrial life was fading into astral life.

III.

As the Sun was setting, Diane Montmaure was sitting by the bedside of Givreuse I. Mystical curiosity continually brought her back to it. She studied the wounded man's untroubled face ardently, thinking about the incommensurable darkness that surrounded the stars and living beings. She was no longer astonished. Did not the simplest life far surpass the feeble imagination of men?

Suddenly, she shuddered to the depths of her being; two large jade-colored eyes were looking at her. Then a sleepy voice stammered: "I'm an only son."

Bewildered, she asked: "Why are you telling me that?"

"Because someone asked me." The eyes fixed themselves momentarily on Diane's pale face, and then turned away. "Where's the major? I've been moved to a different room."

She leaned forward and replied, softly: "You're no longer in the field-hospital."

"I've been asleep, then?"

"You've been asleep."

"For how long?"

She hesitated, but it was impossible to avoid the question. "Two days."

"Two days!" he said, in alarm. "That's terrible. Oh, I know…it was my wounds—I was hit in the head and…where else?"

"In the leg."

"That's right—in the leg. Is it dangerous?"

"Oh, not at all."

"I'll be able to write, then?"

"In a little while."

"Just a few lines…to my mother…and…" He stopped short and looked at Diane. "You're quite sure? Not dangerous?"

"That's the doctor's opinion."

He paused. His face was still anxious, a trifle stiff and somewhat ghostly. "But that long sleep," he remarked. "That's bizarre. Why? I should be rested...but I'm tired, so very tired and weak!"

"That's natural."

"Natural? Perhaps. One might think, though, that something extraordinary has happened to me."

"Why?" she asked, avidly.

"I don't really know...it's just an impression. Everything seems so far away...so far away! Oh, prodigiously!"

"So far away...in space?"

"I don't know. It's as if there were a limitless interval between the moment when I was wounded and now..."

For a moment, they were both plunged into a dream. "I'd like a drink," he said, finally.

She gave him a drink. He drank avidly, but without voracity, then said: "Are we still winning?"

"We're winning."

He smiled, slowly and vaguely. "I thought the time had come and that France was going to die. What saved us? What force emerged from the depths? Or from the depths of men?"

His voice was weak, as if it were breaking up, but serious nevertheless, and possessed of an indefinable timbre, reminiscent of the sound of water falling into a distant abyss.

She could not help asking him: "You say that you're an only son?"

"That's right. I have no brother."

"Nor cousins...born, as you were, in Avranches?"

"I only have female cousins—little girls. The oldest is 13. Why are you asking me that?" She blushed in confusion; he did not notice. "It's just that the major, out there, asked me just as I was falling asleep...and it's bizarre. What interest can he have had?"

"What if someone had been found on the battlefield who resembles you greatly?"

"And who can't be identified?"

"Perhaps."

At that moment Dr. Formental appeared on the threshold of the room.

In the next room, Louise de Bréhannes was by the bedside of the other Givreuse. He had just woken up. A red-haired nurse was giving him a drink. When he had drunk, the invalid looked at the two women anxiously. Then he asked: "Have I been asleep? It seems to me that I'm in a different bed."

"You were at Viorne," Louise de Bréhannes replied, in her beautifully harsh voice. "You were brought here while you were asleep."

"I've been asleep for a long time, then?"

"Two days and two nights."

"Two days, Madame?"

"Two days."

"That's terrible. Why? Are my wounds serious?"

"No, you'll be on your feet in a fortnight."

"I'd like to inform my mother…"

"We'll write to her."

Like the other, the wounded man had an anxious expression, stiff and slightly ghostly. "I'm still very tired," he said, "in spite of that long sleep…"

"You've lost a lot of blood."

"There's no other reason?"

"No, since your wounds aren't dangerous."

"Is it really only my wounds? I feel that something prodigious is going on…"

"Ah!" she said. A curiosity different from that of Diane Montmaure, but just as avid, caused her to ask: "What sort of thing?"

"My memories are confused, like a fog. One might think that it had been a long time…a very long time…" Madame de Bréhannes' hard green eyes were fixed upon him. "I'm still thirsty," he said.

When he had had a drink, he remained thoughtful for some while, then said: "Are we a long way from the front?"

"About 300 kilometers."

"Are the Germans still retreating?"

"Yes."

"What a miracle!"

"It's God's doing!" she affirmed.

He did not reply. His eyelashes fluttered. A profound uncertainty clouded his gaze.

Louise de Bréhannes could not contain her curiosity any longer. "You have a brother, I believe?"

"Someone already asked me that. No, I don't have a brother."

"Or a relative who resembles you?"

"None—I don't have much family."

In the next room, Formental sounded Givreuse's chest with his stethoscope. He found no fever. The pulse was weak, the temperature normal. "Pure blood!" he muttered. The invalid's weakness was evident, however. "Are you hungry?"

"A little."

Formental was agitated. Amid the unleashing of ferocious forces, this incident acquired a mysteriously formidable significance. It was like a disdainful reply by the creative genius that quivers in the heart of things. He exchanged a glance with Diane Montmaure and, divining that she had already questioned the soldier, merely asked: "You're not in pain?"

"Apart from a singular impression of fragility and an inconvenient weariness, no…I'm not in pain."

Like the young nurse, the doctor was struck by that voice, more faint than indistinct, more distant and discontinuous than weak. "It's quite simple," he declared. "Remember that you haven't eaten anything for 60 hours and that you've lost a lot of blood. You won't feel like that for long." He made a discreet sign to Diane. She followed him. In the corridor,

28

they met Louise de Bréhannes and a young man, an intern from the Quinze-Vingts.[5]

"Is the other one awake too?"

Madame de Bréhannes nodded affirmatively. "That was fated."

All four of them went into the chief's den—a drab little white room with wretched chairs in each corner, sheltered from microbes and dreams.

"It's virtually unnecessary to question you," said the major, with a resigned smile. "They've confirmed everything they said *back there*."

Louise de Bréhannes and Diane Montmaure looked at one another. "Everything," said Louise, eventually. Diane nodded in acquiescence.

"Is that terrible or consoling?" murmured Formental, hoarsely. "I don't know. Here I am, open to any mysticism."

"Religion is sufficient!" said Louise, dryly.

"I don't think so," sighed Diane. "No definite religion, at least."

"Nor any faith at all," the young intern put in, softly. He had grown tall, with long arms with which he did not seem to know what to do, but which were singularly skilful. He resembled Pierre Curie. "And why invoke faith?"

"What do you mean?" said Louise, rudely.

"Excuse me, Madame," he replied, bowing. "I mean that facts have always confounded the imagination. For example, however extravagant a philosopher or a storyteller might be, don't the most humble phenomena surpass him? Nature never ceases to demonstrate that it has no regard for logic—but every time it strikes down one of our theories, we hasten to construct another. Why do you want the case of these men to be more astonishing than gravitation, magnetism or radioactivity—or even the metamorphosis of a caterpillar into a butterfly?"

---

[5] A hospital for the blind founded in Paris by Louis IX in 1260.

"More astonishing?" replied Formental. "That's not the issue. It's *outside*."

"Yes, it's *outside*," sighed Diane. "It's on another plane."

"Supernatural, then," Louise specified.

"If our plane is the only natural one—but what does that prove?"

"Let's see," said the intern, softly. "It is, however, certainly happening among us, with the most striking evidence and in the domain most accessible to our senses. We have no need of a microscope, as for bacteria. We have no need of hypotheses, as in the case of atoms. They're here, perfectly visible, in flesh and blood."

"But much more inexplicable than a thousand invisible things," Formental added.

"Presently inexplicable!" the young man insisted.

"Come on!" exclaimed the major, with a hint of anger. "They're not twins; their identity-papers make them one and the same person. Their wounds are identical; the soldiers in their regiment only know one Givreuse."

"Their combined weight makes up the weight of a single man," Diane added, vehemently.

"And who knows whether they might not be twins all the same?" said the aide. "Perhaps one of the sets of identity-papers is a duplicate and only one of the men has served in the regiment. A novelist could arrange that story—I can already see three or four ways to do it. It might be that they know one another and don't want to say, or that they've forgotten as a result of the shock, or that they don't know one another and someone—an enemy or a mysterious friend—has intervened, or that only one of the two knows the other… Note that it's not even necessary for them to be twins—in which case one can have recourse to other conjectures. With imagination, it can all be resolved…"

"But not the identity of the wounds."

"There, we have recourse to another set of explanations. Those who have studied the calculus of probabilities admit all coincidences as possibilities. In the trillions of trillions of millennia that our nebula has existed, why should there not be one occasion on which, not merely two men, but two twins, are wounded in the same fashion on the same battlefield. It's infinitely improbable…but it's not impossible."

"What about the weight?"

"There are men whose weight is low in proportion to their height…men who weigh very little, that's all."

"Both of them?"

"Both of them. Their resemblance virtually demands it."

"It's the most awkward paradox!" declared Madame de Bréhannes, stubbornly.

"I agree, Madame. The truth doubtless lies elsewhere—but the paradox gives a direction to thought."

Formental was scarcely listening. All speech seemed to him to be illusory. He was prey to facts; they drew him towards unknown realities. Finally, he heard the words: "We have to confront them with one another!"

"That's not difficult," said Louise.

"Oh, really? What about the mental effect?"

"I think they'll take it marvelously."

"Me too!" said Diane, timidly.

"You're very reckless," groaned the doctor. He looked through the window at a mild and modest landscape descending to the river. In the distance, exceedingly tall and slender poplars were shaking beneath slate-colored clouds. The plants were dying, their exhausted flowers hanging down on their stalks. Three recently-sheared sheep were grazing miserably. An old donkey raised its head, like a moth-eaten pullover.

"Please don't interrogate them any further as to their origins," Formental said, finally. "And above all, don't distress them with any insinuations. Their nervous state is good, but I believe they're very weak…"

IV.

The Givreuses' health was restored with surprising rapidity. They had no more fever; their wounds healed well and they manifested an avid appetite, which Formental allowed them to satisfy. They remained very thin, though. Their cheeks were hollow, their hands seemed almost translucent and the thinness of their eyelids was slightly bizarre—one might have thought they were eglantine petals.

"They're not getting any fatter," the intern remarked, one morning. "If they were weighed…"

Formental agreed to that. Charles brought his American balance to the bedside of the first Givreuse.

"40 kilos, 110 grams," he announced. "That's amazing. I would have thought that he'd actually got thinner."

Formental and Diane Montmaure looked at one another. They had thought the same as Charles. "In that case," the doctor stammered, "his *density* must have increased."

"I'm sure of it," Diane replied.

After a moment's pause, however, the wounded man asked anxiously: "40 kilos! You don't mean that that's what I weigh?"

"40 kilos, 110 or 111 grams—yes, that's it exactly. There's no mistake."

"Go on!" said the other, with a hint of agitation. "That's not possible. Before I left I weighed 73 kilograms."

There was a long silence. Formental's head slumped on to his breast. Then he whispered: "It's even more peculiar!"

An almost identical scene unfolded with the other wounded man. He too now weighed about 40 kilograms, and he too claimed to have weighed 73 at the time of his mobilization.

Formental resolved then to risk a confrontation—which the state of the wounded men seemed to permit, their sensitivity being moderate, or less than moderate. In a sense, they were

32

already prepared for it. Each of them knew, from what Madame de Bréhannes and Diane Montmaure had said, that he had a double of some sort. Gradual confidences had ended up preparing them for a singular scene.

The scene in question took place at about 4 p.m., the time that Formental judged to be the most favorable. The two Givreuses waited for the introduction impatiently, but there was nothing extreme in their impatience; their nervous excitation remained less than average.

They were brought to the doctor's office almost simultaneously.

They studied one another profoundly. Their breasts were visibly palpitating. Their eyes, habitually slightly lackluster, filled with a joyous gleam. Their emotion was unexpectedly obvious; there was nothing restrained about it; it resembled a sort of ecstasy.

Their hands came together spontaneously.

"Do you know one another, then?" asked Louise de Bréhannes.

"We've never seen one another before," they replied, in unison, "and yet…"

"Which of you is Edouard-Henri-Pierre Givreuse, born in Avranches in 1889?" asked the major, anxiously.

"It's me!" they both said. Only then did they seem astonished.

"Surely only one of you left with the nth regiment," said Formental.

When they both acquiesced, Diane intervened. "Where did you go first?" she asked the first Givreuse.

"To Montargis," he replied. "I arrived in the morning."

"An immense column went up to the barracks," continued the other.

"The enthusiasm was fearful…"

They stopped; their entire manner testified to an intense perplexity, but also the most ardent sympathy.

"And you left from Avranches?" asked Louise.

"Yes," they said, together. Both then added: "I stopped off in Paris."

"At a hotel?"

"No, in my own house."

"Wait!" said Formental. "It would be better if you took turns to speak. I'll alternate the questions. Where do you reside in Paris?"

"15 Rue Cimarosa."

"What floor?"

"My mother and I live in a town house."

"Where did you eat on the last night?"

"At the Carlton."

"How did you get to the railway station?"

"I took a fiacre, for lack of a motor taxi."

"What time did you board?"

"10:20 p.m."

"Do you have any particular memory of your stay in Paris?"

"Yes. As I was coming back from the Carlton, two young women gave me flowers."

The doctor had alternated the questions rigorously. "Are you in agreement?" he asked, in a tremulous voice.

"Yes."

The same shiver seemed to run through all the witnesses; the two soldiers were almost tranquil.

"Very well!" Formental exclaimed, feverishly. "What do you think of your adventure yourselves?"

The one to whom he had turned replied: "It ought to confuse me…and yet, in a strange way, it corresponds to something mysterious within me. Without being able to explain how or why, I have a profound feeling that some extraordinary event has fractured the unity of my being. A part of myself is outside me!"

The other listened, as if he were listening to the echo of his own voice. "A part of my being is in you," he said.

The doctor took out his watch and observed that the confrontation had lasted much longer than he had anticipated. "I hope this hasn't tired you?" he said, with a hint of remorse.

The wounded men smiled gravely. "It's rested us. We're much stronger and we feel better."

"Perhaps we shouldn't continue any longer, though," Formental replied, anxiously.

They lowered their heads. The intern pressed a button controlling an electric bell. Two male nurses came in and, in response to the major's instruction, took away one of the wounded men.

Half a minute went by. "Ah!" sighed the other. "The tiredness! It had disappeared...but it's come down on me again like a block of stone. Everything's slowed down... everything's nebulous and sinister..." One might have thought that he had diminished. His eyes were hollow; a tragic pallor invaded his cheeks. He went on: "*He* has taken away my strength. Doctor, don't leave me without *the other one*. I'm certain of it now—without him, my life is *fragmentary*..."

"I was sure of it!" stammered Diane Montmaure.

The door opened. The intern, who had accompanied the wounded man, came in excitedly. "He's complaining out there—he claims that without his...fellow...he has no more strength and is suffering."

Formental put his hand over his eyes. His lips moved, but nothing audible emerged save for an incomprehensible whisper. Finally, he said: "We must yield to their wishes; they know better than we do what they need."

"Lead us not into temptation," murmured Louise de Bréhannes, "but deliver us from evil. So must it be."

V.

Augustin de Rougeterre was standing under his English oak-tree in his garden in the Rue Malakoff. The oak had lived there through the reigns of kings, the First Republic and the Empire, directly descendant—along with other oaks, over thousands of years—from a forest in Celtic Gaul. It was alone now. It was 700 years old. Its hollows resembled caverns; its bark was like the hide of an old rhinoceros; 20 branches, as thick as trunks, produced myriads of tremulous leaves.

Comte Augustin loved that tree. On stormy nights, he thought he could hear the clamoring of knights and men-at-arms departing for battle, or the voices of ancient bagpipes. He was a bitter, taciturn and pious man. He had fought in wars, on the veldt and the savannah, in the marshes and the mountains—but in August, having wanted to return to harness, he had been betrayed by his infirmities.

As the daylight faded, he was daydreaming fervently. *Le Temps* and *Les Débats* lay at his feet. Between August 20 and the Marne he had almost died of rage and hatred. Then magnificent fables had renewed his vigor. This evening, he was as ardent and as melancholy as the clouds of fire and smoke that hid the setting Sun. He did not understand this war. It was covered in an execrable fog; it buried heroism in its caverns, it revealed enemies more abject than the Niam-Niams or the Flathead Indians.

Le Temps reported favorably. Augustin de Rougeterre made the sign of the cross and said, in a low voice: "Rise up, Lord, in Thy wrath; show Thy power against our enemies. May the evil that they do be returned to them, and their injustice fall upon their own heads." His hands were pressed together; memories of his youth awakened with the prayer.

Then he took a letter from his pocket and re-read it. "What does this signify? Has Pierre gone mad? Or has he written to me while delirious?" He sat down on a porphyry bench

36

and fell back into his torment. The crepuscular clouds passed slowly over the oak-tree.

A servant appeared, carrying a card. "All right! I'm coming!" Augustin got up and marched stiffly toward the house.

Two soldiers were waiting for him in the reception room. He made an abrupt gesture, then became paralyzed, his eyes fixed upon the visitors. Each of them was the perfect image of the other, and *their* image was that of Pierre de Givreuse. A sensation, almost of terror, passed over the old man. In a hoarse voice, he said: "Which of you is my nephew?"

The soldiers exchanged a glance; one of them replied: "We both believe ourselves to be Pierre de Givreuse."

The Comte started in amazement, with a hint of anger. "Is this some trick?" he exclaimed. "The timing is abominably bad."

"Alas, it's the profoundest truth," said the one who had not yet spoken.

Their voices were as similar as their faces. Rougeterre was gripped by a sudden anguish; his temples were covered in sweat. His was a violent soul, in which sentiments emerged wholly formed. At that moment he did not know what to think or believe; the supernatural came in through open windows.

"So," he said, "each of you imagines himself to be Pierre de Givreuse. But you cannot doubt, any more than I can, that one of you is the victim of an illusion?"

They lowered their eyes and made no reply.

"You can't possibly doubt it!" Augustin affirmed, with anguish and indignation.

The one who had spoken first said, in a low tone: "We doubt it!"

This reply exasperated the old man. "One may doubt anything, except the word of God. One cannot doubt the identity of things. There are two of you? You don't deny that there are two of you?" He was trembling with excitement, rebellion and mystic dread.

"We believe that we're two...we aren't sure."

Haggard and wild-eyed, Rougeterre remained silent for an interminable interval. His lips were blanched, his cheeks were quivering. Finally, he stammered: "If this is a trial, O my Lord, have pity on me. I have a contrite and humble heart. Do not abandon me to the snares of the One who has tempted us all since the first woman!" Then, passing his hand over his face, he regained a measure of self-possession. "There's a logic even in the supernatural," he said. "If your minds haven't gone astray, you must be certain that you are quite distinct from one another."

"We can see perfectly well," replied the one who was further away from the old man, "that there are two of us—but we also *know* that our past life is common to us both. We've talked to one another at length. Our memories coincide, without any kind of exception, except from the moment when we woke up in the field-hospital at Viorne. Interrogate us separately regarding our childhood and youth...compare your memories with ours...and you will be convinced, as we are, that nothing that has happened to one of us is foreign to the other. *Nothing!* The duality has only lasted for a few weeks. With respect to everything that happened at Viorne and Gavres, and the incidents of our journey together from Gavres to Paris, our personalities are certainly distinct—with one reservation, however. That is that we only have the full complement of our strength and our faculties when we're together. As soon as we're separated, we become weak; the timbre of our voices changes; our memories are less certain, our thoughts less vivid and less complete; our sensibility is attenuated, our sight and hearing less clear..."

These words drove Augustin de Rougeterre to despair. He tried in vain to escape the certainty that they were emitting and forcing into the very depths of his soul. He did not want to be convinced—or, at least, he had a vague desire not to be convinced *so quickly*. But time seemed to have been abolished; a prodigious abundance of impressions overwhelmed the old gentleman and found a powerful echo in his mysticism.

"Very well," he said, finally, with a sort of fatalism, "I'll put you to the test. Would one of you care to follow me?"

One of them got up. Augustin led him along the hallway to his study. There he opened a drawer, took out a little album, and opened it at the second page. He pointed to an ink drawing that represented a young woman. "Who is that?" he asked.

"It's my great-aunt, Pauline de Rougeterre."

"And who made the drawing?"

"You did, uncle."

The drawing was not signed. Augustin's face showed a trace of tender emotion. He leaned over to the young man and embraced him. The other returned the kiss with evident affection, but with a strange stiffness.

"Let's see," said the old man. He displayed a dozen daguerreotypes and more recent photographs; Pierre de Givreuse recognized all of them. Finally, with a slight tremor, Augustin opened a minuscule enameled box in which a ring set with emeralds was sparkling.

"It's a family heirloom," said the soldier, gravely. "It belonged to my great grandmother, the Marquise Catherine de Givreuse, who died on the scaffold in January 1794."

"There's no doubt about it!" affirmed the old man. "You're my nephew Pierre."

"Wait!" replied the young man, wearily. "You haven't heard my…companion."

Rougeterre shook his head. At that moment, his mind was made up; if the matter still seemed extraordinary, it seemed less supernatural—but he said: "We'll see. Would you care to wait for me in the hall?"

He went out with Givreuse and went to look for the second soldier. Then he showed him the drawing of the young woman. Like the other, he recognized Pauline de Rougeterre and attributed the drawing to his uncle…

The Comte's soul filled with darkness then, and, as the soldier recognized all the portraits assembled in the album, the sensation of a prodigy returned with increased force. "My

39

God, have I lost my mind? Only madness can explain it all. Am I mad?"

He studied himself in a mirror; then he felt himself as one does in a dream. "No, if I were mad, I wouldn't have these doubts. I wouldn't be able to look back at myself. In that case, though, the universe is frightfully different from what I imagined…" From the depths of the unconscious, these words rose to his lips: "One God in three persons…why not one man in two persons…and *perhaps*…why not all men in two persons? Man is made in God's image…and if God is the sum of all knowledge…He is also the sum of all mysteries…He reveals the knowledge and the mysteries to us according to desires and circumstance that *He* alone directs…may Thy Will be done, on Earth as it is in Heaven!"

He turned to the soldier and hugged him to his bosom. "You too are Pierre de Givreuse!" he stammered. Then, noticing that the young man was pale and tired, he said: "What's the matter, my boy?"

"It's nothing—the fatigue of being without him."

"Then let's go rejoin him!" They went. "What shall we do now?" asked Rougeterre when they were all together again in the hall. "Surely you haven't seen your mother…"

"How could we dare? We needed your advice. If we were to appear before her together, unexpectedly, she'd be terribly distressed. And if we were to appear separately, she'd be alarmed by our evident weakness. It's desirable that we aren't separated and that our duality seems merely extraordinary. This is what we thought. One of us will not be Pierre de Givreuse. A resemblance, even an unprecedented one, will doubtless provoke extreme surprise, but not fear or anguish, especially if she has been told about it in advance. Our mother will understand that a fervent friendship has arisen between us, similar to the affection of twins."

Augustin reflected for some time. He had difficulty setting his thoughts in order. The evidence of superhuman intervention now seemed overwhelming. Sometimes he saw a sinister Will at work, sometimes the most marvelous favor of the Beyond. Haggardly, he replied: "I'll do as you wish. Besides, your idea seems reasonable to me. We need to iron out certain details, but…" Pallor was succeeded by redness in his temples. His voice lowered to a whisper. "Don't you have any memory of something strange…a memory that might resemble a dream?"

"Nothing. Between the moment when *I* fell on the battlefield and the moment when *we* woke up, our memory is void."

"Completely?"

"Completely."

"God does not want it known!" said the Comte, putting his hands together. "May His will be done…"

VI.

When Madame de Givreuse had heard the story that Augustin told her, she was bewildered. Then she asked: "And the resemblance really seems absolute to you?"

"Perhaps there are a few trivial—very trivial—differences. I was too emotional to discern them…but it seems to be impossible to maintain that one is more like Pierre than the other!"

"I doubt that I could be mistaken!" said Madame de Givreuse, pensively. "Mothers have a sixth sense, Augustin." She was smiling now. An entire and immeasurable universe seemed to be displayed within her, fading into eternity. Passionately, she exclaimed: "Why isn't he here? Why has he made me wait?"

"Because of his very affection. He feared…"

She interrupted him hotly: "Has he something to hide? His wounds?"

"They're not at all serious—but he's still thin and pale. He would doubtless have notified you of his return, but he feared the uncertainty of the post and the telegraph."

She had already calmed down. Her clear face was redolent with an ardent softness that age had been unable to dull, scarcely streaked by a few wrinkles as fine as virginal thread. She had the same eyes as Pierre de Givreuse and copious hair worn in the Montespan style, whose silky gold was mingled with silver skeins.

"Oh, may he come soon," she whispered.

She was standing up when they came in; she rushed to meet them, but her dash was interrupted, so profound was her surprise—and she stopped, enchanted and consternated at the same time, trying to distinguish between her son and the stranger. Slight differences were manifest to her sharp gaze. The face of one seemed slightly larger than the other's, and the texture of their skin did not seem to be identical, but she could not tell which of them resembled Pierre more.

"My son!" she cried, in the vague hope that the appeal would give birth to some revelatory emotion.

The two faces expressed the same anxiety. Finally, one muted and hesitant voice replied: "Mother!"

She was already hugging the one who had spoken—but she glimpsed a tremulous tenderness in the other's gaze, which upset her. "Welcome," she said, extending her hand to him. "I've been told that your friendship is perfect." She sighed, and added, involuntarily: "And I can understand that!"

Again she embraced the one who had replied to her cry—then, moved by an irresistible impulse, she put her hands on the other's shoulders. She withdrew them immediately. A host of contradictory feelings tormented her, in which constraint was mingled with joy and obscure anxieties corroded hope.

Light footsteps were heard, and a sparkling daughter of men appeared in the doorway. She advanced with the rhythmic step of a Cycladean fisherwoman, but she was tall. She had a Nordic face, fine and fluid cheeks, eyes as variable as the waves; her plaited hair was black with a copper sheen. On seeing the two men she released an exclamation that was almost a plaint. Then she stopped, her pupils dilating while they looked at her, both very pale.

"Will you be any more clairvoyant than me, Valentine?" murmured Madame de Givreuse. "I was unable to recognize Pierre."

The young woman looked at them, concentrating her attention and appealing to the memory of forms and colors that is so sharp at her age.

Finally discouraged, she said: "I don't know."

Part Two

I.

The days went by. Little by little, invincible habitude rendered normality to one of the strangest adventures ever related in the annals of humankind. Madame de Givreuse became accustomed to the double presence of the person she believed to be her son and the fantastic unknown, who had adopted the name of Philippe Frémeuse.

For two weeks, the young men did not go out at all, save for a few furtive walks in the evening, in the most deserted streets. They hardly ever separated. Not only did their strength and their faculties diminish when they were not together, but they were gripped by a sort of dread, the sensation of a frightful solitude.

A very slow metamorphosis took place, however, in their physical and mental being. Their skin became less transparent, their complexion less dull, and their hair seemed thicker. Their density also increased; from the 37 kilograms that they weighed at the beginning of their sojourn in Gavres, they advanced to 44.

It was with Valentine de Varsennes that their relations were most singular. The young woman had been living with Madame de Givreuse for three years when the war broke out. At first, Valentine had seemed to be a child. A firm and fugitive passion for travel had absorbed Givreuse. It was in the two months before the war that he had begun to love the young guest, with a passion that remained secret, because Pierre thought that no transient adventure was admissible. The Medieval right of sanctuary, the privilege of hospitality, conferred sacred rights upon Mademoiselle de Varsennes. Nothing other than a love "for better or worse" seemed acceptable. He waited for time to reveal the true significance of circumstances.

When war broke out, he was no longer uncertain of himself, but he could not discern Valentine's sentiments clearly. She was unaware of them; she was a simple soul. Her inexperience was more complicated than many experiences. In the enchantment of blossoming, suffering is often as powerful as joy, a certain horror is mingled with gratitude, and subtle dread renders every ambition fearful. One is a poor creature subject to powers that often seem brutal, and desire is balanced by menacing mystery. Nevertheless, she experienced a powerful attraction to Pierre; his was the only male face she admitted into her dreams. When they separated, too many evil possibilities veiled the future. At the ominous moment of farewell, there was a great spark between them, but nothing was said.

The two soldiers retained an indestructible memory of that moment. When they saw Valentine again, they experienced a shudder of resurrection, and each of them knew that his impressions were identical to the other's. They did not feel any jealousy. When they reflected, they were abstractedly constrained to consider one another as rivals. Without influence over their sensations, inasmuch as their sensations related to themselves, that conviction had an effect on their relationship with Valentine. They moved silently and furtively; they could not see any outcome of their love; they considered that it would be odious not to conceal it.

This situation disorientated the young woman. She often experienced an obscure distress, sometimes a sort of shame that ramified into the most delicate regions of her soul, sometimes an astonishment mingled with consternation or an ardent and sad curiosity. The palpitant moment of farewell and the great spark that sprang from the unconscious were Valentine's most striking memories; they created the fine substance of those dreams that grow like living organisms, whose roots are steeped in the mysteries of life.

During Pierre's absence, love had come, as furtive as little flowers in the depths of a wood. All the anxiety and all the pain of the war were mingled with it, but also the untiring strength that builds and rebuilds. Its complexity and its detours were nuances of the soul, not ambiguities or equivocations. Since his return, terrifying elements mingled with elements so troubling that the reality of the world was turned upside-down—and yet, love persisted. It persisted fantastically. It was *one* man that Valentine loved—the one who had formerly lived at the Château de Givreuse and whose identity was certain—but how could he be distinguished from the other? When she found herself alone with the one playing the role of Pierre, he no longer seemed to be himself; he was only *partly present*—and that corresponded to a reality. Alone, each of them was clad in an imperfect appearance, ambiguous and bearing less resemblance to Givreuse.

She tried in vain to rationalize it, but all logic became false, insufficient and wretched.

To hasten the recovery of the wounded men, Madame de Givreuse resolved to go back to the country. They returned to the Château de Givreuse, of which only the west wing was habitable. It was the domain of bats; they shared the granite with rooks, seabirds and swifts. A population of gorse and broom had made inroads into the ruins, the Atlantic winds roared over the stunted oaks, and the hedgehogs came out in the starlight like bristling phantoms. The west wing was comfortable, though; the stone was dry, the bay windows opened large eyes to the Sun as it rose over the fields and set into the sea. Crackling fireplaces consumed gorse, pines and oaks. The walls were made of the same granite as the cliffs, coarse, indestructible and reassuring.

In this primitive refuge, the soldiers and Mademoiselle de Varsennes lived an affectionate existence. They were scarcely aware of its strangeness. The entire ambience—the eternal palpitation of the heart of the waters; the rumble of the tides; the storms charged with the odor of distant lands; the immense nights; the ancient stones of the château, which retained the memory of tumultuous generations of yesteryear; and, on the distant deserted plain, the dolmens and cromlechs impregnated with the primitive soul—was amenable to mysterious things.

Love followed its course, like gravitation, like the rays of light that travel through the interstellar darkness, like the avid seeds of gorse and brambles; because it contains the totality of Enigma, it adapts to all enigmas. It increased in Pierre and Philippe, all the more strongly because they were weaker. It increased in Valentine, dolorous and fearful, as chaste as the silver river that seems to run from the Moon in never-ending waves on clear nights.

Meanwhile, the young men's metamorphosis was incessant. Intensive alimentation restored their lost energy and rapidly augmented their *density*—for the troubling anomaly remarked at Gavres persisted. By mid-December, they each weighed about 55 kilograms, without their plumpness changing noticeably. In truth, their faces appeared almost normal; the cheeks were no longer as hollow, but the rest of the body remained slim and lithe.

There was also a psychic, or rather a physiological, metamorphosis. Although they still experienced the same affection for one another, their nerves tolerated separation better. It now required quite a long time for them to experience the full intensity of the impression of weakness, anguish and solitude that the absence of the other caused each of them. To be sure, as soon as a certain distance separated them, Philippe and Pierre soon felt ill, but that ill-feeling was tolerable for more than an hour. It was only then that it began to turn into suffering and communicated a sensation of great fatigue. They did not submit willingly to such proof, but they admitted its usefulness—and someone obliged them to submit, for a wise and energetic individual gave them his attention and imposed his will upon them.

This was the aged neurologist Bernard Savarre, whose sanatorium was located beyond the great cliff, in the middle of a heath. Only strange creatures were cared for there. Four buildings, separated by gardens, sheltered the inmates, classified according to their defects. Although he had lived for 25 years with neurasthenics and the demented, Savarre maintained his own mental health. While the singular influence of nervous disorders—whose contagion is closely analogous to that of microbial diseases—continually struck down doctors, and nurses of either sex, Savarre remained invulnerable, astonished by his own immunity. His was a mind as open as human infirmity permits. He had not replaced his religious beliefs with any of the superstitions of men of science. Nothing seemed incredible to him. According to him, there was no such thing as absurdity, and any contradiction could only be apparent.

"What is reason but a crystallization of ancient experience?" he said. "Since the dawn of history, we have seen several, of our best fleets sunk. How incoherent Plato now seems, and how derisory Aristotle is! And yet, they were incomparable intellects. Be sure that marvelous usage will be made of new constructions, which will yet surpass the maneuvers of Spencer and young Nietzsche."

The case of the Givreuses had astounded him, though. He searched for an equivalent in ancient texts and could not find one. "There are certainly stories as extravagant," he said, "but they're imaginary. The question is whether this one is real. If it is, we've entered into an unprecedented era—and all terrestrial life too."

He doggedly re-checked the proofs. They were as good as those of the surest scientific discoveries. The anomaly of their density struck him most of all. At the time when he received the first confidences, the respective weight of the young men was no more than 45 kilograms. This weight was in flagrant disproportion to the volume of flesh and bone. According to appearances, Philippe and Pierre should each have weighed about 70 kilograms—and it was known, with utter certainty, that before his departure, Pierre had weighed 73.

Savarre also enquired, insistently, about the place where Pierre had fallen; he noted that it was not the same as the place where *they* had been picked up.

"The place where this phenomenon occurred must be of some importance, whether the event was biological, psychic or social," he remarked one evening, when he was chatting to the Givreuse's doctor—a man so reliable that nothing was hidden from him.

"What do you mean by a social event, in this instance?"

"I mean some substitution, so improbable that one is tempted to judge it impossible, but which must nevertheless be taken into account."

They were walking on the outer wall, under a yellow crescent moon that was setting in the placid waves. Their white beards reflected silvery gleams. They were surrounded by the kind of puzzlement that the anthropoids of the Tertiary Era had not yet felt, but which was already tormenting the people who had raised the heavy granite amid the bracken.

"What do you believe?" asked the Givreuses' doctor, timidly.

"Nothing yet. All judgment is suspended—but how many scientific facts are more secure than the unity of these two men?"

The other shuddered, and darted a sideways glance at Savarre. "Unity? So you think they're both Pierre de Givreuse?"

"I think that I've no reason to doubt it. There's no better-established proof in the archives of identity than the proof of that unity, notwithstanding the character of the event. I don't say, mind, that the two men are only one man, or that their duality seems less complete than any other human duality, but I do say that everything leads me to admit that they have been formed out of only one man."

"Come on!" exclaimed Morlay, whose common sense was in revolt. "You don't mean to suggest that each of them is *a part* of Pierre?"

"I mean the opposite. I've gone through all the imaginable combinations—imaginable for me; unless we go back to substitution, I can see nothing but a doubling."

"But that's impossible."

49

"It's merely contrary to all human experience. No one has ever seen a man, a lion, a frog, a fish or a crab become, by binary division, two men, two lions, two frogs, two fish or two crabs—but that doesn't alter the fact that binary division is the primitive mode of generation, and that, for a period that was perhaps the longest in the history of living things, it was by splitting into two that creatures reproduced. And let's not forget, my dear friend, that our bodies contain a multitude of cells that operate in that manner..."

"Then you think that Pierre de Givreuse..." Morlay stopped himself, so crazy did the hypothesis appear.

"I don't think anything yet, my friend; I limit myself to offering one of the two conclusions imposed by my fallible logic. That conclusion, already quite grotesque in itself, becomes even more so if one seeks to make it more precise. It is in fact, necessary to suppose, not only that each of Pierre de Givreuse's cells has divided into two cells, but also that the entire mineral and quasi-mineral part of the body has divided in an analogous manner—that every hair for example, has become two hairs, and that the bony elements have split in two, particle for particle. It's obviously a monstrous absurdity—but absurdity can't always stop us; the history of science shows us that at every step..."

He fell silent. The yellow crescent moon had become red and was about to plunge into the waves. Owls raised their necromantic voices.

"What if it were a miracle, though?"

"It would be a miracle! But what does that word mean? It presumes that we believe natural laws to be *absolute*—and that another absolute is required to break them. I've only ever thought of laws as approximate, susceptible to exception or even to disappearance. What we know about the world is utterly negligible; I've long been wary of building a general theory on so microscopic a basis. I see petty theories as provisional; I'm not their servant...they're the ones that serve me. By what do you expect me to be astonished?"

"And if it were never to be explained?"

"It would be one more little fact to add to the infinity of inexplicable facts. In any case, everything is inexplicable, at bottom. Human explanation only contrives to bring what is unfamiliar to us into the ranks of the familiar—but familiar things are no better understood than the rest!"

II.

It was a mild and pleasant winter's day, when large clouds were pursuing one another over never-ending waves. Fishing-boats were sailing in the distance, clearly visible, even though they were sometimes surrounded by mist. Two frigates with trenchant sails were floating amid the islands and a huge seagull was soaring in the gentle majesty of the moment, while the sea, lifted up by an ample and fresh breeze, seemed to be in the morning of its birth in eternal time.

The two soldiers had accompanied Valentine to the beach. The cliffs rose up like chaotic citadels, hollowed out by caverns, the highest of which still sheltered men of the Middle Ages.

The strollers walked silently for some time. There was a plenitude of life in their breasts. Around them, Nature was—as always—a friend and an enemy. They drew out her strength with every breath, but she also surrounded them with her perpetual threat and her inexhaustible destruction. The love that exalted them was an emanation of her; like her it filled them constantly with joyful energy, and like her, it never ceased to breathe anxiety into them.

The beautiful girl whose skirts flapped in the wind, her pale face more nuanced than the clouds, and the scarlet fruit of her mouth, sang them a hymn more passionate than the equinoctial wind.

They were full of strength now, although their gait had a slight limp in consequence of their wounds. The great emotions of war rendered their affection more serious. They wanted to be reborn in other individuals; the blood of their race was in revolt against sterility. A fatal destiny intended them to be rivals.

They were dreaming as they followed the slender silhouette over the sand and pebbles; they were suffering, but not from jealousy. No jealousy could emerge in them. As on the day when they had seen one another for the first time, they had an inclination toward one another that came from the wellspring of existence, which nothing could ever break. Was it possible that one of the two sufferers would sacrifice himself?

In her innocence, Valentine thought that she was in love with the one who had taken the name of Pierre de Givreuse—but far from being better able to distinguish him from the other with each passing day, she was less able to distinguish him. It seemed to her that they were even more identical than before, and she was not mistaken.

To begin with, a difference in the texture of their skin had been perceptible, and—to a very subtle gaze—a slight difference in the breadth of their faces. Augustin de Rougeterre had characterized it one day by saying: "One is slightly more vertical, the other slightly more horizontal." That difference had disappeared. The texture of their skin was identical; the two faces were no longer distinguishable from one another by any indication, however slight. There was no longer any other indication but the difference in their costumes.

Often, without the knowledge of Madame de Givreuse and Mademoiselle de Varsennes, they exchanged clothes, and then the one who had taken on the role of Philippe became Pierre. These changes answered a sentimental need; they permitted each of them to live, by turns, in the most filial intimacy with *their* mother.

The beach was deserted. They had, however, encountered a shrimp-fisher and then two adolescents. Their resemblance excited scarcely any astonishment; it had become familiar. Everyone knew the story that Rougeterre had told Madame de Givreuse. The story scarcely even seemed strange now; Nature and mirrors have accustomed the human imagination, over thousands of years, to the most marvelous resemblances.

One of the two found himself alone with Valentine; it was the one who was playing Pierre de Givreuse that day. A weak lukewarm breeze had sprung up, coming from the sea, bringing the effluvia of the ocean with a slight hint of a storm. The young woman became nervous.

Because her life had been so perfectly purified by education and a natural docility to regulation, Valentine suffered the instincts that are in all of us, without any enlightenment to clarify them. Her reading, selected with care, had left her in an ignorance that she never tried to break. With regard to everything implicated in the essentials of feminine destiny, she was like a little child, even though, on the other hand, her nature was made for a great amour. What had been born within her agitated her magnificently, like a storm in the darkness. She only knew that she had to partake of the destiny of a man, and she consented to that—but she trembled before a formidable reality: there were two images of the same man. This drama, which she was incapable of working out, troubled her days and her nights.

They reached a fantastic landscape of oddly-shaped stones displayed at the foot of the cliffs in a "mute tumult;" they were reminiscent of cyclopean constructions, primitive cities, granite cemeteries, pointed towers, pyramids and the ruins of cathedrals. Only the sea had labored there, however, for hundreds of thousands of years, with the collaboration of storms and tempests.

Valentine studied the mounting waves. They launched themselves upon the stones with those extended roars that astonished the ancient poets; they were like immense herds of fabulous beasts with white fur and green skin; they surged into granite straits and re-emerged broken. From the open sea, further herds came running, incessantly, which seemed bound to scale the cliffs and drown the land—but the force that heaped them up from the depths was the same that marked their bounds and chased them away.

"Do you remember?" the soldier murmured, timidly. "It was here that we took our last walk…before the war. How many times I've evoked the memory of you, standing on a red rock, with your hair almost in disarray. A ship as slender as a crescent moon was passing in the west…dusk was falling…the fires of a lighthouse and a star intersected on the surface of the sea. It's the most important memory of my life…"

She turned her beautiful Celtic eyes toward him; the mute avowal spoke louder than words; they quivered with youth, ardor and dreams…but when the other drew nearer, Valentine was gripped by an intolerable anguish. She was certain that he also loved her, and that there was no essential reason why he should be rejected, but there was horror, pity and remorse within her. Everything that she might have said died away before an instinct as imperious as it was indefinable.

When they had returned to the château, the two soldiers lingered in the overgrown garden. The one who had spoken to Valentine described the scene as if he were repeating it to himself.

"What do we do now?" said the other. "You've determined the future. One of us will marry Valentine. That's necessary. It will lead to a sane and robust happiness. But what will become of the other? Might he suffer?"

"Another love might save him. Life is many-faceted. It only requires one meeting. Time is on our side…and its metamorphoses."

A raucous flock of rooks rose up from the ruins. The two men remained silent, caught in a tragic uncertainty.

"Which of us, henceforth, will bear our name into old age, and will have Valentine as his lot?"

"Which of us will no longer bear the name…like a foundling child…and might perhaps have no love as his lot?"

The future filled with darkness; they saw the horror of their detached fates; a long lamentation reverberated in their being.

The one who had spoken to Valentine said, in a dull voice: "The resolution is too demanding. We can't take it yet. Life would be equally intolerable for both of us. What are a few months—or even a year—to Valentine?"

The rooks croaked more loudly; an owl raised its mournful voice. The two Givreuses lowered their heads, lost in dolorous meditation. Each of them felt that it was impossible for him to consent to the other's self-sacrifice.

III.

Savarre continued his enquiry. He made a journey to Gavres and Viorne. At Gavres, the hospital staff had been almost entirely replaced; he only found Major Formental there. The latter had retained a clear memory of the event but had gradually come to attach less importance to it. Savarre perceived that. Guided by a jealous sentiment, even more than his interest in the Givreuses, he attempted to minimize the fantastic aspects of the adventure, attributing it to pathological phenomena.

Formental, who admired Savarre blindly, allowed himself to be swayed by his illustrious colleague and recounted what he knew without asking anything in return. The interview communicated no new facts to the neurologist, but he had expected none; he had only come to Gavres to verify the testimony.

At Viorne, he found none of the original witnesses. He had to travel for five days before encountering Major Herbelle and the male nurse Alexandre. There again, as he had foreseen, he found only confirmations. He let Herbelle believe, like Formental, that the "Givreuse case" was the issue of nervous pathology, and that it was, in the final analysis, a matter of a double illusion, provoked by fatigue and the wounds suffered by two men who the hazard of birth had made almost identical and whom singular circumstances had brought together.

Like Formental, Herbelle raised a few objections—but like Formental, he had gradually lost interest in the event and was inclined to believe it less extraordinary than he had initially imagined. He did not insist, and acquiesced when Savarre said, as he left: "A few obscure points remain, but I'm almost sure that they can be explained…"

Savarre explored the battlefield. He saw nothing exceptional, save for the Château de Grantaigle. The local inhabitants he questioned told harrowing stories; he listened to them patiently, but discovered nothing therein that related to his enquiry.

In order to leave no stone unturned, he went to visit an old bone-setter who was reputed to have achieved miraculous cures. The old man lived in the middle of the heath, in a hovel that the shells had spared. He looked like a sorcerer, quite diabolical, with blue-green eyes as dilatable as an owl's, a long face with a goat-like beard and thick hair in serpentine hanks that stuck out wildly in all directions. Savarre's visit alarmed him; he played the idiot. Encouraged by a 20-franc note, however, he decided to impart a few confidences; they were naïve, amusing and quaint. He had recipes, no worse than others, and had at length acquired a certain primitive science—but he could not be of any use to Savarre.

The neurologist explored Grantaigle. An old gardener, deaf and senile, was the sole resident. The neurologist learned that the château's owner had disappeared and that the servants had been killed or had fled. He made a futile visit to the ruins.

The local people gave him a few details regarding the château's owner, Antoine de Grantaigle. He was about 55 years old and had once enjoyed a measure of celebrity; he had three or four discoveries in physical chemistry to his credit. For a quarter of a century he had had no further communication with the Academy of Sciences and had published nothing in the journals, but he had not given up. On the contrary, he had worked obstinately in a large laboratory installed in the château; it was vaguely known that his experiments had as much relevance to biology as to the physicochemical sciences.

Two nephews had come to the château after the victory of the Marne, and had recently reappeared. At first, it had been believed that Antoine de Grantaigle had simply retreated before the invasion, but now there was hesitation between three hypotheses: he was buried under the debris; he had been put to death by the enemy in some corner of the heath or in the forest; or he had been deported to Germany. The nephews had ordered searches which, thus far, had produced no result.

Savarre went to see one of the nephews, who was engaged in the auxiliary services. He was a man of sallow complexion who occupied his leisure in peace-time writing a *History of the Origins of Chivalry* and *Considerations on the Evolution of Heraldic Science*. He had heard mention of Savarre; without being familiar with the doctor's work, he took him for a great man.

The interview took place in a deserted railway station where wagons were awaiting a locomotive. Grantaigle's nephew was satisfied by the vague pretexts that Savarre invoked, and gave him a few details regarding the scientist. "An impenetrable man! We hardly knew him. I believe that he was much occupied with radiations, and the origins of terrestrial life—but no one was allowed in his laboratory except for a young Champenois as secretive as he was, who was mobilized and who perished in the Hauts-de-Meuse. Are you familiar with my uncle's first discoveries?"

"They were remarkable and highly original."

"So they say. I'm not competent to judge. What's certain is that he'd lost none of his intelligence and that his endurance in his work seemed unusual. There's reason to believe, therefore, that he had made other discoveries; my impression is that they might have surpassed the first and formed a sort of whole. If he didn't think it worthwhile publishing them he must have had good reasons—he might have been an original thinker, but he wasn't a maniac, or even an eccentric."

"Do you think he's still alive?"

"No. If he'd been deported to Germany he'd have found a means of notifying us of his fate. He was very clever when he deemed it necessary, and prodigiously skillful. He'd have played his guards like little children and stuffed them with illusions—and the truth is that they wouldn't have been capable of keeping him prisoner even for a few days."

Grantaigle's nephew left Savarre briefly in order to receive a dispatch. "Ah, Monsieur," he sighed, when he returned to the scientist, "what a plague these dispatches, letters and circulars are...the army has to be strong in order not to be contaminated. Is there anything else you want to know?"

"What became of the laboratory?"

"Destroyed—reduced to dust, evaporated into atoms. Nothing remains of it except for a fragment of a pyrometer—which is of no interest—and a piece of burnt paper on which I was able to make out one sentence: *Life came to us from the interstellar realm, and only the interstellar realm can explain it to us...*"

"Ah!" Savarre murmured, pensively. He paused momentarily, then said: "If anything is discovered, would you have any objection letting me know?"

"None. On the contrary—unless it concerns personal secrets...of a sentimental nature, I mean, for the scientific secret is lost if my poor uncle has been killed."

Savarre withdrew, vaguely disappointed. It seemed fundamentally ridiculous to him to establish any connection whatsoever between Grantaigle's work and the enigma of the Givreuses. *It's more likely*, he thought, as the train carried him westwards, *that the adventure is of a superhuman order than a scientific one.*

IV.

Spring had returned. Cruel and charming life deployed its meticulous genius; it was the time when growth seemed to crush the earth and the waters—but death was able to limit life, and even to serve life. There was not a tuft of grass where security reigned. Every insect had its predator, an agile scarab or ant-lion crouching in the depths of its trap, which died in their turn beneath the beaks of birds or the teeth of insectivores. The sparrow-hawk, the pine-marten and the owl gorged themselves on fresh blood. Over everything reigned the strange vertical beast which regulated life and death in the forest, the fields, the hills, the mountains and even the gulfs of the ocean.

The destiny of the Givreuses now seemed even more troubled and more fearful. The young men's anxiety had increased; a new fatality had arrived since the day when one of them had exchanged an obscure vow with Valentine. They were definitely rivals, without wanting to be, without any of the sentiments of hatred and bitterness that comprise rivalry— and their rivalry was all the richer in suffering and dejection. One of them could not sacrifice himself without the other being irreparably unhappy, as if a part of his being had been cut away. That sacrifice seemed impossible; everything within them rebelled against it; life ceased to seem desirable to them.

They loved Valentine as they breathed; one might have thought that their two loves combined and mutually increased one another's force. When they did not reflect at all, when they simply abandoned themselves to their penchant, without thinking about the future, there was an immeasurable gentleness even in their rivalry; they lived in a present that was exceedingly passionate, charming and pure at the same time. Their love was then confounded with the joy of being young, with the beauty of places, of constellations, of cliffs and the ocean. There were no more plans, hopes, fears; they lost themselves in a conscious, ineffable hypnosis that abolished time...

When reflection, or one of those melancholy reveries that project us into the future, brought them back to reality, when they told themselves that it would eventually be necessary to choose between total renunciation and the effacement of one of them, they fell back into even blacker distress.

No scene like the one on the beach had been repeated, or even sketched out. The attitude struck by "Pierre" seemed strange to Valentine, but less strange than might have been expected. She had not forgotten the dread that she had felt among the granite blocks; she never thought about it without a shiver, in which there was fear, unease and the sense of a mystery more troubling than that of the resemblance between the two men. Her consciousness took note of their slightest actions and their merest words, and only a sensitive delicacy prevented her from spying on them.

Their intimacy betrayed unusual features in every respect. It involved no external demonstration; it was taciturn—they chatted with others, but not with one another. There was no hint of dispute, and even less of contradiction.

Valentine was never as struck by this fact than one afternoon in May, when she was sitting on an oak bench at the far end of the overgrown garden, reading. Pierre and Philippe were out in the garden walking. As usual, they were walking side by side. Sometimes, one or the other would pause to study a plant, an insect or a cloud; then they would smile—and that smile implied a kind of parallelism of sensation and thought. Not once did they speak.

In the end, that silence caused Valentine a veritable malaise, almost anguish. It worked within her confusedly, as at times when one is afloat between a waking state and sleep. She thought she was on the point of divining something—a glimmer flickered back and forth—but then everything became dark again. She was in an unknown existence that tickled her intelligence with enlightenment and her avid heart with trust...

The attitude of Augustin de Rougeterre added to these impressions. That austere man of frank actions and simple words was evidently troubled in the presence of the two young men. A certain fearful and indecisive vagueness was discernible in his gestures, his gaze and his speech—which Valentine usually attributed to the embarrassment he experienced in being unable, like everyone else, to tell Pierre and Philippe apart. On occasion, though, it presented a more complicated enigma. Sometimes, Augustin's eyes revealed a sort of sacred horror, which was subtly transmitted to the young woman. But why? She could not have even the shadow of a suspicion as to the reality—what human creature could? She thought in terms of mysterious relations; all sort of vague adventures passed through her mind.

On the other hand, it was impossible for her to prefer Pierre to Philippe, and *it did not seem to her that she had any right to a preference.* She no longer dared to love; she struggled, in distress, against her memories and her inclinations. She thought about running away, of taking refuge far from Givreuse and renouncing happiness. Her affliction, her anxiety and the thousand spiteful shadows that tormented her even in her sleep would, however, have been dissipated—so she believed—if she had not been sure that each of the two men loved her, and in the same fashion, with the same nuances. She wanted to doubt it, but her delicate intuition would not permit it. When she met the gaze of Philippe or Pierre, she read an identical tenderness there; she saw the same hesitation, the same timidity, the same generous sweetness.

The thought of that duplicate love made her blush, as if she had committed a sin. In another person, it might have been confusedly mingled, to some extent, with the equivocal vanity that is found in exceptionally pure women. After all, reverie in a waking state is more or less akin to dream-sleep; how many honest souls sense "rough drafts" of temptation within themselves, whose realization would fill them with horror? It was not like that with Valentine, however. She wished, ardently and constantly, that one of the two would cease to love her. She wanted that one to be Philippe, but she would have accepted it if it had been Pierre.

One morning, Madame de Givreuse went with Valentine, Pierre and Philippe to an abandoned village on the far side of Saint-Michel-les-Loups. It was a sort of pilgrimage. Once, the place had belonged to the domains of the Comte de Rougeterre; one farm a short distance away—the only one that still had tenants—still belonged to the family. Madame de Givreuse had spent some very pleasant days there, which she had not forgotten. Pierre had often been there.

The carriage stopped at the edge of the village. The four visitors sadly considered the houses gathered around a pyramidal bell-tower—a wretched old belfry devoured by moss, lichen and pellitory. An astonishing silence reigned. Almost all of the shutters were closed. There was an occasional glimpse of a window-pane tarnished by time; feral cats hunted among the worm-eaten apple-trees. There was an abundance of spiders and crane-flies. One might have thought that the end of the world had come. Death hovered over the roofs. They pricked their ears involuntarily in search of a human footstep; the absence of children was even more obvious than that of adults.

"We're in France, though!" murmured Pierre. "Thousands of creatures have no shelter at all. Isn't it as heartrending as the ruins of Herculaneum?"

"And sadder!" added Madame de Givreuse.

They went through the village. Jacques Berleux's farm extended beyond a quincunx of beech-trees. It dated from the monarchy. It had once been a microcosm in which all human industry was represented: carpentry, forge-work, spinning, weaving, cart-building, leather-tanning, brick-making and tilemaking. If necessary, the inhabitants would have been able to get by, almost entirely, without the assistance of other humans. A sturdy wall surrounded the orchard, the kitchen garden and the courtyard.

The farmer came forward beneath his centenarian appletrees. He was an old man, an image of Old France, with shaven lips, prudent eyes and a welcoming smile. He performed a sort of reverence as he said: "M'lady Comtesse...and Monsieur Pierre…I'm at your disposal." With amazement, however, he slyly studied the two young men. "I've heard talk…but I didn't believe…they're as alike as two bees…it's almost a miracle…and I can't even tell which one is the other Monsieur…"

Philippe was pointed out to him. He looked at him with admiration and distrust. "It must be a whim of God—that's not chance, M'lady…what must be must be…and even so, all must be satisfactory to you…given the war, I mean. It's taken my two sons, Madame!" He had taken his visitors into his reception-room—a long room papered in red, where one of his daughters with noble features, the mouth of a marquise and gloved hands brought bread made from a mixture of wheat and rye, fresh butter, milk, cream, coffee and shortbread to the hearth.

The meal was perfectly charming; it evoked memories of youth that the octogenarians found in the deep recesses of their desiccated brains. Fresh air came in from the orchard and the meadows through two wide-open bay windows. Valentine, Pierre and Philippe were all smiles.

The farmer showed them letters written by his sons. They were dull and monotonous; the same phrases recurred over and over again—but sometimes, like a wolf suddenly appearing on the edge of a wood, a terrible or plaintive image cropped up, vibrant with blood and suffering.

"I don't complain," said the old man. "What must be must be, lady…one can't…" Then, very softly, he began talking about the land. "It yields, but only crumbs…the arms are lacking, m'lady, and mine are beginning to get rusty…the right one has a rheumatism that runs over the shoulder and down to the fingers. Some of the crop was lost, rotted…there's havoc in the stables…"

Madame de Givreuse knew what the speaker meant. She listened calmly, resolved to give him something, because she deemed him fundamentally honest, while knowing that it was necessary to take the man's complaints with a pinch of salt. "We'll see what can be done, Maître Berleux," she said.

"Times are hard for everyone—and we need money for the widows..."

"For the widows, of course, M'lady...but the land, everyone must live..." He sighed. In reality, although the harvest had been mediocre, Maître Berleux had reaped abundant benefits therefrom. English money was streaming along the shore. "Alas," he went on, "fathers of families who have two sons at the war...at the end of the day, M'lady will see...I know that M'lady loves justice..."

The snack was concluded. "Let's go see the stables, Maître Berleux," said Madame de Givreuse. She finished a piece of shortbread and got up. Because it was a matter of money, the young people did not do likewise, but she gestured to Pierre. "Come on," she said. "It concerns your patrimony."

Pierre followed her.

Philippe and Valentine were left alone. That rarely happened, and only for very short intervals. This time, it was a snare of destiny; Philippe had no pretext to withdraw.

At first they remained silent. Valentine's anxiety communicated itself subtly to the young man. Philippe dared not look directly at her; he looked sideways at her beautiful pale face and the long hair spilling out under her hat. His heart was full of an affection so gentle that it seemed to exclude passion.

He remembered an almost identical occasion, a year before the war, when he had been in the same room with his mother and Valentine. Perhaps there had already been love in his heart, but it had been in a nascent state, quite ready to vanish into the vast gulf of possibilities in which so many sentiments are sketched. Valentine was standing at one of the windows. A light breeze came in, causing a large black feather in her hat to quiver; a pearly glow spread over her cheeks; her large eyes displayed the charming indecision of adolescence. He had moved closer; they had exchanged a few words of little significance—but which he still remembered, because they were linked to an internal evolution.

The memory made Philippe's heart beat faster. The perfume of iris and amber that floated around Valentine was like the pollen of some distant flower. The view was one of extraordinary freshness and delicacy: meadows like the pasturelands of Ireland; a stream straddled by a little bridge covered in the ancient manner; a row of black poplars, Gothic trees that extended steeples tinted with silver and jade toward the sky. It was a mysterious invitation to intimate joy, to peaceful days in which a humble and quiet destiny faded away. "This is a tragic land, though," he murmured. "A land of spoliation and suffering…like all those the Vikings have passed through."

She raised her head; their gazes met and turned away.

"How peaceful it seems, though," he went on. "As if it were an invitation to life."

"Do you think so?" she said. "In autumn and winter, it's bleaker than the cliffs—and I don't much like meadows. I prefer woods…even moorland…"

He shivered slightly. She had just restated, almost exactly what she had said before. He got up and went to the window. A humble warbler was singing somewhere nearby; its voice was full of the promises that such creatures make themselves when Nature is exorable.

Philippe fell into a reverie; the warbler's voice brought forth deceptive echoes that reawakened memories and vows. A refrain came to his lips without his being conscious of it:

> The branch is gilded by the Sun
> And bows down to shelter
> The buds that are about to blossom
> And the bird that is about to sing…

A faint moan made him turn his head. Mademoiselle de Varsennes was standing up, very pale, her eyelids fluttering and her mouth partly open. Her hands were trembling. He understood; his soul filled with fear and darkness. He had just repeated the verse that he had recited when he was Pierre de Givreuse, in front of this same window, where he had stood alongside Valentine.

He took a step forward. She went whiter still; she seemed to be about to faint. Then there was a reaction; her cheeks reddened—but then a sort of vertigo overtook her and she exclaimed, hoarsely: "Who are you? Where did you come from?"

So quietly that she could hardly hear it, he whispered: "Alas, yes! Who am I?"

Feverishly, she went on: "Why did you recite those lines? And why *here*?"

He did not have the strength to reply immediately; the large eyes fixed upon him inhibited him intolerably. "How do I know?" he said, trying to smile. "The lines came into my memory...what could be simpler?"

Her lips moved, but she said nothing more. Confused suspicions, sharp contradictions and the sensation of the Beyond jostled one another pell-mell. Then two tears ran down her cheeks. Philippe, overwhelmed by love, pity and the dolorous mystery of his life, remained where he was, dejected—and although he knew that he was innocent he felt guilty.

That evening, when the young men were alone, Philippe said to Pierre: "It's become impossible for both of us to remain at Givreuse. Our double presence is becoming an evil action. The trial to which we're subjecting Valentine is insupportable; we don't have the right to prolong it. I've never felt it as I did today..." He related what had happened at the farm. "I might have been able to avoid that slip, but will it be possible for us not to commit others—and more serious ones? All our memories are communal; it's inevitable, in a cohabitation as continuous as ours, that the one who isn't playing the role of Pierre will end up giving himself away. Even if it doesn't happen, Valentine will suffer anyway. She knows perfectly well that we both love her."

These words merely repeated Pierre's thoughts. He limited himself to replying: "Shall we both leave?"

That was the question that Philippe was asking himself. Even though absence no longer gave rise to physical suffering, he was frightened of separation—but they understood that the logic of their destiny demanded at least a temporary separation.

"Fundamentally, we're in agreement," Pierre continued. "We'll meet up often..."

"Which of us will go?"

"We can't decide that for ourselves—we have to draw lots."

The lot selected Philippe.

Disheartened, they rested on their elbows for some time, looking out on the nocturnal garden. A warm breeze was blowing from the sea; clouds moved across the crescent disk of the Moon, giving the scene a febrile but charming life. The young men's souls were bitter and rebellious. Both were suffering, but Philippe was suffering more than Pierre; he was going into a tragic and terrible exile. In the eyes of men, he did not exist; *he had never been born*. In leaving his mother, it was as if he were renouncing her conclusively; his love for Valentine would be no more than a torture...

Pierre had an immediate sensation of the passion—in both the Latin and Biblical senses—that the companion from which he had scarcely begun to differentiate himself was undergoing. All the thoughts going through Philippe's head were going through his own. The ordeal suddenly seemed to him to be unbearable. "Don't go!" he groaned.

"We both know that I must," replied Philippe. "Let's obey the law that has divided us, and which is leading each of us to live a different existence. By staying together, we can only render the future more frightful...and Valentine will be irreparably unhappy."

"This parting might not settle anything, though," Pierre said, agitatedly. "I'll be waiting...everything will be in suspense..."

"I expect so," Philippe replied, sadly. "For a long time, it will be impossible for us to consent to one of our two identities being truly sacrificed for the other. My departure will only be a first trial. Who knows whether it will be beneficial?"

They fell silent, bewildered. Never had existence seemed to them so ominous. Their hands gripped one another, and that grip made them more intensely aware of their unity.

"All the same," stammered Philippe, "it's a dream, isn't it?"

"Or a higher truth," murmured Pierre.

Thoughts that had haunted their minds a thousand times rose up; they experienced the vast astonishment, the tremulous incredulity, and the indeterminate suspicions all over again. Then it all melted into imperious reality, and their mystery seemed to be nothing but one more petty enigma in the infinite enigma of existence—except that their affliction remained heart-breaking and inexorable.

They got up the next day after a sleepless night. An early visitor, Augustin de Rougeterre, was waiting for them. He felt a slight frisson as he greeted them. He had not grown used to their double presence; every time he saw them, he felt the breath of which the prophet speaks pass over him.

"I've come to talk business," he said. "We're proposing to extend our enterprise…"

He wanted to talk about airplane manufacture, to which he had patriotically dedicated part of his fortune, and with which he had associated Madame and Pierre de Givreuse. The business was profitable—more so than he wished. "We're increasing the capital by a third," he said. "I wanted to ask your opinion…"

"It's entirely in conformity with yours!"

"I'd also like, since you've undertaken scientific studies…" He stopped, slightly alarmed, as he was every time he referred to their past. "At least, I'd like one of you…to supervise a subsidiary branch near Granville…"

"That will be me," said Philippe. "I'm leaving the château for a few months, to devote more time to my career…"

The Comte looked at him suspiciously, as if vaguely scandalized. "You're going your separate ways?"

"We'd resolved to do so before you came."

Augustin hesitated, pensively. "I didn't dare advise you to do it," he said, finally. "I've thought about it more than once."

They had gone into the dining-room. The table was set; it lacked nothing but coffee and milk. Madame de Givreuse and Valentine were late.

"You'll have to repeat a sort of apprenticeship in life," Rougeterre went on. "Each of you will have to get used to acting on his own account."

8 a.m. chimed on the old clock; a chambermaid passed along the hallway. "Victorine!" called Pierre. "Has Madame not come down?"

"Yes, Monsieur, but…"

She did not have time to finish. Rapid footsteps were heard and Madame de Givreuse came in, her features in distress. "Valentine has disappeared!" she exclaimed.

"That's impossible!" cried Pierre and Philippe. "She can't have disappeared!"

Their consternation was greater than their astonishment; although they could guess the motive that the young girl had to be obeying, they could not understand the abruptness of her action.

"It is indeed impossible," said Rougeterre. "Valentine can't have disappeared like that; she probably went out early and has been delayed on the way back, for one reason or another."

Madame de Givreuse shook her head. "I thought that too, Augustin—but she never went to bed! She must have gone out during the night or very early."

"That's more serious," said the Comte, looking suspiciously at the two young men. "That young woman has always seemed to me to be incapable of acting without consideration."

Pierre and Philippe did not try to hide their emotion. As is only natural, when a person's actions are suddenly in contradiction to her character, they feared the worst…and even the worst of all, irreparable…

"She must at least have left a letter," Rougeterre went on, impatient with the others' silence.

"We've searched—we didn't find anything," said Madame de Givreuse, faintly. She loved Valentine with an affection outweighed only by her affection for Pierre. She had thought she knew everything about the young woman, who was unable to dissimulate, let alone lie.

"There are too many mysteries in this house," Augustin muttered between clenched teeth. Aloud, he added: "All the same, nothing can make me believe that she left without a reason." He alternated his gaze between Pierre and Philippe, his eyes gleaming with curiosity and reprobation.

"Undoubtedly," said Pierre, looking the Comte in the face, "but no one has done anything or said anything—knowingly—that could have offended Mademoiselle de Varsennes."

"All right!" groaned Rougeterre. "Let's stop trying to understand and let's not lose any more time. We have to find her!" He was a man of action; he proposed a series of steps. Philippe, assisted by the gardener, was to explore the beach; Pierre would go to Avranches and the Comte to Granville. Madame de Givreuse would send servants to the neighboring villages and to ask Savarre—who knew the country thoroughly and had a numerous staff at his disposal—for his help.

V.

Valentine had spent a tragic night. The evening, however, had been almost calm. When she retired to her room, she initially experienced a fairly gentle relaxation. It seemed to her that she had recovered, that her agitations had been a waking nightmare and that she had exaggerated the situation strangely.

She was not sleepy; she took a book from her small library; it was *François le Champi*.[6] It was some time since she had read it. She took pleasure in those naive lives, lost in the depth of the countryside. She read continuously, almost avidly, to the point at which Madeleine was crossing the shaking bridge, carrying Champi in her arms...

Suddenly, she felt that sudden hastening of her heartbeat that recalls us to our troubles. She put down the book and watched three midges that were flying around the electric light-bulb. A terrible malaise, dull at first, spread from her diaphragm throughout her being. With painful clarity, she saw Philippe's silhouette again; she heard the four lines that he had murmured at the window. She repeated the lines without being able to remember the last two exactly, and tried for a few minutes to reconstitute them.

What was intolerable was that she could not understand why she was so troubled. She was not in the habit of analyzing her sensations and was perhaps not very good at it. She was suffering from a sort of mystical fear. That fear had abruptly increased and was continuing to grow; in spite of herself she saw something supernatural in the afternoon scene. All of this whirled around in her head without her being able to glimpse an outcome. Imprisoned in her intuition, she had no clear ideas, but was all the more impressed...

Several times, she tried to resume reading, but the book soon fell from her hands and the black dream recommenced, without result.

That lasted for several hours. She was worn out with fatigue, but was afraid to go to bed. Towards midnight, she sat down in an armchair in front of the window in order to breathe in the fresh air; then she was seized by torpor and fell asleep.

---

[6] A novel by George Sand, first serialized in 1847-48, which tells the story of a foundling who is driven from his adopted home when his foster-parents fall on hard times, but returns to rescue his widowed foster-mother, and eventually marries her.

When she awoke it was near dawn; two large stars were setting over the ocean. Valentine shivered. She was feverish; her temples were red and her hands icy. She looked at things in astonishment. A mist filled her brain; everything within and around her was exaggerated. Mechanically, she picked up a mantle.

She went through the overgrown garden, exited by a side gate and found herself on the road just as a melancholy glow mingled with the moonlight. It is certain that she only had a restricted consciousness of her actions. The fever was increasing; her heart and pulse were beating desperately.

She walked through the bracken and grass for some time. The dawn exaggerated the clouds and filled them with its fugitive light. Then a red furnace rose up amid the apple-trees. Mademoiselle de Varsennes continued walking. The fever sustained her and wearied her at the same time. She paused several times and turned in the direction of the château, but an indefinable will impelled her on her way again.

This went on for several hours. When she reached Avranches the Sun was already high in the sky. She headed for the church, went in, and prayed discreetly. Then she stopped in a narrow street in front of an old stone house with a shingle roof. There was a knocker on the door. She rapped.

A woman with a triangular face, red-eyed and already old, came to open the door and uttered an exclamation: "It's you, my dear child!"

"It's me, Madeleine."

They both stood there in surprise; then the hostess took the young woman into a little reception-room—or, rather, a parlor—furnished with low chairs with elongated backs, like those in church, an old oaken table, a carved chest that was somewhat reminiscent of a sarcophagus, and a large chest of drawers with copper handles.

Madeleine Faubert had been Valentine's governess and first instructress. The aged spinster displayed as few faults as human make-up permits. Sincerely modest without being humble, constant and scrupulous, resigned and cheerful, thrifty and generous, sometimes stubborn, a little too secretive, sometimes irascible with respect to pride or egoism, her heart was an inexhaustible reservoir of compassion. She loved Valentine dearly, with a complex tenderness in which her own unsatisfied desires were concentrated: maternal instinct and a mysterious, infinitely pure love that nevertheless reflected the passions of which poverty, chance and circumstance had deprived her. Although as innocent at heart as a little child, she had a penetrating intelligence and experience; she understood sentiments of which she had no personal knowledge. She was the only person to whom Valentine dared to tell everything.

Madeleine studied the young woman without appearing to. She saw her blue-tinted eyes, her feverish cheeks and the distress expressed by her entire person. She pressed her visitor's hands with fingers that were as slender and delicate as Valentine's, but whose joints rheumatism was beginning to inflame slightly. "What's the matter, dear Marquise? One would think that you had a fever." She took the young woman's pulse and observed its precipitate pace.

"Yes, I think I have a fever—and I'm so very tired, Madeleine."

Madeleine had sat her down on one of her church chairs with a hard, stiff back. She sensed that she ought not to ask any more questions. She waited patiently, with the gentle self-composure of women who know how to listen and console.

"Oh, Madeleine!" the adolescent sighed. "Why am I so unhappy? That's nothing—one has every right to be unhappy, when there is so much pain in France…but not like this…not like this!" Her eyes were full of tears. "I have no idea whether you'll be able to understand…I don't understand myself…perhaps I'm mad. I've run away from the château…out of fright…"

"Fright!" exclaimed Madeleine, gripped by the combative spirit that she felt on behalf of others. "No one has taken the liberty…?"

"Oh! No one, my dear. No one has done me any wrong…or even said anything…"

Madeleine scrutinized the pale face closely. In a lower voice, the young woman said: "Perhaps you've guessed, Madeleine, what I've thought about during his absence?"

"I've guessed it, little Marquise. That's fine…it's what I've wished for."

"I'm sure that I loved him already, before his departure…but not completely. It's as if that absence was necessary…and I thought that he…"

"You can be sure of it!"

"When they came back…"

The instructress started. "The other one wasn't coming back."

"Exactly. But how can one tell? It's impossible to detect the slightest difference between them. You know that…"

"That's true. The resemblance is striking."

"It's frightening! I was gripped by it immediately… gripped by one of those revelations that make one so sick at heart. You can't know, Madeleine…I waited for him with so much fervor...I was so impatient and so happy…and suddenly, it's him, and it isn't him…there's another, who is the same…"

"Yes," said the old spinster, pensively. "I hadn't thought…of that. Yes, that must be disturbing."

It was as if a fog dissipated in the young woman's mind. So many dark sensations, so many intuitions, until then indefinable, seemed to have been clarified by the fever.

"It wasn't at all like a familiar resemblance. It was a revelation—a thunderbolt…the destruction of a personality. I spent several days in a veritable bewilderment. Everything was dying within me—at least, I thought so. Then it came back. My dream tried to revive. It lived again. I made an immense effort to accomplish an abstraction of the other one— Philippe—and to *isolate* Pierre. I thought I was succeeding in that, in spite of a persistent anguish, a dark presentiment. There was one beautiful moment, on the sea-shore, among the wild rocks, where we had a memory in common. There, I thought that the threat was defeated…our eyes had found one another again…but when Philippe rejoined us…how can I put it? It was exactly the same gaze…and, I'm fearfully certain, *the same love!*"

"The same love!" Madeleine repeated, pensively. She understood. A fraction of Valentine's disturbance infected her own soul.

"My God!" sighed the young woman. "Again, that's nothing. I thought that one of the loves would fade away, sooner or later…and that that would be sufficient in itself to create a profound difference between them…but in my over-excited mind—is it even in my mind, or rather in my entire being?—a new misery was born. Until then, I could at least distinguish Pierre and Philippe in terms of their past. One of them had lived with me before the war, our memories over-lapped…oh, I still believe that, for how could it be otherwise? But a sentiment stronger than any reasoned conviction devel-oped—that, by some witchcraft or other, *Philippe's memories are the same as Pierre's*. I tried hard to reject it, but the senti-ment increased incessantly, seemingly receiving proof after proof, by virtue of a word, a gesture, or any one of the thou-sand insignificant actions of life. Was I mad? I asked myself that continually.

"Yesterday, all three of us went with Madame de Gi-vreuse to Jacques Berleux's farm—you know, the farm of olden days on the far side of the abandoned village. Philippe and I were left alone while Madame de Givreuse and Pierre were discussing business matters with the farmer. I retained a very dear memory of an hour spent in the room in which we found ourselves. It was almost the same time of year. Sudden-ly, as before, a bird began to sing, and Philippe recited four lines of verse—the same ones that Pierre had recited at the same window. I was seized by a veritable terror…which in-creased last night."

There was a pause. Madeleine was increasingly affected by the young woman's "atmosphere."

"Is it possible," Valentine whispered, "for the memories of one man to be communicated to another?"

"Telepathy," suggested Madeleine. "Besides, dear child, why shouldn't those lines have come into Philippe's mind quite naturally."

"In front of that very window? And in circumstances so similar to those that had led Pierre to recite them? That would be a prodigy!"

"Would you care to tell me what the lines were?"

"I don't recall the third and fourth exactly, but something like these:

"The branch is gilded by the Sun
"And bows down to shelter
"The buds that are about to open
"For the bird that is about to sing...

"There can't be many people who know those lines!"

"That's true. Take note, however, that they concern a bird that is about to sing. Now, both times they were recited before you, a bird was singing. Two minds that resemble one another as much as those of Pierre and Philippe might be subject to the same invocation. It's extraordinary, but not supernatural..."

"If only you were right!"

"I am right, Marquisette! You have to believe me, and set your mind at rest. What must they be thinking back there?"

"My God!" groaned the young woman. "It's intolerable that I should cause Madame de Givreuse any anxiety. What shall I do?"

"Simply send a message. As I can't leave you alone, Madame de Givreuse will come here. I think I'll be able to make her understand..."

"It's so difficult. The slightest allusion might distress everyone..."

"I'm not thinking of telling her the simple truth—or of allowing her to guess..."

The horn of a motor car sounded in the street. The two women looked out of the window. A limousine was drawing to a halt.

"It's Pierre!" exclaimed Valentine, fearfully. "Or Philippe!"

"I'll take care of him." Madeleine opened a door hurriedly and ushered Valentine into a minuscule dining-room. Two blows of the knocker resounded in the hallway.

The visitor's features seemed almost rigid, but his eyes betrayed a dark anxiety. Mademoiselle Faubert introduced him into the little parlor. He looked around feverishly.

"I beg your pardon," he said. "Have you seen Mademoiselle de Varsennes? She…"

"She's here," Madeleine replied, calmly.

A nervous smile played upon the young man's lips. "Thank God!" he sighed. "We were afraid that…on the way, though, I had a presentiment that she would have sought refuge with her dearest friend!" The last words caused Madeleine to conclude that she was in the presence of Pierre. "I don't ask to see Mademoiselle de Varsennes…" he went on, timidly.

"She's very tired."

"There's no place in the world where she'd be safer than here. I'll go telegraph my mother."

There was a short pause. Each of them looked at the other with ardent and anxious curiosity.

"It's impossible for me to leave her alone," said Madeleine, finally, in a low voice. "Otherwise, I'd go to see Madame de Givreuse."

"Perhaps my mother might come here?"

"Of course she may. I think that would be useful."

Pierre hesitated, then said: "Mademoiselle de Varsennes isn't ill?"

"No."

He understood that he should not insist. "When would you like my mother to visit you?" he murmured.

"As soon as possible."

"In that case, I think you'll see her this morning."

Madeleine had scrutinized Pierre's physiognomy attentively. She had seen multiple nuances of emotion pass through it, but no astonishment. *Does he know, then?* she wondered. *Or at least suspect?*

He seemed to want to ask something else, but he did not dare, and withdrew.

Madeleine was thoughtful. She understood Valentine's indefinable suspicions now.

10 a.m. had just chimed on the Church of Saint Saturnin when Madame de Givreuse arrived at Mademoiselle Faubert's house. The visitor betrayed her agitation more evidently than Pierre; her face had the hardness that emotion gives to authoritarian features. She felt a trifle resentful toward Valentine; she did not understand why the young woman had left so mysteriously, but her rancor was founded in offended affection. Perhaps she was also vaguely jealous of Mademoiselle Faubert. She held the instructress in esteem, but had never showed her any real cordiality.

"Excuse me, Madame," said Madeleine. "It wasn't possible to leave Mademoiselle de Varsennes alone."

"I understand that perfectly," the visitor replied, coldly. "We've been very anxious!"

Madeleine thought she could perceive a reproach in her tone. "I was about to send a telegram when Monsieur de Givreuse arrived."

The Comtesse made a vague gesture, and then said, angrily: "Why has she done this? It's so contrary to her nature."

"Circumstances can be stronger than character."

"What circumstances?" exclaimed Madame de Givreuse, indignantly. "What could have happened to Valentine, *in my house?* I assume that no one has shown her any lack of respect?"

"Oh, that's impossible, Madame. Mademoiselle de Varsennes has received nothing but evidence of affection from yourself and everyone else."

"What, then? She's not mad…"

"Merely very troubled."

"For which she has her reasons?"

"Undoubtedly, Madame."

"Could she not have confided them to me? Does she not know that I love her as I would my own daughter?"

"She knows that. She loves you like a mother."

"Well then?"

Madame de Givreuse was generous, devoted and tyrannical; she was not overblessed with insight. She rightly deduced, however, that it was a matter of some sentimental crisis, and she had expected for a long time that Pierre and Valentine would fall in love. She wanted that.

"Alas," Madeleine replied, "the people who love us the most are sometimes those to whom we cannot make certain confidences."

Madame de Givreuse shrugged her shoulders. "Let's be clear, Mademoiselle. Has Pierre said something to Valentine—not offensive, he's incapable of that—but which has frightened her?"

"I don't believe so."

"So she's obeying an entirely private sentiment—is that it?"

"That's it."

"Do you know what that sentiment is?"

Madeleine did not reply.

"Come on," the Comtesse continued. "I need to know. My ardent desire is that Valentine should be happy. I certainly have a right to know why she has run away from us."

"Perhaps she doesn't really know herself. She's so scrupulous!"

"I know what you mean—it concerns Pierre. But in what sense? Is she afraid of love? Is she afraid of being loved?"

"Both, undoubtedly."

"I don't see that that's any reason to run away from us."

"If she wants to escape any influence, however…to be free…"

"How are we constraining her?"

"Oh, Madame, that's not what I mean. I'm talking about the influence exercised by affection itself…the scruples that a

79

young woman might have. How do we know whether Valentine isn't fearful of upsetting you?"

Madame Givreuse smiled, almost softly. "Upsetting me? I only want her to be happy. If she and Pierre were in love, I would be delighted. If she doesn't love Pierre, I certainly wouldn't hold it against her. She's as free as the wind on the sea!"

"She surely has no doubt of it…"

"In sum," the Comtesse went on, "has any event caused Valentine to act thus?"

"Only internal events, I might put it thus…"

"She wants to think things over! That's good. It won't prevent me from seeing her, I assume?"

Madame de Givreuse had raised her voice. The interior door opened and Valentine showed herself, her face tearful. She went silently to kneel before the Comtesse. Her long hair was in semi-disarray; fatigue, emotion and insomnia had swollen her eyelids and her young eyes seemed all the more charming for it. Mollified, Madame de Givreuse drew the young woman to her bosom.

VI.

Philippe's new life was melancholy, but not as much as he had feared. Strength rose up within him from the depths of his being and made him apply himself to his task. He worked hard organizing the workshop that had been entrusted to him. He had a natural technological bent; he was developing a latent talent, and his imagination revealed its ingenuity.

Savarre had fabricated documents that provided the young man with safeguards. He was now named Philippe Frémeuse; his birthplace had been established as New Orleans in the United States. Philippe's papers were authentic; they had passed into Savarre's hands from a shipwreck victim who had died in his sanatorium, whose only son had perished at sea. The father had not had time to register his son's death, and they had no other family. This deception was indispensable and inevitable. No administrative authority could accept the duplicate personality of Pierre de Givreuse, nor admit that a man could exist without official papers establishing his identity. In the meantime, this legal fiction did no injury to any individual or collective. The neurologist intended to perfect it subsequently by adopting Philippe. At the Town Hall of Ennuyères, to which the Château de Givreuse was dependent, no suspicion was raised. Philippe Frémeuse was officially admitted to membership of the community.

All of this, without confirming it, prepared the ground for a renunciation. The destiny of the Givreuses was separated. The one who remained at the château acquired a privilege that the subtle form of circumstances would render definitive. The other suffered thereby, but without bitterness; indeed, a primitive delight was mingled with his trial by ordeal. Philippe struggled desperately to transform his love in memory, and that struggle tended to establish a difference, if not of temperament, at least of character, between himself and Pierre. It multiplied his activity.

To the factory that Rougeterre and his associates had set up near Carolles, it was Philippe who brought the greatest vigilance and tried hardest to perfect the machines. He had succeeded in improving an engine; that small victory over matter helped him adapt himself to his fate. Thus, while Pierre abandoned himself to delightful but passive emotions—taking up, as it were, the life of the species—Philippe accentuated personal life, developing original elements therein. In the particular state of plasticity in which they still found themselves, which offered analogies with childhood and early adolescence, that differentiation had a certain operative breadth.

It happened that the spirit of invention, the will and aptitude for struggle, made progress in Philippe. It was a kind of recompense for his sacrifice; it encouraged him and filled him with confidence in the future. His work became a passion; he strove doggedly to produce faultless machines, sturdy and flexible engines that refused to break down. He became an aviator himself, so bold and so skillful that he soon desired to become a military pilot—but he concluded that he would render greater service as a manufacturer than he could at the front. Tempted nevertheless by the perilous life, he departed in an airplane on several occasions for the East, where he took part in the trials of the Rougeterre apparatus and departed surreptitiously to hurl bombs of his own invention down upon German railway stations, trains and ammunition depots. These exploits satisfied his need for adventure and his hatred of tedium.

One evening, as he returned from one of these expeditions, a projectile struck his engine. The twilight was fading away and night was falling very blackly, overcast by heavy cloud. There was not a star in the sky. Electric searchlight beams rose up from the ground, rotating about the sky. The engine was still functioning, but Philippe knew that it could not last much longer. Guns were thundering, and a few German aircraft were prowling in the shadows.

Is this my final hour? Philippe wondered.

He loved life. On that black Earth, lost in the darkness, years of strength and courage had been promised to him. He thought about *the other one*, his mother and Valentine, with immense affection; he also experienced a strange regret at dying without having discovered the secret of his duplication...

Suddenly, he found himself in a fog—or, rather in a cloud. The searchlights no longer reached him. For ten minutes more the engine functioned; then it stopped. It was necessary to descend at hazard. Philippe made his machine describe a long spiral, and without quite knowing how, found himself in a large, almost bare clearing in the middle of a forest.

Everything was peaceful. The distant artillery-fire was scarcely audible. He waited for a few moments, revolver in hand; then, by the bright light of his lantern, he set about examining the engine. The damage was actually slight, but badly located. He rapidly improvised a repair, and was getting ready to take off again when he heard a voice. A human being had just emerged, scarcely clad in a vague chemise and a ragged skirt. She was still a child; her eyes shone like those of a lynx. He directed the light at a swarthy face beneath a shock of hair that hung down to slim shoulders.

"You're French!" she said "I know you are!"

"I'm French."

She looked at him imploringly. "I've been living in these woods for nearly a year," she went on. "None of *them* has ever found me."

A great pity, tinged with admiration, filled Philippe's heart. "What about your parents?" he asked, softly.

"I have no parents," she sighed. "I'm a foundling."

"Poor child!"

He became more interested in her. This adventure had mysterious affinities with his own. The child's origins were lost in the darkness of being, just as his own were lost in the darkness of force. "Wouldn't you be afraid to come with me?" he asked.

"Oh, don't leave me here alone!" she exclaimed, her eyes shining.

He installed her in the apparatus then, wrapping her up in a blanket. Then, having checked everything, he took his place in his turn and started the engine.

"Above all, don't move!"

The apparatus moved forward and took off. It cleared the tree-tops. The child showed hardly any astonishment, and soon became accustomed to it. The darkness was profound. A mist was settling over the forests, the hills and the plain; the airplane became invisible.

A few hours later, Philippe landed, far beyond the enemy lines.

Philippe placed the little girl with an instructress. He went to see her every day when he was not on his travels.

She was fearful, abrupt and wild at first; she moved like a captive beast; she could not break the habit of being on her guard and fleeing at the slightest suspect sound. He liked her oread's face, her wide sparkling eyes and her supple forest-dweller's figure. The child demonstrated an unbridled and jealous affection for him. The night when he had lifted her up into the sky inevitably remained the most magical night of her life. He also became attached to her. He was delighted to have found her in the unknown, among innumerable enemies. The connection that linked him to her became ever stronger, and gave him more courage.

One day, he found her in the instructress's garden. The equinox was already approaching. A stormy wind was blowing from the sea. Storm-birds were circling, squawking stridently; soaring birds[7] with trenchant wings quit the heights and made long feverish swoops over the cliffs. He walked beneath the apple-trees with little Jeanne; spiders like little crabs were spinning their webs there. Her movements were furtive and rhythmic.

What will become of her? he wondered, anxiously. *What path will she follow through incomprehensible life?* He wanted her to be happy. Obscure emotions rose up in him, but he preferred them to be obscure, for fear of all the possibilities that might so easily become impossible. Eventually, he asked: "Are you happy, Jeanne?"

She turned her clear dark eyes toward him and replied in a low voice: "I'm happy when you're here."

He shivered; he foresaw the child's future, the mistreatment of the adolescent. "That won't always be the case," he murmured.

There was indignation and fear on the swarthy face; the eyes became quite black, so dilated were the pupils. Then she laughed hoarsely. "Only until I'm dead!"

---

[7] The term Rosny uses here is *apodes*—which can be directly, if rather obscurely, transcribed into English with reference to fabulous birds that have no feet—but the metaphorical reference is merely to birds that rarely seem to land.

"Dead!" He felt the force and depth of the intonation; there was no doubting it. At the fatal hour, the love that was born within this child, like pollen in a flower, would be irrevocable. It would be a jealous love.

They walked together for a while, side by side. The wind blew the sea-mist away; a black nimbus formed and deepened, bordered by phosphorescence. A vision developed its confused vicissitudes. Philippe glimpsed the twists and turns of a destiny in which there was no more loss or sacrifice, in which pure days would emerge, one after another, like stray buttercups in the mountains.

Warm raindrops fell upon the apple-trees; something intense and delicious welled up from the autumnal grass—but a rhythmic image suddenly stood out against the cliffs and pain began to beat again in Philippe's breast. Once again, he saw the open window overlooking the landscape of Old France, while lines echoed implacably in his memory:

The branch is gilded by the Sun
And bows down to shelter
The buds that are about to blossom
And the bird that is about to sing...

He took the little girl's arm, and led her back to the house.

Part Three

I.

Pierre suffered more than Philippe. The strangest remorse accompanied him even into the depths of sleep, often waking him up with a sudden shock. Then, in the shadows, he was subject to an unconscious nightmare, which filled him with horror and disgust. While Philippe steeped himself in active life, Pierre curled up within a dream. He prowled through the immense château like Hamlet, wandering in the sinister cellars where prisoners had suffered hunger, torture and cold.

Madame de Givreuse's affairs gave him scant employment; she put such activity into them that the young man's involvement was virtually unnecessary. He took refuge in the old library, where strange books solicited his curiosity, or wandered beneath the cliffs, living with the wild sea-birds and enigmatic animals, which emerged from the depths of the strand as if from the depths of the ages.

Like the knell of doom, one single thought resounded in his head. He wanted, incessantly, to call Philippe back. Whenever they met up, though, Philippe opposed that call and insisted that the ordeal was necessary. These disputes revealed the first differences born of their separation; there was more precision in Philippe, more fever and subtlety in Pierre; they began to anticipate the progressive dissolution of their unity.

Valentine had not returned to the château; she visited Madame de Givreuse once a week. Pierre became furtive during these meetings; he spoke rarely. The young people hardly dared look at one another. After Valentine's departure he fell into a black depression, without knowing whether it was regret or the sense of his own impotence. He spent hours analyzing his state of mind, but the more he analyzed it the more indecipherable it seemed; he got lost within himself as if in a virgin forest.

One day, he went out of the château and headed for the heath. He came within sight of Dr. Savarre's sanatorium, a part of which was now given over to wounded soldiers. It was one of those days when the atmosphere is saturated with all the adventure of life. A muted storm that could not burst rendered the air delicious and hardly breathable, supersaturated with pollen. There were brief palpitations, the beginnings of a breeze, as abortive as the thunderclaps within the clouds.

Pierre stopped beside the high wall that had hidden and sheltered so much misery. The silence was punctuated by the rustle of the bracken and broom, reminiscent of the distant rippling of skirts. He saw a female form sliding along the wall with hectic and uncoordinated movements—surely a madwoman.

She caught sight of Pierre. She stopped, stepped back, tensed. She had wild and fearful eyes, exceedingly pale in color. Suddenly coming to a decision, she launched herself toward Pierre and grabbed him by the shoulders. "Silence!" she whispered. "Don't make a sound! The giant frogs are coming...the sea is full of them...they're worse than crocodiles! Oh!"

A bright gleam seemed to spring from her dilated pupils. Her mouth was partly open; it was the same as Valentine's mouth: scarlet, with glints of mother-of-pearl.

"Is it you?" she said. "Do you still love me? The hour has come, my love...it's sounding down there...the black-and-red hour...the tide's rising...the giant frogs will flood the cliffs...all the way to the stars. Listen! Oh, how they growl...they've put the sailors to flight, you know...in the torrid sands. Clutch me to your heart...save me..."

Two warders had just appeared around the corner of the wall. They were coming forward, heavily but rapidly. The madwoman uttered a loud scream. "There they are! Quickly! Anda! They're going to devour us!" Her grip became convulsive; her charming mouth quivered, a continuous groan rising from her throat.

Abruptly, she ran away. Then, seeing that the warders were about to recapture her, Pierre shut his eyes, gripped by an abominable sadness. When he opened them again, the warders had hold of the fugitive.

She did not scream again; she followed them, mute and somber—but when she passed close to Pierre again, she cried in a heart-rending voice: "Why have you abandoned me?"

He fled across the heath. He saw that white face, those excessively clear eyes, and especially that mouth—so fine and sparkling—without any respite. Inexpressible presentiments ran through him like electric currents. He took massive strides.

Dusk was falling when he saw that he was in a town; it was Avranches. The Church of Saint Saturnin loomed up into the haze. A bell had just finished chiming; a bright star was twinkling. He went into the church. Women were kneeling therein, and also a few men. He studied them in the wan yellow candlelight. He was bizarrely surprised not to see Valentine and Mademoiselle Faubert. For a few minutes he hoped that they might come; then he left, disheartened.

Two women were passing by in the twilight; he recognized their gait. Having been surprised not to find them in the church, he was even more surprised to see them there. Valentine's face was turned toward him. She shuddered...

Mechanically, he began walking alongside Mademoiselle Faubert, drawn by a force that interrupted the train of his thought. His exacerbated sense of smell perceived a subtle perfume of iris and amber. He was no longer thinking about Philippe; it seemed that his past and his future belonged to him, as to other beings. He heard Madeleine's greeting and replied mechanically.

After a short time, they found themselves outside the old house. The oblique moonlight surrounded Valentine with a magical glow. Her face shone like a water-lily flower in a twilit pool; her dress fell about her in harmonious waves and her partly-open mouth was as innocent as a child's.

88

Captive love expanded in Pierre then, like spring-time. It was a blossoming of his entire being; he no longer understood—or, rather, no longer perceived—his scruples; the imperious voice of generations overwhelmed the feeble psychic voice...

That scene had profound echoes in Pierre's consciousness. It contributed to the increase of his personality. For the first time, he sensed the possibility of being jealous of Philippe. It was still uncertain and intermittent, but, in the final analysis, there were moments when he thought about making the best of the other's renunciation. Simultaneously, his love for Valentine underwent a metamorphosis; it became more feverish and more suspicious.

Thus far, he had enjoyed a rather singular security. He gave no thought to external rivals; the issue was a private matter between him and Philippe. Perhaps because he had felt an initial manifestation of jealousy, he began to dread a change of mind on Valentine's part. The separation, which had previously been an inchoate sadness, became a source of precise and corrosive anxieties. That too tended to create a sharper notion of his new self. From then on, he waited impatiently for the young woman's visits; he spent longer in conversation and he did not succeed in hiding his agitation.

Valentine was less timid. Pierre's metamorphosis reassured her instinct. She found that he resembled Philippe less, and the hope of discovering sensible differences between them made her existence more exciting.

One Thursday she arrived unexpectedly. It was a day when Philippe had chosen to return to the château, and the young woman knew it. Drawn by an ill-defined need to compare the two men, she wondered anxiously whether Pierre's transformation might be a mirage created by her imagination.

She found Madame de Givreuse alone.

The Comtesse had just returned from her military orphanage; seated on the terrace, in the shade of the large palmate leaves of a fig-tree, she was enjoying a momentary peace. As she had received the gift of quietude, she knew how to forget the bustle of activity during rest; retaining the fine days of the past, she threw the others into the dungeons of unconsciousness. Today, she was particularly content. She did not know why; actually, she loved the double presence of Pierre and Philippe because, deep down, she loved the latter almost as much as the former. "Good day, little bird," she said. "We have a visitor." She did not notice the flutter of Valentine's eyelids. "A visitor you haven't seen for some time…"

A chambermaid, with the curly hair in which Soldi[8] believed he could read the mysterious cosmogony of the men who had raised the cromlechs and built the first pyramids, came to set the table for tea. There were muffins; Madame de Givreuse loved them.

Pierre and Philippe appeared around a quincunx of English oaks. At first, their resemblance seemed just as exact to Valentine—but when they came closer, the young woman smiled. Philippe's complexion was more tanned than Pierre's, and there was something more resolute in the contours of his features; his eyes seemed clearer and bolder. There was a fever in Pierre's pupils; his mouth was indecisive and sensitive; his entire being was inclined toward visions and the interior life. Both of them resembled the young man who had answered the call to arms less than they had before, with the result that she did not know which of them was in better accord with her memories. She did not ask herself which she might prefer. Her heart was still full of uncertainty, but she no longer doubted that a preference was possible. Above all, she felt the mystical fear that had caused her so much suffering begin to decrease.

A short time afterwards, she saw them together again in Augustin de Rougeterre's house, this time by chance. Perhaps because she had thought about it so often and so passionately

---

[8] The sculptor and engraver Emile Soldi (1846-1906), who fancied that he could make anthropological deductions from ancient and folk art.

in the interval, she found the lack of resemblance further accentuated. All three of them went to the bank of a little pool over which Babylonian willows extended their melancholy drapes. Madame de Givreuse and Rougeterre were walking ahead; the ringing voice of the Comte was making the frogs hop.

All three of them loved that spot, where they had spent delightful moments at one time.

"Do you remember," Valentine suddenly asked, observing the young men closely, "the squirrel that we saw here at the end of autumn?"

The first three words had put Philippe on his guard. His physiognomy gave nothing away, while Pierre replied: "We haven't seen him since! He disappeared before the war..."

She laughed lightly, marking her internal joy. Her eyes met Pierre's; she read a painful ardor therein, and whispered to herself: "He's the one who's suffering more!"

From that day forward, she thought of Pierre more often. She exaggerated everything within him that was not identical to Philippe; she created a new image, which she superimposed on the images of times past. Philippe, however, retained a mysterious power; at times, when she thought she had rid herself of him, he reappeared like an evocation and a reproach.

A month passed, which remade hearts and the vegetation. Valentine found herself by the same pool with Pierre and Rougeterre. A domestic arrived, bringing a visiting-card. The young people were left alone.

Their hearts were as indecisive as their words, but Pierre knew that he was gradually becoming a normal person in the young woman's eyes. She no longer had the charming embarrassment of timid creatures. At intervals, he turned toward her; never had she seemed so multifaceted. All the gracefulness of living creatures was concentrated in her. The interplay of boughs and clouds, the twitter of woodland birds, the silvery corollas of arrowheads and the gleam of the water were transformed, and became more intoxicating...

Valentine leaned forward to pick a pink flower that was growing in a shady spot. The friable earth yielded; Pierre scarcely had time to grab it and pull it up. Valentine uttered a little cry of alarm; she remained pressed against Givreuse's bosom. He had not expected that violent sensation; he went pale, as if he were about to faint; his heart skipped a beat and his face was momentarily buried in her scented hair…

"Thank you!" she said, in a faint voice, trying to smile.

What he could see in her beautiful, still-tremulous eyes separated him from everything else. He forgot Philippe completely. He only remembered him again when she had gone. Until nightfall, he examined his conscience. It was ardent and distressed, tormented by a remorse that could not succeed in making him forget the cruel joy of the embrace.

What have I done, though? he wondered. *My gesture was necessary. Am I master of my sensations?*

But he had prolonged those sensations! He resolved to talk to Philippe.

They met up in the ravine through which a meager river ran down to the ocean. Heavy stones loomed up; a field of gorse had been burned, leaving a black funereal void.

"Are you unhappy?" Pierre suddenly asked.

"I don't know. I live…my life isn't repulsive. I'm gradually adapting to people…"

They were moving through sage, yarrow, umbellifers and St. John's wort. Little batrachians were hopping about intermittently. Pierre found it difficult to make his confession. That difficulty was itself demonstrative of the changes that had taken place; previously, he had talked to Philippe as if he were talking to himself. Finally, he said: "Don't you want to cut your ordeal short?"

"No, no!" said the other, swiftly. "I'm sure that would be absolutely fatal."

"I'm privileged."

"That's inevitable."

"But what if Valentine were to choose me?" Pierre went on, confusedly.

Philippe stared at him, astonished by his tone. "We have no right to dispute Valentine's choices."

"Of course—but think of what the consequences will be of the circumstances *we* have created."

"We ought to desire them, since it's necessary for us to be two people. For Valentine, most of all, the separation is necessary. It would be intolerable for us to fight over that innocent creature. Whatever happens, I shan't complain."

"What if you're sacrificed?"

"Sacrificed? By whom? It wasn't you or me that decided that I should leave—it was fate."

"We could both give her up."

"Why? That would be breaking two hearts instead of one…and perhaps a great pain and a bitter memory for her. If she chooses you, I'll bow down to the inevitable."

"You'll suffer…"

"Undoubtedly. I've learned to cope…I'm learning to cope with that suffering every day."

Pierre heard the muted tremor of a soul beneath the words. There was stoicism in Philippe's attitude. Pierre felt badly about his companion's distress, but he felt nevertheless that a secret life was now beginning to separate them. Twice he tried to make his confession, but he could not do it. Each time, an equivocal instinct stopped him.

Philippe divined that confusion confusedly; it troubled him, but he was determined not to attempt to overcome it. "Whatever you do," he said, with a sudden surge of affection, "I shall have no reproach to make to you. When I left the château, we were exactly the same as one anther. It's the separation that has created a difference…if not fundamentally, at least superficially. Whatever you have done, I would have done!"

"Don't think that I've mentioned love to her!" said Pierre, plaintively.

"Don't feel constrained to remain silent!"

They looked at one another; their unity was manifest once more, more powerful than any passion or any affection...but Pierre did not say what he had resolved to say.

Philippe experienced a tremendous weariness, weighed down by a moral burden, and he had no other consolation than the little girl he had plucked from the unknown wood.

"I forgot," said Pierre, insouciantly, "to show you this...I got it this morning." He took a note out of his wallet and held it out to Philippe.

Philippe read:

Dear Friend,
I shall soon leave on a very long voyage. Perhaps you would come and bid me farewell at "The Gladioli," where I shall be staying for a few days in order to see my friends.
Best wishes from,
Thérèse de Lisanges.

Philippe found the note intriguing.

"It's impossible for me to go, of course," Pierre remarked.

"I'll go, then," said Philippe.

Pierre looked at him in amazement. "Under your new name?"

"Of course...but on your behalf."

"She'll believe..."

"She'll believe what I tell her. I suspect that she already knows something—she's always been able to keep abreast of things."

Pierre made a gesture expressing indifference.

Philippe went to *The Gladioli* the following day. It was a small manor house entirely surrounded by gardens. A sleepy-eyed servant introduced him into a drawing-room with tall wood paneling and sturdy old Norman furniture. After a pause, a fascinating and complex young woman came in. Beneath a fine layer of powder, a Catalan or Latin-American complexion was discernible. The finest blood nourished ardent lips, scarlet in the center; her eyes were soft but ironic, with a hint of insolence, as black as oil, with glints of topaz. Her charming figure was in continual flux, seemingly changing its shape as she moved.

She fixed Philippe with a gaze that suddenly seemed affectionate: "Pierre…"

"No," he said, smiling a trifle wanly. "I'm not Pierre de Givreuse."

Amazement immobilized the young woman's features. "I was told about that!" she said, putting her hands together. "I didn't want to believe it!"

Embers of the past, of a bitter and incendiary love that lit up Givreuse's life for a year, threw out a violent spark—but something else rose up, which was new, and which would not have been possible in normal circumstances.

She studied him with avid curiosity. "I've never seen anything as fantastic!" she continued. "And the voice too… even more faithful than the face…and the accent…you're not playing games with me?"

"I'm Philippe Frémeuse, Madame."

"I have to believe you," she sighed, with a little ambiguous laugh. "But it isn't you that…" She hesitated.

"It isn't me that you were expecting," said Philippe. "It's just that Pierre isn't able to come."

Her attitude became cold, hard and stern. "I don't understand."

He had expected that. Although he had thought long and hard, he had found nothing to excuse his visit. There was an insurmountable distance between him and this woman, who had summoned him but did not know him. Anxiety and excitement alternated within him, and a spirit of adventure rose up within him like a flock of migratory birds.

"Pierre asked me to offer his excuses," he stammered. "He is…he regrets…" He floundered.

She began to smile again, ironically and indecipherably. She wanted to know where this meeting might lead. There was an inextricable mixture of curiosity, violent memories and nascent impressions. In sum, this young man, so similar to Pierre, took her back to a past that she would have liked to revisit one more time, and mingled with that past was the possibility, if not the promise, of a renewal. "That's all right!" she said, interrupting him. "If Pierre de Givreuse has reasons for not paying me a visit, those reasons are of no interest to me. As for you, Monsieur, although your presence might be... unusual...I consent to excuse you—but the fact remains that I don't know you!"

How easy it would have been if he were able to adopt his true personality! It was annoying—but at the same time, the adventure seemed to him all the more exciting. It involved a recommencement of something whose absence had extinguished all inclination and all passion. The Thérèse sitting in that massive Gothic armchair was no longer the Thérèse from which he had once separated himself, because the mysterious flame had gone out.

"Let's try to chat," she said, in a bantering tone. "This can't be very comfortable for you. Let's see—let's take up a thread at hazard. Have you been in combat?"

"Yes, Madame."

"You've been wounded?"

"Yes."

"And what are you doing now?"

"I'm employed in aircraft manufacture, under the patronage of Monsieur de Rougeterre."

"A worthy patronage—he's a man who is held in very high esteem. There are so few estimable men..." She made a weary gesture. "I know six or seven, at the most, who are alive. As for the rest...what smoke!" Her disdainful gesture indicated an invisible multitude. Her trenchant and ambiguous laughter resounded again. "What about you? Are you estimable?"

"I don't know...I'm trying to find myself..."

"That's a start. Those who are trying to find themselves form an élite of sorts. The masses never think of trying to find themselves…one would think that they know in advance that it would be futile…"

She fell silent, and remained thoughtful for half a minute. Her long gray velvet sleeve, dangled over the hard arm of the chair; she had tilted her head back, revealing a shapely and striking neck. Her exceedingly long hair shone like a starlit pond; every undulation emitted the primitive but very refined sensuality that always emanates from beautiful hair.

He studied her surreptitiously, abandoning himself to a plaintive and intoxicating disturbance; everything in him wanted to forget his bitter life. A scent of freshly-cut grass floated around this woman.

"We've conversed but we've said nothing," she sighed. "The difficulty is obvious. I think you must have fought bravely."

"Was it fighting? One no longer knows. Everything comes from the depths of the invisible. Everyone is in an immense torture chamber…and heroism doesn't reside in fighting, but in suffering patiently."

"Yes, that must be so," she sighed. "Our poor soldiers of France!"

She had softened her tone, but behind the softness, the woman was on watch, and womanly desire, in every era, war has given them more power! "Have you suffered much?"

"A few weeks of pain count for nothing," he said, forcefully. "And I haven't stopped fighting!"

"Bravo!" she exclaimed.

There was a pause. He thought that the visit had lasted long enough, and stood up. Then, timidly—but affecting a timidity greater than he actually felt—he asked: "Will you permit me to come again?"

"I wouldn't have permitted it a little while ago! I'm at home almost every day…at 4 p.m.…for the whole month. After that, alas, I have to leave for Chile, where I have important business to transact. My mother is Chilean." She held out her hand to him. It was a small, very nimble hand, which squeezed the young man's hand very slightly.

II.

He returned to *The Gladioli* several times. Their conversations were bizarre and fascinating. Both of them were partly reliving and partly remaking the past. Philippe recognized all of Thérèse's coquetries, reservations and ambiguities; it was not a simple return to previous things but a new idyll. Everything had changed, but the change was not a renewal, as among those with whom we begin life. In sum, Thérèse had a charm that she could never have had again for the Givreuse of yesteryear. She seemed rejuvenated. There was less instinctive cruelty in her, a livelier freshness of sentiment.

For Thérèse, the renewal was of another kind. She too saw the past phantasmagorically rejuvenated, but with the certainty that Philippe was someone other than Pierre. What she rediscovered of Givreuse's voice, gestures and ideas was only a repetition, in the same way that the flowers of spring are a repetition of those of previous springs. What had seduced her in one man she found again in another, and, as she retained a nostalgic regard for Givreuse—who had been the great love of her life—she experienced an intoxicating rebirth of her destiny.

She had no idea what she was going to do, though. A widow, she had only succumbed to temptation once, after long resistance. By nature, she was correct; after the break-up with Pierre, she had sworn never to accept love again, except within marriage. But did she love Philippe? She could not tell. She surrendered to the impulse of the moment, to a sort of psychic miracle that could have no future. Everything was contained in conversations punctuated by languorous silences, during which she thought about the brevity of existence and its bitter uncertainty. One day when he had stayed longer than usual, she said to him: "It's rather late to go back to Carolles. Do you know what? We'll dine together."

She regretted her invitation immediately; then, thinking that within three weeks she would be crossing an ocean full of snares, she shrugged her shoulders.

They dined on the luminous terrace in front of huge copper beeches and Hungarian linden-trees, separated by an extensive lawn beyond which garden flowers and wild flowers grew randomly. It was the season when the lindens were beginning to emit their magical scent; it arrived at the whim of the breeze, expressive of the obscure desire of that which is determined to grow and multiply.

The evening passed extraordinarily slowly. Bats circled the treetops and flew along the wall, melancholy dancers in the dusk.

"I've detested the evening twilight for a long time," said Thérèse, as she nibbled one of those little elongated strawberries that are neither entirely domesticated nor entirely wild. "It seems to me to be the hour of anguish, of evil expectation. I imagine that those great fires illuminating the clouds are about to set fire to the Earth and the sky."

"I've always liked the evening twilight," Philippe replied.

"Are you sure of that? Children don't like it at all...nor do most animals. That's perfectly natural. It announces the advent of nature's mourning-dress—the night."

He contemplated the enchanted silhouette, over which the occident spread a variegated light. A few bright stars were beginning to appear. A cricket trilled in the grass; another soon replied from the far side of the lawn. Glow-worms lit their little pale green lanterns.

"Is it possible that we're at war?" she said, her expression suddenly darkening. "And that so many others..." She did not finish the sentence; she lowered her head. Both of them shared in the bitter pain she had evoked.

The coffee evaporated its aroma, replete with promise and consolation. Night had fallen. Insects fluttered around the candle-flames; with every passing minute a tiny roasted corpse fell upon the tablecloth, agitating its minuscule limbs for an instant before falling asleep for eternity.

"That's strange!" she said. "Why do these tiny creatures come to die in this fashion? Life is full of impenetrable stupidities!"

"These insects seem to us to be automata of a sort—but what about the thousands of birds which precipitate themselves at lighthouses and break their bodies thereon? Yes, an incredible stupidity is mingled with the ingenuity of creatures—and we're just as much animals as those insects!"

"More, perhaps, for we can foresee events—and look at what our foresight does for us! I assume you smoke..."

"Not much—only at times when the sadness becomes too great."

"For the mirage?"

"Tobacco doesn't provide me with any mirage. It dissolves and disperses my ideas. This evening, I prefer the odor of the linden-trees." In the dancing and indeterminate light, he breathed in that accompaniment, which seemed to spring from a magical Earth. "How sweet it is to look at you," he murmured, in a tone that she recognized.

She started slightly, and plunged into the depths of the dream. "Really," she said, with a hint of mockery. "Are you being sincere?"

"Is it possible that I might not be? Are there many Frenchmen for whom you would not be a marvelous spectacle?"

"Marvelous! That's a rather extravagant word..."

"Since the gods are dead, what remains to man of the marvelous, except for woman?"

"Good—if you're talking about all women."

"I'm talking about those of whom old Priam said: 'It's right that one should die for them!'"

"Priam was an old fool." She shook her head. "Let's go for a walk in the moonlight—it's rising behind the copper beeches."

She got up and went down to the lawn, bare-headed. He followed her, all a-tremble. Confused glimmers of light guided them. He knew her too well not to know that it was a provocation, but he also knew that she was provocative by virtue of caprice, curiosity and the spirit of bravado.

"At heart," she said, "I'm a country-dweller, with a slight hint of savagery. It's not because it's beautiful that I love nature, it's because it's redoubtable."

At first they walked on the lawn; then Thérèse took an oblique pathway that led through the beeches. The delicate odor of the young woman dominated the odors of the vegetation; he listened to the rustle of her skirt. When she turned round, he perceived the whiteness of her face, whose form was vaporous, and a dark mass that was her hair…

Blood rose to Philippe's head; he seized her little hand and squeezed it.

"Oh!" she said, reproachfully. She snatched her hand away, and her laughter gushed out, silvery and slightly hoarse. "You shan't catch me!"

She had disappeared. He heard her light footfalls in the shadows. A sort of gleam shone momentarily beneath the trees, then was lost in the darkness. Philippe shivered; all the ancient dreams, all the amorous fables concerning forests, nymphs and elves, intoxicated him. He ran at hazard, losing his head. Suddenly, laughter burst forth behind him; turning round, he saw her pale silhouette three paces away.

"You see," she said, "I can't be caught. And here's what we're looking for…"

A phosphorescence insinuated itself between the trees, then the glimmer of a night-light; there was a sensation of an immense presence. Finally, the red, cold orb stood out amid the colonnades.

"Here's the hand that you wanted to take," she said, with an equivocal softness. "It's a friendly hand."

He took the little hand fearfully; he knelt down to kiss it.

"Are you really paying court to me? Be careful."

"What else can I do, if I love you?"

"Love me? Do you think so?" She took his arm and drew him back to the lawn, which resembled a vast green pool.

Noctules were flying hectically back and forth; a toad was croaking its obscure love-song. "What you just said to me is frightening!" she murmured. "But it's not true…"

"Not true!" he groaned. "As true as my life itself…"

"That would be even more frightening. It's not permissible to love so quickly. And if you really love me, unfortunate boy, remember that I shall soon be leaving…that you won't see me again—if you ever do—for a long time. One doesn't squander one's love in such a manner!"

"Does our will ask such questions? Besides, to suffer because of you, Madame, is a further delight."

She looked at him amicably, but she made no reply.

For a week, their meetings were brief. She displayed variable moods; there were moments when she treated him as a stranger, others when she was almost wheedling. Neither of them thought about the denouement. Thérèse had the countless reasons that women have for not wanting to do so. Perhaps she would have restricted herself to a platonic remembrance even with Pierre—she did not know. With Philippe the adventure unfolded all the more equivocally for being a combination of the love of yesterday and the love of today. The attraction that she experienced with regard to Givreuse's fantastic double, however, increased with an unexpected rapidity. Although born of the resemblance between the two men, it was quite different; the new love had, in Thérèse's view, a greater intimacy than the other…

One day, when she was listening to Philippe, she experienced a sharp suspicion. The same suspicion had occurred to her several times before, but it had seemed so absurd that she had not entertained it for a moment; this time, it was irresistible. She watched Philippe slyly, and asked him insidious questions…

He was on his guard. Mademoiselle de Varsennes' crisis had taught him to mistrust his memories; he only spoke about the past with extreme prudence. Thérèse did not catch him out in any mistake, and yet the suspicion lingered. There was even a moment when she was convinced that Pierre de Givreuse was with her, playing the role of Philippe.

That's idiotic, she thought. *Why would he do that?*

The suspicion persisted, however, equivocal and manifold.

And what if it were Pierre?

She was not a woman to live in doubt. She had the two men watched; she knew, in broad terms, what they were doing and where they went. She obtained information on Mademoiselle de Varsennes that was fragmentary, but decisive for a mind like hers.

Is that why Pierre hasn't come? she wondered. *But if my suspicions are accurate, that might explain why he's playing the role of Philippe with me. That would be abominable and cunning—he'd have the old love and the new, without any risk!*

The female imagination dabbles in the impossible, especially when the impossible is mixed up with the age-old battle of the sexes. She laughed at herself; even so, she went to take a peek at the Château de Givreuse and keep watch on Pierre's movements.

One day, flushed with excitement, she lay in wait for him. He found her suddenly in front of him, on the road. Hypnotized, his gaze fixed itself upon her, with a naïve stupefaction that could not be feigned. "Thérèse!" he stammered.

She examined him with avid curiosity. Very quickly, she saw that he had thinner cheeks than Philippe, a paler complexion, and something in his entire bearing that was dreamier, more indecisive. *This is Pierre*, she said to herself. *It's him that I loved...*

She felt, with muted joy, that that love, once so profound and so terrible, now left her almost indifferent. It had disappeared conclusively into the gulf of dead things. Only Philippe moved her. She divined a similar indifference in the young man, and that was the only reason that she felt slightly resentful. "I've seen your double, you know," she said, slightly sarcastically. "The resemblance is certainly uncanny —but I wouldn't be deceived by it."

They stayed there briefly, exchanging remarks that were of scant interest to them; then she offered him her hand, without rancor.

Pierre thought that he ought to telegraph Philippe, who arrived at the château that evening. "I ran into Thérèse," he said, as soon as they were alone.

Philippe went pale, suffering a sudden surge of jealousy. "Where?" he asked, hoarsely.

"On the Avranches road."

"She must have contrived it."

"I don't think so. The conversation was brief and insignificant."

Philippe walked with his head bowed for some time. A profound wrinkle brought his eyebrows closer together; an anguished severity contracted his lips.

"I don't need any exaggeration of my ordeal," he said, finally. "I'm conforming strictly with the lot; I didn't want there to be any *de facto* rivalry between us. Thérèse is completely indifferent to you?"

"Completely."

"Good! For myself, I love her…"

"You love her!" Pierre exclaimed. The evolution of his own life bore such scant resemblance to Philippe's that he was dumbfounded. He could not understand how, having loved Valentine, one could revert to loving Madame de Lisanges.

"Yes," said Philippe. "And take note that my loving her is not a return to the past—the past is almost an obstacle. I love her by virtue of *a renewal of my person*, and of hers— which is as inexplicable as our unity. Doubtless I have not entirely ceased to love Valentine, but now the abandonment of that love is no longer tragic. Even if she does not love me, Thérèse has saved me…to suffer for her sake is an ordinary suffering. Do you understand why I need to be entirely certain of your indifference?"

Pierre listened, fascinated. The youth of the universe entered into him again, all the scattered favors that illusion gathers together in heaven and Earth. He was hopeful, as one breathes in the fresh morning breeze.

"Is that true?" he stammered. "Oh, if you knew how remote Thérèse is...how she has faded into the darkness..."

"That's more than I asked for. Be free. Between you and Valentine, there's no longer any obstacle..."

They had stopped in a covert resplendent with vagabond flowers; they looked at one another with that expression which surpassed affection—but they made none of the gestures that display the amity of men.

III.

Thérèse was playing one of those Slavic sonatas vibrant with the same rebellious, dissatisfied and fraternal soul as *War and Peace* or *Crime and Punishment*. Phantoms were passing over the steppes in the surge of the sea-wind; waves of mysticism were swelling hearts; men were bewailing their bitter destiny and their eternal isolation.

Philippe contemplated her harmonious figure and her neck, as round as the neck of the Shulamite,[9] overhung by her fabulous hair. The sonorous enchantments evoked his own destiny. He was astonished not to find it even stranger.

"Do you like it?" she asked.

---

[9] "The Shulamite" is the addressee of the Biblical *Song of Solomon*, but the more immediate reference that Rosny almost certainly has in mind is a relatively recent "scène lyrique" based on that poem, *La Sulamite*, first performed in 1885, with words by Jean Richepin—a writer with whom he was personally acquainted—and music by Emmanuel Chabrier.

"Sometimes it's too fluid...everything escapes me...then there's an imperious envelopment, almost morbid but very gentle nevertheless..."

The dark lashes of Thérèse's changing eyes fluttered; love radiated from her like the perfume of linden-trees—and Philippe remembered, with astonishment, that she had been his mistress, although she did not know it, and that they were now confronting one another like people in love with one another for the first time...

It was necessary to conquer her! She sat there, enigmatic and new, and he, who had pressed her to his heart on countless occasions, did not even know whether he would obtain a kiss on the lips...

"Will you love me forever?" she asked, with a mixture of coaxing and sarcasm.

"You're too womanly not to be sure of that!"

"Sure? The most deceptive of words. How can creatures around whom everything changes, and who change themselves, be sure of anything?"

"*E pur si...*"[10]

"You think so—and it isn't false...but it's impossible that it should *already* be true...or, if so, it's a poor love, of which it's necessary to be afraid."

"Don't say that," he said, in a pleading tone. "Who knows whether a great love might not be born in a matter of days?"

"All right...let's say that it's not verified. I'm a classic-ist; I have a sense of time...and I only have faith in that which lasts! First, I have to know whether the love I'm offered will be a *great* adventure—if not, what good is it? In this tragic world, where we receive so little happiness and so little beau-

---

[10] This partial phrase is quoted from an apocryphal anecdote in which Galileo, having been forced by the Inquisition to recant his assertion that the Earth revolves around the Sun, murmurs as he gets to his feet again: "*E pur si muovo*" [And yet it moves].

ty, what remains to a woman if love is merely a caprice?" She inclined her sparkling head. "You don't displease me... but how do I know whether I can love you? How many times shall I see you before my departure? Perhaps ten. And how many times have I seen you already? We're strangers—is it possible that we shall cease to be within such a short interval."

"But what if you were to fall in love with me?"

"Well then," she said, with her little ambiguous laugh, "I would love you, and that's all. You can't think that I'd surrender at the last moment, like a thunderclap. That would be the surest means of being forgotten."

"I wouldn't forget you."

"What do you know about it? You're not yet at the age when a man knows himself; and I don't know whether that age ever arrives for one in 1000! What I do know is that perfidious masculine moralists have lied throughout the centuries in charging woman with the infidelity that is the very essence of man!" She had drawn closer; she put her little hands on Philippe's shoulders and looked him in the eyes. "Mystery! Mystery" she whispered.[11]

He shuddered. With an irresistible gesture, he took Thérèse in his arms and drew her to his bosom. She scarcely resisted. Her hair was there, so soft and wild; he plunged his lips into it recklessly, and felt the young woman's delightful body shiver. "Thérèse!" he stammered.

She detached herself from his grasp with a brisk and lithe movement. "You don't have the right to call me that!" she protested. Momentarily, emotion retained its grip on her and twisted her mouth. Her pupils were dilated to the point at which the iris was no more than a shining ring. She collected herself; her face became serious and severe. "I'm on my guard, you see!" she said, defiantly. "Don't count on any surprise!"

---

[11] Given her previous remark, Thérèse probably has *Revelation* 17:5 in mind—as Rosny surely must.

He knew her well. He knew that she would remain mistress of herself, until the moment when she consented freely…

The clock chimed 6 p.m. "I'm expecting a visitor," she said. "Shall I see you tomorrow?"

"I don't know. We're trying out an electric boat—a large pinnace, unsinkable, which might, when it's perfected, be useful against submarines…"

"Ah!" she said, interestedly. "They say that there are submarines close to the shore. How could a pinnace combat those monsters?"

"The boat is extremely fast…an advantage increased by its smallness. It could launch a light torpedo, which is believed to be effective.

Anxiety spread across Thérèse's features; she squeezed Philippe's hand nervously. "Come as soon as you return…it doesn't matter what time!"

Dawn was on the point of breaking. A few ragged streaks of light extended over the sea and into the immense darkness of the sky. There were silky threads, wan reflections, and a vague and fugitive phosphorescence. Then clouds became discernible, some the color of iron filings, others the gray of mud. In the pale orient, shafts of daylight extended over the wild plains of the ocean; woolly clouds wadded the firmament.

A small boat had just emerged from the cliffs. It was almost the same color as the waves, and the two men aboard were like fragments of the hull, their clothes being the same shade—except for the parts of their upper bodies emerging from two concavities hollowed out in the upper surface of the craft.

They steered around a two-pronged rock feared by navigators and headed south-west at top speed. That speed was surprising for such a small boat, and must have attained nearly 30 knots. One of the two men aboard was old, with a red beard flecked with white, a face like tanned leather and two marcasite-colored eyes beneath coarse bushy eyebrows—a mariner's eyes, swift and sure. The other was Philippe.

The sea was rumbling feebly; the waves were long and very slow, but high-peaked.

"She holds steady!" said the old man.

Philippe nodded his head. The old man was steering. In front of Philippe there were levers and switches. There was no other communication between the inside and the outside of the skiff; above as below, the entire hull was tightly sealed. The boat was named the *Insubmersible*, and it was.

The seaman's eyes could just make out a few ships far out to sea. One of them was more visible than the rest, and much closer; it was toward that one that the boat was heading. It was traveling north-west at top speed—a speed considerably inferior to that of the *Insubmersible*. Within ten minutes, the distance had diminished noticeably.

Through his telescope, Philippe made out the name of the ship: *Old Queen Elizabeth*. It was presumably a cargo vessel, already old, between 500 and 2000 tons, with two funnels.

"Look out!" muttered the old mariner. His finger indicated something at the surface of the waves, which Philippe could not see immediately. "A periscope!" the other specified.

Philippe could just make it out, minuscule upon the immensity. "You're right."

"No mistake, Monsieur…that boat out there has been spotted…the filthy beast is out hunting."

"Underwater?"

"She must have her reasons…you can't tell me that she hasn't seen her!"

"To the *Queen Elizabeth*, comrade…circuitously."

The old man gave a connoisseur's wink; the boat began to describe zigzags and parabolas. In the distance, a sort of apocalyptic beast was emerging.

"It's coming up, Monsieur, take Pierre Salaun's word for it. "There'll be a chase."

"We must follow that one now!"

It was a submarine of great breadth, a powerfully-armed cruiser much faster than the freighter. There was more than six kilometers between the two ships; the *Insubmersible* formed a near-equilateral triangle with them, being about five kilometers from each of them.

For some while, the three vessels sailed on silently. Finally, there was a puff of smoke, soon followed by a detonation.

The *Old Queen Elizabeth* maintained its course.

"Too short!" sneered the old man.

The submarine was five kilometers away from the freighter, the *Insubmersible* three kilometers from the submarine, for which it was headed at top speed.

The submarine continued firing. Gradually, its projectiles homed in on the fugitive.

"*Touché*," muttered Philippe, angrily. He could see the hole made by the shell.

"They've seen us now, Monsieur!" groaned Pierre Salaun.

Until then, the submarine's crew had not appeared to notice the presence of the *Insubmersible*. The pinnace was merely an insect lost at sea. When he finally saw the insect maneuvering, the cruiser's captain seemed astonished.

"I told you so!" Salaun remarked.

A shell had just fallen into the waves three or four cables away, and others swiftly followed. The extreme speed of the *Insubmersible*, its swerves and its small size made it a difficult target.

For the *Old Queen Elizabeth* the situation was becoming serious. There were large gaping cracks in its hull. One of which was on the water-line. The water was pouring in; the ship was starting to list; they crew were hastening to the lifeboats. An enormous jet of steam and a prolonged detonation testified that the engine-room had been hit.

"Poor fellows!" murmured Salaun, rapidly making the sign of the cross. "They're on fire!"

The pinnace was now only a few hundred meters from the submarine. Projectiles were raining down furiously on all sides, but the little boat, as rapid as a seagull and as disconcerting as a swallow, seemed to be playing hide-and-seek with the shells.

"Ah! Damn!" muttered the mariner. A projectile had just sunk less than ten fathoms away. "Not that one!" Salaun shouted, wildly.

"Slow down, then stop...aim straight at them!" Philippe commanded, placidly.

The old man obeyed. In the distance, the *Old Queen Elizabeth* was sinking, puny boats fleeing over the gray plain. The men on the submarine were laughing.

"Stop!" said Philippe, his eyes fixed on the enemy. He pressed three electric switches in succession. There was a muted pressure, a wake, then a wave crashing against the flank of the submarine, and a clamor of curses. "Got them!" the young man added. "Out to sea!"

The *Insubmersible* drew away at top speed. The submarine seemed unscathed; it continued bombarding the boat.

"It hit her, all the same," the old man remarked.

A quarter of an hour went by. The *Insubmersible* was out of range. The *Old Queen Elizabeth* had sunk. The submarine was still on the surface.

"Gently!" said Philippe. He had taken up his telescope again, and was examining the enemy. "Something's definitely going on!"

"Hey!" exclaimed Salaun. "Look over there...further out. Something's coming..." Salaun lifted his own telescope. "Heads up! It's a destroyer—but that swine of a submarine will dive..."

The destroyer was coming forward at high speed.

"The submarine isn't diving!" said Philippe.

"It's because it can't, then—our pill must have put something out of order. Look out! Hurrah!" A distant cannon-shot had just rung out. "Too short!" Salaun observed.

111

The cannonade increased; the submarine was properly bracketed. It attempted to reply. "Off target, you old hound!" Salaun exclaimed, jubilantly. "She's within two kilometers—and you're still not diving, I see..."

A jet of fire and smoke rose up from the submarine. Pitiless fire riddled it. The monster listed and began to sink. Two large shells struck home; it sank into a maelstrom. Soon a large oily sheet extended over the waves.

"The beast's punctured!" exclaimed Salaun, making the sign of the cross. "And you know, Monsieur Frémeuse, we're the ones who started the job. Without our little torpedo, the big fellow wouldn't have had the time...the shark would have gone down into the sea. David's beaten Goliath."

A strangely abstract joy filled the young man's heart, while there was a wild explosion in the old man. The *Insubmersible* was getting close to the place where the pirate had vanished. The greasy and silky sheen was beginning to disappear. A few corpses were floating in the water.

"Assassins!" howled Salaun. "God knows how many brave men they've done away with!"

But there was one that was moving...

A man was struggling feebly on the surface of the gray immensity. He appeared to be still young, his face beardless and his cheeks thin.

"Where can we put him?" asked the old man.

"We'll see."

The man disappeared, only to surface again further away. Philippe threw him a line; the shipwreck victim grabbed it. He murmured something, then his arms opened and his head dipped beneath the waves. He did not reappear.

Scattered clouds came together to form a colossal mass. Blue fissures became visible again, then disappeared with phantasmagoric rapidity; a deceptive wind whirled around and the cloud-mass became a nimbus the color of smoke and slate, bordered with quivering gleams. Brisk, rough waves made the pinnace shudder.

"Dirty weather's on its way," muttered Salaun. "We have to get back to the coast double quick."

The coast was eight knots away when the full force of the storm burst. The frail *Insubmersible* was tossed about dangerously, its propeller periodically spinning in mid-air. The pale and attentive Salaun, hunched over and scowling, tried to avoid dangerous passes.

Suddenly, everything stopped—the engine was no longer functioning.

"We're in the Devil's hands!" said the mariner. "That would normally be all right by me...but not today. There's still those swinish reefs..."

For nearly an hour the boat drifted at the whim of the storm, the two men doing their best to fight it. Livid glimmers streaked the sky; the depths of the firmament were so dark that it gave the impression of being the end of twilight. A large reef formed by three rocks rose up to their left...

The rain was falling in torrents; a leaden veil covered the Atlantic. In spite of his long experience, Salaun no longer knew where they were. They peered into the distance; the little boat was like an item of flotsam, borne by the whims of the weather. Suddenly, a sinister profile loomed up out of the mist...

"The reef!" moaned Salaun.

The *Insubmersible* yielded a dull cracking sound; they were among the rocks...

There was an indentation between two solid blocks, forming a sort of long, narrow gully.

"We might be able to make fast," declared the old man. "If we're not holed...there might be a way to get out of this...later..."

They succeeded in securing the boat effectively to a granite projection and they disembarked.

Half an hour went by; the *Insubmersible* did not sink; it was shaken by the occasional breaker, but the storm was already easing. A pale gap in the clouds appeared overhead.

"Luck, Monsieur," Salaun remarked. "The boat seems to me to be sound...if we can just get the engine going."

"That'll be difficult—perhaps impossible. The boat's own design is opposed to it—it requires a special tool to get inside!"

They had taken refuge in the cleft. In the center, it formed a sort of cave with a split ceiling. The near-horizontal floor was slippery, polished by the waves. At high tide, it was submerged.

"We'll be all right for a few hours...and at high tide, it might be possible to climb...there's a sort of niche that will hold two..."

"The weather's easing."

"We'd need luck to get up there. Bah! We might be found before..."

Philippe was no longer anxious. He was content. The tiny *Insubmersible* had just rendered a service that far surpassed its commercial value, although chance had done three-quarters of the work—to be sure, Philippe had known that one or more submarines had shown themselves within sight of the shore, but that was no guide, inasmuch as one day's indications signified nothing for the next. His experiment had been a success; if the pinnace was not perfected, it had nevertheless demonstrated its potential...

While Philippe was thinking, the good weather returned, with a suddenness that seems even more frequent at sea than on land.

Salaun had gone back to the boat. He tinkered with it for some time; then his blurred silhouette stood up straight. "It's all right, Monsieur Philippe—the engine's working!"

It was 10 a.m. when Philippe arrived at Thérèse's house. She appeared in a long woolen garment, still damp from her bath. Her hair was not yet dry; she looked at Philippe in bewilderment.

"Excuse me—you told me to come, no matter what the hour."

"What! It's finished already?"

"We went out before dawn. It was over some time ago."
He had changed his clothes. Nothing betrayed the expedition
that he had just completed.

"You've tested the boat?"

"In the most favorable conditions…"

"The sea was calm?"

"That's not what I meant…"

A voice was heard in the next room. "Madame! Madame! You don't know…they've sunk…"

Thérèse opened the door curiously. "Sunk what?"

"A submarine, Madame—within sight of Granville."

Thérèse turned to Philippe. "Did you know that?"

"Yes. The submarine had just sunk an English steamer,
the *Old Queen Elizabeth*…a destroyer sank it in its turn."

"You saw it?"

"As clearly as I see you."

"It happened while you were at sea?"

"Yes."

"Oh! Tell me what happened!" She turned towards him,
her expression mingling the naivety of a little girl with the
ardor of a woman.

He told her what had happened. He did it soberly, without emphasizing the role of the *Insubmersible*. Avidly, she
plied him with questions; she had a violent desire for Philippe's role to have been decisive, and reconstructed the tale of
the frail boat attacking the huge pirate in her own fashion.
"It's you who wounded it!" she affirmed. "It was you!"

"We'll never know."

"But it's certain. Why else wouldn't it have dived?"

A pink tint invaded her pale cheeks. Philippe saw the
fiery glimmer in her eyes that had once preceded their em-
braces. The past was reincarnate in the present and Philippe,
losing his head, put out his arms to seize the young woman.
Two little hands met his own simultaneously, and held them,
while a firm voice whispered: "No! You're dear to me, Philippe…but I don't love you yet!"

Doctor Savarre had just come back from his clinic when he was handed a visitor's card, accompanied by a letter. The name printed on the card, unknown to Savarre, nevertheless took on a particular significance by virtue of the address that followed it: *Château de Grantaigle.*

"This isn't a servant's card...but the laboratory assistant is dead." He looked at the letter, but did not open it immediately. He liked to exercise his powers of divination. "What if *he* isn't dead?"

Finally, he unsealed the envelope and read:

Monsieur,

Monsieur Charles Gourlande is the assistant—or, rather, collaborator—about whom I spoke to you during your visit. At that time he had disappeared and had been erroneously crossed off the list of the living. He will be able to inform you much better than I was able to do myself; moreover, he knows exactly what the discoveries were that my father wished to keep secret—if not forever, at least for our generation and the following one—because he judged them to be harmful.

You may have confidence in Monsieur Charles Gourlande; no more honest man exists.

Please accept, Monsieur, my sincerest good wishes.
Abel de Grantaigle.

Savarre read the letter again. "Harmful discoveries? Shall I really learn something?" He shrugged his shoulders—a gesture expressive of uncertainty—and instructed that Charles Gourlande should be shown in. He was almost a giant. Above massive and rigid shoulders he displayed a diamond-shaped face liberally but patchily strewn with hair. His lips were set in heavy jaws. His vast and deep-set eyes gave evidence of nyctalopia.

"Thank you for coming," said Savarre, extending his hand.

The other advanced an arm that was still very stiff as a result of recent wounds. There was a short pause, during which Savarre and Charles Gourlande looked at one another anxiously.

"I don't know what you want to know, Monsieur," the latter eventually said, "but, as you've probably learned from Monsieur Abel de Grantaigle's letter, my confidences will be limited by promises—formal and unconditional—that I made to my master. His death has not released me from that obligation."

"Is he really dead?"

"There's no possible doubt—his mortal remains were found buried in the ruins."

"You know all his secrets, I believe—I mean the secrets of his laboratory."

"Not all. There are a few essential formulas and a few crucial experiments that he kept hidden even from me. My master was certainly the most powerful scientific genius, by a wide margin, that has ever appeared on Earth. Faraday, Ampère, Carnot, Maxwell and Curie, great as they are, could not be compared to him…"

Savarre experienced a flash of ill-humor. He discerned that it was a mixture of indignation, jealousy and disdain—but he had exercised objectivity for far too long for that stance to be so easily compromised. *Besides*, he thought, with an irony addressed to himself, *he's dead, so…* He smiled, and the smile signified that skepticism had replaced the jealousy.

"You don't believe me," said Gourlande, smiling in his turn. "That's entirely natural. In any case, it's of no importance. Let's get back to the matter in hand. What do you want to know?"

"I'd like to know the nature of Monsieur de Grantaigle's discoveries," the neurologist replied, with some slight hesitation, "and their actual results…I mean, their *realizations*. It's not curiosity that leads me to ask."

Gourlande bowed his head thoughtfully, then said: "Do you, perhaps, recall the object of his first endeavors?"

"Not exactly. They were concerned with polarization, I think."

"My master refined a part of the theory of rotatory polarization and, on the other hand, created a sort of mechanical polarization, but only for circular or pseudo-circular systems. In his final paper, which remains underappreciated to the present day, he advanced a theory regarding the transformation of transversal waves into longitudinal waves, and *vice versa*. From that moment on, he stopped communicating with scientific societies, and also with individual scientists. He was beginning to get too far ahead of his contemporaries. His discoveries multiplied, becoming more and more profound and diverse. I can tell you about his research on the polarization of electricity—not with respect to negative and positive polarity, but to the polarization of individual electrons, or, if you prefer, atoms of electricity. That discovery led him to the phenomena of pre-electricity. The most astonishing result of his research was the bipartition of atoms."

Savarre started, and his temples swelled.

"It's necessary that the term be unambiguous," Gourlande continued. "The bipartition of atoms is a phenomenon quite different from the bipartition of animal cells. In the latter, two polar nuclei are formed, which preside over the formation of new cells similar in every respect to their mother cell. In the bipartition of atoms, there's also a formation of two complete atoms, but each of reduced mass and formed of pre-atomic elements, orientated in each new atom at right-angles to the pre-atomic elements of the other. One thus obtains two systems of simple bodies—for example, two hydrogens and two oxygens, and, in consequence, two kinds of ordinary water and oxygenated water. For the same volume, these hydrogens, oxygens and waters have half the mass, and, consequently, half the weight of ordinary hydrogens, oxygens and water molecules. They also have particular luminous and electrical properties..."

Savarre had risen to his feet. A violent emotion was up-setting his eyes; a flood of light dazzled him, to the utmost depths of his unconscious. He could not hold back an excla-mation: "That's prodigious!" He suddenly had no further doubt; what Gourlande had said fitted in perfectly with the enigma of the Givreuses. "I dare to presume," the neurologist murmured, hoarsely, "that Grantaigle extended his discoveries to organic matter."

Gourlande fell silent. His nyctalopic gaze, strangely dis-tant, seemed to be coming to Savarre from the depths of a cave. After a long pause, he went on: "Yes, but my confi-dences must stop there. The formulas that I can communicate to you do not extend that far. They stop at pre-electric pheno-mena. To obtain the bipartition of atoms, it's necessary to solve problems that will not, I believe, be solved for 200 or 300 years—for a man like my master might never be produced again, as none was ever produced in the past..."

"I'm sure," cried Savarre, with extreme agitation, "that Grantaigle has applied atomic bipartition to living beings."

"Sure!" said Gourlande, gloomily. "Sure?"

"Absolutely sure."

They remained standing face to face, their eyes fixed, quite pale.

"Monsieur," said the visitor, softly, "I've answered your questions, to the extent permitted by the sacred oath that I swore to my master. You will not refuse, in your turn, to an-swer me this: why are you interested in his discoveries? They have no connection with your own work..."

"I'll tell you—but first, I want to make a conclusive veri-fication, in your presence. Can you spare me half an hour?"

"I'm free all day."

Savarre went to the Château de Givreuse by automobile, where he asked to speak to Pierre. It was nearly dinner-time; the young man was in the garden.

"Would you care to entrust me with your individual sets of identity papers—which I suppose you have at the château—for an hour or two?" the neurologist asked.

Everything seemed perfectly normal to him, so Pierre went to fetch the identity papers without asking any questions, knowing that if he had something to say, Savarre would say it spontaneously.

The doctor returned home, rummaged around in a cupboard, rapidly carried out a few experiments with a magnifying glass, made two or three weighings in a little precision balance, and then went to find Charles Gourlande.

The latter was waiting for him, leafing through a journal. He had not entirely recovered his tranquility; his face betrayed a certain anxiety.

"Excuse me," said Savarre, "if I ask you to keep secret what happens here, and what I have to say to you."

Gourlande smiled sadly. "With regard to everything that does not affect my honor and my honesty, I promise you silence."

Savarre sensed that these were not vain words. He showed Gourlande one of the two sets of Givreuse identity papers, and another set that he had taken from the cupboard. "Materially," he said, "by which I mean only taking account of the paper, these two objects appear to be almost identical—but if I'm not mistaken in my conjectures, they must differ profoundly. One of them is polarized."

Gourlande's nocturnal eyes appeared to fill with deeper shadows. He looked at the two sets of papers very intently, then said, suspiciously: "Why should they be polarized?"

"Look at the transparency of the sheets, and compare them! An indefinable difference between the pages of the two sets of papers is perceptible. It's more obvious under a magnifying glass. With respect to the Givreuse papers, one perceives that the light passes more easily in the direction of length than in the direction of breadth; with respect to the others, there's nothing similar. Then again, the weights differ in a surprising manner."

Savarre drew a little balance towards him, weighed the documents successively, and observed: "The ordinary papers weigh almost exactly twice as much as the Givreuse papers! And that's not all…"

The neurologist took the second set of Givreuse papers from his pocket and superimposed them on the first on the balance.

"Put together, these have the same weight as a single set of papers—and if you compare them under the magnifying glass, the apparent transparency is equal in the two documents, but in perpendicular directions!"

Gourlande carefully verified each of Savarre's assertions. "Exactly right," he agreed. "Where are you going with this?"

"You've already guessed," the doctor replied, softly. "I affirm that these two sets of identity papers come from a single set, divided by Grantaigle's methods!"

"It's not impossible—and as an experimental fact, that does not surpass the confidences that I'm authorized to impart."

A fever had gripped Savarre; forcefully, he exclaimed: "The papers belonged to a soldier—who was carrying them on his person at the time of *the experiment*!"

Gourlande shivered. "Is he still alive?"

"He's alive—*they're alive*!"

A kind of fearful joy appeared in the nyctalopic gaze.

"You knew!" said Savarre, imperiously.

Charles Gourlande raised his eyebrows. "Do you understand," he said, in a low voice, "why my master wanted his experiments to remain secret? Do you understand how dangerous they might be in the human era, still so barbaric, in which we're living? Above all, don't hold it against him. He's innocent. He didn't want this frightful thing to happen. The note that I found is brief, but clear. It was quite by chance that the wounded soldier arrived in his laboratory. It was entirely accidental that he fainted *at the exact spot on which the polarizing energies were focused*. My master was also wounded and unconscious. When he came to, the metamorphosis was complete. *They fled.* My master just had time to write the note—then he and the laboratory were destroyed."

"But still, you knew."

"I knew what the note told me. I discovered it recently, after my return from Germany, where I had spent long months, very ill and badly wounded. On my return, the first thing I did was visit Grantaigle. As you must have been told, the laboratory was annihilated. It was then that I found my master's last notebook...the note moreover, was comprehensible only to me. I must say that I had doubts about the reality of the event. I supposed that my master had suffered some sort of nervous breakdown, accompanied by delirium and hallucinations. It was only natural that his hallucinations should have related to the subject that had preoccupied him day and night for so many years..."

"So you considered the experiment impossible?"

"In those conditions, yes. Until then, my master had only obtained successful results with rudimentary organisms. The bipartition was successful with batrachians, particularly with newts. The duplication of newts generally produced resistant individuals, which were 'completed' in a matter of weeks. Most of the time, the newly-formed frogs were inviable. My master duplicated moles, mice, even birds, but they didn't survive the experiments, or only survived for a few hours. It's remarkable—and this will interest you—that the months of July and August 1914 were extraordinarily favorable to the experiments. During that period, several duplicated mammals survived for quite a long time. My master inferred that the Earth was traveling through an interstellar medium particularly rich in pre-electric energies; he demonstrated the fact by experiments in atomic transformation. At any rate, his discoveries multiplied, and he thought he was on the point of rendering duplication inoffensive for higher organisms. Then the war took him..."

Charles Gourlande buried his face in his hands. A harsh sob elevated his bosom. In a barely-audible voice, he murmured: "When I saw Monsieur Abel de Grantaigle again, I was gripped by anxiety. Your approach to him could not have been motiveless. I was obliged to wonder whether it might be connected to what I had believed to be my master's hallucination. At that time, I thought that the adventure must have terminated in the death of the duplicated man—and I still don't know whether..." Gourlande fixed the neurologist with an imploring gaze.

"Not only are they alive," said the latter, "but, after a period of torpor, they haven't ceased to develop. Presently, they have all the appearances of normal human beings..."

"That's more than I dared hope. Undoubtedly, the etheric circumstances must have been more favorable than ever on the day of their metamorphosis, and continued to be excellent in the months that followed. Oh, if only my master had survived! He would have saved us all, for he would have resigned himself to war work. He would have manufactured radiations that would have paralyzed and immobilized millions of enemies."

"Why did he stay at Grantaigle?"

Gourlande shrugged his shoulders. "He had made Grantaigle into an immense accumulator of energies, which depended more on situation than equipment. It would have taken him years to rebuild such an apparatus."

There was a profound silence. Then Savarre observed, with a sort of wry satisfaction: "So the occurrence wasn't supernatural?"

"It was superhuman. My master was not only the greatest of men; he was, in himself, a new humankind."

Epilogue

Thérèse was walking with Philippe in the shade of the copper beeches. It was the day of her departure. In a few hours, Madame de Lisanges would set forth across the vast Atlantic. She was experiencing a dull distress and bitter regrets. At intervals, she looked up at Philippe feverishly.

He, sadder still, was ravaged by his love as by a disease. A wild astonishment surged through him in gusts; how was it possible for him to desire the woman that had been his mistress with that new force? Because she believed him to be another man, she had become another woman herself! In a sense, she was even more enigmatic than if she really had been unknown to him. He no longer strove to understand; his agitation was too extreme—but he sensed that he alone, among human beings, was able to perceive so fantastic a metamorphosis.

Such sensations were alien to Pierre; his relationships with familiar individuals remained, if not identical, at least comparable...

A slow old-fashioned chime sounded in a nearby belltower. "In a little while, we'll no longer be alone," Thérèse whispered. Suddenly, she gripped Philippe's arm and said, in a vehement tone: "Forgive me, Philippe...I fear that I've caused you genuine suffering, and must appear very cruel to you..." Her hand was so agitated that it trembled on Philippe's wrist. "I could not do otherwise! Since you wanted proof—it's you who forced the issue!—and as you did not displease me...what could I do? Love isn't a game for me...I've always feared it as the worst misery and desired it as the highest beauty. The longer I live, the more I want it to be profound and durable. So I had to discourage you immediately, or subject you to a long wait, had I not? I couldn't discourage you—you were dear to me, Philippe! You brought me the most extraordinary mixture of the past and the future. I needed time...and the certainty that your own love was no mere caprice. Philippe, are you perfectly sure that you love me? Will you have the strength to wait for me…more than six months…two seasons? If not, is it worth the trouble?"

The passionate voice cut through Philippe as the equinoctial wind cuts through the woods. He replied, violently: "I love you, Thérèse—the very love that you desire, patient and resigned."

They were in the middle of the wood. Nothing was audible but the light rustle of the branches; a jay fled into an aerial pasture; the odor of vegetation spread out like an emanation of eternal life.

She sighed, let her head fall on to the young man's shoulder and half-closed her eyes. "I've loved you for several days already…but it was necessary not to say so…I was afraid…there's so much uncertainty between souls. I wanted to be sure that you'd wait for me." She smiled ironically. "Now, you'll wait for me!"

He leaned down; the scarlet lips were no longer evasive; their mouths exchanged an avid promise.

"Here are my friends!" she said. She had drawn away; she darted a long glance at him, in which there was a victory and a prayer.

He did not regret not having possessed her; he would wait for her as one waits for Destiny.

Two days later, Valentine, Pierre and Philippe were walking along the foot of the cliffs. Although it was summer, the day was oddly similar to the mild and charming winter day when large clouds had pursued one another over the inexhaustible waves. As they had then, boats were floating in the distance, clearly visible, although blurred. Frigates were sailing beneath the cloud-mass; the sea had the same ample and regular beat—the beat of an incommensurable bosom—but there was not the same anxiety in their souls.

Philippe was as strong as ever; destiny was no longer stifling him; his hope had the appearance of a certainty.

Valentine had forgotten those sinister evenings when the two men seemed like revenants to her. She no longer confused them with one another. Philippe's gaze scarcely reminded her of Pierre's; she no longer discovered the love therein that made any choice impossible. Pierre alone was close to her...

She bathed in the delicious wind; it told her the hazardous legend of creation; it gave her cheeks an eglantine shade; her young innocent mouth had taken on a red flush and the gleam of pearls still steeped in sea-water.

As on the winter day, Pierre found himself alone with Valentine in the region of shaped stones. The tide was beginning to lay siege to them; it arrived in the gullies with its moist plaint.

"Valentine!" the young man murmured.

She lowered her head, deeply moved. She recalled the two episodes of souls mingling on that spot—but the second was faded; it was the other that mingled with the beast of the waves.

"Would you like my life...all my life?"

She did not reply immediately. Her dress danced in the wind; a stray wisp of hair eddied around her temple. She savored the joy of holding her destiny, and Pierre's, in suspense...

Then, nodding her head with a smile, she determined the future.

When they came back to the cliff-top, they saw Dr. Savarre walking near a Calvary, beside a man of gigantic stature.

Savarre stopped; his companion looked at the young people with a singular avidity. All five of them followed the narrow path through the bracken.

The neurologist drew Philippe to one side and asked: "Everything's settled? You're resigned?"

"I have no need to be."

Savarre pointed at Pierre and Valentine. "Nor them?"

"Nor them."

Savarre shrugged his shoulders vaguely and rejoined his companion. The Château de Givreuse appeared, silhouetted against the clouds. While Valentine, Pierre and Philippe continued on their way, the neurologist and his companion paused, in front of the resounding sea.

The tall man—Charles Gourlande—said: "I'm glad to have seen them. They seem robust..."

"They are. Everything suggests that they are reconstituted for a long life."

"I feared the contrary. How well they have stood up to the metamorphosis! It was a thunderbolt, after all—but in terrestrial organisms, everything is progressive, save for death."

"Even that! When the end isn't sudden, the agony undergoes a gradual evolution. Dr. Barbillion[12] has described, with remarkable talent, the *sequence of deaths* that precedes the real death. First we lose intelligence, memory, will, speech... everything that constitutes consciousness..."

"Is that certain?" Gourlande asked, interrupting him abruptly. "It would be a great consolation..."

"I have no doubt of it; as soon as the agony begins, *we no longer know what is happening...*"

"But the dying man breathes...he moves, his heart beats..."

"He does not know it! The medulla continues to regulate movement. It passes away in its turn; our skin can then be burned without the muscles reacting. We're still breathing in the meantime, but our respiration is awkward, as if reversed; it only ceases after the sound that has frightened men since time immemorial—the 'soft and prolonged' sound that is the last breath. Many people, even intelligent ones, believe that consciousness is only truly extinguished with that breath. At that moment, which is not the supreme moment, as so many intelligent men believe, there is no longer the slightest trace of

---

[12] Presumably Lucien Barbillion, a physician who published various scientific papers and a history of medicine in the last decades of the 19th century.

consciousness. The heart still beats, however, as it did at the dawn of life, in the fetus. When the heart falls silent, general death is consummated, but the series of local deaths lasts a good deal longer!"

"In sum, we always die *from top to bottom*?"

"According to Barbillion's apt expression, 'we take off our clothes at night in the reverse order to the one in which we put them on in the morning; it is the same with life…'"

Gourlande remained thoughtful for a moment, then said: "In the Givreuse case, the division must have resembled an instantaneous death, but a death of the *whole*, in which there was no *normal* passage from consciousness to unconsciousness, even less from the higher faculties to the inferior ones."

"You think that because it wasn't the organs that were subject to division, but the infinitesimal elements of matter. Even so, might not the division have commenced preferentially with certain elements?"

"Perhaps with the *inferior* elements. It must, in fact, have been the less complex molecular groups that were duplicated first. In consequence, the phenomenon was a kind of death in which the agonies were in an inverse order in comparison to ordinary death. All that gives a scant idea of the event, though. The duplication of organisms is extremely rapid; it begins with a vanishment. There's reason to believe that at the decisive moment, there's a veritable atomic explosion of the entire being. To make it a little clearer, I might draw a rough comparison with the explosion of radium atoms dividing themselves into atoms of radon and helium, except that the phenomenon is much more delicate."

"I'm not competent to judge!" muttered Savarre. "In any case, the reconstitution had nothing explosive about it, even though it has been quite rapid. Pierre and Philippe have taken long months to recover something approximating to normal density. If that's attributable to nutrition and normal growth, the weight they've regained is prodigious. The phenomenon is nevertheless gradual—and there are inferior creatures that double their mass and volume much more rapidly."

"One can offer two hypotheses. Either each atom is re-constituted gradually, or, each atom being reformed with the rapidity of radioactive phenomena, there's an indefinite series of reconstitutions. In the second case, everything happens as if there were an evolution *of the whole individual*."

"Which hypothesis do you prefer?"

"The second. It conforms more closely to what we know about atomic and pre-atomic activity."

They walked on for some time without saying anything; then Gourlande asked: "Do the Givreuses know anything of what I've revealed to you?"

"Nothing. It's better if they don't know. Their lives will become normal. I've been able to regularize the situation of the one who calls himself Philippe with the aid of papers left to me by a poor fellow who died suddenly in my clinic. I attributed those papers to the second Givreuse without doing anyone any harm. In addition, I'll adopt Philippe. I have a strange affection for him, and his future fascinates me."

The wind increased over the Atlantic; the waves roared, full of the mysterious fury of the elements.

"Life! Life!" sighed Savarre. "What did your master think about Life?"

"It drove him to despair. He investigated it by means of prodigious experiments, but it didn't yield up its secrets. It remained as enigmatic to him as to the humblest women kneeling in the half-light of churches. Nevertheless, he thought that it had its ultimate origins in nebular space.[13] Terrestrial life is but a moment, presiding over mysterious individual or general metamorphoses."

"Individual or general!" Savarre exclaimed. "But if they're individual, we don't conclude them here. Did your master believe in immortality, then?"

"Believe? No, he didn't believe; he limited himself to hypotheses. To begin with, he proposed that the individual,

---

[13] Rosny inserts a footnote here: "Grantaigle is probably referring to interstellar space."

wherever it might be, is multiple. Unity, as it has always been conceived by spiritualists, is not manifest anywhere. In spite of that, he imagined immortal entities."

"Souls?"

"Not exactly. In man, for example, there are several kinds of structures. The first kind form *a being composed of beings*, and thus without essential unity, but *individualized* and *partly indissoluble*. The others form a body that's more-or-less coordinated but subject to an intermittent dissolution during terrestrial life and total dissolution after death. By contrast, the relatively indissoluble being only loses a tiny fraction of its elements, and even grows, *with infinite slowness*, if I might put it that way."

"What do you mean by that? Is the extremely slow growth compensated by extremely slow losses?"

"In part. The increase outstrips the decrease."

"So the development of a being might extend infinitely?"

"No more than certain mathematical series, which increase without limits but never surpass a determined sum. The relative indissolubility conceived by my master was, moreover, of a particular kind. The different beings that compose the indestructible being may be more or less distant from one another, without ceasing to be narrowly unified; in consequence, the *total being* is sometimes subject to dilatations and sometimes to contractions; it may have a variable extent, according to the environment in which it evolves…"

"I don't really understand," said Savarre. "Are the total being and the beings that compose it material?"

"According to my master, matter, energy and spirit are merely human concepts; he was only concerned with actualities. I'll try to explain it to you later."[14]

---

[14] Rosny adds a footnote: "It is possible that Grantaigle's theory will be enveloped by us in an article or a pamphlet entitled *A New Theory of Immortality*." I cannot trace an article with that particular title, or anything similar, and the direction in which Rosny developed his pluralistic ideas in the articles

"Very well. After death, though, what becomes of the relatively indissoluble part of a human being?"

"It returns to the nebular world. I suppose that in the course of its eternal evolution, it might often re-formulate beings analogous to terrestrial beings."

"How can that be reconciled with the duplication of Pierre de Givreuse? A part of Pierre was indissoluble by definition."

"If my master's hypothesis expresses a reality, that part could not be divided either. It was coordinated with one of the new bodies. Another being rejoined the second body."

"Another being!" Savarre exclaimed. "How did it happen to be at Grantaigle at the very moment of duplication?"

"I don't see any difficulty in that, if my master's hypothesis, or even the ancient hypothesis of spirits, is admitted into the equation. In any genesis—and I have no need to remind you of the seemingly-capricious events on which human geneses depend—it's necessary that a nebular being is present. One supposes that it is alerted in advance, and that seems to me no more mysterious than the propagation of light or gravity…"

"But each of the two men believes himself to be Pierre de Givreuse!"

"On Earth, no matter what the origin of beings might be, we only have terrestrial memories. The one that was not Pierre de Givreuse found his memories already formed."

---

he published in the *Mercure de France* in the 1920s and 1930s do not include any notion of immortality, although the notion he developed of a tightly-packaged "fourth universe" would be easily adaptable to some such notion, by analogy with the Spiritualistic notion of an "astral plane" parallel to the observable world, in which spirits can move freely. The story "Dans le monde des Variants" (1939; tr. in vol. 2 as "In the World of the Variants") provides an oblique illustration of the manner in which such a hypothesis might be elaborated.

A storm was chasing the innumerable flocks of the oceanic sea, and raucously clamoring storm-birds were intoxicating themselves on the unleashed elements.

"Man will never know!" murmured Savarre.

"If he were meant to know," said Gourlande, softly, "everything would have been revealed to him at his dawn!"

ADVENTURE IN THE WILD

I. The Black Tiger

The huge tiger stood up, ready for action, every inflection of its body expressing pride in its countless victories. Even giant buffaloes, struck down from behind, whose carotid arteries it had severed, succumbed beneath its sovereign claws. Because it had been awakened with a start, fury ignited green and yellow fire in its eyes.

All around, the forest seemed deserted; its formidable odor chased away the creatures with subtle nostrils and sharp eyes with which it nourished its flesh. It was not hungry yet, but it was thirsty, and as the daylight faded it sought the expanse of water where, for some time, it had been accustomed to drink. Its large body was too heavy not to make the ground tremble, but it was a subtle tremor that did not extend far and became lighter still when it was in search of prey. Going to drink did not require as much prudence; who would dare to dispute its passage?

Deer and a wild boar scented its approach, without it catching their scent—its sense of smell not being very powerful—and without it seeing them, for they remained at a respectful distance.

Soon, it reached the sheet of water and, as in the jungle, was alone with small creatures: frogs; mud-rats; parrots bristling in the branches; two monkeys at the top of an ebony tree; insects for which the tiger might be prey itself. The parrots squawked and the monkeys chattered, almost sarcastically, advancing their flat-nosed faces, as it began to drink, insouciantly.

A grating sound caused it to raise its head; through the reeds, in the distance, in the valley beyond the forest, it saw a cart, horses and men.

"The horses have scented a tiger!" muttered Hendrik de Ridder, checking his rifle.

A tall Dutchman with nickel-blond hair and green eyes, he had a complexion as dark as the mongrel Chinese-Hindu cart-driver or the Sumatran servant crouched at the rear. He was mumbling, in rather coarse French, while a young man and a young woman sitting on the bench covered with tanned hides and red-brown fleeces listened to him. "It would have been better to harness buffaloes, although they're slow beasts...they're not afraid of tigers. The old buffalo Donders has gored two of them! Donders is a champion..."

Hendrik took out a little telescope in order to examine the area.

"Daar!" said the Sumatran servant, unsheathing his dagger. He pointed at the reeds on the shore of the lake.

"A fine tiger!" Hendrik said.

The massive head rose above the reeds.

In his turn, the young man seated on the cushioned bench examined his rifle. As tall as the Dutchman, but of another race, with an agile face and curly hair, he glanced anxiously toward his female companion, who had hair the color of old gold and a mouth as red as a cockerel's crest. "Would it dare to attack us?" he asked.

Hendrik was one of those Dutchmen for whom dissimulation is painful. "Anything can happen with tigers, especially black tigers..."

"Are there black tigers, then?"

Hendrik continued to watch the reeds. "They're so-called because the black stripes are broader and darker than those of other tigers. Our ancestors were unfamiliar with them—it's a new variety, a sort of abrupt mutation, in Hugo de Vries's terminology...perhaps the most beautiful tigers that exist, and the largest!"[15]

"But look!" the other replied. "There are four men here. I thought tigers were prudent."

"Sometimes reckless! A tiger like that believes in itself. Everything is at peril beneath its claws—everything that can fit in its belly!"

"Won't it attack the horses first?" asked the young woman.

"A tiger has its own ideas, Mademoiselle. This one probably knows that men are more dangerous...so it will begin with them!" He continued in a low voice, as if to himself: "And can we really count as four men? I'm not a good shot. I've wasted my time in Europe! The driver won't even defend himself; the Sumatran only has his kris. What about you. Monsieur—what sort of a shot are you?"

"Quite poor...although I've fought in war..."

"So, you see, we're not worth four men. Here, a man is someone who can aim quickly and shoot straight."

The tiger suddenly stuck half its body out of the reeds. Its granite head, almost black, its pale breast and its formidable paws symbolized primitive power.

The Sino-Indian's face became ashen; his ears blanched. Less cowardly, the Sumatran squeezed the hilt of the kris, and the three whites felt the "queen of terrors" looming over them.

The red furnace was beginning to sink into the west, but the enormous Moon, still nebulous in the scarlet radiance, was rising behind the forest.

---

[15] Hugo de Vries (1848-1935) published his book on mutation theory in 1900-03; the theory was obsolete by the time Rosny wrote this story, the sudden gross mutations in de Vries's theory having been replaced by the much subtler mutations of Mendelian genetic theory, but the terminology persisted, and the notion was retained in a great deal of popular fiction.

"It's hesitating…or waiting for some other prey," Hendrik remarked. "Nothing's lost. Within a quarter of an hour, we'll have reached the Refuge, where even the horses will be sheltered. Without them, the route would be too difficult!"

When the Sun had set, before the end of the rapid dusk, the tiger's eyes lit up like beacons.

"Isn't it afraid of firearms?" asked the young woman.

"It's doubtless unfamiliar with them, Mademoiselle— and it would be dangerous to fire, unless one's a good shot, like my father…or the Grafina de Gavres.[16] Tigers are irritable animals. It would be child's play for that one to leap into the cart, kill one or two of us and carry off a third…"

"We won't let it do that!" riposted the young man.

"No!" said Hendrik, with a small, very soft laugh. "I expect we'll fight like good soldiers. But a tiger is a thunderbolt. We might be able to kill it, but is that worth the life of a man or two? Ah!"

Emerging from the reeds, the wild beast slowly and nonchalantly set about following the cart, at a distance.

"It's reflecting," Hendrik went on, "after its fashion. I suppose it would prefer a deer or a wild boar…"

While the night spread forth its fine ash-grayness, the Moon, like a colossal orange, distilled a light that was still weak, filtered by the high branches. The tiger drew closer. Two or three times it uttered a kind of bark. The Sino-Indian was holding the reins with a tremulous hand; the frightened horses snorted.

"Man is a feeble creature!" the Frenchman exclaimed. He had indignation in his voice—the indignation of a young man who has been to war. His memory was full of the unspeakable horror of days of battle, when the human creature unleashed forces similar to those of volcanoes, capable of annihilating all the wild beasts on the planet…

---

[16] Rosny inserts a footnote to explain that Grafina—*Gravine* in French—is a Dutch title equivalent to the French Comtesse (or the English Countess).

With a burst of machine-gun fire, that huge tiger would have been destroyed more rapidly than a brown rat in the teeth of a ratcatcher's dog. A simple grenade would have blown it away...

In the solitude of the night, Frédéric felt the sovereign preeminence of the beast all the more profoundly. His heart alternately speeded up and beat more ponderously, and he darted glances full of humiliated affection toward his sister Corisande. He was, however, skilled in physical exercises, apart from shooting. On campaign, an officer from the start, he had scarcely made use of firearms.

The young woman did not have a clear conception of the threat posed by the brute, which was not as tall or as massive as a buffalo or a horse. Perhaps, without meaning to, the Dutchman was exaggerating?

"Yes," Hendrik replied, after a pause. "*Here*, man is a feeble creature compared to the tiger. Only a man who is sure of lodging a bullet in one of those eyes, or full in the heart, is the Master. On the other hand, we've already won half the game. In seven minutes, if it continues to hesitate, we'll be safe."

He had taken out his watch and was speaking in a placid tone, but his voice seemed more guttural than usual.

Suddenly, the tiger became invisible.

Hendrik pointed out a ribbon of tall grass and brushwood on the left. "It'll be easier for it to watch us and plan its move." To the Sino-Indian driver he said: "Look out!"

The cart steered slowly toward the right, in order to avoid a bushy outcrop from which the beast might have reached the cart in two bounds. Perhaps it was conscious of the maneuver; a brief hoarse sound was heard.

"As long as it isn't too annoyed!" said Hendrik. "If it's angry, nothing will stop it. A few more minutes gained. Not so quickly, Chandra, not so quickly...speed might excite it."

The man stammered a few words, through chattering teeth.

"He says that it's the horses," the Dutchman said. "And it's true...they're crazy with fear. Ah! The Refuge..."

Corisande and Frédéric could not see anything. Hendrik gave his telescope to the young woman, who made out a grayish mass at the far end of the valley; soon, a cyclopean building became visible to the naked eye.

"Oh! We're not safe yet!" said the Dutchman. "We need to get inside and close the gate, before it arrives...*God de here!* Here it comes!"

The tiger, springing from a clump of almost-arborescent ferns, was running in large bounds; as Hendrik had feared, the gallop of the horses had excited it—and the horses, perceiving the pursuit and seized by panic, took the bit in their teeth. The heavy vehicle pitched so violently that the travelers instinctively held on to their benches.

Hendrik had shouldered his weapon. He fired four times in succession—in vain. Frédéric did not hesitate to imitate him, with no better luck. In such conditions, the shot would have been awkward even for a good marksman; the detonations only served to increase the horses' stampede, without stopping the tiger.

The Sino-Indian was cowering in the depths of the vehicle; the Sumatran, although terrorized, was still clutching the hilt of his kris.

"Here's the caravanserai!" cried Hendrik, seizing the reins. "They're going to overshoot, and then..."

Scarcely 30 yards separated the beast from the cart. In spite of the crazy speed of the horses, that advance could be covered in a moment, and then...

"Damn!" the Dutchman could not help groaning. With a terrible effort, he tried to stop the horses, to steer them toward the Refuge—but the frantic beasts went past, and the tiger was arriving with lightning speed...

There was nothing more to do but await the attack.

Hendrik, abandoning the harness, took up his rifle again. "Fire at point-blank range, if possible," he advised.

A few more bounds, and the men would perish, save for some salutary stroke of luck. Then the Sumatran let out a raucous cry: "Look! Look!"

Six thickset beasts had just sprung forth from the Refuge: six dark beasts with sturdy heads and abrupt jaws. One might have taken them for small-scale jaguars, but their howls left no doubt as to their species.

"Gavres' dogs!" Hendrik exclaimed.

The dogs arrived at great speed, with an indomitable ardor.

Frédéric and Corisande watched them in amazement.

"Will they dare to attack the tiger?" asked the young woman.

"Will they dare!" Hendrik replied, with a kind of ecstasy. "They can kill it! If the tiger consents to fight, it's dead!"

The Sumatran had started laughing—convulsive but confident laughter—and the Sino-Indian was making a frightful racket.

Surprised, the tiger turned round. It was undoubtedly unfamiliar with those howling beasts, but their stature scarcely exceeded that of wolves, an entire pack of which would not have dared to take it on. Disdainful, it only hesitated for half a second—but the big dogs needed no more.

Already, the first mastiff was attacking the wild beast's throat, while the other five made for its flanks and thighs. The battle was obscure, atrocious and formidable. The enormous body of the tiger, the muscular torsos of the dogs, the seven ferocious mouths, rolling in a frantic mêlée, punctuated by snarls and furious gasps…

One of the dogs went down; another projected from two yards away, immediately resumed the attack; red springs opened wide. The tiger, clawed and bitten, occasionally shook off the stubborn pack, but nothing could prevail against the obstinacy of animals more warlike than all the brutes of the forest, the savannah and the sea.

"It's prodigious!" Frédéric exclaimed, while one of the six dogs, its entrails streaming over the ground like reptiles, and two legs half-detached from its body, blinded by scarlet fluid, opened up a passage into the tiger's belly with one final effort...

The dog died with its head literally plunged inside the cat, which stumbled, while the fire in its yellow eyes became duller and two red holes were hollowed out in its throat.

"It's finished!" Hendrik concluded, contentedly.

The tiger only got up again heavily and awkwardly, its extended claws raking empty air, almost blind in the fog of its commencing death-throes. It collapsed, its flanks palpitating feebly. The dogs resumed tearing it apart.

Once more, the sovereign beast stood up, in the stupor of defeat and impotence, then fell slowly back with a dull exhalation of breath, and died.

The men howled with delight.

II. The Man with the Mastiffs

The horses continued their frantic flight. Hendrik had taken up the reins again, in vain; the maddened animals remained insensible to the bit. Although it was broad, low-slung and well-equilibrated, there was a danger that the cart might overturn.

Hendrik, however, spoke to the beasts in a soft and serious voice: "*Vos! Zwarte! Hy is dood... Stil! Stil! Stil!*"[17]

The cart oscillated like a ship in a storm. The Sumatran, thrown on to the bench, collided with Frédéric, and the Sino-Indian uttered a groan, while the cart, plowing into a large

---

[17] Rosny inserts a footnote, which translates the first part of this speech as: "Vos, Zwarte! The tiger is dead..." He does not translate "*stil*" at this point in the text but subsequently translates it as "silence." Here, it obviously means "whoa."

bush, came to a standstill. Trembling on their legs, snorting and panting, the exhausted horses were pulling desperately, but when the Sumatran had thrown covers over their heads they calmed down almost immediately.

"They'll be manageable within three minutes," affirmed the Dutchman.

In the moonlight, the dogs were still harassing the cadaver. A man of short stature, exceedingly stout, with thick legs, advanced toward them.

"That's Jan Cats," said Hendrik, "*Jufvrouw* de Gavres' kennel-master."[18]

Jan stopped next to the tiger and examined his dogs. One of them, flat on the ground, would not see the light again; a second was scarcely any better off, and all the rest bore some wounds...

While the Sino-Indian driver saw to the horses, Hendrik, Frédéric and Corisande went to join the man with the mastiffs. Young Hendrik addressed the man in Dutch. "They fought like heroes, Jan."

"It's in their blood," Jan replied, and, having bowed respectfully, resumed his careful examination. "*He* is well-defended, in his fashion. Beasts and men are what they are. A fine tiger, Mynheer—but he was dealing with the best dogs in the world!" He shook his head sadly. "Poor Leeuw is dead—he's the one that led the attack. Duyvel's hanging by a thread...but the others seem almost unharmed—scratches. Those four still have strength enough to defeat a second tiger. All the same, the mistress will be sad...but I couldn't let Christians—including a de Ritter!—be killed. No, I couldn't."

The cart came back slowly, the horses led by the driver and the Sumatran.

"Would you mind, Heer Hendrik, if I saw to Duyvel now...and Leeuw too?"

"Our saviors! I should think so, Jan. Come on!"

---

[18] Rosny's footnote defines *Jufvrouw* as "Demoiselle" [Miss].

Hendrik helped to carry Duyvel, who looked at the humans with an extraordinary expression, having scarcely uttered a complaint, in his rude courage. His belly was open; blood was running from the nape of his neck; the thrust of a claw had opened the skin of his skull all the way to the nostrils.

"Do you think he'll have the same valor, if he recovers?" asked Hendrik.

"The same valor!" Jan riposted, indignantly. "Be sure that he'll be as ready for battle as he would if he'd never sustained a scratch. It's the tiger that would never have started again. And yet, the tiger…"

They arrived at the caravanserai. A large gate with two battens was wide open. Surrounded by high walls, the courtyard preceded a large house, a primitive stable and a shed serving as a coach-house.

"A building from the old days!" Hendrik said to the Frenchman. "It's solid; it'll last enough two centuries—and now that the country has become dangerous again, following the earthquake and the floods, one is very glad to find such a refuge on one's route!"

The Sino-Indian and the native took care of stabling the horses. Jan, aided by Hendrik, transported the wounded dog into a low-ceilinged room in which two candles were burning. He examined the wounds more attentively.

"I think he'll be able to pull through," he said.

He took a few improvised instruments from a square box, along with a stout needle and a reel of hempen thread. Then, having pushed the entrails back in, he sewed up the dog's abdomen.

"Temporary," he said. "I always have what's necessary for the beasts, and even for men."

After unhooking a lamp quite similar to the lamps of olden days, Hendrik assured himself that it contained oil, and lit it. "The beds are only heaps of dry grass," he said, "but there are blankets in the cart for the *Jufvrouw*. Apart from the main hall, there are a few bedrooms…or, one should rather say, a few cells. Excuse us! I believe we can go by the occidental route."

He spoke softly, having become timid again. In this primitive place, by the yellow light of the lamp and the candles, the young woman seemed to be a creature of luxury, harmony and splendor. Hendrik was not insensible to feminine grace, but he had not a single impure thought.

"We'll be fine!" she said.

He admired the delicate gestures and elegance of the daughters of France, but he was not one of those men who was immediately submissive to sharp impressions; he needed time.

"Aren't you hungry?" he asked Frédéric, not daring to ask Corisande.

"It's only two hours since we ate."

Hendrik went to get a box from the cart that contained bread, ham, cheese and beer. Having spread these provisions on a granite table, he soon demonstrated that the excitement had had a considerable effect on his appetite.

Jean Cats came to join him. He set about eating too, but it was the remains of a meal interrupted by the tiger. Besides, for reasons of deference, he sat at a different table from the young Dutchman. They both ate religiously.

"There's no need to be astonished, Heer Hendrik," Jan said, "if other vermin are prowling around the vicinity. The earthquake and the floods have chased out many dirty beasts…and I'm told that there were several black tigers in the forest. There's also been mention of brigands. A farm has been pillaged and the inhabitants burned alive. We're living in dark times."

Hendrik did not think he ought to pass on this information to the young French people. "We're safe for tonight," he said, "and tigers sleep by day."

"If they're not hungry!" Jan Cats retorted. "The four dogs can still demolish one, but against four, it's rare for a tiger not to kill three before dying. The Grafina will be very sorry…she loves her dogs."

Frédéric and Corisande were listening. Jan amused them, with his face as wide as the face of a hippopotamus and the surprising breadth of his torso. He had eyes the color of soda, faintly tinted with violet; his voice, almost ventral, sounded like the voice of a trombone.

"Why does the Grafina breed these dogs?" Hendrik asked. "She can put a bullet in a tiger's eye at 100 paces. That's more economical than getting dogs killed. It seems to me that retrievers are worth better than that."

"She likes that sort of thing, Heer Hendrik—as I do. She likes handsome fighting buffaloes, the fastest racing pigeons, big grayhounds capable of chasing down a deer…I'm like the Lady, no disrespect intended." Jan took a large swig of beer and went on: "If Duyvel recovers, all will be well!"

For politeness' sake, Frédéric and Corisande had accepted a glass of beer. Hendrik thought that it would not be courteous to prolong the conversation with Cats. He turned to the young woman and explained: "I'm gathering information, Mademoiselle. In the wake of the cataclysms, there have been changes in the terrain—and we're talking about Comtesse Louise de Gavres."

"But that's a French name," said Corisande.

"It is a French name. The Gavres' came to Holland after the *dragonnades* of your Louis XIV.[19] Later, a Gavres emigrated here. It's now a mixed family, but Comtesse Louise hasn't forgotten her origins or her native tongue. The Gavres' have always spoken it. As I've told you, she is, along with my father, the best shot on the island. A tiger is no more redoubtable to her than a panther or a boar!"

"It's rather humiliating, in these forests, to be a poor shot!" said Frédéric, with a hint of bitterness. He was robust, courageous, and animated by a spirit of adventure; the vain role he had played during the tiger's pursuit still rankled.

---

[19] Louis XIV's fervent persecution of French Protestants came to be known, familiarly, as the *dragonnades* because of his fondness for unleashing troops of dragoons in rapid raids.

Corisande was listening as one listens to fairy tales.

"You're right," said Hendrik. "I'll take lessons from my father...doubtless you'll do the same."

"Is Mademoiselle de Gavres still young?" Corisande asked.

"She's only 23, Mademoiselle."

After what Corisande had seen from the cart, a woman for whom a tiger was not redoubtable seemed a legendary creature.

Having finished his snack, Hendrik said: "You must be tired?"

"I don't know," Frédéric replied.

"Nor me," said Corisande, laughing. "But as you say, we must be."

An hour later, the men and animals in the caravanserai were sleeping in the midst of the carnivorous expanse. In every part of the forest, beasts with phosphorescent eyes, sharp canines and trenchant claws were in search of the creatures that were to surrender their living flesh and warm blood. Desperate flights, gasps of terror and cries of agony mingled with the infinite rustle of branches and the hoarse cries of the victors...

It was a night to which the Ages were indifferent; billions of creatures trembled and died in this manner in the ancestral forests, and billions of avid throats cried out in the same way. *Sicut erat in principio, et nunc, et semper, et in saecula saeculorum!*[20]

The dogs woke the travelers an hour before dawn. The Moon, very low in the sky, shone weakly, and was beginning to take on an orange tint. The barking of the dogs was furious and continuous.

Jan got up first, then Hendrik and Frédéric.

"What's happening?" asked the young Dutchman.

---

[20] "As it was in the beginning, is now and shall be, forever and ever" (from the Lord's Prayer).

"Something serious," Cats retorted. "Our dogs know how to distinguish between animals and, at the end of the day, there's only one that's capable of putting them into such a rage."

"A tiger?"

"Yes, a tiger. And men…but to excite them like that, they'd have to be prowling round the caravanserai! If they were only passing by, the dogs would content themselves with a brief serenade. We'll go and see!"

Hendrik translated these words for the young French couple, while Jan made a tour of the Refuge. The façade, like the surrounding wall, had no windows; a few narrow loopholes replaced them.

"Men?" said Frédéric. "What men?"

"In this region there are only Malays, who are always untrustworthy. Those who remain quiet for years can suddenly devote themselves to savage deeds. The Malays here are, moreover, the most excitable of their kind. I don't think that we have anything to fear, though."

Jan had just come back. "I wasn't mistaken," he said. "Two splendid tigers have invaded the valley."

"After the one yesterday evening, that's incredible!"

"Everything's been turned upside-down, Heer Hendrik. Would you like to see?"

Hendrik and Frédéric followed the dog-handler. Through one of the loopholes they made out formidable silhouettes. One was no more than 300 meters from the Refuge, the other some 200 meters further away.

"What can they do?" the Frenchman asked.

"Nothing now, but we have a day's journey to make. With them, one never knows. They could soon be far away…they might also come back unexpectedly. It's a male and a female…"

"Let's try to kill them!"

"We could—but I fear that it would be a waste of ammunition."

Frédéric looked at the tigers, feeling a return of the humiliated anger that he had experienced in the cart, on realizing his impotence. He would have admired their redoubtable strength had he been able to fight, but the thought that he was like a defenseless animal continued to exasperate him.

He went in search of his rifle and, having carefully taken aim at the nearer tiger, fired three shots in quick succession. The bullet passed over and to one side of the astonished tiger, which growled dully. Beside himself, the young man tried to rectify his aim; this time, the bullets seemed to bury themselves in the ground 20 or 30 meters in front of the wild beast. Even if they had attained the correct distance, a slight rightward deviation would have rendered them harmless.

"I give up!" he exclaimed, resentfully.

"You might as well!" said Hendrik. "That's six bullets that might have been useful in a fight at close quarters, or at point-blank range."

The enraged dogs continued barking, and the male tiger, vaguely disturbed by the presence of invisible beings, retreated into a thicket, into which the tigress soon followed him.

Jan Cats, who had witnessed the scene, concluded: "It would take eight of our dogs to tackle them—four for each beast. When there are only four dogs, the tiger generally kills three before going down. At daybreak, I'll inform the mistress."

"How?" asked Hendrik.

"By pigeon! Whenever I go away I bring a few fine travelers of the Antwerp variety—the best in the world!"

"What's the purpose of informing the Grafina?"

"Firstly to let her know what's happening. Then, she'll be glad to know that there are tigers in these parts. I'll wager ten stuyvers to a florin that she'll come to our aid. That's the kind of woman she is."

"Should we wait for her?"

"I'll wait for at least half a day, myself. The pigeons can cover 50 kilometers in an hour. They'll arrive quickly; the mistress will be at home…it only takes three hours on horse-back. She has the finest horses. That's five hours, at the most, to wait after sunrise. Why don't you wait too?"

Hendrik, thinking that there would be an inconvenience in remaining in the caravanserai for half a day, turned to Frédéric and told him about Cats' proposal.

Corisande had arrived. The story excited her. "Do you think she'll come alone?" she asked.

"With one or two dogs," said Jan, when Hendrik had translated the question. Not mastiffs—hunting-dogs, from which no beast can conceal its presence, either by night, in a thicket or underground!"

"Ah!" said Frédéric, pensively.

The day did not take long to break; hardly had the dawn sketched its light when the fiery red orb rose over the forest. Jan went to fetch a brown canvas sack, at the bottom of which was a wooden board. He plunged his hand into it and with-drew a large pigeon, colored like a ring-dove, with orange eyes. A silky rainbow set a gloss upon its round throat and black stripes cut across its wings; its entire body was quiver-ing.

Corisande looked at it approvingly, and Jan, full of pride, said: "Even an eagle can't fly faster! Would you like to hold her for a moment, Heer Hendrik?"

Hendrik gripped the bird carefully, and Cats brought out a second, slimmer creature with a paler underbelly and a less iridescent throat. "She's no less agile, and has no less stami-na." He fixed the ring that he had prepared. "Hup! On your way…"

The beautiful birds flew upwards with a flutter of wings, circled momentarily in the sky, and, having determined their route, disappeared.

"No sea-dog, armed with his compass, can orient himself like those pigeons."

"Now we wait," Hendrik concluded, with the phlegmatic patience of his race.

III. The Horsewoman of the Wilderness

Li-Wang artfully served the coffee, milk, honey and warm bread. In the garden, the plants were growing hectically, so rapidly that their life was perceptible; the stems thrust upwards from the ground avidly, and the flowers throbbed like beating hearts.

Li-Wang was as furtive as a serpent, and every gesture revealed a balanced and skillful meticulousness. The Grafina's footsteps scarcely caused him to raise his head, but he pricked up his ears like a wolf.

Louise de Gavres emerged into the light, a tall woman with flexible hips and a fine, ardent head. The daughter of a brown-haired race, her vast and commanding eyes were that opaque black color that extinguishes light. She was beautiful in body, seductive of face, harmonious in her movements and resistant to stress. Dressed in white, with a short skirt, she was reminiscent of Artemis the huntress. Any weapon would have suited her, even if she had had scarcely practiced with it.

Her gaze caressed the garden. Then she opened a very old Bible bound in pigskin and read, with a grave, almost emphatic joy: "Who is this that cometh from Edom, with garments dyed red; that man glorious in his apparel, traveling in the greatness of his strength?"[21]

She repeated the ancestral gesture, and the history of the Pastors of the Desert, the Exile, the cold Netherlands, and the

---

[21] The Grafina is reading or paraphrasing *Isaiah* 63:1; the words in the Authorized Version do not correspond exactly to those she uses, so I have improvised slightly to align the quotation more closely with a translation of her actual words. (The question is rhetorical, but it refers to a visitation of the Lord, promising redemption to "the daughter of Zion"—i.e. the Children of Israel, although the Grafina is obviously construing the passage metaphorically, with reference to her own family.)

first virgin forest, came to her from the depths of time. She remembered, still full of rancor toward those who had subjected her family to the dragonnades—and she retained an indignation against France, mingled with affection.

The young woman never thought about death and hardly ever of the future; she lived according to her intuition, but that intuition was vast and numerous, containing hardly any fictions, no lies, and no other mysticism than that which muted the profundities of life. Honest, she did not disdain trickery when dealing with an enemy. Thus constructed, formidable and seductive, she was elevated to a superior level in any human or animal order.

Her forefathers had left her vast lands; she considered them as an extension of her personality. Having been brought up to it since childhood, she knew how to make plantations prosper, whether of coffee, tea, sugar-cane, tobacco, saffron, camphor or cinnamon. The domain was a fatherland of perfumes, which filled the nights and days with incense. Louise de Gavres could not imagine any severance between herself and that fecund earth; her wealth was as natural to her as her sin.

Li-Wang, with a face of stone, finished setting the table. He knew how to laugh, like a child, but in front of his mistress and strangers he never lost control of his face any more than Louise lost control of hers. The habits of mastery had been ingrained in her by ten generations; she maintained all its disciplines by means of her own self-discipline, and the individuals under her sway, Chinese, Malays and Hindus, obeyed with the precision of well-designed clocks.

She esteemed Li-Wang for his prodigious silence, the agile sureness of his actions and his phantom footsteps. The Chinese man's respect for his immutable mistress was seasoned with a little love and a little hatred.

Three dogs came to lie down around the table, one as black as soot, the others as red as foxes. Their gestures revealed, to anyone who knew animals, that their primary perception of the universe arrived via their nostrils.

The Grafina ate heartily of the bread, the butter and the honey, in the stimulating atmosphere of the coffee. All her nerves and all her senses participated in the meal. As happy as her senses of taste and smell, her sight devoured the garden and her hearing rejoiced in the delicate sounds of the hour.

In the depths of the sky an eagle appeared, which frightened the small birds, and caused the parrots to fall silent in the palms and the fowl on the lawns. Louise, thinking about Jan, the mastiffs and the pigeons, enjoyed the trenchant flight and the soaring relaxation of the raptor.

Then her expression darkened. "My carbine!" she ordered.

Li-Wang's eyes, between the narrow curtains of their lids, were as piercing as the Grafina's. He too had seen the pigeons appear in the gap between the hills. He disappeared like a puff of smoke, and, a few seconds later, brought the long-barreled carbine.

The eagle was soaring at 1000 meters and, gripped by terror, the pigeons flew lower. Had they been wild, they would have hidden in the grass or the bushes, but the dovecot attracted them like a magnetic pole, and they arrived almost at ground level.

The eagle plummeted like an aerolith; the pigeons were flying frantically, and for 30 seconds their fate was undecided. Then the eagle got so close that, in the natural order of things, at least one of the fugitives would have perished. Three thrusts of the pointed wings, and it was all over! But the woman had what was needed to surpass that sovereign velocity. The large carbine was only immobilized for a second; scarcely had it thundered when the eagle fell, wings and all, its head shattered.

"Go fetch it!" said the Grafina.

Li-Wang brought the magnificent raptor back. Millennia of endeavor were concentrated in the immense wings; the Grafina understood fully that all perfect adaptation is genius.

"It's beautiful!" she said, regretfully. But it is vain to regret that which is necessary, and she went in search of the

pigeons that had gone into the dovecot. They too were beautiful, agile offspring of nature and serfs selected by humans.

Mademoiselle de Gavres detached the messages.

Jan Cats had written, without emphasis: *The dogs have
killed a tiger to save Hendrik de Ridder and two white travelers. Leeuw is dead. Duyvel has a ripped abdomen. There are
two more tigers. I shall remain in the Black Valley Refuge
until 2 p.m.*

"Leeuw must have led the attack," murmured the Grafina. "Two more tigers?"

Her heart grew heavy. She loved her dogs. Then, having
put back her weapon and released the pigeons, she finished her
meal without haste—for everything had to be done in its own
time.

In the kennels there were six more dogs, ready to die in
battle, all armed with jaws of granite and sturdy muscles. The
Grafina's stable comprised six saddle-horses and eight car-
riage-horses. She selected two animals with velvety chestnut
coats, slaves possessed of fire and courage, always ready to
make the supreme effort. When they felt their mistress's hands
on their rumps, they shivered wildly.

"Saddle them up quickly," said the young woman to the
grooms. "Full nosebags…we've got a long way to go."

She took a change of clothing, twin carbines, a large cut-
lass, two dogs—not fighting dogs but expert trackers and
hunters. Man or animal, any suspicious prowler would be revealed.

Half an hour later, the horsewoman passed into the wilderness. Brush, forest, savannah and heath were as familiar to
her as to the panther, the orangutan or the wild boar. She had
roamed around them while still a child, in the hollows of old
trees, on the rivers, in the bushes and the caves. As primitive
as she was civilized, she knew how to light a fire with flints
and, in every circumstance, to do what the aboriginal inhabitants of the forest did.

Proud, generous and passionate, benevolent to the weak,
she was pitiless when the necessity arose. At rest, she had as

much indulgence for the tiger as for the deer, for the eagle as for the sparrow. She did not judge nature, and never thought that the immense genesis and immense destruction might be criticized, or desired any change in the cruel order of things.

An indestructible sense of hierarchy brought the chain of being into conformity with her instinct; she had never been able to imagine that Jan Cats was not superior to Li-Wang, or Louise de Gavres superior to Jan Cats. She was a redoubtable mistress, with whom those who accepted their function could live in a profound security, but who despised rebels and expelled them from her domain. The basis of her hierarchy was not immutable, though. If Jan had shown himself to be as intelligent as his mistress, she would have recognized it; as things were, she valued and respected him as a great animal-handler.

She would probably have shown more reluctance in admitting that a yellow man, a Malay, or even a Hindu, might ever be worth as much as the sons of men from Western Europe. She did not consider them as entirely human, but she never offended the dignity of any of them; she measured out the portion of servitude to which it was necessary for them to submit and the portion of freedom to which they had the right. When they had as much character as Jan, she liked them, and when, like Li-Wang, they mingled hatred with their attachment, she did not despise them.

In the forest, the dogs ceased to describe ellipses. They watched the horses' surroundings, extending through space the subtle and almost infallible net of their sense of smell.

For centuries, a bridle-path had been maintained with picks and axes, but the frightful vegetation was ceaselessly renewed and recreated obstacles; in a matter of days, it expanded its green foliage, its menacing flowers and its sly serpentine roots. The Grafina's agile eyes, nourished by images as well as instincts, detected the signs of peril without difficulty, by courtesy of constant vigilance.

Nourished by humus and water, life streamed forth from every terrestrial pore: the bamboos were the grasses of giant meadows; the "traveler's palms," whose leaves served as tiles for poor people's homes, extended their arches; the patriarchal banyans, the teaks, the iron-trees, the ebonies, the pala-quiums,[22] the rasamalas, the phantasmagoric orchids, the ferns as tall as oak-trees and the perfidious population of lianas fought with a sacred fury, an energy sharpened by hundreds of thousands of years of vegetal warfare.

The Grafina loved to be enveloped by that force, in which every living thing exterminated another; the memories streamed through her mind, with a violence all the more intoxicating for being mingled with the gallop of horses.

At about 9 a.m. she stopped to let the animals rest and drink. They had covered 30 kilometers, but, being creatures of fortitude and valor, they gave no evidence of tiredness. Stroking their velvet noses, she studied their fine heads, sharp little ears and red-tinted eyes affectionately.

Panting with jealousy, the ardent dogs awaited their caress.

The place had been a landmark for centuries. In times unknown, the forest-dwellers had accumulated variously-sized blocks of stone there, which framed a vast doorway; made with trunks of ebony and ironwood, it would have withstood the assault of 50 elephants. A spring emerged from the stones, from which the young woman, the dogs and the horses drank.

That wild place, eaten into by the forest, overlooked a lake-shore, frightfully beautiful and vivacious: the leaves were flowers, the flowers fabulous creatures, vases of splendor and perdition, tabernacles of light, grace and death, beds of frantic amour, poisonous incense-burners whose every oscillation exhaled intoxication, sensuality or fever.

---

[22] Trees of the genus *Palaquium* are best known as the source of gutta-percha.

Having sheltered the animals in the ancient cyclopean structure, Louise opened the door with ebony hinges and bolts of teak. She had often stayed here, through magical mornings and avid nights; she studied the site with the nostalgic gaze of the past, on the lookout for animals. Through them, she had known her empire and the incomparable palpitations of peril.

The first one to emerge, baroque, derisory and dull-witted, had the rudimentary trunk of a tapir. It was a kind of rhinoceros, a tapir with a black back, shoulders and head, whose thick muscles would have been able to give battle, but which, flustered by the smallest adversary, could only preserve itself by cunning prudence. Some disturbance must have chased it from its lair; it was sniffing the ground and the water in a ridiculous manner.

The approach of some carabaos caused it to flee through the undergrowth. In their coarse beauty, rich in warrior vitality, ready to take on a tiger and throw a panther ten yards, the carabao buffaloes advance on to a promontory.

Dried mud coated their bellies; their heavy wild eyes blindly menaced the enemies that surged from all the fissures of the world—and yet, they stopped at the sight of a living creature more solid than themselves, for which the biggest cats would have been mere playthings. It could defy any moving creature, even an elephant. Covered with a hide more impenetrable than the shell of a tortoise, hideous and caricaturish, with its facial horn and its nasal horn, it lived in a morose security, punctuated by obtuse fits of wrath. Although there were six of them, the buffaloes gave way and the colossal brute plunged into the lake. It only stayed there briefly, crushing a few roots in its muscular jaws, and emerged heavily.

That was the moment when the Grafina was about to leave. If her horses had been able to get under way, the rhinoceros would be negligible; although it had a rapid trot and plenty of stamina, the impetuous beast would have outrun it without difficulty. It was, however, climbing the slope toward the cyclopean enclosure; Louise no longer had time to open the door and mount a horse; it was necessary to wait and see what the monster would do.

It did not come in; it stopped, moved by a caprice or a memory. Its myopic eyes could scarcely see in the gloom, but its sense of smell announced the presence of several creatures. Advancing its formless muzzle, gripped by impatience and anger, it poked the ironwood planks.

The Grafina studied it, irritatedly. In its immeasurable stupidity, the brute, thinking it was threatening lives, risked its own existence. With a single gesture, it could have crushed the young woman, but that gesture was impossible—and it was she, without armor or claws, who could annihilate the immense organism with a single movement. She took aim at one of its eyes, as sure of hitting it as she was of reaching the rump of a horse with her hand—but she did not fire. She was reluctant to deliver the colossus to the hyenas, jackals and vultures.

"Go away, beast more stupid than the serpent, the tapir or the tortoise!" she muttered. "I need to get past."

An absurd symbol of prideful power, eternally self-destructive, the rhinoceros snorted and uttered a ridiculous whistling sound.

I can wait another few minutes, the Grafina said to herself.

She did not have to wait. The brute started circling around the enclosure. Swiftly opening the door, Louise rapidly mounted the horse that had not yet carried a burden and spurred the beast away. With a noisy gallop the rhinoceros retraced its steps and started its charge, heavy and redoubtable. The Grafina and Rulf formed but a single creature, and the other horse, unladen, had an excess of energy.

It took 30 seconds for them to reach top speed, and the young woman started to laugh: the heavy mass was defeated. Moved by an opaque obstinacy, however, it continued the vain pursuit.

"Hup, Rulf! Hup, César!" There was an intoxication in guiding these agile machines. The Grafina laughed with pleasure; periodically, she turned her head to the colossus, which was beginning to shrink. Come on! There would be no battle.

Moving into a basalt corridor between two black walls, the young woman began to slow down. At a turning, she shivered: a tree had fallen there, its roots on the path, blocking the exit.

If the monster had not given up, the adventure would be turned around. Louise's thoughts combined with quick instinct; already, she had turned round and was making Rulf and César retrace their steps.

The brute had not given up! It was running on at its granite trot; it must have reached the entrance at the same time as the Grafina. Because it was pitching like a boat, its head oscillating, even Louise de Gavres might miss its vulnerable spots. It would have been necessary to dismount from the horse, and hoist herself up on a rock—but the horsewoman did not want to sacrifice her horses. Concentrating hard, silent and determined, she continued traveling at top speed—the greatest speed, perhaps, of which humans had made use for 1000 years. No Numidian cavalier, no desert Arab, had ever raced more rapidly. Three seconds! Gain three seconds!

When the *Jufvrouw* was no more than ten strides from the exit, the rhinoceros arrived…

The Grafina shouted: "Up! Up! *Honden! Taïaut!*"[23]

The dogs launched themselves forward. Lithe and cunning, they feigned an attack on the colossus—then, moved by a subtle instinct, barking loudly, they stood aside while the other swerved.

That was the moment when the Grafina reached the exit. Taking a strong hold of the bit, and squeezing with her knees, she turned sharply, putting her soul into the muscles of the horse.

The immense muzzle, and the horns that could pierce the belly of an elephant, were very close…one single leap would make the difference between mortal impact and deliverance…

---

[23] "Hounds! Tally Ho!"

The monster charged, but Rulf and César had bounded away—and again the horsewoman headed into open space.

Luckily, there was a clearing here; the horses and dogs made light of the pursuit, and the centauress turned, saw the wrong-footed rhinoceros, whose enormous mass was beginning to decrease, whirling around.

The threat had been averted. Louise de Gavres tasted the rude joy of peril braved; her voice stroked the dogs and horses alike.

The Grafina soon recovered the millennia-old track. Rulf and César bounded over the equivocal but supple ground. The air was beginning to vibrate as insects multiplied their unwelcome and unvanquished legions. There, even where humans have purged the land of carnivorous cats, annihilated the bears, wolves and hyenas, the devouring insects defeat them. Winged, or leaping on steely feet, or crawling in the darkness, or hidden in hair as if in a jungle, the insects attack us as they did in the earliest times.

Poisonous clouds enveloped Rulf, César and Mademoiselle de Gavres. She paid them no heed; she seemed invulnerable. The joy of being alive was accompanied by a vertigo in the balance of her organs. In another hour, she would arrive at the Refuge; she would see these beings descended from those who had exiled her ancestors, and the dogs that had defeated the tiger.

She thought herself mistress of the moment.

"Hup, fine beasts! We'll rest when we're there!"

Scarcely had she said it when her certainty crumbled. Victorious nature had extended its traps—the route was not clear. The cataclysm having excavated ravines, the water, which no issue leaves inert, had formed a lake between the forest, which had become dense again—where the horses could not pass—and marshy ground.

Open-mouthed, the Grafina contemplated the obstacle.

"It's 11 a.m.!" said Jan Cats, taking out a fat watch. "If she's going to come, the mistress won't be long now."

The heat of the Sun seemed almost sinister to the two Europeans. Without water, that heat would have been deadly; where there was water, it accumulated frightening and ferocious life.

Corisande and Frédéric were waiting without impatience. On leaving Europe, they had said farewell to the past. It was in this unknown land, to which they had never given a thought before, that they would find their destiny. It would doubtless take more than one season, so what did one day matter? But the sort of self-recrimination that had arisen in Frédéric the day before persisted, and tormented him. Humiliated by an impotence that stemmed from such feeble causes, he thought almost with malevolence about the woman who was going to arrive and would be the protectress of five armed men—men as well-armed as she was herself.

The restlessness of the dogs testified to the proximity of the tigers; they would be out there in the brush, sleeping lightly. Were they hungry or satiated? Two or three days sometimes passed before a tiger could eat, a victim of its overly strong odor and the subtle senses of its prey.

"Can't we set a trap?" Frédéric asked.

"We've thought of that," said Hendrik, "but tigers aren't so stupid. They must be suspicious of the Refuge. In any case, we're going to cover the cart: the driver and the Sumatran know how to do it. We have plenty of wood here. It's also necessary to protect the horses."

"I've read that tigers rarely attack during the day," said Corisande.

"That's true, Mademoiselle—so we have a good chance of getting past. If they've hunted successfully, there's no danger. If I were alone with my men, I'd risk it, but I'm responsible for your safety…"

Corisande and Frédéric looked at one another.

On Hendrik's orders, the Sino-Indian and the Sumatran took bamboo stalks and branches of teak and ebony from the wood-heap in a shed, in order to improvise a shelter for the travelers.

"Thus protected, we'll be able to fire at leisure," Hendrik remarked.

"The Mistress will be here!" muttered Jan Cats.

The dogs stood up. Cats cocked an ear. At first, no sound troubled the silence of the wilderness—a silence more profound beneath the midday Sun than in starlight. Then Jan broke into a smile. "The Grafina!" His chubby face expressed a slow and intense joy; the dogs leapt about madly. Corisande was agitated by an ardent curiosity.

As the horses arrived with lightning speed, they saw a brunette woman with the head of a Ligue member crouched over the neck of her horse. A thin, short man with olive-colored skin was almost lying on Rulf.

At the threshold of the caravanserai, Mademoiselle de Gavres leapt down. The dogs assailed her as if they were going to devour her, drunk on the young woman's caresses.

Corisande and Frédéric looked at the beautiful, luminously-costumed huntress avidly. She seemed as fresh as if she had only just got dressed.

The Grafina fixed her black eyes on the travelers with a start of surprise and a certain malaise—*for she recognized them.*

Were they not the people who had sheltered the bloody dragoons on the day of the massacre, who had appeared on the double perron to welcome them, dragging Jacques de Gavres, the Martyr, who was burned alive on November 17, 1697?

The Grafina studied, in amazement—almost with hatred—the charming young woman coiffed in light, with the fine French face and the little poppy-red mouth, and the young man with the military bearing. She replied to their greeting with a solemn bow, repeated in the fashion of her ancestors, and, noticing the young man's *croix de guerre*—which was for her a mysterious emblem—she murmured: "The ordeal was stern—the entire Earth has trembled."

Her bell-like voice gave a majesty to the old French accent that her Huguenot forefathers had retained. Then she said to Jan: "Give the man I pulled out of the water something to eat. Will Duyvel live?"

"He'll live, Mistress!"

The Grafina turned to Hendrik, to whom she spoke in French. "The tigers are nothing. The Sumatran I saved had told me that the Carabao-Men[24] have been driven back to the Blue Forest."

"Bad news!" said the young Dutchman.

That mysterious horde, living deep in the marshy forest, practiced a vile and ferocious religion. They were accused of combining the flesh of man and beasts. They never penetrated any domain without killing everyone, except for the women of child-bearing age, reserved for the use of their males. Their rites were older than the centuries of history.

"Three days to reach your fort is too long," Mademoiselle de Gavres continued, "especially with the young woman…" Her voice hardened on the final words, and that malevolence awoke an obscure anguish in Corisande. "You can come with me, Heer Hendrik. We'll arm the servants, and your father, with his household, can come to meet us." She turned to Frédéric, smiling weakly. "We don't have any machine-guns or grenades. I'll get some!"

To avoid the flood, the travelers had to follow a route even wilder than that followed by the *Jufvrouw*.

The Sumatran led the saddle-horses. Louise de Gavres, sitting in the back of the cart, watched the forest. Jan led the

---

[24] The term Carabao (Rosny renders it *Kérabau*; it is derived from the Malay word *Kerbau*) is usually applied to a particular variety of domesticated water-buffalo, one of many employed throughout South-East Asia, but Rosny appears to be using it more generally. It seemed more appropriate to use the English equivalent rather than referring to the people in question as "Buffalo-Men" or "Kerbau-Men."

dogs on a lead—except for Duyvel, who had been laid on a bed of dry grass. The dog had a fever; green gleams ran around his pupils.

For half an hour, there was no sign of enemies.

"I suppose," Jan remarked, "that the tigers are behind us."

"A tiger's territory is vast!" the Grafina replied. Her dark eyes followed the movements of the retrievers, which penetrated the mysterious invisible spaces more profoundly than the mastiffs.

The route was about to make a deviation when the black dog stopped, nose to the wind; the other immediately shared its anxiety.

Mademoiselle de Gavres left the cart with a single bound. She glided to where the dogs were, almost as silently as a wild beast, then went on ahead of them, while the vehicle followed ponderously.

At the turning, the Sino-Indian uttered a dull exclamation. The tigers were there; the body of a fine stag lay across the route. It was not dead; it was still breathing, but its blood was already being drunk and it was being eaten.

At the sight of the Grafina, the regal beasts, amazed and furious, raised their flat-faced heads, with growls that increased in volume.

Corisande recalled the scene of the day before: the impotence of humans, the power of beasts. A rush of terror took her breath away. Louise's silhouette stood up, tall, slender and lithe, before the thickset beasts. The dogs were howling, seized by madness, scarcely subdued by Jan's harsh commands.

"My God!" moaned Corisande.

The larger of the two tigers had leapt forward. Ten more of those giant leaps and the Grafina was doomed. With her head inclined to the right, she shouldered her weapon. Four shots sounded, with chronometric regularity—and the miracle was accomplished. The beasts spun around, roared, collapsed—and died before the deer did.

Frédéric's heart filled with a savage enthusiasm. Stupefied, he looked at the young woman, the monster-slayer, who was as tranquil as if she had shot two jackals. "Oh! Splendid! Splendid!" he shouted, with an admiration that overwhelmed his self-contempt.

Hendrik nodded his head in placid approval. "My father's pupil," he murmured. "A pupil equal to the master."

Jan, the Sumatran and the Sino-Indian loaded the spoils on to the front of the cart, which resumed its course through the jungle.

As evening approached, the dogs gave further signs of disquiet. The Grafina and the man she had saved studied the route ahead.

The Sun was orange by the time Mademoiselle de Gavres picked up a bizarre object carved in jade: a colossal needle with an eye as long as her hand and a triangular point.

"One of the Carabao-Men's weapons. The native isn't mistaken." To Frédéric, who was leaning forward avidly, she said: "Some of these weapons have been in existence for 1000 or 2000 years. Some have been found in the tombs of the Carabao-Men that must be as old as the earliest pyramids. Take care—the needle is almost certainly poisoned."

"How has the race been able to survive?" asked Corisande. "Isn't it hated?"

"Execrated! It takes refuge in frightful terrain, in the marshes. Other men die there like flies. The Carabao-Men suffer no harm."

"Are there many of them?"

"20,000 or 30,000, it's believed—men, women and children. The race is dying out."

"They're no longer seen," Hendrik added. "None have appeared in the vicinity of our lands in my lifetime."

"Nor in the vicinity of mine!" said the Grafina. "One might have believed that they had disappeared. Even my father only ever saw one of them. What I know about them I learned from my great-grandfather and a forest-dweller."

"Something extraordinary must have occurred to cause them to leave their marshes," Hendrik added.

"Are they really so very dangerous?" asked Frédéric.

Louise de Gavres looked the young man up and down in a strange manner. "Their bravery is boundless, their patience prodigious, their instinct infallible, and they're indomitable. When captured, if they can't escape after a few days, they kill themselves."

"So nothing is known about them?"

"They're known by their actions. My great-grandfather told me the story of their incursion in 1833. It was disastrous for the sparsely-scattered colonists who had settled here at that time."

"Yes," said Hendrik. "The forests were virgin then."

They arrived at the Grafina's home during the night.

IV. The Ancestral Simulacra

The day after their arrival, the Grafina said to Corisande and Frédéric: "Would you like to see your portraits, as they were painted in the 17th century?"

Although she had offered the French couple a sumptuous and refined hospitality, an ominous malaise persisted. Louise de Gavres spoke to them with a cold reserve that occasionally seemed hostile.

"Our portraits?" they said, bewildered.

Their hostess's attitude was serious; it would have been absurd to believe that it was some sort of trick. "Yes, your portraits."

She led them through a dark corridor and into a solitary room, where the only furniture was very old.

"Look!" said Louise de Gavres.

She pointed to a large painting on the wall, which caused them to step back in astonishment.

At the top of a double perron, coiffed like Madame de Montespan or Madame de Grignan, and clad in a silvery dress, stood a young woman, on whose hand a captain of dragoons had placed his lips. Beside her was a bare-headed young man and, further away, a tall prisoner with an obstinately bold and proud face.

Corisande and Frédéric, nonplussed, recognized their faces, their hair and their eyes, very nearly as they would have appeared in a mirror—and the captive bore a strange resemblance to Louise de Gavres.

"Who are they?" asked Corisande, curiously.

"She," said the Grafina, slowly, "is the Marquise Anne de Tamares. The young man is her younger brother. The prisoner is Jacques de Gavres, the martyr, burned alive—although he was a gentleman—on November 17, 1697."

Corisande's face was fixed on the woman's. "Why do I resemble her?" she said. "There's no link between us…"

"I haven't told you the name of the young man: Philippe de Rouveyres. Aren't you descended from him?"

Stupefied, almost terrified, in an atmosphere of sorcery, they remained silent.

"We don't know," Frédéric said, eventually. "Our family, impoverished since the Revolution, has become almost bourgeois; we've only heard slight mention of a Comte Charles de Rouveyres, in the reign of Louis XV—never any de Tamares."

"We're ancestral enemies nevertheless!" said Louise, enigmatically.

There was a smile in the corners of the Grafina's dark eyes. Corisande, full of suspicion, suddenly felt herself invaded by some obscure combative spirit—as if she were host to the soul of Madame de Tamares and Louise that of the proud Jacques de Gavres.

"They were inexpiable times!" said the Grafina, in a bitter voice. "Those people"—she pointed to the Marquise—"expelled from France the purest of her children."

"Oh—the purest!" Corisande retorted. "If they had been able to, wouldn't it have been them who expelled the others?"

The Grafina went pale. "I don't believe so!" she said.

"Do you imagine that there are two sorts of men? Haven't the English treated Catholics as badly as our people have treated Protestants?"

Frédéric remained silent, but his gaze met that of Louise—and they both became aware of themselves with a singular ardor, he as a Catholic, she as a Huguenot. They were separated by a silence as hard as a wall.

Eventually, Louise resumed speaking: "In two days, everything will be ready for your departure. I hope the delay won't inconvenience you."

"No," said Frédéric. "Our time isn't limited—but I'm confused by everything you're doing for us."

"I'm not doing anything. I'm only following the rules. You're my guests. Until Dirk de Ridder can collect you, my responsibility will remain entire!"

"Outside this house, we'd cease to be your guests."

"Not now."

"Why?"

"All the roads are dangerous."

"You're not the cause of that."

"I'm responsible," she said, rather dryly. "That's the de Gavres law."

They felt the weight of that protection.

"How long will it take for Monsieur de Ridder to get here?"

"We'll know that when I've received his message."

It was necessary to submit to the will of this haughty woman; they were profoundly humiliated by that necessity.

The day went by slowly. Men and dogs explored the region; the Grafina went out more than once herself, with her large retrievers.

That evening, Hendrik asked: "Has any trace of them been found?"

"No," Mademoiselle de Gavres replied. "Nothing except the traces already found. Since then, they must have moved away. Perhaps it's a trick. No one knows."

Although there were electric lights installed there, the table was only lit by large candles; others burned in the cressets along the wall, and the light had a restful softness about it. The night slept beyond the mosquito-curtains; the palm-trees were murmuring in the gentle breeze, and the great flap of the punkah refreshed the guests.

Li-Wang and a Sumatran servant were silently serving lobsters from the Red Bay.

"I'm expecting grenades and two machine-guns," said the Grafina. She turned to Frédéric and added: "Will you consent, Monsieur, to instruct us in their use?"

Frédéric's face became animated; the humiliating sense of inferiority from which he had been suffering since the incident with the tigers seemed less intense. "I'm more familiar with launching grenades than the operation of a machine-gun—which, in any case, will be child's play for you."

"We'll see!"

The leg of a wild boar was brought in, prepared according to an old Malay recipe, with sago, roasted nuts, raki, red pepper and cloves.

A dog growled in the darkness, then another—and all around the house, the voices of retrievers, mastiffs and basset-hounds resounded frantically. The Grafina sat up straight, listening attentively; the sound of hoof-beats became audible. Li-Wang appeared, and said in a cold voice: "It's *Jufvrouw* Ruyter."

Mademoiselle de Gavres seemed astonished, but she got to her feet and went to meet the nocturnal visitor. A few minutes went by before they saw a young woman appear, followed by their hostess. Tall and athletic, with hair as blonde as maize-straw, a bold mouth and fresh cheeks, she turned her wildly gleaming eyes to the guests. Their color changed like the shades of the ocean. Frédéric looked at her in amazement.

"Mademoiselle Suzanna Ruyter," said the Grafina, introducing her to the French couple.

She bowed and held out her hand to Hendrik, while the servants set an extra place at the table.

The tall woman lit up. "It's chaos!" she said. "The rivers overflowing, the ground opening up, lakes spreading in the valleys, the forests expelling their beasts and their humans..." She spoke in French because of the guests, in a soft voice with a harsh accent.

"Mademoiselle Ruyter has encountered the Carabao-Men!" said the Grafina.

"I'm not sure about that!" said Suzanna, serving herself a slice of pork. "A mass of hairy individuals attacked us furiously. My men fired into the pack, but had to retreat before the weight of numbers. Two horses were wounded."

"When did they strike?"

"Half an hour ago."

"They shall die!" said the Grafina. "Were any men hurt?"

"No—we were able to flee in time." She was eating with heroic insouciance.

"Their weapons are poisoned!" Mademoiselle de Gavres continued.

Frédéric looked at each of the striking young women in turn. A dazzling sadness overwhelmed him. The dreams of ephemeral humankind passed through his inner being like migratory birds—those tyrannical dreams that are born and die within us, but are sufficient to create hope or melancholy. Even a young man bears a thousand aborted destinies.

"Is there no remedy for their poison?" Suzanna asked.

"Yes—a red hot iron, applied within ten minutes, or Kannour liquor."[25]

---

[25] I have transcribed Kannour directly; I am not certain whether the reference is to the place in France from which the French surname "Kannour" originates, or to the southern In-

"No one knows that!" Hendrik remarked.

"Except me. I have the recipe, and even a supply, enough for 200 men. It doesn't spoil."

A silence. In the distance, a plaint, then a hoarse cry; primitive life was prowling around, ready to submerge the work of humans come from arctic lands.

"Do you think they'd dare to attack the house?" asked Hendrik.

"I think they'd dare," the Grafina replied, "but I've heard my grandfather say that, although they're always ready to die, they know the value of prudence…"

Barking sounds came closer, and they saw Jan Cats appear.

"Well?" asked the Grafina.

"Men from the Blue Valley, Mistress."

"How many?"

"At least 50, according to Vandalen and Devos."

"What sort of men?"

"Carabao-Men."

"We'll see!"

Jan withdrew, and Louise did not think it necessary to translate what the servant had reported for the benefit of her French guests. When the coffee had been served, however, she left to give her orders.

When she came back, her face was impassive, but Corisande, who could see through the expression, divined the presence of obscure forces.

Young Suzanna finished the meal placidly. She was related to Louise's family via a great-grandparent; her Dutch heritage had brought her a great deal—the heroic and temeritous heritage symbolized by the great name of the Ruyter who

---

dian district of Kannur or Kannoor, which would also be rendered Kannour in French.

had led his fleet up the Thames into the formidable port of London.[26]

"The red Moon will rise soon," said the Grafina. "Would you like to see the night?" She was talking to Frédéric.

"The nights are as beautiful here as in the high mountains!" said Suzanna.

In spite of the rising Moon, the stars stood out clearly. An exceedingly soft breeze, charged with the scent of flowers, brought a blue gleam, and Corisande alternated her gaze between the Southern Cross and the black holes of the Coal Sack, immeasurable etheric solitudes. In the ever-more-vivid light of the rising Moon, Frédéric continued to be subject to Louise's hostile spell and the evident grace of Suzanna. Because he was adrift in a strange world, without any thought of the days to come, the young man tasted the double charm without anxiety or hope.

Suzanna smiled periodically; a pearly spark mingled with the electric light of her vast, enigmatic, vaguely sensual eyes, full of boldness and defiance. Louise, more serious and intense, exuded the seduction of dark-haired races, along with their mysterious and despotic voluptuousness.

"We'll soon be able to see clearly enough to read a book, Monsieur," said the Grafina to Frédéric. She drew him gradually to one side and, when they were some distance from the group, she said: "I'd prefer to learn how to throw a grenade tonight."

"You think the danger's imminent, then?"

"In reality, no—but my duty is to act as if I thought it was. Haven't I my guests to think of—and also my servants?"

---

[26] Michiel de Ruyter (1607-1676) was a Dutch admiral who inflicted a humiliating defeat on the British navy during his raid on the Medway in 1667; he did not quite contrive to reach London, but his victory was decisive enough to bring the Second Anglo-Dutch War to an end. He had earlier fought in the First, and was later to fight in the Third.

She spoke in the tone of leaders for whom authority is a right, but also a servitude.

They had moved on ahead; behind them, Suzanna and Corisande were two silvery blurs. Having rounded a clump of bushes, they found themselves in front of a quadrangular building closed by a sturdy door. The Grafina opened it and flicked a switch; a stone hall appeared, deep and high-ceilinged.

"Here are some empty grenades. Others will soon arrive, charged."

She listened to Frédéric's explanations, and demonstrated that she understood them marvelously. Then, imitating the young man, she threw an uncharged grenade several times, with the skill of a javelin-thrower.

"You've already mastered it!" said Frédéric. "There's almost nothing to teach you."

They went back, in the gleam of the night-lights eternally illuminated in the boundless ocean. The night, gentle and implacable, saturated with perfumes and buzzing with insects, was ardent with life and charged with death. In the depths of the Ages, Frédéric perceived a similar night, when the same pale form had appeared, bringing an immortal promise, symbolizing the desirable agitation that fills the guests of a blade of grass and the guests of a forest with joy.

Corisande and Suzanna had already reappeared.

"Where did you go?" asked Suzanna, as they drew nearer.

"To try out weapons."

The Dutch woman laughed lightly—a laugh reminiscent of April and lilies of the valley. Frédéric thought that the velvet moment, the perfumes, the light breeze and the stars themselves were all feminine in that austral night. Then, with a shiver, aware of the strange beings roaming that savage land, he turned a gaze full of anxious affection toward Corisande.

She was the charming center of his life and his perpetual tenderness, the memory of which went back to a time when everything dissolved in limbo. Protector and protégé at the same time, he felt that he was ready to die for her; he willingly followed her advice, the intuitive wisdom of which he was well aware. "What did our hostess want?" she asked.

He never lied when she questioned him. "To try out weapons."

"At this late hour! What is she afraid of?"

"She isn't afraid of anything, but she wants to guard against the unexpected. She's a leader, Corisande!"

"A leader of what?" she murmured, slightly annoyed.

"I mean that she was born to command, as others are born to serve. She's a great person."

"Do you think so?"

"I'm sure of it."

"I fear that she might be narrow and intolerant—a Huguenot of the olden times. She makes me keenly aware of having been born *in the other camp*."

Corisande's tone surprised the young man. "One would think that you don't like her."

"She doesn't seem likeable to me—but I haven't forgotten that she probably saved our lives yesterday."

"Why don't you like her?" he asked, almost naively.

"I've just told you."

"That's hardly sufficient."

"Yesterday, I would have thought the same. Now, for indefinable causes, it's enough for me. I understand the past."

"So you're still mystically inclined!"

"Perhaps without being aware of it—and there's also the painting. Oh, how sharply I feel the presence of our ancestors!"

Had he not perceived that too? Yes, but in another way, as an enemy of the family but a subject of the woman, submissive to that primitive attraction which, throughout the ages, has amalgamated the flesh of victors and the vanquished. He did not persist. Through the mosquito-curtains, they saw a shooting star; a nocturnal bird was singing plaintively in the garden; the calm was so profound that he might have believed himself in a deserted wilderness.

V. The Carabao-Men

The Southern Cross rotated slowly around the eternal clock-face. The island was just about to escape the black gulf and bathe in the abysm of light when the dogs raised their warning voices. The raucous thunder of the mastiffs alternated with the clearer voices of the retrievers and the baying of Malay dogs, akin to the howling of wolves.

Corisande woke up, anxious, and put on a dressing-gown. In the pale moonlight, she saw men gliding under the palm-trees; then the tall figure of the Grafina appeared, soon followed by the squat silhouette of Jan Cats.

Noisy words were spoken, which she did not understand.

Cats said: "Should we release the dogs?"

"Not until I give the signal. The retrievers first."

Three minutes later, Cats came back with the retrievers; then Corisande saw her brother arrive with Hendrik.

"What's up?" asked the latter.

"We don't know yet," said the Grafina. "Something unfamiliar in the domain." Leaning toward the dogs, she murmured a few familiar syllables, which would determine their conduct.

They disappeared, followed by Louise and Li-Wang.

"Don't come *now*," Mademoiselle de Gavres had said, to the Dutchman and the Frenchman. "We're going on reconnaissance…"

Cats remained with the guests and the time, stretched by expectation, went by with excessive slowness.

There were howls, a gunshot, distant shouts…

Corisande, astonished and shivering, looked out. Abruptly, she sensed a presence. Arms folded around her; a bestial, musky and marshy odor, spread through the room.

As she turned round she saw a monstrous head, with eyes as phosphorescent as a leopard's, a square forehead and ca-

173

nines elongated into tusks. The colossal face was covered with hair the color of iron; one might have thought it a man and a buffalo at the same time.

Corisande looked at this formidable creature, terrified. She tried to fight. She was a vigorous young woman, but in those hairy arms she realized that she was as weak as a child. Besides, the entire structure of the enigmatic individual revealed a power comparable to that of big cats.

He carried the young woman along a long corridor, penetrated by the bluish moonlight. Corisande had called out once already; her voice, enfeebled by fear, was only a raucous murmur. When the initial surprise had passed, the courage of an energetic race awoke once again in the young woman, and she released a piercing scream.

A man emerged at the end of the corridor; she recognized Frédéric.

He leapt forward and fell upon the brute, his fists hammering the giant skull. With a groan, grinding his long canines, the Carabao-Man squared up to his aggressor.

Frédéric was a muscular athlete, agile, and skilled in most sports, but his strength had to be much inferior to that of his antagonist; if the other succeeded in getting a grip on him, defeat was certain—he would be killed in a flash.

The wild beast's hand went to a jade axe hanging by his side, but before he could succeed in detaching it, two impetuous blows landed on him, one on the chin, the other behind the ear. It would not have needed any more to knock down an ordinary boxer, but they only shook the Hairy Man—who, abandoning the attempt to release the axe, rushed at Frédéric.

A terrible fist nearly reached him, but the young man stepped back, moved sideways, and three times, with mechanical precision, he struck his adversary on the chin and the solar plexus.

The Carabao-Man went down.

"Bravo! That's magnificent!" cried an earnest voice—the voice of Hendrik, who had just appeared, preceded by the two retrievers and followed by the Grafina, Jan Cats, Li-Wang and other servants.

Gravely, Louise de Gavres studied the brute extended on the floor. "Tie him up," she said to her men. Then, turning to Frédéric, she continued, her astonishment tinged with respect: "That's very good, what you just did!"

"Admirable, even!" added Hendrik, adding, with Dutch sincerity: "I wouldn't have believed it!"

In spite of the joyful excitement that still gripped him, Frédéric experienced a sort of hectic pride: the sensation of impotence that had humiliated him since the adventure of the tiger vanished; he had ceased to be a useless combatant, paltry and almost despicable.

Corisande, rescued from the hideous peril, contemplated her brother with prideful affection.

Meanwhile, Louise examined the captive, who had already emerged from his daze; his eyes, surmounted by bushes of stiff hair, shone like the eyes of a lynx, and his open lips displayed two rows of stout teeth the color of jade—which seemed to be their natural color. He had small, pointed ears, and exceedingly short hands—because the fingers were only half as long as an ordinary human's. Like the face, the hands produced a dense fur.

The Grafina spoke to him, and then tried to make him understand by signs. The man remained vague, distant and bestial.

"They never *wanted* to understand!" Louise remarked.

"Wanted?" said Frédéric.

"Yes, wanted—for I don't doubt that they're skilled in sign language—more skillful than the indigenes, and even more skillful than us. We won't get anything out of him—and the others are out there, waiting."

A brief ferocious grimace animated Li-Wang's inscrutable face.

"Are you going to put him to death?" asked the Grafina.

"Nothing else to do, Mistress!"

Louise de Gavres raised her eyebrows. "Yes, Li-Wang, we can do much better than that. We can set him free."

"Free!" Cats protested, involuntarily.

Hendrik translated the hostess's words for Frédéric. "Why?" asked the latter.

"It's quite simple. If he doesn't come back, they're capable of wanting to avenge him. By releasing him, we have a chance—a very small chance, but a chance nevertheless—of inclining them to peace. All the more so since he can report that we're strong."

"Wouldn't it be better to hold him as a hostage?"

"We'd have to be able to negotiate with them—which is impossible."

The Carabao-Man maintained an apparent impassivity, belied by the glaucous fire in his eyes.

"Is he really human?" murmured Frédéric.

"I'm not sure," the Grafina said. "In any case, I'd be astonished if his race had any direct relationship to any other human race!"

"You think that they're not descended from the same ancestors as other men?"

"No. Anyway, if no one has any objection, we'll release him."

"Here?"

"No—outside the limits of the plantation proper."

Mademoiselle de Gavres said a few words to Li-Wang and the Sumatrans. They gathered around the Carabao-Man and took him away, accompanied by the retrievers and the mastiffs.

"I want to see him leave," said Frédéric.

Frédéric and Corisande followed the group. Eventually, the retrievers, for whom space was a vast reservoir of effluvia, began to show agitation. A few natives emerged from the shadows, with more dogs.

"We're nearing the boundary," Hendrik remarked. "The house is almost in the middle of the plantation, which covers 3000 hectares."

"How can such an extent be defended?"

"The Grafina has 200 servants of a warrior race, and her dogs—and the Carabao-Men don't attack plantations as rebel Malays do."

The retrievers growled dully, and the mastiffs barked.

Li-Wang ordered the servants to halt.

"They're close by, aren't they?" asked Hendrik.

"Very close," the Chinese man replied. "We must do as the Mistress ordered now."

Hendrik agreed. Li-Wang spoke briefly; the Sumatrans stood aside and he pointed to the west for the Carabao-Man's benefit.

The wild beast, fearful of a trap, remained motionless for some time. Finally, he took a few steps, with an extreme slowness, and, observing that the dogs did not move, retained by the servants, he accelerated his pace, took flight, and bounded toward a clump of ebony-trees mingled with tall ferns, into which he disappeared.

Raucous cries, acclamations or threats, rose up and faded away.

Li-Wang remained inscrutable.

Again, Hendrik asked: "Are they really human?"

In the morning, the Grafina said to Frédéric: "The pigeons have brought a message. Dirk de Ridder will set out tomorrow, with 30 men. We can set out at the same time, if you wish. There's no sign of the Carabao-Men in the west.

"Won't they pick up your trail?" asked Suzanna Ruyter.

"Everything's possible, cousin—but if our dogs, our men and our instruments don't warn us of the presence of 1000 of them, we'll know almost certainly that the road is clear..."

Frédéric looked down at Louise de Gavres and Suzanna Ruyter with vague regret; they were the symbol of Possibilities that incessantly appear and disappear on the horizons of our destiny.

"What have you decided?" asked the Grafina.

Frédéric hesitated. "We don't want to expose you to any further danger," declared Corisande.

Louise de Gavres shook her head disdainfully. "Danger is everywhere! It's here every hour of every day. Everything and everyone poses a threat!"

Early the next day, the Grafina received news from all directions. Carabao-Men had been sighted in the south-west, and a small group was heading north; the west was completely clear.

"They're coming from the south," the Grafina remarked. "During their last incursion, they never crossed the Groenheuvel, and yet they were much more numerous than now. They're not great travelers; the area that extends from their marshes to the edge of the domain must be largely sufficient for their aims. We'll head westwards to start with, then steer northwards. We should meet up with Dirk in three days."

"What about the domain?" asked Frédéric.

The Grafina smiled coldly. "There's a telegraphic connection and two pigeon relays. If my presence becomes necessary, I'll be alerted. The distance the carts will take a day to cover, I can cover in three hours on horseback."

"What if your men are taken by surprise?"

"There's no fear of that. The dogs and the scouts are sufficient to prevent any surprise. The servants will always be able to take refuge in the fort—which is impregnable." She concluded, in a different tone: "Let's go! A hostess has a duty to her guests!"

VI. The Caravan

That night, they camped in a clearing, which the indigenes kept free of trees and brushwood. Five huge fires surrounded the encampment, dissuading wild animals from approaching. All around was the enormous vegetal region in which humans were still permitted to eke out a primitive existence. The beasts were prowling around as in the time when the tiger, the elephant, the rhinoceros and the great buffalo were the only dominant creatures.

"Would a tiger dare to cross the line of fires?" Frédéric asked.

"It's improbable," the Grafina replied. "Audacious as they are, those fires are too hot and there are too many men. The ordinary tigers that live here habitually know our race well enough not to attack a company."

"What about black tigers?"

"It was only by chance that you encountered one. They're rare, and don't usually frequent this region—but even black tigers are afraid of fires. Besides, what does it matter?" Mademoiselle de Gavres had a contented smile. "Our dogs would denounce them."

Frédéric darted an involuntary glance at the young woman's rifle. He experienced one of those surges of astonishment that renew the novelty of adventures. The beautiful woman, in the snowy candor of her garments, with her vast black eyes in which flames reverberated, seemed more mysterious. She inspired in him a dread full of charm and, at times, a kind of animosity. Because it was from one woman to another, that animosity was keener in Corisande; it arrived as they exchanged untender glances, broken as courteously on one side as the other.

She doesn't like us, the young man told himself. Again, he saw the large painting, the handsome Huguenot all bloody, the Marquise who resembled Corisande's twin sister—and his own image surged forth from the depths of time.

Would he, like those people, have been an implacable enemy of the captive? He found himself transported back in time two centuries, and could see Jacques de Gavres on the pyre, distinctly. The flames were rising up, as they did this evening in the forest; they were enveloping a man. Corisande, in the guise of the Marquise Anne de Tamares, and he,

Frédéric, becoming the Chevalier Philippe de Rouveyres again, were watching the torture.

He woke up with a start, and saw the dark eyes that were watching him with an extraordinary intensity; one might have thought that they could see the images unfurling within him quite clearly.

The amber and copper glow beneath the arches of the forest made the branches quiver, and the old earth, bitter, magnificent and malevolent, manifested the ardor of life and the fury of death with equal force.

"It's horrible!" murmured Corisande.

"And more beautiful than horrible!" retorted the Grafina.

Dogs and scouts had searched the undergrowth before dawn. The pleasant odor of coffee mingled with the effluvia of plants. A Sumatran prepared the conquering beverage with pious care, while another toasted slices of bread over the red embers. The meal brought the humans together in a joy as fresh as the silver morning.

Time went by quickly, the life of men diffused in the life of the forest and the grasslands. Frédéric dreamed of a whole-hearted joy, without surprises, without anxiety, without anticipation, in which tomorrow evaporated in her bosom of slow duration. Abandoned to that state of mind as one abandons oneself to sleep, memories rose up in him, vaguer than clouds, becoming so confused that, in the end, he could not recognize them.

His tranquility would have been perfect without the slight frissons he felt at the approach of the Grafina. In the young woman's shadowy face, he discerned a hostile mistrust.

Toward the middle of the third day, Mademoiselle de Gavres said: "There's nothing more to fear. The Carabao-Men have never come this far. We'll meet up with our friends to-morrow."

Frédéric and Corisande looked at one another; a similar emotion passed over their faces. The legend of the man of whose inheritance they had come in search rose up in their minds. He had been a soldier of fortune, perhaps more passionate for adventure than money, and yet, he had made a fortune all the same.

Fortune had not hoarded its gifts from him. As clever with his hands as a Japanese conjuror, rich in effortlessly-acquired knowledge, an artist with neither difficulty nor vanity, a lively talker, ingenious and surprising, Raymond de Claverol seemed made for victory. There were no weapons, tools, instruments of which he had not learned to make use with a disconcerting facility, and there were few men he did not know how to please or could not amuse.

He would probably have succeeded in his native land, but the instinct of a wanderer had drawn him away into the great world; no other man had traveled so many deserts, climbed so many mountains, sailed on so many rivers, lakes and seas, or visited so many cities.

The fortune had been made all the same—at least, it seemed so—and quite unexpectedly: neither gold, nor legendary gems, but a wealth that was not that of other centuries, which a mountain had yielded to him in the midst of a rocky desert, where not a single tree or bush grew. He called it the Regal Stone. It lay there, having erupted from unknown depths, near a volcano that had been extinct, had reignited and then died down again.

The Regal Stone contained oxides and salts containing barium, lead, silver, bismuth and copper, and also uranium, polonium, actinium, radium and regalium. The radium was in very small quantities, but the regalium ore proved to be abundant—*and the radioactive power of regalium was almost equal to that of radium.*

"In a ton of regal stone," Claverol had written, "one finds a little more regalium than the radium contained in a similar quantity of pitchblende. Its extraction is certainly difficult, but less so than the extraction of radium. I estimate at more than 100 grams the quantity that can be extracted from the stratum and a more considerable proportion in the whole deposit. I've bought the land, with all the exploitation rights. Dirk de Ridder is holding a sealed letter, which he will give to you; that man, whose honesty is certain, will facilitate your moves and grant you a limitless hospitality. You cannot exploit it yourselves; it will be possible, even easy, to find an American, British, Dutch or even French 'consortium' that will pay you a fortune to associate itself with you in the enterprise. You shall have the wealth that I wanted to share with you, but which is escaping me; I'm returning to the original dust. No hope my poor children. The illness will have carried me away in a few days' time. I have hardly known you, but have loved you profoundly—you are my family! Adieu..."

The letter from his uncle had been combined with one from Dirk de Ridder, written in a strange but intelligible gibberish, which announced Claverol's death and invited the young people to come, if they could, to claim their inheritance. Dirk put at their service his knowledge of the country and its peoples...

"Is it possible?" Frédéric had murmured. "Might uncle have been mistaken?" For he had that innate hunger for a fortune that is the predatory instinct accumulated by humans over time and space. Corisande scarcely thought about it. Her dreams were more concerned with the uncertain happiness that wealth brings, the lure of creatures attracted to pleasure.

"No!" she had affirmed. "He wasn't mistaken. What he knew, he knew well. You'll be rich, my dear Frédéric."

"I want that more for your sake than mine."

"What would I do with it? A simple life is sufficient for me."

"Too simple."

"Everything is within us—wanting too much from outside, my dear Frédéric, eats into us."

"It's not a matter of wanting...it's only a matter of taking."

"Well then, take it!" she had said, with a little laugh.

The forest opened up into a broad pastureland, punctuated by small hills and gorges, where mountain springs nourished the green flesh. Sometimes, they perceived a few herds of buffalo, guarded by a savage herdsman, a distant deer or a few seemingly surly wild pigs. Harsh sunlight stung the caravan, and a ferocious multitude of insects buzzed incessantly.

The Grafina was worried. She sent selected men out several times, especially when they went along the hillsides, accompanied by the wisest dogs.

As evening approached, the caravan was moving alongside a deep gorge. The gleam of water was discernible in the darkness of the abyss; stunted grasses and stubborn lichens led an indigent life therein; a few trees grew there, lodged in interstices in the rocks, extending a few pitiful branches toward the light.

Rak the Black, the best of the track-beaters, seemed to spring forth from the rocks. As supple as a python, with a face the color of cinnamon, the man looked at the Grafina with eyes reminiscent of the wing-cases of a scarab beetle, and said: "In truth, Mistress, we're being followed by Carabao-Men."

She took notice of him, having been warned by the mysterious signs of the desert and the noses of the dogs. "Have you seen them, Rak?"

"I've only seen one, Mistress—but there are several sets of tracks."

"There can't be very many of them, Rak. Otherwise it would have been impossible for them to hide while we passed over the plain."

"I don't think there are very many...not as many as we are!"

"They've never come as far before, Rak."

"I don't know, Mistress—I've hardly heard talk of them. The one we captured on your land was the first I ever saw. The second is the one in the gorge."

Why have they followed us this far? thought the Grafina. *It's not for loot...what do men matter to them?* Aloud, she

said: "That's good, Rak. You'll always be the king of trackers."

A grave smile formed on the ancient face. Rak claimed
to be descended from "the men before men"—by which he
meant a race that had preceded all the invasions of the island.

"Find out how many there are, Rak!" she added. "Thanks
to you, nothing will happen without my being warned."

"Rak will hear all that his ears can hear; he will see all
that his eyes can see."

"Go!" she said.

He had already disappeared; he was instantly invisible.

The other scouts had not seen any Carabao-Men, but
they had all found traces. The Grafina watched over the cart
that was carrying Corisande. From time to time, however, she
went ahead of the caravan, mounted on her big black horse,
accompanied by infallible dogs. *They knew.* The expanse
yielded to them the secret of a presence that made them growl
when it came closer—and they would have set off in pursuit
had the horsewoman not stopped them.

The valley opened up, as broad as a plain, a grassland
sown with a few spare clumps of trees; another numerous party could not approach without revealing its presence. The Grafina's sharp eyes searched the tall grass, surveyed the hills and
the stray blocks of stone occasionally washed down by torrents.

Dusk was falling when she distinguished a thickset form,
which vanished in a flash—but Louise de Gavres had seen it
as distinctly as if it had lingered. Rak was not mistaken. Carabao-Men were following the caravan.

Why? Louise repeated to her self. *Especially as there
can't be many of them*!

Night was about to fall, abrupt and streaming with stars.

A river interrupted the caravan. Beyond it was the Red
Forest, swarming with wild beasts. The water ran in a torrent
at the bottom of a rocky bank, but on the other side, an indomitable vegetation devoured millennia-old humus; one could
see occasional siamangs on watch in the branches, and furtive

184

herbivores coming to drink. Three crocodiles were asleep on an islet, as motionless as blocks of granite.

One could divine the implacable war of living things, plants or animals, avid to accomplish their savage work, the consumption of earth and flesh, the formidable pullulation of births filling up the abysms of death incessantly...

Some 400 yards from the river, the Grafina saw a rocky mass, which she went to examine with Rak and Hendrik. "We'll camp here," she said.

It was a circle of granite open to the west by means of a large breach, from which the Copper River could no longer be seen. Three enormous stones, almost pyramidal in form, were balanced on their truncated points.

Rak, who had just reappeared, lay down, prone, with his arms extended, murmuring a melody with singular modulations in a plaintive voice. When he got up again, his eyes as phosphorescent as a panther's, he looked at the Sumatran servants in a hostile manner. "These are the stones of the Gods and the Ancestors," he said to the Grafina. "Our ancestors raised them when the world was newly born, long before those who have stolen our heritage."

Having said that, he prostrated himself again, and continued: "It's my duty to worship them, Mistress. Perhaps they'll help me. I was only able to count nine Carabao-Men. They can't be more numerous—of that, I'm sure!"

"There are 34 of us," said the Grafina.

"Yes, Mistress—we would be able to defeat them in combat, even without you—but you're more redoubtable than the entire caravan..."

She wore a faint smile, in which there was pride, assured that no visible man could escape her shot. "Rak," she said, "it's necessary to get rid of everything that might hide them during an attack. No one can oversee that work better than you..."

The caravan went into the enclosure with its carts, its horses and its buffaloes. The Grafina made sure that the men and beasts were camped no less than 100 yards from the rocks or the opening, while Rak began cutting the grass, clearing the bushes and removing large stones—although he had to leave a few, which were too heavy. To move the Ancestral stones would have required an army, but, situated as they were, with the others, in the very center of the camp, they could not facilitate ambushes by aggressors.

When the preparations were complete and the sentries in place the Grafina had the opening barricaded.

"Is there some danger, then?" Frédéric asked young Hendrik.

"I don't know," the latter replied. "We're obviously taking very careful precautions."

Without waiting for darkness, Louise de Gavres had the fires lit. The Sun was, at any rate, low on the horizon: a vast scarlet furnace setting the opening ablaze. It set. The night quickly devoured the twilight; the Southern Cross shone forth brightly in the black sky and the siamangs commenced a mournful howling at the edge of the forest.

As the Grafina passed close to him Frédéric repeated his question. She seemed taller in the firelight, very straight in her snow-white garments. Her large black eyes held a coppery reflection of the nearest fire.

"There *ought* not to be any danger," she said. "A few Carabao-Men are watching the caravan, or at least keeping watch on it by day. They are too few in number to attack us."

"All these precautions, though?"

A disdainful smile formed on the magnificent face, and Frédéric sensed himself blushing.

"Our duty is to take *all* the precautions that a company on the march can take. It's stupid to neglect any—and you know that very well, since you were a soldier during that frightful war... I don't believe that the Carabao-Men will attack us, but they might set traps—attempt to capture some of us."

Her voice had become mysterious; Frédéric sensed threats that were all the more disquieting for being vague. "What good would that do them?"

"I've been asking myself that. Memories keep coming back to me. My grandfather spoke to us about human sacrifices. The Carabao-Men aren't very avid for loot. They often transform what they pillage into fetishes. Captives destined for sacrifice naturally have an essential value. Besides which, they eat them after having immolated them, and such meals must have a religious significance."

Louise fell silent, pensively, and Frédéric did not extend his interrogation any further.

The siamangs were howling frightfully; gigantic bats with wingspans comparable to an eagle's fluttered beneath the stars.

Toward the middle of the night, the Grafina awoke abruptly, but without a start, having been accustomed since infancy to emerge from sleep instantaneously. Her dog Donder was standing up beside her, with his head raised, sniffing the air. It was probably him that had woken the young woman up.

"What is it, Donder?" she murmured, very softly.

In the dog's dark head the eyes were shining like a wolf's. Louise de Gavres had a profound confidence in his nose and his cleverness. He rubbed his cranium against his mistress's shoulder, with an almost imperceptible growl. She sat up, listening, then put on a garment that was narrowly fitted to her body and checked that her revolver was loaded.

The fires were going red; copper gleams were reflected from the rocks. The sentries were at their posts, each one accompanied by a dog.

First, the Grafina made sure of the presence of the guests; they were asleep. Then she made a tour of the camp. Everything seemed tranquil in the starlight. The night was mysterious, wild and soft. Only a few distant voices denounced the immense tragedy that was still incessant in the region. Occasionally, a breath of wind conveyed the liquid melody of the river.

The Grafina interrogated the sentries as she passed; they had not seen anything. Rak was not among them; he had not been assigned a fixed post—his mission was to roam. He only slept by day, at the hour of the siesta in the morning, while the caravan was making preparations for the day's journey, and during the pauses. He went to sleep instantaneously as soon as he consented to it, but he could have stayed awake for three days without feeling fatigued.

It did not take Louise long to reach the opening. It had been barricaded with tree-branches, in such a way as to prevent any abrupt attack. Two sentries were lying in ambush at the closure itself. The Grafina examined the place attentively, then moved to the right, where a granite wall loomed up. Donder manifested an increasing but mute agitation.

"*Stil!*" murmured the young woman.

The dog lifted his shining eyes toward her, expressive of submission and impatience.

"*Stil!*" she repeated.

He lay down, quivering with fervent instinct, while Louise started creeping along the wall. She crept like a leopard, rendered invisible by a bulge in the granite. When she reached the corner of the outcrop, in front of the open ground that extended to the river, she stopped.

She could hear the sound of the water distinctly—the sound of a torrent or rapids. By the light of the constellations and a hidden fire, she could see the flat ground and the large trees by the bank. To the left, the grass was dense; she slipped into it and steered obliquely toward the river. When the vegetation was high enough, she walked, then resumed creeping.

After ten minutes, she found herself next to the river and stopped, on her guard. The noise of the water drowned out all other noises, but the wind carried an indefinable odor: a bestial, musky and marshy odor that Louis de Gavres recognized.

She resumed walking with even more prudence, and reached a thicket. Through a gap in the rocks she perceived a beach some 80 meters below her hiding-place, which would be flooded in the rainy season.

In a feeble light, which seemed to spring from the rocks, a dozen silhouettes appeared, two of which were upright.

Were they definitely men who belonged to a species incapable of reproducing themselves with other humans, except in the limited manner in which onagers reproduce with horses? Jan Van de Casteele affirms that in a brochure published in Amsterdam in 1830 or thereabouts. He wrote (we are translating from the Dutch): "The Carabao-Men are, by comparison with other humans, as zebras are by comparison with horses or donkeys. If they abduct a woman, the woman's children are afflicted with sterility. It is well-known that such anthropologists believe that Neanderthal Man belonged to a different humankind from our own. Perhaps several human species had appeared in the remote past. Perhaps the Carabao-Men are descended from one of those species; they have only ever been encountered in Sumatra, where their habitats are marshy, and situated in the bosom of the most inaccessible regions..."

The Grafina contemplated the encampment with less disgust than astonishment and interest. She was perennially fascinated by powerful or strange creatures. These, with their rounded faces, their green eyes—more phosphorescent than those of tigers—and their giant shoulders, were sustained by torsos of surprising depth whose sides came together like a prow, by short legs, with thick but smooth thighs and much-reduced calves, and by prismatic feet reminiscent of the multiple structures of bears, bovine animals, and tapirs. Their rounded faces, however, were intermediate between human faces and those of buffaloes; their hair also justified their name, by its nature and its color...

The strength of their musculature had to be far in excess of the strength of human musculature, although their short legs could not permit them to run very rapidly.

Although they had a sense of smell nearly as keen as that of wolves, they did not detect the presence of Louise, who was positioned both downwind and higher up than them. The rock that bore the thicket at its summit was vertical until half way up; a ledge projected there, which barred the route of any projectile except at the opening.

That opening, narrow and sinuous, made any precise aim impossible; a bullet or an arrow would almost certainly have ricocheted. Even so, Louise counted four men that she or Dirk—but no one else—could certainly have shot.

A tremor in the grass caused her to turn round; something, man or beast, was moving there. Louise de Gavres cocked her revolver. A slight hum that was only perceptible, even to animals with the keenest hearing, at a range of a few paces, and a branch raised up twice, signaled the presence of Rak. In a trice he was beside the Grafina,

Meanwhile, Louise took aim, one after another, at the four Carabao-Men accessible to bullets, to assure herself that she could shoot them down.

"It's a bad thing to spare them!" said Rak. "Aren't they pitiless?"

"They haven't attacked us, Rak."

"They're attacking us by following us!" replied the primitive, full of disdain for such vain scruples. "Oh, if I could shoot like the mistress…!"

"Why are they following us?" she murmured.

Rak's shoulders shook. "For the mistress…for the young woman who has crossed the ocean…or both," he replied, anxiously. "The Carabao-Men have always stolen women. Didn't the Graf or the Graf's father tell their descendants that?"

Rak looked at the young woman with a submissive ardor. He admitted that they were separated by an abysm, but he loved her crudely, as a man loves a woman above all those of her race. She did not deign to know that.

"Let's get back to the camp!" she said.

All the fires were still burning strongly and the sentries were at their posts. With its circle of rocks, the majority overhanging, the camp ought to have been able to withstand the attack of a company much more numerous than the defenders. The only weak point, the western opening, had been fortified under the surveillance of Rak and put under the guard of two sentries with three dogs.

We've taken enough precautions to stand off 100 men, the Grafina thought. She smiled disdainfully. There would be no attack. Only trickery on the part of the Carabao-Men was to be feared. They were only a threat to the Grafina herself or Corisande—but the tent in which Corisande was sleeping was in the center of the camp. To reach it, it was first necessary to cross the cleared ground, avoiding the vigilance of the sentries, then cross the lines occupied by men and dogs—men almost as prompt to awake from sleep as the beasts.

The abduction of Corisande was thus impossible, and also that of the Grafina, with her infallible dogs, which an emanation as strange as that of the Carabao-Men would have woken up even before they had crossed the cleared zone. Even so, Louise de Gavres decided to watch while Rak slept.

Rak shook his head and considered the camp suspiciously. "The sentries aren't all reliable, Mistress."

"The dogs are. But I intend to watch myself while you sleep."

"Rak isn't tired."

"Rak hasn't slept for half a night since we set out. I want him to have all his strength for tomorrow. Do you trust me?"

"More than all these sentries put together!"

"Then rest as best you can when you're not fearful of any surprise."

"I shall be dead until the Mistress wakes me up!"

The Grafina made a second tour of the camp. The white silhouette doubled the vigilance of the men. She encouraged them with a brief word, and all of them, while they accepted her leadership, were subject to the seduction of her person.

There was none who did not desire her, weakly or energetically; in their savage souls, fable scarcely surpassed the illusion of primitive desire. According to their natures, though, the desire was servile or bold, precise or confused; the most ardent were no less pliable to the will of the woman, with whose indomitable character they were familiar, and whose audacity, skill and agility they respected.

As she terminated the inspection, she saw Frédéric in front of her, and looked at him without benevolence. "Be careful not to cross the boundary of the camp!" she said, rudely.

"There's danger, then?" The lusterless face and immense eyes fascinated him, although he still had a hostile ferment within him, which seemed to be increasing without any reason.

"In the wilderness, one must always believe that there's danger."

"I sense that you're afraid of a particular danger…"

She raised a shoulder impatiently and, ceasing to shield him, said: "We're being followed by Carabao-Men. Not numerous enough for us to fear their attack—that would be easily repelled—but they might set a trap for us, if the circumstances favor an abduction."

"An abduction?"

"Yes, the Carabao-Men abduct women—and even men. They sacrifice the men to their gods, if one can give that name to the elements they worship. They let the females live—whose fate is abominable."

Frédéric studied the fires, which were projecting a bright light over the cleared zone, the sentries on watch and the dogs, which were drowsy but whose senses remained alert to the surroundings. "A surprise seems impossible," he murmured.

"Humanly, yes…it seems to me…"

"Outside of humans, what is there to fear?"

The large eyes enveloped Frédéric with a disdainful expression. "Outside of humans, there is nature: nature is always the stronger…even in your lands where humans imagine that they have tamed everything. Was there not an earthquake in Messina that killed 100,000 of those conquerors in ten minutes?[27] And I remember a cyclone which, passing over one of your cities, killed the schoolchildren playing in a courtyard surrounded by railings. Five minutes before, everything had been resting in a profound peace; the storm passed by, and those poor children were no more than a memory."

She uttered a silvery laugh, which he found charming in spite of himself.

"Who knows whether an aerolith, in the abysms of the sky, might not be on its way to crush us? But then, everything is calm, the precautions are taken; there would be no point in being anxious. Rest, man from Europe!"

Two hours before daybreak, clouds covered the stars; a wind rose that whirled through the camp. Louise was still on watch; Rak soon came to relieve her. She breathed in the wind and found a stormy odor therein. In the distance, above the eastern rocks, one constellation was still apparent. The clouds swallowed it up.

Rain and tempest! thought Louise.

The horses were beginning to wake up; their muscular heads could be seen stirring, and their large violet-tinted eyes shining in the firelight. Dogs were sniffing the feverish emanations of the weather. The sentries waited, impassively.

The advance-guard of the tempest got under way. The winds, ceasing to swirl, arrived in immense waves of vast extent, which had galloped over the ocean and were now mounting an assault on the forests, savannahs and mountains. The clouds lit up; having come from the occidental abyss, lightning-bolts were flashing all the way to the Eastern horizon.

The meteorological phenomena were alive, palpitating like racing hearts, with a power superior to that of all the carnivores and herbivores on the planet; the thunder growled like

---

[27] The earthquake that struck Messina in Sicily on December 28, 1908, and the associated tsunami, were indeed reported to have killed more than 100,000 people.

100,000 lions, and deluges of water streamed from the sponges of the clouds.

The camp-fires writhed then; thick smoke was choking the men and filling the animals with terror. Dizzy horses bounded around the circle of granite. Then, in the immense stream, everything was extinguished; the wind and the rain held sway over an ocean of darkness. And in the boundless night, in which the herds of the tempest collides frantically with the hordes of the water, a sudden sense of impotence and resignation paralyzed the men and the animals.

Before the rain, Rak had appeared in front of the Grafina, as impassive as if he had been death itself, and said: "It's the Ancestral Gods. Rak wants to watch over the Mistress…"

"No! Let Rak watch over the foreign guests. Their lives must come before mine."

"All would be lost if the Mistress were lost!"

"Why lost? The tempest will pass…"

"If the Ancestral Gods wish it! It might squash us like flies, but if we survive and the Mistress has disappeared, the Carabao-Men will steal the foreign woman and eat the foreign man." He lowered his head and murmured, fatalistically: "The fires will soon go out. It will be as black as the tomb…"

Louise de Gavres adopted a commanding tone: "Watch over the foreigners' tents!"

He bowed and, without adding a word, headed toward the French couple's tents.

Before the rain extinguished the fires, the Grafina covered herself with a leather mantle and lit a little horn lantern—but a whirlwind carried the tent away and the feeble light flickered and went out.

Momentarily enveloped by the canvas and partly knocked over, the young woman found herself devoid of shelter in a flood almost as dense as the waves of a torrent. Everything around her was invisible. The howling of the storm did not permit any human or animal noise to be heard. In spite of everything, Louise's violent soul loved the brutal victory of the elements and the power of the universe; she was intoxicated by the taste for risk and peril that she had inherited from her ancestors.

Nevertheless she was anxious about the fate of her guests; in the chaos that abolished all responsibility, she felt responsible all the same. Groping along, she attempted to rejoin them. She had nothing to guide her. In that unlimited darkness and those torrents of water, any attempt at orientation was vain to the point of being derisory. Debris interrupted her progress—one hundred objects carried away by the tempest. Like her own tent, the foreigners' tent had surely been uprooted...

She moved forward regardless, or moved, at least, sometimes in one direction and sometimes in another.

Abruptly, she felt herself seized.

Two arms had closed around her—two arms that seemed very long and whose strength was evidently enormous—but the Grafina's slender muscles were packed with strength and the formidable tension of the muscles of a big cat. She made a rapid about-turn, her fists landing forcefully on an invisible face. The grip relaxed.

Louise de Gavres leapt backwards and found herself with a kris in her right hand and a revolver in her left.

She was not in any doubt: the marshy and musky odor that the wind had initially carried away from her had been revealed during the attack: the Carabao-Men had invaded the camp.

Cries of distress, rage and agony, followed by a sharp scream and a female call for help, confirmed the disaster.

All her senses taut, the Grafina attempted to grasp some indication—but the odor had disappeared; the enormous deluge, combined with the wind and the darkness, rendered any action vain.

They've abducted the young woman, and perhaps killed her brother! Louise said to herself, filled by an anguish that she would never have felt on her own behalf.

She had a religious sense of hospitality, so profound that the idea of not having been able to help her guests plunged her into a wild despair. What could she do about it, though? Nature had intervened, and Nature was the stronger. Not stronger, however, than the Carabao-Men, since they had invaded the bivouac, killed one or more men and abducted Corisande!

The idea that she was powerless against them filled the Grafina with a fury that made her spine quiver; then the anguish returned, mingled with an inexpressible shame...

She ran at random, bumping into obstacles and slipping in the mud—but that frenzy soon stopped; nothing was more contrary to the mentality of the young woman than futile movement. It was necessary to wait.

She waited—and the wait seemed, in accordance with the rule, immeasurably long.

The rain ceased almost instantaneously; a hole was hollowed out in the clouds, allowing the first star to appear.

Weak glimmers of light filtered through the darkness. Rak appeared, holding a bamboo lantern in his hand. Somber, humiliated by his vanquished sense of smell and his deceived vigilance, he struck his breast scornfully and murmured: "Rak is a blind infant! But the Carabao-Men are the sons of the Water; they can plunge themselves in it for as long as pythons."

"Rak is not at fault!" said Louise de Gavres, softly.

No other words could have moved the man so profoundly. He bowed, moaning: "Rak would give his life to get the foreign woman back..."

"I know that; everything that a man can do to pick up a trail, Rak will do...and no one is more skillful than he is."

She lit her lantern again, and the track-beater's lantern; other small glimmers of light joined her own. Savage faces surged forth, still upset by the disaster, and the Grafina made a tour of the camp in silence.

Animals and humans formed a chaotic mass there; the tempest had ravaged the carts. Two men were dead, found face down on the ground with jade daggers planted in their backs; another was dying in agony. As Louise had expected, Corisande was not found, nor Frédéric.

"They've abducted him too!" cried Hendrik, who was following the Grafina. "I thought they killed the men."

"They always end up killing them," Louise replied, "but sometimes they take them for sacrifice."

While giving orders, she searched for a trail with Rak and the most skillful of the sentries. The inundated soil did not retain any trace capable of guiding a human eye or a canine sense of smell and a pursuit at hazard, in the dense darkness, would have been a waste of effort. They had to wait until dawn.

Even so, the *Jufvrouw* thought it useful to explore the Carabao-Men's encampment. Rak was ready as soon as she said the word.

"There's no hope of finding them there, though?" murmured Hendrik.

Louise shrugged her shoulders. "There's little enough hope of finding some vague clue. If we only consider their intelligence, by our standards, the Carabao-Men are probably as stupid as the most stupid natives, but for their noses and cunning, they give nothing away to any race." Through clenched teeth, she added: "Tonight, they're the victors—they've inflicted the worst possible shame upon us by carrying off our guests. I shall not rest until I've recovered them or avenged them. I'll go with Rak and three other men. You'll be responsible for the caravan…and you'll go to meet your father."

"I'd rather go with you. The kidnappers…"

"What good would that do? It's necessary to know one's strength and one's skills. You left this country a long time ago. It gives me no pleasure to tell you so, but in the pursuit you'd be nothing but a burden. You'd slow us down. In entrusting the caravan to you, I'll give you trustworthy aides. Besides, now that they have their captives, the Carabao-Men won't come back again. If Dirk wants to come after us himself, that will be the most powerful of reinforcements."

"There's no doubt that he'll want to!"

"Dirk is the finest rifleman in the islands, with a nose as good as Rak's and the strength of a tiger!" said the Grafina, enthusiastically—for there was no man she admired more.

"He says that your rifle is as good as his!"

"But will he be able to catch us up? He'll need to pick up the trail here. Tell him that I'll leave the sign of the Trefoil as I go…here's Rak!"

Rak was panting, having come back to the camp at a run. "The Carabao-Men have gone along the river, Mistress. They've built a raft—the bank still bears the traces. Rak doesn't think it's a trick, since that route is the quickest—the only quick one, when it's necessary to transport prisoners or loot."

"Dangerous for them if they stick to it! We'll risk nothing by following it right away—any other would be impossible before daybreak. Saddle the horses!"

A quarter of an hour later, Louise de Gavres was galloping along the river, followed by Rak and three other horsemen. A few stars had reappeared and, low in the East, a pale light was diffusing through the clouds.

VII. Into the Unknown

The Carabao-Men were carrying away Corisande and Frédéric, who had been captured in the same elementary fashion—seized by exceedingly long arms, whose grip was as powerful as that of a python. Corisande had scarcely been able to struggle, overwhelmed by crushing force. Frédéric, agile and robust, had resisted for more than a minute, but the grip that enveloped his arms and torso had tightened further, taken away his breath and paralyzed him.

They were carried off into the howling night, whose darkness seemed to be made of tempest and rain. Their horror participated in the frenzy of the weather; it was as if they had been captured by men and the elements at the same time. They had cried out and they had protested, but their voices were lost in the immense wind.

It seemed that Nature itself had gripped them—the Nature that had dominated their ancestors for hundreds of thousands of years; civilization seemed like a fugitive minute in eternity.

Their anguish was increased by the stink of their captors. All terrible things weighed upon their souls: degradation, torture and death. Humiliated by being in the power of brutes, impotent to help Corisande, Frédéric was convulsive with fury.

The kidnappers were advancing slowly through the deluge, over the muddy ground. They finally stopped, without anything visible revealing the surroundings; a noise fused with other sounds that advertised the proximity of the river; the prisoners found themselves under shelter, presumably in a hollow in the cliffs or a cave.

"Corisande!" the young man called. In this refuge, the racket of the elements was attenuated.

"They've taken you too!" replied a weak voice.

Raucous cries interrupted them; the Carabao-Men began talking, all at once. A rough hand fell upon the young man's mouth, and then he felt himself being tied up. The storm was beginning to abate, however; the rain was slackening. Frédéric and Corisande were lifted off the ground, carried to the river and deposited on a vacillating surface that must have been a raft—and which soon moved away in the darkness, pitching continually.

Can these monsters see in the dark? Frédéric asked himself.

Whether they could see, or some subtle sense of touch supplemented their sight, they steered the skiff through the fast-flowing waters. By the time the rain ceased completely, they had covered ten miles; the speed of the current was equal to that of a trotting horse.

We're doomed! Frédéric thought, horrified.

He had come close to dying so many times during the war that a glimmer of hope persisted, but the hideousness of the ordeal was rendered intolerable by the capture of Corisande, an extension of his person with whom he had shared his joys and pains since infancy.

Because anguish, like all human sensations, has its rhythm of increase and decrease, Frédéric and Corisande eventually fell into a sort of torpor, which prolonged the sentiment of complete impotence. Everything within them was suspended; their very thoughts were losing themselves in a confused future.

First light and dawn appeared, fugitively, rapidly replaced by daylight. Frédéric and Corisande saw that they were on a large crude raft, surrounded by some 15 individuals who seemed to be as much beast as man.

Those sturdy heads, those formidable muzzles that stuck out like the muzzles of baboons, those short legs, those exceedingly long arms, the boar-like hair that grew all over their bodies and the green and yellow eyes, which gleamed in the half-light, revealed a race of men perhaps inferior to the mysterious race that had lived in Chellean times.[28] All their weapons and tools were made of wood or hard stone: jade or malachite. There were clubs, axes, harpoons, strange grooved assegais, and other weapons made of jet, twisted into an elongated helix, scrapers and masses that must serve as hammers. The raft was made of branches tied together with lianas and covered with bark.

Frédéric took stock of the Carabao-Men and their equipment mechanically, as he had once spied on German

---

[28] The Chellean period, so-called by virtue of the fact that its typical stone tools had been discovered in some profusion in the vicinity of Chelles, on the Marne, was one of the subdivisions of the Stone Age identified by Gabriel de Mortillet (see the introduction to vol. 4).

redoubts. Corisande kept her eyes closed almost constantly, in order not to see the hideousness of the creatures.

For some time yet the raft sailed down the river, which had broadened out, the current slowing. Soon, the flow of the waters was no more rapid than a man's walk.

The image of the Grafina rose up periodically in Frédéric's memory. What was she doing? Was she dead or a captive? Alive, she would not resign herself to the occurrence; she would organize a pursuit. At that idea, Frédéric's heart beat more powerfully, and escape plans multiplied. He knew, having heard it from Louise de Gavres, that the agility of the Carabao-Men was quite mediocre. He was a good runner, also trained in boxing and fencing; only shooting had been neg-lected—from the outset, during the war, command had been substituted for individual action on the part of officers, and he had only rarely, in exceptional circumstances, had to fight with a revolver or a sword.

What good would it do me to be able to shoot, anyway? he said to himself, with desperate irony. *If I succeed in run-ning away, only my legs will matter, and perhaps my fists, or one of those hatchets, if chance puts one my way—or even a club!*

If he succeeded in escaping, though, could he abandon Corisande, even temporarily? He had an absurd feeling that his presence was necessary to the young woman. *Madness!* he murmured, in his fever. *How can I rescue her, if I'm not free?*

The Carabao-Men stopped the raft in a haven and disem-barked. Immediately, they crouched down in a clump of trees rendered thicker by tall ferns. From there, they could see out while being invisible themselves. They were manifesting a sort of good humor, and one of them—the most thickset, whose enormous teeth shone like human shells—offered a slice of badly-roasted meat to the captives.

The kidnappers ate voraciously, in the manner of wolves and dogs, devoting two or three thrusts of their teeth to every mouthful, with grunts that doubtless expressed their pleasure. In this manner, they devoured an enormous provision of meat that was nearly raw and bloody—after which, having become sluggish, it seemed that they were about to go to sleep.

Several of them had closed their eyes. The man who had offered the meat to the prisoners watched them as a cat might have watched them. His monstrous face became immobile; his eyes and his mouth revealed confused impressions by slight movements. His eyes were larger than those of the others, a brighter green in color; they gleamed in the shade as much as, and perhaps more than, the eyes of a lion.

What's passing through that head? Frédéric wondered. *What bizarre instinct led them to pursue the caravan? Why haven't they killed me? Oh yes...their sacrifices to some unknown forces or beings...I have to die ritually...and Corisande...*

A long shiver passed down his spine. He loved life, but Corisande's fate touched him even more deeply than his own. The marshy and musky odor increased the young man's horror singularly.

"Corisande?" he murmured.

She was lying a few feet away, her legs hobbled like his, sometimes terrified, sometimes seized by an astonishment so profound that it almost abolished the reality. Sometimes, too, she went numb; a sense of fatality took hold of her and the monstrous adventure scarcely troubled her. In response to Frédéric's appeal she raised her head and tried to get a better view of the young man through the fern-fronds that separated them. She could only perceive a broken image, rendered more indecisive by the gloom—and he could only perceive a paleness in which dilated eyes glistened.

"My poor Frédéric!" she replied. "What will become of you?"

"Ah! You, especially," he groaned.

The thickset man got up abruptly and headed toward the young woman. He studied her with an ardor that seemed almost benevolent. He spoke in a raucous voice reminiscent of the lowing of a buffalo. His words had no more meaning for them than the melody of the river.

What he said, in a language that went back 30,000 or 40,000 years, in which no consonants could be distinguished and in which the vowels resembled howls, whistles, coughs and sighs, was: "The Pale Girl and Man will not escape the Sons of the Marsh. The Sons of the Marsh can see in the dark; their strength is greater than that of all other men. The Pale Girl will belong to Hourv, the Red Eagle, when the Moon of Jade follows the Moon of Reeds. The following night, the Pale Man will be offered as a sacrifice to the Great Marsh. The waters shall receive his entrails, his feet, his hands and his eyes. Hourv shall have his heart; the chief of chiefs shall have his head; his body will belong to the Eagle clan."

Thus spoke Hourv, the Red Eagle, as his ancestors had spoken for millennia, without any ferocity, his soul being almost gentle—but his race saw no more cruelty in the immolation of the foreigner than we see in the immolation of oxen, whose cadavers we eat so placidly.

Without any hatred against Frédéric, he conceived for Corisande a sort of love mingled with primitive desire, and he had such a profound sense of the morality of the ancestors that he would wait, for the accomplishment of the rites, until the present lunar cycle and that of the Moon of Reeds had elapsed. In the meantime, he would defend the lives of his prisoners as he defended his own, and he had the right to kill them if the other races arrived with sufficient forces to deliver them.

Although he was sure that his prisoners did not understand any of what he said, he added: "If the Pale Captives succeed in running away, the Red Eagle and his warriors will put them to death. But how can they succeed? For those of their own race they will be invisible in the hours of darkness, when the wind comes from the mountains, heavy rain extinguishes fires, or a mist rises from the waters—but for the Sons of the Marsh they will always be visible; our watchers will know every one of their movements! Has Hourv not seized the Pale Captives from their camp, in the midst of their warriors, blind in the night without fires and stars?"

Corisande and Frédéric listened to that animal voice in amazement. Although Hourv was demonstrating by speaking that he was a man, they could not bring themselves to believe it. The stigmata of the beast were as obvious in him as in a gorilla or an orangutan. His apparent gentleness reassured the young woman vaguely, but Frédéric did not allow himself to be taken in. The war had informed him with what insouciance, when he has the right—and especially when he has the duty—one man can cut another's throat. Rape, an even simpler act, appeared to innumerable savages, sometimes benevolent in their customs, as normal as hunting.

"Perhaps," the young woman murmured, "if we knew how to make ourselves understood, they'd accept a ransom?"

"Perhaps," he replied.

He did not believe it; he remembered what the Grafina had told him: throughout the centuries, there was no memory of any material or moral exchange between the Carabao-Men and the Sumatrans or the Europeans. No one had ever learned the language of this singular race; rare escaped captives had scarcely reported a few sketchy syllables, reminiscent of the language of wolves, dogs, buffaloes or crows. Thus persisted a mystery that would undoubtedly never be unveiled.

Abruptly, Hourv sat up, listening—a gesture imitated by his companions. Then, all their faces turned toward the other bank.

"Something's happening," Frédéric murmured.

He was not mistaken. Through the curtain of foliage, he saw several riders surge forth, followed and preceded by dogs. With a great palpitation, he recognized the lithe body and clear face of the Grafina. He was about to cry out—although the cry would not have carried to the other bank—but brutal hands gagged him, and Corisande too.

As if some obscure divination had altered her, the Grafina came to a halt and examined the location, while two dogs explored the surroundings. In the luminous morning, she looked magnificent; Frédéric's piercing eyes discerned the night-black eyes that seemed to see through the foliage. It was an illusion; at that distance, the thicket was impenetrable to the eye, although its occupants could see distinctly through the thin interstices.

She hasn't abandoned us! Frédéric thought. A kind of intoxication passed through his distress. The dull hostility that he had felt toward Louise vanished; nothing remained but admiration for the woman's beauty and courage.

There are only four of them! he said to himself—but he remembered the Grafina's skill; if discovered, the Carabao-Men would have been slaughtered by the infallible carbine. Their instincts and millennia-old traditions inclined them to ambush; if direct combat became inevitable, they would go down like rhinoceroses...

Louise de Gavres and Rak had dismounted. Aided by the dogs, they were searching the river-bank for traces. Frédéric knew only too well that they would not find any; even so, an immeasurable hope increased within him as the sagacious seekers prolonged their research. Perhaps some sign would indicate to them that they had to go over to the other bank.

At first, that idea awoke an uplifting image of deliverance; then the young man shuddered as he thought that Louise might fall into a trap. Around him, attentively, all their senses taut, with their axes and assegais in their hands, the Carabao-Men were waiting.

In the end, the Grafina and Rak, having discovered no traces, leapt into the saddle and departed with their companions. The riders drew away. Soon, they disappeared over the horizon and grunted, while a deadly despair gripped the captives, the Carabao-Men grunted half-joyfully and half in disappointment—for they had thought momentarily that chance might deliver the Grafina to them.

A short time later, Hourv gave the signal to depart. Eight Carabao-Men picked up the raft, which 15 Malays would have had difficulty dragging, but which they transported without bending under the strain. Hourv threw Corisande over his shoulder, and a warrior took possession of Frédéric.

The forest, bristling with horns and armored with brushwood and lianas, opposed a strenuous resistance to the invaders. Four men were incessantly hacking down the vegetation with axes or cutting through it with knives. The further away they got from the river, the less difficult the passage became; the shade of old trees limited the pullulation of bushes and grass.

An indeterminate time went by, and then the forest became denser; the axes and knives recommenced hacking and cutting. Finally, the Carabao-Men uttered a raucous screech, which was a cry of victory. Another river was there, as rapid as the first.

The left bank of the river ceased to be a grassland; the Red Forest now occupied the whole extent. Louise de Gavres ordered a halt, dismounted, and signaled Rak to come closer.

"The raft can't have got this far," she said. "We would have caught up with it some time ago. "We have to look for the trail on the other bank."

"Rak thinks so too, Mistress. If you wish, he'll be the one who will go over to the right bank, with one of the dogs. He'll recover the trail."

Louise hesitated momentarily. She was sure that the Carabao-Men would not have been able to navigate on the Yellow River as far as the confines of the savannah without being seen by Rak or herself. On the left bank, their emanations could not have escaped the dogs.

The Grafina did not doubt that they had embarked initially, and Rak agreed. Afterwards, they must have gone deep into the forest—where they would conserve their advantage, for the obstacles would slow down the fugitives and the pursuers equally; moreover, the latter would lose time looking for traces.

"Rak can go over to the other bank," the Grafina said. "He will know how to become invisible—and he will take Vos with him, the best dog in the islands."[29]

Vos was already beside her, as lithe as a leopard, with child-like eyes full of the fire of life, the ears of a wolf, in which the slightest frissons of the grass vibrated, and a sense of smell that continually notified him of the mysterious presence of creatures that had crossed his path or were moving in the vicinity.

Louise put her hand on the dog's head, then, drawing him toward the track-beater, she murmured: "Vos must follow Rak!"

The retriever, understanding the gesture, uttered a feeble growl; on the warpath, he did not like to leave his mistress—but he was able to obey. He sniffed the adventurer as if he wanted to know him better than he already did, and when Rak went into the river, he went in with him. Rapid as the current was, it could not stop the man or the beast.

Having come ashore on the other bank, they went back upstream while the ascendant Sun dried the man's garments and the animal's hide.

The Grafina and her servants followed in parallel on the left bank. An hour went by without any track being discovered.

The Grafina thought that the Carabao-Men must be far away in the forest—unless, having kept watch on the pursuers, they had re-embarked further downstream. As she was reflecting, Rak and Vos stopped. Their attitude left no doubt; they had picked up the trail; it was necessary to rejoin them.

On that side, the vegetation was too dense for the horses to be led. The young woman confided them to one of her

---

[29] The reader may remember that Hendrik had previously addressed one of the horses pulling his cart as Vos; Rosny—who was evidently dictating the novel to an amanuensis—might have forgotten that he had used it previously, or misremembered the context.

207

companions; the other two were to cross the river with her. It was mere child's play for the three of them, habitués of woods, brushwood and savannahs, accustomed since childhood to overcome natural obstacles. On campaign, Louise never forgot to bring an impermeable sheath, light and able to float, which kept her weapons and ammunition, of which one often had sovereign need in the wilderness, sheltered from water.

By the time she came ashore, Rak had already explored the forest for 500 meters from the bank.

"Have they headed into the forest?" she asked.

The scout held out a wisp of blonde hair, which would have been sufficient to show that Corisande had been disembarked there, but the revealing traces of the camp were numerous. The Carabao-Men had deemed it futile to take precautions that would have been vain. They were too numerous to be able to hide the vestiges of their passage from clever trackers. They were counting, naturally, on the start they had and the difficulties of the pursuit, in order to reach the bulk of their horde before any attack. Then they would be by far the stronger.

"Do you think they might have re-embarked further on while we were heading upriver?" asked the Grafina.

"This river leads to inhabited lands."

And it would have taken them in the direction from which Dirk is coming, Louise thought. "Rak's right," she continued. "Let's follow the trail."

Their passage through the vegetation was facilitated by the passage of the Carabao-Men themselves, and besides, although thick, the forest became less difficult as they drew away from the river. They lost no time, so clear was the trail, not only for Vos's infallible sense of smell but even for the men.

Evidently, the fugitives had neglected all precautions, sure of having deceived their pursuers long before. Nevertheless, their negligence astonished the Grafina. The Carabao-Men might believe that their lead is long enough for them to have nothing to fear, or might even be hoping that their tracks would be found too late to allow any chance of pursuit, but their immutable traditions, like their savage instincts, should have maintained their mistrust and made them act as if peril were close at hand.

Louise suspected a maneuver that would put them out of range. She thought about it, evoking all the possibilities that her imagination and knowledge of the locale could suggest. Perhaps reinforcements were waiting for them in the forest? That was improbable. The chance that had delivered Corisande and Frédéric into their hands was unforeseeable in time as in space...so a strange coincidence had favored them.

Suddenly, an idea flared up in the young woman's mind, and she asked: "Are we far from the Vampire River, Rak? Do you think that might lead to one of the lands where the Carabao-Men live?"

There was a tremor in the tracker's features. "I'm sure of it!" he said. "My grandfather saw them in the region that extends to the fork of the tributary and the larger river—they nearly captured him. It's one of their three homelands, Mistress...I thought of that as soon as you mentioned it."

"In that case, Rak, I've little doubt as to their intention. The stream is fast-flowing. They'll embark upon it—and by the time we reach the bank, they'll be far away!"

"So far," murmured the scout, "that we can only catch them up in their marshes...after days on end..."

Louise de Gavres lowered her head, gripped by a humiliating sadness. Then she said: "They never sacrifice their victims straight away..."

"No, Mistress. They consult the waters, the Moon, and also their elders. Sometimes, my grandfather said, the date is fixed before they've taken their male and female prisoners."

"We shall go on until the end."

Rak acquiesced with a nod of his head. His race was stoical; it did not attach an excessive importance to life.

The Sun had passed its zenith by the time they reached the shore of the Vampire River. The young woman was distressed to see that she had guessed rightly. The Carabao-Men had embarked, almost certainly, for their marshes.

"They're less than three hours ahead," the Grafina murmured. "If we try to follow them through the forest we'll travel much more slowly than their raft. We're not equipped to construct a raft ourselves—which would take a long time, in any case."

She fell into a bitter reverie. She would rather die than abandon her guests; she would fight on as long as the faintest chance remained. Even so, she did not want to be defeated, especially when she had been attacked. The stubborn soul of ancestors who had sung psalms on the heath, in the forest and among the antique cliffs was within her. Like them, she was always ready for trials, always resolved to put her duty above life and ruination. No duty seemed more sacred to her than the one we contract toward those who have eaten our bread and whom we have tried to bring into port.

"Rak," she said, "pursuit would be vain. We need a boat and reinforcements—but the trail should not be abandoned, even if we were completely certain that we know their route... and we're only half-certain. Rak will follow the left bank, Kalava the right. You're both more rapid runners than the Carabao-Men and you won't let yourselves be taken by surprise. I'll catch up with you further on, and we'll be able to continue our pursuit on the water."

Rak listened, his face and body as motionless as if he had not been a creature of flesh. He limited himself to replying: "Very good!"

A short time later, he went over to the other bank and Louise de Gavres gave her instructions again to Kalava, who was already on his way. Less cunning and subtle than Rak, Kalava nevertheless had flair and cunning; he was seconded by a little Bornean dog that belonged to him, in which he had a superstitious trust. He was a very small man, as fleshless as an old fakir, with skin the color of raw coffee beans and opa-

que and unreadable tarry eyes, which seemed to be asleep but
were as piercing as an eagle's eyes.

"You understand completely?" asked the Grafina.

"Kalava has understood completely and will not let himself be caught." He looked down at the little Bornean dog, the
color of mud, which had hair so sparse that its skin seemed
naked, and eyes that were more vulpine than canine. "Nor
Gaour," he said, passing his hand over the animal's bare back.

The words of the Book rose up from Louise's memory:
"And they shall fight against you, but they shall not be the
stronger!"

Ten minutes later, the horse Rulf was carrying her back
to the caravan.

VIII. The Men of the Forest

The caravan was finalizing its preparations for departure
when the Grafina reappeared. Three Sumatrans were finishing
burying their companion, killed by the Carabao-Men, whose
funeral rites would have to be celebrated later, according to a
centuries-old formula.

Louise de Gavres considered her servants in a melancholy fashion; they were not warriors. The majority, however,
knew how to use a kris and did not lack bravery; three or four
were capable of following a trail, but none could match Rak,
or even Kalava. In sum, they were mediocre auxiliaries to
fight the redoubtable men of the marsh. It would have required
a solid nucleus to set out immediately in pursuit. It was better
to go to meet Dirk, who was equal to all the tricks of beasts
and men and was, with the Grafina, the best shot in the mountains.

Hendrik had supervised the preparations for departure as
best he could, but his inexperience was too visible to give him
an effective authority. As soon as the young woman reappeared, all the men, still tired and distressed by the cataclysm,

211

recovered their courage, and the caravan got under way. It was necessary to go back upriver as far as Green Rocks Ford. There, the river broadened out to form a lake, randomly sewn with enormous blocks of stone. The carts were able to cross there without overmuch difficulty; the men were no more than waist-deep. On the other shore, a pathway went through the forest—a thousand-year-old path formerly sketched out by buffaloes and wild beasts and finished off by the indigenes.

For two-thirds of the way, the caravan moved through a dark forest still inhabited by barbarous tribes, which were usually inoffensive, but could revert to ferocity in troubled times. Knowing the bravery, cunning and skills of these men, Louise de Gavres considered recruiting some of them for the pursuit. It was not impossible; the Amdavas, avid for firearms, which they had difficulty procuring, consented to enroll in the service of anyone who promised them some. It was necessary not to ask them to do any skilled or domestic work, but they were marvelous guides, incomparable hunters and obstinate combatants.

Toward evening, two horsemen caught up with the caravan: a Dutchman and a native.

"Karel!" exclaimed Hendrik, joyfully. It was his younger brother, like him a son of the blond race, with the same jutting skull and tall stature—but Karel, more suntanned than a Moor, had the bright eyes of Achaeans and riparian Frenchmen. When the two brothers had greeted one another, Karel said to the Grafina: "Father is a day's march away."

"Half a day, since we're going to meet him," said Louise de Gavres.

"Where are our guests?" the young man asked.

The Grafina's expression became very dark; her voice trembled as she replied: "They've been captured by Carabao-Men."

"Carabao-Men!" cried Karel, amazed and consternated. "I thought they no longer existed." And he could not help adding: "Father will be desperate."

212

"No more than me," muttered the young woman. "If they're not rescued, it will be the shame of my life."

Karel remained silent. He turned away so as not to display the reproach that rose up in him. Hendrik, guessing his impression, interjected: "No one in the world could have foreseen or prevented the abduction. Everything was devastated by a tropical storm. The rain put out the fire and the lanterns; the dogs lost their sense of smell, the men couldn't see anything in a darkness as black as the tomb. All creatures have their gifts—the deluge and the darkness didn't prevent the Carabao-Men from seeing and moving around as if in broad daylight!"

"Has their trail been lost?"

"No," replied Louise, untroubled by the young man's disapproval. "We know that they embarked on the Vampire River, which leads to one of their homelands. Rak, the best scout on the island, is following them on the left bank, Kalava on the right." She paused and, for a moment, her beautiful dark eyes stared into the void. Then, gesturing broadly toward the caravan, she continued: "There are a dozen reliable men here, just about. The rest would be a burden. That's not enough to fight—out there, in their marsh, the enemy is numerous—but your father is worth 50 natives, and I intend to recruit the men of the Red Forest.

"I know their language!" said Karel, proudly. "And my father knows it even better. They'll give us warriors!"

Dusk was about to fall; the caravan prepared to halt, and Louise de Gavres, because she was young and accustomed to conquer, and because the young man brought new energy and a soul less somber...

The next day, toward noon, Dirk de Ridder appeared at the head of ten native horsemen. He belonged to the doomed race of giants. Even in Norway, his height and the amplitude of his chest had been unusual. Once, no doubt, the lands of the North had produced men of that sort in profusion; over the centuries, their number had dwindled.

He had the face of the pirates who left their glacial lands in their bridge-less ships to strike fear into whole populations. His glacial blue eyes, calm at rest, shone in battle or in anger. His head, powerful but not heavy, covered with hair the color of a cougar's fur, long but cut short at the temples, with a face with singularly fine cheeks, exhaled a tranquil and almost innocent bonhomie, which gave no hint of the cunning that the Dutchman employed against his enemies. His honesty was legendary and, very polite with his friends, he became rude to the point of brutality when he did not like someone. He was as incapable of breaking his word as he was of committing a crime.

His strength was in proportion to his stature. Such a man could tackle sovereign wild beasts with a hatchet or a kris; he had proved that by slitting the throat of a tiger in a formidable close-quarters combat, and by felling buffaloes seized by the horns. Nature had not inflicted any defects upon him. That colossal body was well-constructed in every part; the muscles did not form the compact knots that one sees in so many athletes; his hands, truly vast if one compared them with ordinary hands, were small for his size.

He arrived at a gallop, on an enormous horse, and when he had greeted the Grafina his eyes scrutinized the caravan in every direction, with the gaze of those who are accustomed to seeing everything at a glance. As he did not see the people he was looking for, his face displayed his astonishment, and he asked, in his bell-like voice: "Where are the guests?"

The Grafina turned her eyes away. He was the only man before whom she sometimes felt timid; it was probably to him that she owed her infallible aim and her subtle knowledge of the forest. "They've been abducted," she replied.

"Abducted!" he cried. His voice rose like a roar. Then stupor held him immobile. He did not understand; he thought he had misheard. "You don't mean, *Jufvrouw*, that they were abducted *en route*?"

"Yes," she replied. "The Carabao-Men…"

Hendrik intervened, as on the previous day, and attempted to describe the unexpected violence of the weather, the absolute obscurity, the impossibility of hearing anything. "Even the dogs were deceived," he concluded. "Including Vos, who scented nothing...while the Carabao-Men..."

"I know!" said Dirk. "It's their gift."

An immense sadness darkened the clear eyes and stiffened the mouth of the Dutchman. "I promised my dying friend to help his heirs in everything," he murmured. "May the Lord grant me the power to keep my promise."

"They were under my guard!" replied the Grafina. "The life of guests must be placed before our own."

The pale eyes and the dark eyes exchanged a long glance. Each of the interlocutors had a boundless esteem for the other.

The Grafina did not rate any man above Dirk for skill, strength and bravery, and he had more confidence in the young woman than the most redoubtable hunters. Together, armed with their rifles, led by their instinct, their intuition and their knowledge of savage nature, they could stand off 20 creoles or 50 natives.

"Let's put our confidence in the sovereign master," said the baas.

Night was about to fall; the formidable clamor of the siamangs filled the solitude. The rapid dusk sparkled and died; the two caravans were combined and the first fires made the stars pale.

The Grafina, Dirk and Karel were up before dawn. The fires were dying down; the carnivores had feasted on living flesh; through the branches, the Southern Cross could be seen descending.

"Karel will go to talk to the Amdavas," said the giant. "In that part of the forest, they know him better than me. I've only made alliance with those in the north as yet...and if you wish, *Jufvrouw*, we'll follow the trail right away. Karel and the Amdavas won't have any difficulty catching up with us."

"So be it!" said Louise de Gavres.

When daybreak came, they had chosen 16 men for an escort, 10 of whom had been borrowed from the planter's caravan. There was no need to think about bringing horses. As they could not embark on the river, they would have had to travel through the virgin forest, and would have signaled the presence of pursuers at too great a distance.

When they reached the Vampire River half of the men followed the right bank and the other half the left. The trail was followed rapidly; after two days marching they caught up with Rak and Kalava. They had found traces of the Carabao-Men on the bank twice, but never further away.

"They were pauses," said Rak, "to sleep for a few hours and let their captives sleep. The current is too strong and inconsistent to permit sleep."

"Shall we construct rafts for pursuit, then?" asked the Grafina.

Dirk acquiesced with a nod of the head. Because the construction had been foreseen the men of the escort had brought some pieces of squared timber to serve as frames for the vessels. Two hours later, they had assembled the materials necessary to make three large rafts. The servants, adapted to various tasks by their adventurous life, worked rapidly.

They waited for Karel and the Amdavas. Rak had marked the trail to guide their progress.

"I hope that Karel hasn't run into any difficulty," the Grafina murmured, during the midday meal.

The planter, endowed with an appetite proportional to his size, ate large slices of venison in silence. Even the most overwhelming emotions did not affect his physical equilibrium any more than his mental equilibrium. One might have thought that sadness and anguish had no purchase on him; on the contrary, he was sensitive, ever-ready to fight for his family and friends and keenly afflicted by their misfortunes—but no agitation threw that powerfully-equipped organism off balance, even momentarily. He was one of those who accept death without blanching or flinching.

Louise de Gavres, although equally self-controlled, was more subject to the hammer-blows of emotion on sleep and the appetite—but she had resources of energy even more profound than the planter's, and, above all, a resistance to privations that left her, after fasting and insomnia, as precise in her movements, as sure in her resolve and as lucid in her mind as in tranquil periods. It was even the case that privations combined with suffering sharpened her faculties, rendering them more intuitive and more perspicacious, without reducing her redoubtable skill at all. Having received her share of the commanding spirit and the gifts necessary to exercise it, she had dominion, for large enterprises, over the colossus, Dirk—who had a unique respect for her, instinctively felt.

"Karel in difficulty?" said the Dutchman. "I think, *Jufvrouw*, that he has succeeded. He knows the Amdavas well." He added, with pride: "He's a man! When he's entirely mastered his rifle, I don't see anyone except for you, *Jufvrouw*, who'll be able to match him on the mountain or in the forest." His granite teeth crushed a morsel of biscuit as hard as brick, and he went on, with a hint of melancholy: "He has the soul of our fathers. How many will have that tomorrow? Who will know the woods and the beasts, *Jufvrouw*, as you know them? Men are degenerating!"

"Aren't those in Europe and America working miracles?"

"I'm afraid that they're only doing so for their own perdition and ours. All these machines serve only to soften bodies and souls. They make life too easy—and they're packed like sardines in the lands from which our ancestors came. When there are too many of them—and that will happen within 200 years—they'll be like ants in an ant-hill. It's a disgusting existence! Oh, I'm glad to have still been able to live the *true* life!" He finished off his meal with a draught of water mixed with lemon juice, and went on: "The Amdavas are brave, *Jufvrouw*, very brave. They're afraid of poison, though, and that of the Carabao-Men is terrible…"

"I've brought the antidote," the Grafina replied.

217

"The antidote? I've heard talk of it, but the recipe has been lost in my family."

"It has been conserved in mine—I don't know why I've always attached such importance to it. Like the poison itself, the antidote is effective in small doses. I've brought enough to protect more than 200 men." Louise pointed to a small box full off brown globules, scarcely larger than pin-heads.

The planter looked at them in astonishment. "They're very small!" he murmured.

"But quite sufficient. It only takes one to save a wounded man. It wouldn't just be unnecessary, but even harmful, to take more. A dose of seven or eight no longer acts as an antidote—they'd even augment the effect of the poison."

"I've heard talk of things like that," said the planter, shaking his head. "There are incomprehensible things everywhere, *Jufvrouw*." He remained pensive for a moment. "Everything is incomprehensible," he murmured, after a pause. "A blade of grass that grows is already a miracle. At any rate, that little box encloses more power than 50 men! Perhaps it will save us, *Jufvrouw*…even more than our rifles. It's necessary to make it known to our servants and the Amdavas, to increase their confidence. Without confidence, our forefathers said, men would be beneath tigers and buffaloes. It's confidence that permitted our ancestors to cross the immense sea to come to a country that's the most beautiful on Earth!"

Louise liked that candor—which was mingled, in the colossus, with the finest cunning as soon as he entered into competition with the forces of nature and savages.

A movement caused them to raise their heads. The dogs became agitated. Then they saw Rak reappear. "The Amdavas are coming, with the son of the giant baas," he said.

Dirk and Louise listened; the progress of a company was just becoming audible, and Karel soon appeared, followed by some 40 men, short in stature and very thin, with olive-colored skins and bright eyes. They stopped at the sight of the camp, attentive but impassive. The majority were armed with old rifles, a few of which were still loaded via the barrel. Five or six possessed more modern weapons; each of them carried a kris, a bow, a well-sharpened hatchet—able to serve them both for combat and for clearing a path through bushy regions—and, finally, a light but solid elongated shield.

"There!" said Karel. "I've promised them a new rifle each and 100 cartridges, after the expedition, plus a payment of 25 guilders. They don't doubt my word—but I think they'd like it to be confirmed."

Dirk marched over to the Amdavas; the chief came to meet him, so small by comparison with the Dutchman that he might have been taken for a dwarf.

"My son's promises will be kept!" said the planter, in a loud voice. "And you shall each have an extra 25 cartridges."

In spite of their traditional impassivity in front of foreigners, the majority of the Amdavas manifested a slight excitement; nothing in the world, after improved rifles, delighted them as much as ammunition.

"The Amdavas know that the family of the giant baas never lies!" replied the chief. "The Amdavas also do not speak two ways. They will fight as their fathers have fought since the trees first grew in this land..."

IX. The Marshland

After six days of navigation, the Carabao-Men disembarked. Since the previous day, the flow of the stream had relented; as broad as a river, it now ran without haste between flat and sinister banks strewn with marshes. There were poplars as tall as cathedral spires; monstrous willows reminiscent of enormous batrachians; innumerable hosts of mushrooms, often of colossal size; mangroves nourished by the mud; black reeds stained with red, like huge rusty blades, from which the breeze drew a strange susurrus; wild bamboos, banyans, teaks and an abundant population of lianas, orchids and epiphytes.

On the waters there were nenuphar lilies with leaves as big as canoes, on which mating frogs assembled in myriads in the evenings. The mire of the marsh nourished lizards almost as immense as prehistoric saurians, foul and voracious fish, formless larval creatures as soft as oysters but deprived of shells, and pythons as long as tree branches.

When the Carabao-Men had sheltered the raft among the mangroves, Hourv stood up before the ancestral land and extended his arms, proclaiming in a resounding voice: "Marshes, from which our forefathers emerged when the first suns rose in the blue water, we bring the salutary captive to the race of chiefs and the captive that will give his heart and his blood. Your strength, marshes, will be renewed in our breasts!"

Having said that, he turned his heavy muzzle toward Frédéric and Corisande, who had been untied, and spoke to them gently. "Your descendants, daughter of Other Men, shall be mingled for generations with the descendants of chiefs, children of the earth and the Waters. Those to whom you shall give birth will be similar to the Sons of the Marsh, but you will live on in them when all the men of your race have long disappeared. Only the race of Carabao-Men will survive until the Last Suns…

"You, foreigner, as white as the flowers of the water-lily, shall die at the Moon of Jade; your heart shall enter into the body of chiefs, your blood shall be drunk by the warriors, and your limbs will be shared among 20 warriors. Thus your flesh will live again in the flesh of Invincibles."

He fell silent. His companions intoned a slow and dismal chant, which their forefathers had chanted at the dawn of centuries, which resembled the croaking of giant frogs. Then the chief gave the signal to depart.

Corisande and Frédéric were no longer hobbled, and were permitted to walk side by side.

"They're no longer afraid of anything," said the young man. "Oh, Corisande, I bitterly regret having brought you to this odious land. I should have come alone."

"Who can tell, my poor Frédéric? Isn't every moment of life a threat?"

"Yes," he replied, somberly. "We're surrounded by traps from the moment of our birth—but at least you would have avoided this degrading peril. Oh, how ashamed I am of my weakness!"

"You're not weak," she said, tenderly. "Haven't you saved me once already, heroically? Even if you had been a giant, what could you have done during that storm? Even the dogs lost their sense of smell; the men were reduced to impotence. Don't blame yourself, my dear brother. You have nothing for which to reproach yourself. The catastrophe was inevitable."

Corisande's little hand sought the young man's hand. A tragic gentleness was within them, the certainty of an affection born in the limbo of infancy, against which nothing could prevail. These poor creatures had always shared their vicissitudes and hopes; they would not have been boasting in affirming that each of them would have sacrificed their own life to save that of the other.

"You see," she continued, "it's not necessary to despair yet. *She* will find us. I didn't like her, Frédéric; I felt a rancor against her that seemed to have been born *before me*, but when I saw her pass by at the river, I understood all that she will do for us."

"I too felt an animosity toward her, but only an animosity. Yes, she will do anything, nothing can intimidate her. She's indomitable, Corisande—and very resourceful."

He turned his gaze toward the men leading them. The chief was marching at the head, a stout human being with the muscles of a bull and a bestial head—but one might have thought that returning to his marshy fatherland gave him a kind of serenity. The others also seemed placid.

"Perhaps these people are not as cruel as they say?" she murmured.

But he, remembering the war, thought of the atrocious actions carried out by men accustomed to the peaceful life of

221

cities. He knew, too, that savages and barbarians kill without ferocity, with the simplicity of a carnivore killing its prey, and that even tortures, when they are rites, require no malevolent emotion.

Toward evening, they perceived a strange multitude of stone blocks reminiscent of the ruins of a fantastic city. They were not ruins, but the intact work of the Ancestors. Some of the blocks resembled columns, some confused statues of men or animals; each of them was hollowed out at the base and enclosed a cavernous dwelling. Around that sort of cyclopean city were marshes traversed by stone causeways, which were also the work of men of ancient times, maintained by their descendants.

As the expedition arrived, a crowd of men, women and children appeared, which soon formed a coherent mass of 500 or 600 individuals. At first, they uttered clamors similar to the bellowing of buffaloes and the howling of wolves; then a chant went up, which must have been as old as the primitive city.

It's a sort of brutal civilization, Frédéric thought, *perhaps comparable to the civilization of the Stone Age.*

The chant ended. A moment later, the captives were surrounded by the crowd. They were stared at without hostility, and with evident joy.

We're their Prey! the young man said to himself—and as Corisande repeated "Perhaps they're not so very cruel!" he shuddered, for he guessed that the absence of hostility would not prevent a fatal outcome for him, and perhaps worse for Corisande.

In response to a signal from an old man, whose head seemed to be encrusted with lichen and whose face was pitted like a frost-split stone, the crowd parted. Then, four men silently surrounded Frédéric and separated him from Corisande.

An atrocious presentiment and an irresistible instinct made him raise his fists, but his arms were immobilized by four enormous hands, and he saw three women, even more hideous than the males, lead the young woman away. She turned to her brother, trying to smile at him; a terrible emotion tightened his muscles.

The crowd remained calm; even the men restraining Frédéric did not manifest any ill-humor.

"Corisande—my dear sister!" he cried, with a sob.

"Nothing is lost yet, Frédéric," she said. Her voice trailed off; she looked at him dolorously, with an expression in which affection overcame fear. Soon, she was out of sight.

Meanwhile, the four men dragged Frédéric away. They led him over a granite causeway across a marsh. The ground on the other side was black; a strange forest of stones, also black—enormous columns of basalt—extended as far as the eye could see. Frédéric's guardians and the crowd following them stopped, while the old man, his arid head lowered toward the ground, resumed the ancestral chant, which the crowd hummed in subdued voices.

They all went into the basalt forest. The further they went the more sinister it seemed; one might have thought that they were in an Archean world, in which no plant had yet assaulted the mineral world.

Finally, a kind of clearing appeared, surrounded by immense rocks; in the center, there was a funereal block, rectangular in form, about six meters high. Next to that stone, which the crowd surrounded in silence, nine short, thin Sumatrans appeared, as if they had sprung from the ground, led by colossal guardians. A rapid dusk was dying away in the western forges when the old man approached the captives and, raising both hands, spoke to them in a slow, soft voice.

"The Men of the Marshes are the strongest of men. One day, they will chase all the others from the mountains to the plain, and from the plain to the sea. How will your people be able to resist? Your warriors have the bodies of dogs, ours have the strength of buffaloes. Even those who have come from distant isles, the men with the silver faces, will be exterminated."

Some distance away, three large fires were lit. An immense bellowing rose up. The old man made a sign, and one of the captives was hoisted up on to the rectangular block. He was lain down upon it after his clothing had been removed. The chant rose up again and, while an enormous Sun disappeared in the west, a red Moon rose above the granite forest.

The old man declaimed: "Thou, who rose from the Marsh before the birth of the Sun and who gave birth to the nurturing planets, thou who watched over our ancestors and will illuminate their victory, see the blood of the vanquished run over the stone where enemies without number perish."

Two men held the Sumatran down on the basalt; a third came forward, armed with a jade knife, plunged it into the victim's entrails and split the skin all the way to the diaphragm.

The howls of the Carabao-Men drowned out the screams of the victim, and the sacrificer, plunging the blade into the breast, brought out the heart, which he held out toward the Occident.[30]

Frédéric saw himself already extended on the stone, his blood shed as the blood of innumerable humans, offered by their peers to the hidden forces of the world, had been shed before. Because the war had accustomed him to murder, he maintained his self-control, and thought about Corisande again. He knew only too well what fate was in store for her; his anguish at being condemned to death was mingled with a bitter and impotent revulsion.

Meanwhile, the other victims were immolated and their hearts, still beating, extended toward the Star. After the torment of the last one, there was a frenetic clamor, and the Carabao-Men and Women precipitated themselves toward the Black Stone from every direction.

---

[30] The puzzling implication that the Moon rises in the west is repeated, more explicitly, at a later point in the text. In other works by Rosny, as in reality, the Moon rises in the east, and the repetition makes it unlikely that the error was due to a momentary lapse of concentration; the significance of the suggestion remains unclear.

Four men butchered the cadavers there; the chiefs presided over a kind of distribution.

Isn't it my turn, then? Frédéric asked himself, astonished.

No one was paying any attention to him any longer, except for his guardians, each of whom went, one at a time, to claim the morsel of blood flesh that was due to him.

Soon, the clearing was deserted; the men and women were assembled around the fires where they were roasting the meat.

All right! I'm not to die yet! the young man said to himself.

In the distance, the feast commenced. One might have taken it for a peaceful tribal meal on the evening after a hunt, when the warriors have brought back deer, tapirs or siamangs. There was joy, however—a grave and mystical joy—because the prey had been immolated on the Black Stone.

If I'm not to perish, Frédéric asked himself, *why have I been brought here?*

He had not forgotten Corisande. He remembered what the Grafina had said; he felt a great surge of distress and terror...

The meal was coming to an end. The Moon was paler, smaller and brighter above the basaltic forest. At a signal from the old man, the diners rose to their feet; once again, the chant reverberated in the night. Then there was a great silence. In the distance, toward the marsh, lights were moving, and soon six women were seen, escorting Corisande. Her loose hair was floating magnificently over a wolf-skin with which the captive's shoulders had been covered. As pale as a corpse, she was walking courageously, surrounded by her hideous guardians.

Frédéric's heart skipped a beat; he thought he was about to die of horror and pity.

Is it possible that those things happen among human beings? Remembering soldiers disemboweled, asphyxiated and burned alive, however, skulls smashed and heads blown off by shells, he lowered his head with a sob.

The multitude had returned to surround the Black Stone. It left a wide corridor for the six women who were bringing Corisande. The men were looking avidly at that abundant hair, which sparkled in the moonlight, and the face as white as the mountain snow.

Behind the six women marched the leader of the band that had captured the young couple.

Frédéric's guardians had come back. At a sign from the Ancestor, they led the captive to within a few paces of Corisande; he believed that he was finally about to be immolated.

She had turned toward him; they looked at one another with a terrible tenderness.

"Adieu, my brother...my brother, whom I have always loved most of all."

"Corisande! Oh, beloved sister!"

Three women took hold of the young woman and transported her to the black altar, where they laid her down after having removed the wolf-skin. Resigned, she prayed. The avid crowd gazed at her fine shoulders and brilliant torso.

The Ancestor brandished his jade knife, then, leaning over, made an incision in the left breast. A red trickle ran down, which one of the women collected in a nacreous shell. Another woman was already dressing the wound.

Then the old man cried: "May the blood of the woman with the face of a flower run in the veins of Hourv, the Red Eagle. And may that be done to her which is done to all the women consecrated to the Sons of the Marsh."

He handed the shell into which the blood had run to Hourv. The man drank the living fluid and, raising his arms toward the Stars, uttered three resounding cries.

The female guardians took hold of Corisande again and, having dressed her in the wolf-skin again, gave her back to Hourv. The man lifted her up in his arms and carried her away.

She had fainted.

Frédéric leapt up frantically, causing one of his guardians to stagger and another to fall down, but ten formidable hands restrained him.

Hourv, before whom the crowd parted, emerged from the granite forest and reached the other shore of the marsh. When he arrived at his cavern, he stopped to gaze at the unconscious young woman. The Moon enveloped her with a silvery light; her scintillating hair ran over the wolf-skin; the harmonious body, with its delicate bones and finely-sculpted face, symbolized the long evolution of races infatuated with beauty. The Red Eagle, with his thick skull and bovine muzzle, clad in thick fur, seemed to be the first sketch of man in times immemorial.

With a joyful grunt, he went into the cavern and deposited Corisande on a buffalo-skin.

X. The Escape

Frédéric, immobile and extended on the bare earth, with his limbs tied up, could not stop seeing Corisande on the Black Stone, the Ancestor declaiming incomprehensible words and the bestial man carrying the young woman away.

There was no uncertainty as to the meaning of the adventure! The pure daughter of Gaul had been delivered to the brute; the vile deed had been consummated.[31] At the thought of that, his heart seemed to burst. Then a dolorous torpor ex-

---

[31] Frédéric's inference is understandable, but seemingly inconsistent with Hourv's earlier assertion that Corisande would only belong to him "when the Moon of Jade follows the Moon of Reeds," a time apparently more than four weeks away. The text subsequently seems to assume, however, that Frédéric is right, perhaps because Rosny had forgotten or repented of making provision for a useful delay.

tinguished his palpitations. He knew full well that Corisande would think about death, but he did not want her to die, and he was sure that she would not kill herself while she believed that he was still alive.

While he got a grip on his thoughts, mournfully, one of his guardians lifted him up on to his shoulder. The crowd of Carabao-Men had already gone across the marsh. Frédéric found himself back in the cavernous city, and was thrown into a fissure, three feet wide and so low-ceilinged that he was not able to stand upright there. This burrow was closed by a wattle-and-daub barrier.

The moonlight filleted in through the seal; Frédéric could see the inhabitants of the city circulating in all directions before disappearing into the bosom of the rocks.

He tried to make his captive presence known, shouting "Corisande!" loudly.

A plaintive voice replied, seemingly from not far away. The door opened; he understood that he was about to be gagged, and hastily added: "It's necessary to stay alive!"

A violent hand closed over his mouth.

Silence had fallen among the men; apart from a sentry, crouching in front of the cavern where the prisoner was lying, there was no other creature to be seen. In the distance, frogs were croaking, and an occasional hoarse cry or a muffled howl announced the distant presence of a carnivore.

For the first hour, Frédéric remained motionless. Bound, gagged and guarded by a man with the hearing of a wolf, it seemed that any escape was impossible. It was, however, about escape that he was thinking.

He thought about it more intently when, on moving his arms, he observed that his bonds were not holding his limbs very tightly. Then, with very slow movements—silent by virtue of that fact—he tried to free one of his hands. By groping around, he eventually discovered a sharp projection, against which he gently rubbed the cord around his right arm.

The sentry became drowsy, still crouched down with his chin on his knees and his enormous face turned toward the cavern. Frédéric knew that the other had senses as subtle as those of wild beasts and that he would come to his feet at the slightest suspect noise. He had already raised his head two or three times, his phosphorescent eyes fixed on the plug—but it was natural that the captive would turn over and change position periodically, and the barrier could not be removed without colliding with the sentry.

The erosion of the cord took a long time, as much because of the slow movements that Frédéric made as because of the frequent interruption of his work. In the end, the arm was liberated and it became possible to liberate his whole body.

There was, however, plenty of time. Finally able to move freely, Frédéric examined the crude door with his hands. The seal was ensured by a branch whose thin ends were embedded, not very deeply, in cavities in the rock. The branch, whose thickness was mediocre—a stout stick—was flexible; an abrupt and energetic pressure, by bending it considerably, would almost certainly disengage it—but every action would have to be effective; if Frédéric did not get out immediately, the escape would be nipped in the bud.

As he was calculating his moves, the sentry stood up and stood there listening, his ears directed toward the cavern. Then he stretched himself, with a sort of groan, and took a few steps to get the numbness out of his limbs. His jade hatchet was still lying on the ground, where it had formerly been within arm's reach. He marched back and forth, in complete security.

Frédéric took advantage of the moment when the sentry was ten meters from the cavern to launch himself forwards.

The branch bent under the impact without becoming disengaged from the rock, and Frédéric was already thinking that his attempt would be abortive when one of the ends gave way and the barrier yielded.

The sentry bounded forward. Like the majority of Carabao-Men, he was compact and sturdy, with powerful muscles. He arrived just as the prisoner stood up outside the cavern. In

229

a hand-to-hand struggle, his grip would be irresistible, but Frédéric, who knew that very well, immediately threw a punch that struck him full in the face. Although slightly stunned, the man extended his hands to seize the escaper. A second punch on the chin, and another in the solar plexus, caused him to stagger. He uttered a stifled shout to warn the tribe...

Frédéric was already brandishing the axe that he had seized in passing, fleeing with the speed of a champion athlete.

The guard's cry had, however, woken up the tribe.

Warriors were springing from the rocks like ants surging out of an ant-hill. With large strides, the young man hurled himself in the direction taken by Hourv.

He had nothing to fear from those who were following him. His agility was far superior to the fastest of them—but a dozen men were surging forth in front of him and might well be equal to the task of stopping him. If one of them got a grip on him, even if only for a second or two, the others would succeed in surrounding him; it would be sufficient for one of them to get his long arms around him, more tenacious than the tentacles of an octopus.

Frédéric swerved in order to pass between two warriors who were far enough apart. They anticipated the maneuver, and moved toward one another as fast as they could, but he arrived with lightning speed, when they were no more than a meter apart. His speed was sufficient to brush past the hands that reached out to grab him, but which did not have time to close.

The way was clear.

A furious horde was, in fact, in pursuit of the fugitive— but that horde was losing ground continuously. Assegais whistled through the air, one of which brushed Frédéric's neck; soon they could no longer reach him, and he felt the intoxication of escape, the energy of a man concentrated by a primitive instinct, which thrusts all other emotions into the darkness of the self. It seemed that, in liberating himself, he was conquering the world of possibility, hope increasing as the clamor of the Men of the Marsh sounded ever more distantly.

The black locale, the stagnant waters, the marsh-plants, the fugitive beasts and the croaking of colossal frogs—the entire world devoid of men—affirmed his ephemeral victory...and then, all seemed lost.

On the isthmus that separated two large marshes, a man had just surged forth, as tall and as thickset as Hourv, the Red Eagle.

He was occupying the narrow part of the isthmus: a tongue of land four meters wide at the most. Agile as Frédéric was, it would undoubtedly be impossible to avoid combat. With his axe in one hand and an assegai in the other, the man had taken up a position equidistant from the two marshes. The fugitive slowed down, then stopped and considered his adversary. Turning round, he observed that the pursuers were continuing their chase.

He feared the assegai more than the axe; its point was almost certainly poisoned.

Warily, he got under way again.

When he came within range, the giant lifted his arm and launched the javelin with a muffled cry. Frédéric could see the flight of the weapon perfectly well. During the fraction of a second that it took to cross the distance that separated the antagonists, he judged its trajectory instinctively—thought would have been too slow—and veered sideways with sufficient precision for the assegai, which would have struck him full in the chest, to pass by a few centimeters from his shoulder.

The adversaries found themselves face to face; their axes whirled. The giant's would have cleaved Frédéric's skull, but a parry turned it aside, and the Carabao-Man staggered, his shoulder struck.

The way was free again.

Narrow at first, it gradually got wider; soon, a capacious strip of land on which he could move in any direction appeared in the silvery moonlight; there, his superior speed protected the fugitive against immediate pursuit. To surround it would have required hundreds of men disposed in every direction.

"Free!" he murmured, in the intoxication of victory that subjugates time and space.

The image of Corisande passed through his mind. The darkness became heavy again, the plain strangely menacing, the vegetation sly and venomous. To free her, he would have to return to the midst of the very people he had just fled, to prepare a double escape a hundred times more difficult than the one in which he had just succeeded.

Was that even possible? Perhaps, if Corisande had been as agile as himself, but, although fond of sport, she would be overtaken by her pursuers. Without pausing in his progress, he searched feverishly for ruses. He multiplied projects that all revealed themselves to be illusory, for he could not count on any surprise. With their lupine senses and their night-vision, the Carabao-Men would perceive any approach from a distance.

He had not forgotten the Grafina, sure that she would be seeking to free those who had been her guests, and whom she had led into the wilderness. Could she pick up the trail, though, or deduce what the Men of the Marsh intended?

"I can't do anything without help! Anything at all!" he murmured.

He would have died rather than abandon Corisande, however.

He continued his course for a long time, slowing down at intervals. In the middle of the night he estimated that he had gained several kilometers, assuming that the pursuit had not been abandoned.

Stopping on the bank of a small shallow stream to recover his breath, he realized that nature was offering him the elements of a stratagem used by beasts as well as men. Instead of continuing his route on firm ground, he took off his boots and walked on the stream-bed, only stopping when the water became too deep.

They'll lose a lot of time picking up my trail again, he thought, *as he went through a little wood, and even when they find it, they'll have been fatally delayed by their search.*

Toward morning he reached the larger river, where he found the raft that Hourv had not thought it necessary to destroy. Although the current was much slower here than it was further upriver, it was almost impossible for a single man to go upstream using that heavy and somewhat formless vessel. Nevertheless, Frédéric resolved to go over to the other bank, which, once again, would render the pursuit more difficult.

"It's very little," he murmured, "but at the end of the day…"

When he had accomplished the crossing, with considerable difficulty, it was almost daybreak. The Southern Cross and Alpha Centauri suddenly began to fade. The morning twilight was barely sketched before a fiery dawn was completed in a matter of seconds, and the grace of the Sun expanded over the waters and trees. The diurnal animals ceased to dread the formidable darkness. The hour, marvelously young, seemed to be the beginning of the world. Nothing announced as yet the terrible heat that the furnace was going to pour out over the forests, plains and expanses of water.

Meanwhile, the idea of another elementary ruse had occurred to Frédéric. Instead of mooring the raft in the reeds, he abandoned it to the current. It drew away slowly, rotated in an eddy, and ended up running aground more than a kilometer from its point of departure, in a creek where it was trapped.

That circumstance might perhaps slow down the pursuit more than the young man imagined, for the river, broadening out in the vicinity of the creek, formed a shallow fork. The fugitive would have been able to employ the same stratagem there as in the little stream; the Carabao-Men would probably be almost certain that he had not neglected it.

Upriver, after several hours' march, the forest became very dense on both banks; the trees had become very abundant, the marsh-plants were scaling the bank, rich with an ever-renewed energy and capable of populating a world.

Frédéric went forward in a sepulchral half-light, overwhelmed by a humid heat, flagellated by thorns, gripped by lianas, sinking into spongy ground and harassed by implacable insects. The homicidal fecundity that surrounded him seemed avid to devour him. A rain of dew streamed over his clothes; the trees intermingled their branches like vast wrestlers; the giant ferns and ferocious grasses hindered his progress as much as the lianas and the pools of water.

In that frightful forest he felt weaker than a child; he would be unable to discern the Grafina and her men if, as was almost certain, she had taken the watery route—nor would she perceive him.

My efforts are becoming futile, perhaps deleterious, he thought, bitterly. *Wouldn't it be better to go back?*

Instinctively, he sought some ruse by which he might hide his tracks; in that game, he was as inferior to the Carabao-Men as a blind man pursued by the sighted. Besides, whether he went forwards or backwards, the peril was equal—but in the open, at least he would have the resource of his agility, while, hindered by vegetation, he would be inferior to men accustomed to the forest. Furthermore, the large wild beasts might approach him in the undergrowth without his perceiving their presence.

He resigned himself to retracing his steps. The heat, suffocating under the trees, murderous in uncovered places, aggravated a nervous depression in Frédéric due to the combination of insomnia and successive emotions.

Soon, the weariness became irresistible. The fugitive's head was boiling; his eyes were covered by mist; he began to reel in semi-unconsciousness. Mechanically, he was seeking a refuge in the direction of the river when a rocky mass appeared through the foliage. Moved by a hypnotic impulse, he concentrated his last forces in order to reach it.

It was on the bank, in the midst of low vegetation; facing the flow, it comprised a kind of cavern no more than five feet

234

wide and scarcely any higher. Frédéric slid inside and, because of the relatively cool temperature, was slightly reanimated. He made an effort to stay awake, but the exhaustion was too great; he slipped into unconsciousness.

When he woke up, the Sun had covered two-thirds of its march; the shadows of the trees on the plain and the river were growing longer; a weak breeze tempered the heat.

Natural pasturelands extended on both banks: grass that was often dry, punctuated by clumps of trees. A few meters from the river there were two clumps of banyans, each sprung from a single tree that had extended itself gradually, forming veritable chambers of verdure, in which primitive people might be able to live.

The projects succeeding one another in Frédéric's brain were rendered impractical by the necessity of staying close to the bank. He would have been able to go downstream, but that would render the Grafina's task more difficult, and he had decided against going upstream. It was therefore necessary to stay where he was, while risking a few brief excursions to procure food. His hunger was already becoming unbearable.

Screeches caused him to turn his head. A hairy mass precipitated itself into the vault; he saw a beast as large as a cougar, breathless and palpitating: a siamang. Outside, another creature was on the prowl, dark in color and no larger than a wolf: a black panther.

Instinctively, Frédéric picked up his axe.

For half a minute, the man and the cat looked at one another; then Frédéric shouted loudly, brandishing his weapon. The panther became invisible, but it remained in the vicinity, hidden among the lianas and the reeds.

That presence complicated his situation dangerously. In stories of adventure that he had come across by chance, Frédéric had read that black panthers are more robust and more aggressive than others. The jade axe did not seem a very effective weapon with which to fight an agile foe endowed with great vitality. Any wounds it sustained would increase its stubbornness.

There was, however, a simple means of getting rid of the predator; it would be sufficient to give it the siamang. At that idea, Frédéric experienced the same repugnance as if he were meditating a treason—and, in spite of his distress, he looked at the refugee with a quasi-fraternal pity.

The young gibbon was also showing all the signs of a sharp agitation: dilated eyes, shivers, palpitations, rapid and raucous breath. A nervous, emotional animal, it turned so human a face toward Frédéric that the man's scruples were exacerbated.

An indeterminable time went by. The river pursued the course that it had followed for millennia, always so similar to itself and yet so different, always composed of new waters.

It's necessary to make a decision! Frédéric told himself.

Leaning out of the cave, he examined the reeds and the bushes. In the half-light, two phosphorescent gleams denounced the presence of the cat. It would remain there, with the patience of its race, for hours on end. Only the proximity of another prey would cause it to neglect the siamang.

"Shall I sacrifice you, poor creature?" murmured the young man, turning toward the monkey.

The two of them stared at one another. The animal released a faint plaintive cry; Frédéric had the impression that its confidence had grown, that it was only asking to familiarize itself to him. What should he do, though? The situation was getting worse by the minute. On the one hand, the panther; on the other, the Carabao-Men, who would no longer be far away.

He was making a tour of his refuge when he perceived a fissure at the rear, partly masked by a rockslide. Moved by instinct, he pushed a few stones aside; the fissure grew. It seemed that it would permit the passage of a man, provided that he crawled on one side, not on his belly.

Where will that take me? he asked himself. *Perhaps there's another way out? With their bulging torsos, the Carabao-Men couldn't get through.*

He glimpsed circumstances that might work in his favor and he tried to advance into the narrow corridor, crawling on his side with his arms outstretched. He succeeded without overmuch difficulty and attained a spacious cavern, lit by a feeble glow coming from a lateral corridor. On following that corridor, he did not take long to arrive at an exit overlooking the river, which was similarly very narrow but sufficiently high for Frédéric to get through it in an upright position, moving sideways.

A rather deep creek was extended there; further away, there was a lush green islet, where two crocodiles were asleep.

A breath made him turn round; the young siamang had followed the man almost as if it were a dog.

"Now you're safe from the panther!" Frédéric murmured. "You can flee…"

The anthropoid leaned out over the river, uttered a faint cry, and hurled itself backwards. Frédéric, having advanced his body obliquely, recoiled in his turn. On the two shores of the creek, Carabao-Men had just appeared.

XI. Outside the Cavern

"The forest ends here," Dirk announced. "We're arriving in marshy ground, perhaps the Black Country in which those vermin live."

Louise de Gavres nodded her head as a sign of assent. The evening was drawing near. The yellow Sun lit up the dismal locations, patches of grass and boggy ground, while the river broadened out again and flowed with increasing nonchalance between low banks punctuated by rocks. Two rafts and four long bark canoes were transporting the expedition: Dirk, his son, the Grafina, 20 servants and 50 Amdavas, together with seven dogs with infallible senses.

It was the latter who gave the first signs of disquiet, but they calmed down when the flotilla had veered to the left to move around an islet haunted by crocodiles.

Vos, however, the Grafina's favorite—a large dog with topaz eyes—remained attentive for longer than the others.

"There's some danger on the right bank!" the Grafina affirmed.

That was Dirk's opinion too. He scrutinized the reeds, bushes, rocks and tall grass carefully. There was no evidence of a human presence, nor that of a tiger. "We have to disembark," the giant replied, "but this isn't a good place to do it."

Karel, a taciturn listener, shouted an order to the foremost canoe. The Amdavas chief who was commanding it accelerated its pace, and the canoe did not take long to gain a lead on the convoy. It soon reappeared.

"A raft, over there," the chief announced.

"On the right bank?"

"No, the left."

That bank, flatter than the other, seemed to be easily explorable. The raft appeared in a little haven where, apart from a few reeds, the view was uninterrupted.

"Vos?" murmured Louise de Gavres, stroking the dog's head. Vos raised his intelligent head, sniffed the air and pricked up his ears, but showed no more anxiety than the other dogs.

"We can disembark," the Grafina said.

The disembarkation was, however, undertaken prudently. Scouts and dogs explored the surroundings within a radius of 1000 meters, without discovering any indication of a human presence. All the Amdavas were trackers almost as perfect as Rak. The dogs, nevertheless, detected a trail to the north; the traces ended at the river, upstream of the creek.

"A company of men came from the marsh at sunset," Rak reported. "The emanation is no longer very fresh. In a short time even Vos won't be able to discern it."

"How do you know that the emanation isn't fresh?" Hendrik asked.

238

Dirk and Karel started laughing. "Because the dogs are hesitant," said the giant. "Rak and most of the Amdavas understand dogs."

"Especially Vos," said the tracker.

"Are the traces extended along the bank?" the Grafina asked.

"Not far, Mistress. Less than 100 paces."

"I was right in thinking that the danger was on the right bank," said Louise. "If we hadn't come around the islet to the left we'd doubtless have found that out."

"Perhaps it's better this way," said Karel.

The giant remained pensive. "Were they really coming from the west?" he asked.

"From the west, baas...at least in the latter part of their journey."

"It can't have any connection with our search."

Silently, Rak held out a crumpled and dirty strip of paper, and the Grafina uttered a slight exclamation. "Our guests have been on this bank!" she affirmed.

"But have they been taken westwards?" de Ridder demanded.

"I found the paper 600 paces from the bank. No other trace. The dogs haven't said anything. The emanations no longer exist. The people traveling toward the marshes came before nightfall."

"In that case, the return of the Carabao-Men cannot have any objective that concerns us," said Louise de Gavres, "unless the captives—or one of them—has escaped."

"Anything is possible, *Jufvrouw*," muttered the giant. "We need to bear that in mind...and also to find out what's happening on the other bank, if anything's happening at all. Karel, send a few Amdavas..."

"I'll go with them," Karel declared.

"With Rak..."

Half a dozen Amdavas, with Karel, Rak and the dog Vos, embarked for the other bank. Having arrived there, they fanned out, each one taking responsibility for exploring an area. They advanced slowly, all their senses on the alert, accustomed since infancy to profit from the smallest bush, tall grass or a slight unevenness in the ground to remain invisible.

Rak and Vos, who were closest to the bank, did not show themselves once—but, by the same token, sight would not have sufficed to reveal enemies hidden among the reeds, the lianas or the bushes. At short range, Vos's sense of smell was worth more than the keenest eyesight. He did not take long to show signs of agitation. Rak stopped and waited. Head extended, the dog sniffed avidly. The tracker put his own head to the ground and murmured—as Louise de Gavres might have done: "Tiger?"

The dog continued sniffing, as if he had not heard anything. Rak knew that the word was familiar to him and that he would have straightened up in response if he had perceived the presence of the big cat. There was no more to do than pronounce the other redoubtable word: "Man?"

Vos turned his head and looked at the scout, twitching his ears. There was no doubt: men were nearby—and who could they be but Carabao-Men?

Should he advance further, or should he wait?

Rak waited, but not for long. Nothing abnormal revealed itself to his sight or his hearing, but, because he had been warned, he discerned—very weakly—the strange marshy and musky odor of the enemy.

There was no doubt. They were there—and it became imprudent to linger.

Rak retreated slowly, at first, then more rapidly. It was easy to see in Vos's attitude that the Carabao-Men were not pursuing them—which probably implied a stratagem, for, having certainly been informed of the presence of the expedition since the flotilla had passed close to the islet, they must be following the advance of the Amdavas and Karel every step of the way, if not Rak's.

In any case, it became a matter of urgency to signal the enemy presence. Although it was doubtless a vain precaution,

Rak imitated the croaking of a giant frog with a perfection that would have deceived the animals themselves.

At that moment, Karel had come within a few javelin-throws of the rock "inside" which Frédéric was hiding. He stopped. His dog, although endowed with a keen nose, was nevertheless inferior to Vos; it did not sense any presence, from which the young Dutchman concluded that there was no human being within a 30 to 40 meter perimeter. He beat a retreat, however, sure that Rak and Vos were not mistaken.

Suddenly, the enemy, although still invisible, clearly revealed their presence 300 meters from the bank. An Amdava stood up abruptly there, and started running. A slender assegai had just struck his shoulder. It was evidently barbed; Karel observed that the warrior had some difficulty removing it—but the Carabao-Men remained invisible.

The wounded man fled, taking large strides, toward the creek, where an Amdava was guarding the canoe that had made the crossing. It was necessary to hurry. Rak, fearing an enemy advance to the river bank, where the vegetation would render them invisible, shouted an alarm-call. Karel, in his turn, urged the Amdavas to retreat rapidly.

They were seen emerging from thickets and tall grass and running over the bare ground, where they could not be taken by surprise. When they all arrived at the canoe they found the wounded man and Rak, who was already gripping the oars. "Quickly! Quickly!" cried the scout. "They're nearby."

Two assegais sailed over the reeds. One of them hurtled at Karel, who ducked with the rapidity of a leopard and caught the weapon in flight. The other javelin sank into the river. The canoe sped across the river and was not long delayed in reaching the creek.

On the bank, the colossal figure of Dirk was standing beside the lithe silhouette of the Grafina.

First, the planter examined the Amdava's wound. It was quite deep, but narrow, not very dangerous in itself.

"The assegai was poisoned, I suppose?" he murmured. "If the antidote isn't reliable, he's probably a dead man."

"It's reliable," affirmed the Grafina. "The man won't die."

The giant studied the river meditatively. Then he said to Rak and the Amdavas: "None of you actually saw them?"

No, no one had seen them.

"They're skillful hunters," he continued. "Here, fortunately, they can't take us by surprise. I assume that their presence is significant. It's not impossible that they've been warned of our approach in advance...and yet, I have a suspicion that it's something else."

"I'm almost certain that we weren't expected. This is a chance encounter. They were camped level with the islet when we appeared—the dogs warned us!"

"Yes, the dogs warned us and Rak understood their language. If that was the case, they weren't there waiting for us." Dirk studied the young woman's face and concluded: "I see that you have an idea, *Jufvrouw*."

"Yes, but it's only an intuition. I think they're here for the captives."

"Who have escaped? That's very improbable...especially both of them."

"It's almost impossible even for one of them. However, I'm wondering whether Frédéric de Rouveyres might have taken advantage of a favorable opportunity. He knocked one of those men down with a punch in my house, and as he's agile—much more agile than them—if he got free, he would have been able to escape their pursuit, temporarily."

"Yes, that's worth checking out. There wouldn't be any great peril in going upriver as far as the islet and going around it. The two arms of the river are wide enough for the rowers to stay out of range of assegais—and I presume that these savages aren't prepared to attack on the water. There are risks, though..."

"It's necessary to run them!" Karel interjected. "We can reduce them by first passing between the island and the right bank. If they put one or two canoes in the water we'll probably have time either to retrace our course or, if we're too far forward, to come around the islet. You've seen our Amdavas at work; they're skilled canoeists. I'd be astonished if the Carabao-Men are as skillful and as swift."

"Tradition shows them to us sailing on rafts or equally heavy boats."

"Good—let's go!" said the young man. "We'll take the best canoe."

"You're going to risk yourself, then?" said the Grafina.

Silently, Dirk enveloped his son with a grave and melancholy gaze. His soul was affectionate, but stoical. Risk was a religion to him.

The best of the canoes, carrying six Amdavas, Karel, Rak and the dog Vos, was not long delayed in moving upriver again.

They got within a few cables of the isle without any incident. Everything was profoundly, almost solemnly, tranquil. The orange-colored Sun was approaching the horizon, growing incessantly. Innumerable nocturnal insects were forming clouds on both banks and on the face of the waters.

In an hour, the Sun will have set, Karel thought, as he scrutinized the banks, which revealed no presence except for an occasional furtive beast that had come to drink, and which fled into the reeds and grass. Several times, the dog Vos growled dully.

"They must be more numerous near that rock," said Rak, pointing at a granite mass.

Karel nodded his head in acquiescence. He slowed the progress of the vessel, then gave the order to move a little closer to the right bank. "The Carabao-Men don't use bows and arrows?" he said.

"No," said Rak. "The ancestors have always said so...and we haven't seen any *en route*."

The granite mass revealed a fissure to their piercing gaze, in a region that neither the reeds nor the grass reached. A minuscule promontory extended in front of the fissure, only covered by a few lichens.

"If we fire into those reeds, perhaps we'll flush out one or two men lying in ambush?" Karel suggested.

"I don't think so, Master. Even when wounded, they observe their rules. I think they know how to die without uttering a cry, as our Amdavas do."

Suddenly, a voice was heard, which seemed to spring from the very rock. Karel straightened up in surprise; Rak and the Amdavas displayed no emotion.

"Are you Mademoiselle de Gavres' men?" asked the voice.

Rak did not understand these words, spoken in a language unknown to him, but Karel knew a few words of French. "Yes," he shouted. "*Jufvrouw* de Gavres. Where you?"

"Inside the rock." A face appeared in the fissure.

"You alone? No other men?" He did not know how to translate the word "Carabao."

"No—the Carabao-Men are hiding."

Karel guessed rather than understood the meaning of this statement, astonished that Frédéric had not been followed into his refuge.

"The chests of the Carabao-Men are too broad, Master," Rak explained. "Only their children could get through that fissure."

"You're right. And yet...well, the Grafina or Hendrik will get an explanation from him." He raised his voice. "Me Karel de Ridder, friend. You Frédéric? *Jufvrouw* or Hendrik coming. *Zuster* Corisande...not?"

"No," Frédéric replied, dejectedly. "She's a prisoner...out there." He looked at the long canoe, which the Amdavas rowers had immobilized 100 meters from the cavern, with a mixture of anguish and hope. He evoked the image of the Grafina with a profound gratitude and an affection that seemed suddenly-born, like those flowers of India that flower in a moment. Scarcely had he questioned himself confusedly when his entire being was inclined to action, to a violent determination to escape. "Thank you!" he shouted. "Thank you, with all my heart." His emotion increased visibly at the sight of this tall Dutchman, who had come to a distant land to rescue someone he did not know. "Is it possible that that man is risking his life for me?" he murmured.

Meanwhile, Karel replied: "No, no thanks...adieu... *Jufvrouw*, Hendrik..."

Already, the Amdavas were ceasing to combat the current. At first, the canoe went with the flow, then they sent it forward more rapidly, under the impulse of swift oars.

It became invisible, and Frédéric sighed. All the threats of men and nature were surrounding him. The image of Corisande rose up unbidden, so precise that the young man instinctively put out his arms to take hold of her.

The canoe quickly reached the haven where the flotilla was sheltered. While still some distance away, Karel shouted: "The Frenchman's over there!"

On the bank, Dirk and the Grafina hurried toward him. When he had briefly reported what he had seen and heard, Louise asked: "He was alone?"

"Yes, alone. I think the young *Jufvrouw* is a prisoner."

Dirk and the Grafina looked at one another. "I'll go see!" she said.

"Not alone," the planter retorted. "If I understand correctly, two good marksmen won't be too many."

"Nor a second canoe," added Karel. He was too well used to running risks to envisage anything other than a means to succeed as fully and as quickly as possible. A second canoe was added to the first. The Grafina and the planter got into it, in order to coordinate their actions better.

While going back upstream, Dirk and Louise discussed the rescue plan, but before making a firm decision they waited until they were level with the rock. Having arrived there, they began to call out to Frédéric, while examining the location.

The young man's head appeared in the fissure. Having recognized the Grafina he was gripped by an emotion that rendered him momentarily incapable of saying a word.

"We know that you're alone," said the Grafina, "unless Karel misunderstood."

"I'm alone," replied a voice that grew firmer as it spoke. "Corisande's a prisoner. I was able to get away, taking them by surprise." Rapidly but precisely, he told the story of his escape.

The Grafina translated as he went, and Dirk said: "He's a man! We shall save him."

The lie of the land dictated the maneuver. In front of the rock was the little rocky point—the minuscule promontory observed by Karel. On either side of the promontory there were reeds and tall grass, in which men were surely hiding.

"Can you swim and dive?" the Grafina asked the prisoner.

"I've been diving since childhood."

"Can you dive long enough to get close to one of the canoes?"

Frédéric measured the distances with his eye and replied: "Yes, I can go between 120 and 150 meters underwater, without too much difficulty.

"The two canoes will take up the most favorable position. Then we'll keep the enemies under fire on both sides of the rocky point. It will be difficult for them, in those thickets, to throw assegais without revealing themselves; if they dare to do that, we can each shoot several of them down in a matter of seconds. Get ready. When I give the signal, jump into the river."

"I'm ready."

"When I say *go!*"

As she went along, the Grafina translated her own words for Dirk's benefit. The two canoes moved closer to the bank, always staying out of range of jet weapons.

Louise de Gavres gave the signal: "*Go!*"

Frédéric sprang forth from the rock, almost naked, and reached the river in two bounds.

Three men stood up in the reeds, only allowing a glimpse of fragmentary silhouettes. Their arms had no time to act; three shots rang out; the three men went down with muffled exclamations. A frantic clamor went up, but the lesson had struck home. The Carabao-Men, recognizing the redoubtable power of their adversaries, remained invisible. The few darts that emerged from the curtain of vegetation could do nothing to hurt the fugitive.

Frédéric had become invisible.

Some 15 meters upriver, two men completely hidden by a projection of the river-bank had dived in. They were swimming like seals and, aided by the current, were not long delayed in getting close enough to Frédéric to perceive a pale form. Frédéric was unconscious of this pursuit and was making rapid progress toward the canoes, with a sufficient start to reach his goal before being caught, when a new enemy appeared.

A descendant of great prehistoric reptiles, although reduced in size, it was a formidable combatant, with its giant maw armed with countless teeth, its eight-meter-long body, enveloped by scaly armor, and its muscular tail. Slow and awkward on shore, it was moving in its element now, not only swimming much more rapidly than a human but any terrestrial animal.

Within a few seconds, it would be within range of the fugitive, ready to close its jaws and saw through the naked body. Direct combat was impossible; it would inevitably end in the victory of the beast. Furthermore, the Carabao-Men had stopped.

Louise de Gavres, Dirk, Karel and the Amdavas could see Frédéric and the reptile quite clearly, and the two Carabao-Men more vaguely.

The canoes were already on the move.

Four shots rang out, and a rain of javelins fell upon the reptile's mouth.

Because of the refraction, neither the rifle-shots nor the javelin-thrusts had the precision that they would have had in the open air. Nevertheless, the formidable beast, stunned by several wounds, went astray. It zigzagged and turned instead of following a straight line toward its prey.

Frédéric was able to take advantage of that in order to reach the nearer canoe, and as the fusillade continued, further javelins and arrows bombarded the crocodile. Its instinct became confused; it no longer sought to do anything but escape these inconceivable things that were pricking its body in every part, and which it probably took for a swarm of hostile creatures.

An athletic hand had grabbed the half-asphyxiated Frédéric, and deposited him next to Louise. While he was recovering his equilibrium, he experienced a moment of ecstasy in seeing the beautiful face with eyes of black fire leaning over him; it was quickly dissipated by implacable memories.

When the canoes had reached the haven again, the Sun was setting behind the forest, the fugitive dusk was lighting its forges, the Southern Cross was palpitating in the depths of the sky and the camp-fires were being lit.

Reanimated, Frédéric recounted his adventure. As he went along, the Grafina translated the story for Dirk and Karel.

It was almost a scene from prehistoric times. The three fires, lit on the river-bank, displayed the savage heads of Amdavas, the attentive giant, and the beautiful adventuress...

"We shall do everything that human strength permits to save the woman that our friend Rouveyres sent to us," said Dirk, inflating his giant torso.

"Yes, everything," murmured the Grafina.

They studied the location thoughtfully. No surprise was possible. Any enemies who dared to cross the boundary that nature rendered propitious to traps and ambushes would fall to the fire of the two infallible carbines. Karel, moreover, was not a bad shot, and out of six bullets, at 100 meters, would only miss with two or three. The Amdavas were reliable; two of those who possessed rifles could use them with some skill; all of them handled their bows marvelously—and, knowing that the enemy was throwing poisoned assegais, they had poisoned their arrows.

"Yes," said the planter, "at this point of the river-bank we can easily keep 200 men at bay. Further on, surprise attacks will become possible, and in hand-to-hand fighting, our enemies would have the advantage over our slender auxiliaries. Their strength far surpasses that of other men."

"Not yours!" retorted the Grafina. "And Monsieur de Rouveyres has faced up to them with his fists. It's not just a matter of strength. With their krises, my men have no fear of adversaries far more vigorous than themselves."

"The Amdavas are also very redoubtable with their own weapons," Karel added, "and they use their shields with extraordinary skill."

"All right!" said Dirk. "Although the Carabao-Men's big clubs seem to me to be more redoubtable in a mêlée than krises. In any case, while we're on enemy ground, where the Carabao-Men know how to render themselves as invisible as they are on the shores of this river, our company isn't worth 200 men any longer."

"No," the Grafina agreed. "It's not even worth 100…if we're advancing into covered land. But let's see!" Addressing herself to Frédéric, she continued: "You've traveled the country as far as their villages. Is all the ground covered with plants high enough or thick enough for men to hide themselves therein completely?"

"On much of the ground the vegetation is low. I also think that if we can reach the largest of the marshes, navigation might be possible there."

"On the marsh we'd be continuously in sight," said Louise, "and disembarkation would become very difficult— but we'll see. Do you think that by making detours we could move forward without risk of falling into an ambush, until we're within two or three miles of their lair?"

"I think so…in fact, I'd swear to it, if we can clear a few strips of territory here and there."

Dirk and the Grafina looked at one another. "We have to risk it!" said the giant. "On the way back, though, the ground will be prepared for ambushes."

"Who knows? Our scouts, with Rak to lead them, almost all the Amdavas and you know how to avoid traps."

"Yes," said Dirk, gravely. "Then again, we need to have confidence in the Invisible!"

Frédéric contemplated these humans, ready to give their lives for an unknown woman who had come from the other side of the world, with admiration. "My God!" he murmured, turning his head toward Louise's beautiful face, on which the coppery firelight was dancing. "Your devotion and your heroism surpass anything I would have dared to imagine."

"Guests are sacrosanct," she replied.

And when she had translated the young man's words, the giant said: "The men of my race would rather die than abandon those whose protection they have assumed."

XII. Toward the Men of the Marsh

With the benefit of detours, the expedition was able to cross half a dozen miles without hindrance. Two or three times, curtains of vegetation would have been able to hide a watchful enemy, but the curtains proved less profound than one might have thought; neither the scouts nor the dogs signaled any suspicious presence.

"I suspect," the planter said, "that they're retreating deliberately, in order to draw us to where we don't want to go."

"They're surrounding us," said Louise.

Neither of them was mistaken. The Carabao-Men had surrounded the travelers at a considerable distance and, knowing how many they were, were counting on exterminating them in the vicinity of their habitat, with the aid of the entire tribe.

The weather was dreary, the sky leaden, with thick dull clouds that harmonized with the stagnant waters, the granite ground and the marsh plants. Water oozing out of the soil often formed pools in which mud-loving creatures were swarming: corpulent reptiles and soft, fetid larval monsters.

In making their detours, they encountered the hard soil of the earliest ages, as hard as cast iron but nevertheless eroded by wind and water, and by stubborn lichens, indefatigable corrosive forces that created fecund soil by devouring the rock.

Toward midday, they came up against a thick barrier of vegetation and marsh. The place through which Frédéric and Corisande had passed with the caravan was so propitious for ambushes that they had to avoid it. Taking a slanting course, they reached a chain of rocks.

In a black region in which basalts were dominant they formed truncated pyramids, often strangely regular prisms or towers; one might have imagined them to be the work of savage architects, even more elementary than those who had built the megalithic monuments. Full of corridors, they permitted passage everywhere, but were manifestly suitable for a stubborn defense.

The scouts, the Grafina and the de Ridders searched for the best passage, but all the corridors included turnings that might hide enemies completely.

"If they want to engage us in battle in there, they can!" muttered Dirk, examining a labyrinth with broad passes.

Louise de Gavres, who had gone on ahead with Rak and the dog Vos, came back to join the colossus at that moment.

"The most favorable passage is through there," she affirmed, pointing to an enormous rock, which loomed over the other rocks as a cathedral looms over a group of houses.

"Let's go see," Dirk replied.

The base of the giant rock, which was quite straight, formed the western wall of a broad corridor bordered on the other side by irregular masses. The corridor only deviated after 100 meters, forming a very obtuse angle.

"It's necessary to go that far in order to see whether there's a practicable exit," Louise said.

"Rak can go there with Vos," said the scout. "If the Carabao-Men show themselves, Rak will be able to escape them."

"If they're here, it's hardly probable that there are many of them," the Grafina replied. "They must be looking out for us everywhere, as far as the marsh, and thus must be widely scattered."

"*Regt!*" said Dirk. "It would, indeed, require an extraordinary freak of chance for them to be concentrated around here. Let's act rapidly. I propose that Rak and Vos go on ahead and that several of our men follow them. Initially, we'll spread out—as if we were continuing to search for a way through—and then we'll reassemble a dozen men unexpectedly."

There was nothing to do but agree.

"The men must be ready to reassemble as soon as the signal is given."

Karel was charged with transmitting the orders. A dozen servants and Amdavas rapidly joined the Grafina, Dirk and Rak; the last-named went into the corridor first, with the dog Vos, and advanced silently, but at speed.

It was not long before the dog showed signs of anxiety. Half way to the bend, Rak slowed down, then began creeping. He disappeared.

Louise and Dirk de Ridder advanced, ready to fire. The Amdavas held their assegais in their hands. There was a whistle, and a brief bark from the dog, and Rak reappeared, running. A club appeared at the corner, but the hand holding it could not be seen. Two or three assegais whistled through the air.

Rak continued to beat his retreat. A fist holding an axe became visible through a gap. As agreed, the Grafina fired first. The axe fell; the wounded hand withdrew, while a long groan echoed from the basaltic walls.

Rak arrived at the gallop. "There are only four or five," he said. "The corridor broadens out and opens on to the plain."

"Will we have to force a way through?" the planter asked Louise.

"I believe we can, especially behind the Amdavas' shields."

"Then let's not delay."

Dirk gave a light whistle, to which Karel, who was standing at the corridor entrance, immediately responded. "In five minutes, the greater number of our men will follow."

The Amdavas, the Grafina's servants and Dirk started running as the signal was given. The five minutes had not yet elapsed when everyone was ready for the attack.

"Whenever you wish, *Jufvrouw*!" said the giant.

She nodded her head. Dirk whistled again, while Karel arrived with the remaining Amdavas. The men of the forest, understanding what was expected of them, disposed their shields in order to form a kind of overlapping wall, broadly reminiscent of the Roman *testudo*, and got under way.

When they arrived at the bend, a few assegais flew—and then the Carabao-Men, small in number and disconcerted by the marching wall, beat a retreat.

As Rak had said, the corridor broadened out considerably; they could see a leprous plain, dotted with pools, planted with low grass, a few clumps of trees, and giant reeds growing on the edges of the pools.

"Forward!" commanded the Grafina. "The quicker we go, the better."

"Forward!" Karel repeated, in the forest-dwellers' language.

The Amdavas had not waited for the order. They were excited. Their bellicose instincts were urging them to battle;

they were almost unaware of any fear of death, not thinking about it.

They arrived at the exit from the corridors without any interruption. The Carabao-Men had become invisible. To make sure that they had not remained in the vicinity, several Amdavas, protected by shields, inspected the rocky walls. As three or four of them were searching a fissure, a Carabao-Man abruptly sprang out. With a blow from his axe he split the skull of an Amdava; with a thrust of his formidable shoulders he knocked down three others; one might have thought him a bull charging goats—and he had raised his axe to strike at those who were running when a formidable hand seized his wrist. Dirk had come to the rescue.

Taken by surprise, the Son of the Marshes dropped his weapon. He turned toward the colossus in order to knock him down. Although the primitive's head did not reach the planter's shoulder, his chest was so profound and his arms so muscular that he must have had the strength of six Sumatrans or three or four Dutchmen. He tried to free his wrist, but the hand that held it would have resisted the pull of a tiger—so he thrust his granite head at the giant's breast.

His shoulder hardly having been touched, Dirk seized the man's other wrist and threw him to the ground with a double twist. For a moment, the Carabao-Man fought back, with extreme violence, but then, recognizing the sovereign strength of his adversary, he became motionless.

Amdavas, Sumatrans and whites watched this scene as the keen-eyed Achaeans and the horse-taming Trojans had watched heroic duels.

"It might be useful to keep him," said Dirk, with one foot on the breast of the defeated man. "He'll need to be tied up."

On a command from Karel, three Amdavas bound the prisoner's body with a kind of slender liana, resistant and elastic. Rak thought it advisable to secure the wrists with jute cord.

"What use will he be to us?" said Karel. "We'll have to carry him. He'll reveal our presence everywhere."

"We can't march in a troop without being seen," the planter replied, "and as we're advancing slowly, by necessity, carrying him won't inconvenience us much. I confess, son, that I'm not sure what use he'll be to us...but I've recognized the usefulness of hostages more than once in my life." The colossus paused, then continued: "Anyway, it has never seemed appropriate to me to kill a man who has ceased to defend himself. I hope to die without having done that—and you wouldn't have done it either!"

"No," said Karel. "I wouldn't have done it."

"Thou shalt not kill, says the Book. I've only killed when it was necessary to save the lives of others, or my own. I also regret having been obliged to come into the Carabao-Men's territory as an enemy. They gave me no choice! A man is a slave to his destiny."

The Amdavas had picked up their wounded warrior. The axe had made a large dent in his skull, without penetrating as far as the brain. Dirk examined the wound. "He might recover!" he said.

"He will recover," said one of the Amdavas, dressing the wound with herbs gathered from among the rocks. Antisepsis has been practiced by many savages for thousands of years. The plants selected by the forest-dwellers were aromatic; the wound was washed in their juice, as carefully as by a conscientious nurse. In addition, the man chanted magical formulas, punctuated by gestures, which were also an aspect of ancestral therapeutics, designed to enhance the morale of invalids.

Frédéric watched the primitive medical procedure with amazement, thinking that the wounded men collected on the battlefield were hardly any better cared-for, and perhaps no more intelligently, than the forest-dwellers.

Further away, Dirk attended to the Carabao-Man, who, while fighting frenziedly, had sustained a wound on the nape of his neck that was bleeding copiously. The Son of the Marshes had thought, at first, that the giant wanted to kill him or subject him to torture. When he understood that his wound was being dressed, a strange stupor rounded his wild eyes; he watched his conqueror, sometimes with hatred, sometimes with a despairing resignation, in which the primal worship of Strength was mingled.

"It's dangerous not to kill him," said Rak.

Dirk paid no heed. Before that fantastic human being, who revealed a race of an extreme vigor, he experienced the sentiment that he experienced in confrontation with large wild animals—especially tigers, for which he had an extreme admiration. To tell the truth, he killed them whenever he encountered them, out of a sense of duty, but with a confused reluctance. That sentiment was no stranger to Louise de Gavres, who was also seduced by dominant animals, even those as hideous as rhinoceroses or crocodiles.

"Why do these brutes feel the need to attack other men?" Dirk complained. "Are they not safe in their own lands? For a long time, the whites, the Malays and the Amdavas have not dreamed of disputing with them."

"Men have always fought men," Louise replied. "They're obeying the same instinct, albeit more obscure, that summoned our ancestors here—and our ancestors were ferocious, as you know very well, old friend!" She turned her beautiful face and dark starry eyes to Frédéric. "You know that too, Monsieur de Rouveyres, you whose ancestors killed mine like dogs, or condemned them to infamous tortures..."

"Alas, yes—you have made me see that. My ancestors behaved cruelly toward yours—but you, you have twice risked your life for Corisande's and mine. Oh, men are not simple creatures, since they can also be as heroically generous as you and your admirable friends. Will you permit me, Mademoiselle, to have as much affection for you as if we were members of the same family?"

Hendrik translated these words in due course, and the giant, affected by them, cried: "We would curse ourselves like the mire of these marshes if we did not defend our guests."

He held out his colossal hand, into which the Frenchman's hand disappeared completely. Louise had lowered her head. Her face was inscrutable. In a low voice, she said: "We accept your friendship, Frédéric de Rouveyres." Her profound and soft voice set all the young man's nerves tingling.

"Now," Dirk declared, after examining the location, "I think we can advance for several more miles. Our trackers and dogs can't be taken by surprise. There are two or three places, at the most, suitable for an ambush, but with too few men to attack us. I'm almost certain that the Carabao-Men won't attack us until they feel that they're the stronger. They've found that their jet weapons are powerless at distances that our rifles can cover without difficulty, and even at a distance at which our Amdavas archers can reach them without them being able to respond."

"Furthermore," added Louise, who had just examined the surrounding area with a little telescope, "the rocks and thickets where they might try to hide are easily avoidable; they'll have to choose between retreat and encirclement."

"*Regt!*" said the planter. "But the time's approaching, *Jufvrouw*, when we'll need to make a plan—which we'll rectify, naturally, according to circumstances. First of all, we can't think of penetrating their ant-hill *en masse*."

"Their termitary, rather," Karel remarked.

"Even if we took possession of it," said the Grafina, "there are numerous caverns there, as Monsieur de Rouveyres has told us. How could we storm them, if they're defended? And won't they communicate with avenues of retreat, which these savages will have attained long before we can find them? A small number of our people will have to recover Mademoiselle de Rouveyres, while the remainder distract the attention of our enemies."

"But how?" said Hendrik.

"Impossible to be more precise as yet. That will only be possible when we're within sight of their rocks. Let's continue our advance."

The expedition marched on, after a brief meal. For several hours all obstacles and all the places where ambushes might be set were surrounded by the agile Amdavas and then passed by.

The presence of Carabao-Men was obvious to the scouts and signaled by the dogs, but the enemy remained completely invisible. Their tactics were invariable; they included a continuous retreat. Evidently, they had taken account of the futility of a battle in which the feeble range of their jet weapons put them in a position of inferiority of which they were now convinced. The infallible marksmanship of the planter and the Grafina had made a powerful impression on them; they believed in the presence of other marksmen just as redoubtable. From a distance, a few of them had seen Dirk flooring his antagonist without apparent effort. They were not afraid. Fear was almost unknown to them. Their warriors did not recoil before mortal peril when it was necessary to fight—except that the supernatural struck terror into them, and they did not know whether some superhuman power might be aiding the white colossus and the woman with the eyes of black fire.

When the Sun was ready to disappear into the occidental waters, the expedition stopped in a broad defile, a granite causeway dividing two marshes. The Amdavas and the Sumatrans cleared the ground along a length of 200 meters, felling some clusters of small trees, and a few bushes and tall ferns. The relatively low-lying plants and the taller trees were left. Then they made up the camp fires.

The rapid dusk was beginning when Rak and the dog Vos appeared. "They're 500 paces away, over there, in the reeds, and a little further on, in the banyans, and they're more numerous than before."

"Might they risk an attack?" said Karel.

"I doubt it," murmured Louise de Gavres. "The sky's clear; no storm is near. Only a cyclone and a storm like the one that permitted the abduction could tempt them. Nevertheless, they aren't concentrating their forces without reason. Do you think there are more than 100 of them, Rak?"

Rak raised his arms to signal his ignorance. "How can one count them, Mistress? The banyans and the reeds could hide more than 1000."

The fires crackled; high flames, springing out of the smoke, became brighter as the darkness increased. When night had fallen—a night white with stars—a coppery gleam swept the causeway for some distance

"At 100 meters one could hit a target as easily as in broad daylight," Dirk remarked, raising his eyes toward the scintillating Southern Cross.

Myriads of giant frogs were croaking madly; one might have thought that a herd of fabulous beasts, aquatic buffaloes, was hidden among the marsh plants. Clouds of insects precipitated themselves toward the flames—a snow of moths, a rain of mosquitoes and vertiginous beetles falling into the red braziers—while dozens of bats somersaulted through the air in pursuit of hypnotized prey.

Inconceivable nature! thought Frédéric. *"So much foresight, such subtle instincts, prodigious organisms, from the tiniest flies to tigers and cachalots... all of it sacrificed to absurd and baroque hazards!*

Meanwhile, the Grafina, Dirk, Karel and the Amdava chief made their rounds in order to render the camp safe from surprises.

"The dogs are restless," Louise remarked.

"Yes... increasingly so," the planter agreed.

Rak stuck his ear to the ground, while the dog Vos scratched the earth. The *Jufvrouw* did not hesitate to imitate the tracker. She heard muffled sounds in the ground: hammering sounds or imprecise noises suggestive of digging.

"Something's happening down there."

Already, Dirk and Karel were taking account of it for themselves. The dog Vos scratched the soil more excitedly and sniffed urgently.

"Isn't it, Rak?" asked Louise.

"Yes, Mistress. They're underground."

"Do you think they're Carabao-Men?"

"I think so—and Vos is sure of it."

Louise knew the dog too well not to be convinced. She put a hand on Vos's head, saying: "Enemies, Vos?"

The dog growled dully, raising his eyes—which shone with intelligence—toward Louise.

"No doubt," said Dirk, then. "The Carabao-Men are here. Either they're planning to attack us unexpectedly, or they're going to try to make us fall into their caverns—for I think that there are caverns beneath our feet."

"We need to know whether the caverns extend across the entire causeway," Louise continued.

"If that's not the case, I imagine that only a part of the ground will collapse."

"There's hard stone almost everywhere," Karel remarked.

"Granite. So I presume they're attempting to knock down the walls or columns supporting it. Let's try to figure out exactly where they're working…and command the men to disperse."

When the orders had been given, Rak, the Grafina, the Dutchmen and several Amdavas listened attentively to the subterranean noises. The noises were not always produced in the same places. There were neutral zones, and others where the activity was concentrated. By cross-checking, they were able to identify those zones fairly clearly.

"Nothing's certain, though," Dirk remarked. "The collapses won't necessarily be limited to the places where they're working."

The most suspect zones were evacuated; supplementary fires were lit at various distances, to avoid the darkness advantageous to the Carabao-Men—although the glare of the stars provided an ashen light in which men accustomed to the savage life could see to fight and to shoot—albeit less precisely than by firelight. The Moon would not rise for another three hours.

The wait, with its procession of frightful images, anguish and impatience, seemed long—but was less fatiguing for men of adventure and nature than for nervous city-dwellers. Intermittently, the work ceased. The zones were now very localized. Even so, noises were heard elsewhere, though never for a long time, raising the suspicion of feints intended to disorientate the listeners.

Everything was ready for a complete evacuation, which had been delayed until now for fear of traps, which the enemies might have had time to prepare under cover of darkness. Beyond 300 meters, it was impossible to discern anything, except scattered vegetation and occasional large blocks of stone.

"The Earth trembled," Rak declared.

He pointed westwards. Amdavas, lying on the ground, confirmed the indication. The Grafina, Dirk and Karel decided to evacuate that zone, and then to mount a general retreat eastwards. They were then about 75 meters from a thick curtain of plants, which overlapped the two sides of the causeway and might hide 100 men. It would have been dangerous to retreat any further.

In that part of the causeway the subterranean noises were less distinct, as the whites and the indigenes both observed.

Abruptly, the Earth shook. Several detonations were heard, and the fires died down. Four Sumatrans and two Amdavas disappeared, uttering loud cries.

In the place where the encampment had formerly been located, there was no more than a vast hole, a chaos of fallen rocks from which long flames and thick smoke were escaping.

"Let's try to save the poor devils!" said the Grafina.

Two of the buried Sumatrans were in her service, the other two had come with Dirk. Shouts—ominous plaints—rose up from the depths. Louise did not hesitate to precipitate herself into the debris, quickly followed by Dirk, Frédéric and several Amdavas.

"No one else must come down!" ordered Louise.

"Karel, Hendrik, go back up!" said the giant imperiously. "The camp can't be left without commanders!"

Louise and Frédéric were the first to pull out a wounded man. Another was moaning lamentably, pinned beneath a block of stone that four ordinary men could only have lifted with great difficulty. Dirk threw it back without apparent effort. The other victims could not be found for some time. In the end, the Amdavas discovered two mangled bodies, with their skulls split and their entrails hanging out.

"A bad night!" said the giant, in a melancholy tone, when he got back to the causeway with the Grafina. "If the retreat had been ordered ten minutes later, the whole expedition would have been annihilated. And now..."

Amdavas and Sumatrans formed a confused mass beneath the constellations. Here and there, a jet of flame lit their faces more brightly, and then everything fell back into the gloom. There was no point thinking about building fires; all their remaining combustible material was buried.

The sinister darkness extended over the marshes. The clamor of giant frogs, the furtive apparitions of reptiles in the starlight and the flight of enormous bats were suggestive of a subterranean world, stifling and phantasmagoric. Invisible enemies, who had just shown themselves to be even more redoubtable than anyone imagined, were watching the expedition. Death floated in the atmosphere.

It's terrible, Frédéric thought, *that all these people are risking their lives for us!*

His gaze settled on the silhouette of Louise de Gavres. At intervals, he glimpsed her white face, imprecise but nonetheless full of charm; the thought of what this marvelous creature was doing for him and for Corisande made his heart swell with gratitude and affection.

Meanwhile, the leaders disposed the men, in anticipation of an abrupt attack. To the west, and to the east, lines of Amdavas who would stand up immediately in response to a signal, covered by their shields; in the center, the Sumatrans. It

262

did not matter much what positions the Grafina, Dirk and Karel took up; in a flash, they would be ready for battle.

If we aren't attacked before moonrise, all will be well," said Karel.

"It's especially necessary to beware of the debris," the Grafina remarked.

A space of 50 meters separated the collapse from the curtain of aquatic vegetation but it was evident that the Carabao-Men might surge forth from underground, so the Amdavas advance-guard was doubled on that side.

Pensively, Louise glimpsed a subterranean existence, doubtless very ancient. From now on, nothing was more probable than a ramification of the caverns, which would become increasingly numerous once they approached the base. The shelters identified by Frédéric, those habitations in the bosom of the rocks, appeared revelatory. Everything became more redoubtable; it would be necessary to advance one step at a time—but as always, the young woman wondered whether it might even be possible to derive some advantage from the situation.

When the half-full Moon appeared in the west, no attack had occurred.

"I presume," said the planter, "that they were counting on inflicting heavier losses upon us, throwing everything into disorder and sowing panic among the survivors."

"All in all, their coup has failed," said Karel. "We were lucky."

"Yes—but luck wouldn't have been enough. We were able to retreat from the most dangerous zone."

"They'll try again, though."

"It's not impossible, Karel—although it's not very probable that a similar opportunity will present itself. I presume that we're camping on terrain that has been mined for a long time...and which would have ended up collapsing of its own accord. That must be quite rare; it would require singularly bad luck for us to camp in similar conditions for a second time."

"That's true!" the Grafina interjected. "I anticipate further pitfalls, though, favored by their subterranean life. We probably have nothing to fear tonight."

"I think so too," replied the giant, placidly lighting his pipe. "So it's necessary that the men sleep. They'll need all their strength. Give the order to the Amdavas, Karel, and you and I, *Jufvrouw*, will take care of the Sumatrans."

The Moon, initially immense, red and dull, shrank and became paler as it climbed into the sky. Gradually, a brighter light spread over the marshes. The Amdavas and the Sumatrans began to feel safer, although a superstitious anxiety persisted in their primitive souls. That anxiety was especially keen in the Amdavas, who were always ready to risk their lives in combat but fearful in confrontation with mysterious dangers, which they attributed to superhuman interventions. It was important to reassure them. When the sentries had been disposed and the majority of men had lain down, Karel summoned the chief of the Amdavas and the warrior who attended to the wounded.

The chief was a sturdy 40 year-old of medium height, with a triangular face, prominent cheekbones and hard yellow eyes. He listened impassively to the eulogy of the dead and said: "We are born for few seasons. Those who die young are less unhappy than those who die weighed down by days...and the best fate of all is that of those who die in battle." Then, turning his eyes away and lowering his head, he said: "Our dead have not been in battle, and we came to do battle."

"Glorious chief of the forest," said Karel, gravely, "on the warpath, it is necessary to expect all perils."

"All those that come from men, beasts, water, air and earth, yes," replied the Amdava, "but not those that come from hidden things."

"No peril has come from hidden things," the giant affirmed then. "The Carabao-Men live under the ground and in the earth. Many others live thus!"

The chief bowed respectfully. He had seen the colossus lift up the stone that had resisted the efforts of four men, and he also knew that his rifle, like that of Louise's, never missed its target. His heart was full of mystical admiration.

"Lambda, son of Sorgoi, has only one thing to say," the chief replied. "He will follow you until death."

The other Amdava, his face reticent and his eyes oblique, remained silent. The Grafina fixed her eyes of black flame upon him. "Our enemies have only one redoubtable secret," she said, "and that is their poison. You know that we have a remedy stronger than their poison. What can they oppose to our rifles and your bows? If they had great sorcerers, would they still be armed with axes, clubs and assegais?"

These words, the Grafina's gaze, perhaps her beauty and the mystery of her presence impressed the Amdava. He lowered his head and replied: "The Amdavas will follow their chief!"

The night passed without any alarm. When the Sun rose above the marshes, the men were rested and the scenes of the previous night were already becoming blurred in the insouciant brains of the Amdavas and the Sumatrans.

The Grafina, Dirk and Rak examined the debris. Heaps of rocks lay in a large hole, without any obvious breach having been opened to the waters—which, nevertheless, were filtering in slowly and would end up attaining the level of the causeway. Already it would have been difficult to pass through.

The opening of a subterranean passage was visible to the west. There could be no thought of exploring it; in addition to the invading water, the Carabao-Men might be lying in ambush therein—but the passage gave rise to a host of possibilities and sketchy projects in Louise de Gavres' mind.

When the expedition had finished the first meal of the day resolutions had been made. They would cross the gap with the aid of Amdavas canoes. The crossing was promptly executed, in spite of the marsh plants that formed obstacles in places similar to those that travelers have observed in the Sargasso Sea.

There was no trace of the enemy.

"How did they get underground?" asked Karel. "Perhaps there's an opening nearby."

"We've thought of that," said Louise. "Rak, Karel and the other scouts will receive orders."

No fissure and no evidence of any cavern were discovered on the causeway and the plain that followed. Nor was there the slightest indication of the proximity of Marshdwellers. Vos and the other dogs remained calm.

"I believe that they're following us and preceding us, though," said Louise, when the expedition called a halt at midday.

The march had been difficult, over terrain that was alternately rocky and boggy, beneath a blazing Sun. The protective clouds had disappeared. From a harsh blue sky, the solar furnace poured torrents of heat.

Sometimes, thickets of hectic and suspect vegetation barred the way; it was necessary to go around them—and the deadly legions of insects never ceased to assail the humans.

They had reached a granite outcrop where overhanging rocks provided shade.

"Do you think we're close to the objective now?" the Grafina asked Frédéric.

"A few more miles at most," the young man replied. "Although I followed another, more direct route, I noticed these rocks on my arrival." He pointed to the south-west. "The Carabao-Men's caverns are in that direction. I think we could see them from the top of one of these rocks." He pointed at the highest part of the outcrop, a steep red rock with black veins, which must have risen up to an elevation of 100 or 120 meters. "Anyway, I'd like to know," he added.

Dirk, for whom Hendrik had translated the conversation, murmured: "Let's examine the terrain first."

Two clefts separated the tall rock from the others and permitted them to make a tour around it. The scouts having observed nothing suspect, Frédéric rapidly scaled the less awkward of the declivities. Apart from one section, where he had to raise himself up by his arms, the young man executed the ascent without any great difficulty. During the climb, he noticed a rather large fissure, which he resolved to explore on the way back.

When he stood on the slanting narrow platform that formed the summit, he distinctly recognized the rocky circle that sheltered the enemy tribe, three or four kilometers away.

The air, which was very pure at that moment, permitted him to see everything precisely.

Frédéric's heart was beating violently. *Was she still alive?* Funereal thoughts and frightful visions crowded his mind tumultuously. If she was still alive, how could they reach her? And even if they reached her, would not the savages cut her throat at the final moment?

In spite of his agitation, he carefully observed the details of the location. By the time he began the descent, he knew enough to guide the expedition.

The fissure stopped him. It seemed to be deep; he could not resist the temptation to go into it, groping his way. After a few steps on rocky terrain he perceived a slope. Passing from gloom into obscurity, it soon became invisible. He advanced with extreme prudence, but was soon obliged to stop by the increasing darkness.

Who knows? he said to himself, thinking about the previous night's episode.

The Grafina, Dirk and Karel were waiting for him down below, ready to climb the rock in their turn.

"Their lair is close by," said Frédéric. He gave a summary description of the access routes and told them about the fissure.

Louise listened with keen interest. "We need to explore it!" she said.

"Shouldn't we fear a trap?" said Karel.

"It's possible—but if there are men in there, the dogs won't fail to warn us in time…and it's very difficult to take Rak by surprise. Monsieur de Rouveyres and I will go together, with Rak and a few natives." As Dirk manifested a desire to go with them, she added: "The men must not be left without a leader."

Dirk acquiesced. In addition to Karel, Rak and Kalava, they chose six Amdavas from among the best trackers of humans and animals, and the dog Vos was joined by the little Bornean dog and three others with sharp noses.

The men and animals rapidly scaled the slopes that led to the fissure, and then they went into the depths of the rock.

The Amdavas' primitive little lanterns and the brighter lanterns carried by the Grafina, Karel and Rak projected a sufficiently vivid light on the side walls and the ground for them to be able to advance without uncertainty.

First, the little troop descended a steep slope that sometimes became abrupt, but always over a sufficiently short extent for a lithe and agile man to be able to continue on his way. Sometimes the tunnel broadened out, and sometimes it narrowed to the point of only letting two or three men through at a time.

Rak and Kalava, preceded by the dog Vos and the little Bornean dog, took the lead. The other dogs sometimes followed and sometimes went on ahead. None of the subtle creatures signaled the slightest presence, with the result that they covered hundreds of meters without anything, save for natural obstacles, causing the expedition to pause.

Twice, intersecting tunnels necessitated a precautionary exploration; they were found to be dead ends. Everywhere, they found traces of the passage of men, but these traces were revealed by evidence of stone-working that undoubtedly dated back to remote eras. There was no evidence of erosion by water.

"It seems to me that the ancestors of the Carabao-Men enlarged, and even opened, more than one passage," Frédéric remarked. "The place was routinely frequented once, but it seems to be more-or-less abandoned now."

"It seems so," replied the Grafina.

As they were speaking thus, they came into a deep cavern that immediately struck them as having once housed men.

Weapons were scattered on the ground. Frédéric, who had made several digs in the company of a friend who was a prehistorian, examined them. They were axes, covered in calcareous deposits, which probably dated from 1000 or 2000 years ago, and wooden clubs, mostly decomposing. In a sort of niche they discovered two skeletons swathed in furs, the greater part of which had been destroyed by the humidity.

The Amdavas discovered other weapons and other skeletons in niches hollowed out by human hands.

"This is a sepulchral crypt!" said Frédéric.

"Let's not linger!" said the Grafina. She instructed the Amdavas to take shelter behind their shields and gave the order to resume the march.

The corridor that followed the cavern with the skeletons had obviously been carved out.

"The cavern and this part of the tunnels must have been in regular use once," said Frédéric. "It's strange that it reveals no vestige to our dogs."

Louise turned her beautiful face toward Frédéric and her large eyes of black fire met the brighter gaze of her companion. A frisson passed over the nape of the young man's neck. He had arrived at that time of life in which a woman's graces took on a gripping intensity. Dazzled by the sight of a femininity so various and so flexible, combined with a heroic nature, he was charmed by Louise's every movement. "Yes," she replied. "The Carabao-Men have often passed this way—but not recently. Their traces are visible to us, but non-existent for the dogs."

Meanwhile, the tunnel extended interminably, although no other intersections were discovered. The slope, increasingly gentle, was on the point of disappearing. For some time, they walked on ground that was almost flat; then a new slope appeared. This time, it was necessary to go upwards.

"We've been walking for nearly an hour," Karel murmured. "We must have covered several kilometers."

"And we're close to their lair," said Louise, "for I think that we've been walking in the same direction for almost the whole time."

The declivity became steeper, and a glimmer began to increase, which soon became bright light. Then a sort of cyclopean stairway appeared, terminating in a platform. In the middle of that platform a block of basalt rose up, similar to the one on which Frédéric had previously seen the captives slaughtered. When he had told his companions this, Karel and the Grafina rapidly examined the surface of the block. Several jade axes were visible there, and a large number of skulls, arranged in a circle.

"It's obviously a place of sacrifice," said Frédéric, "and a kind of sepulcher. We must be close to their habitation."

Less than 50 meters away, they discerned rocks disposed in such a way as to enclose a sort of amphitheater.

The dogs were becoming agitated, and an immense howl suddenly went up, which must have been uttered by a multitude of invisible human creatures, both men and women.

At the same moment, Rak discovered the opening of a chasm reminiscent of the oubliettes of the Middle Ages. Spiral projections permitted an agile man to descend and climb up along the side wall.

After a brief silence, the howling began again, just as loudly but more rhythmically, with a strange sepulchral quality.

"We need to know what's in there," said Karel, leaning over the chasm.

"I'll go!" said Frédéric. "I'm used to rock-climbing. I've done plenty."

Louise and Karel attempted to dissuade him, but the young man was obstinate.

"We'll draw lots," said Louise.

The draw sided with Frédéric. Before he set off, Louise and Karel attached fine but very resistant cords to him which they always carried on hazardous expeditions.

Armed with Louise's lantern, Frédéric went down slowly. The descent proved to be easier than one would have thought *a priori*; the projections were conveniently disposed, the majority being reshaped to be more accessible. It only took five minutes for Frédéric to reach the bottom of the chasm. It was a hexagonal cavern, which seemed to have been inhabited.

Frédéric had no doubt that it must have an exit. He examined the walls and the ground at length, feeling them and trying to introduce the blade of his knife into various interstices. For a long time, he found nothing that licensed belief in any sort of doorway or displaceable block of stone, but chance favored him. While supporting himself against the side wall, he felt a slight quiver. He pressed the same spot and its surroundings, doggedly, without any further result. He was already getting discouraged when the quivering increased and the wall appeared to see-saw. He redoubled his efforts, using both hands. A block pivoted and, through an opening large enough to allow a man of considerable girth to pass through, the exterior light entered the cavern.

At the same moment, a clamor louder than all the preceding ones went up from the facing rocks. The roaring voices of men and the strident plaints of women were discernible—but, as always, these individuals remained invisible.

For an instant, Frédéric appeared in broad daylight, not out of bravado but in order to discover more. Assegais sprang from a thicket, but they did not cover a quarter of the distance required to reach the young man.

A mere threat! he said to himself.

He stayed there for five minutes. Silence fell again. No further projectiles were hurled. "Now I know!" he murmured, attempting to close the exit again.

271

After a few attempts, the block, apparently immovable to begin with, pivoted on its axis again. Frédéric found himself in semi-darkness again.

"I have to go back up!" he exclaimed.

The climb, as is often the case, seemed less perilous than the descent, although it took slightly longer.

He imparted his discovery to Louise de Gavres and concluded: "I'm almost sure now that they won't even try to attack us here. There must be some fetishistic reason. The place where we are has become inviolable...perhaps only for a time...but in the meantime, we're protected."

"If that's the case," Louise murmured, "and I'm inclined to think so, it might perhaps facilitate our task. Let's try to find some means of making sure. In any case, for the time being, let's hold this position."

XIII. In the Depths of the Rocks

Corisande was the captive and slave of Hourv. At first, she thought of death, but it seemed impossible to her to die without having seen Frédéric again. In her ignominy, even more than before, there was an immense affection in her, entirely consecrated to the companion of her life. If it were necessary to die, she wanted to do it by his side.

Deep down, without formulating it in any interior speech, she sensed that she would be able to live again in his shadow; she hoped for some inconceivable future that would purify her.

Was Frédéric still alive? She had understood what he had said, in the darkness, at the moment of his flight, but had he escaped his pursuers?

She had been assigned a large niche hollowed out in the basalt. She lived there alone, save for the times when Hourv came to her.

It was a solitary place, where narrow cracks hollowed out in the rock by the weather intersected. The men, women and children of the Marsh rarely passed by—but there was always a sentry posted a short distance away, sometimes two.

Hourv demonstrated a sort of gentleness. Sometimes, he talked, with abundant signs. The crude sounds, similar to grunts, had become familiar to the young woman during the journey on the raft and the march over the marshy ground. She could make out a few words. She tried to find out whether Frédéric had been recaptured, and thought she understood that he had not, as yet.

Then, in spite of everything, she had hope. Youth, the creator of illusions, thrilled within her; thinking about the Grafina, she did not doubt that the strange young woman would dare anything to rescue the prisoners.

The time—the interminable time—of the captivity and the horror went by, as it had gone by for the wretches buried in the depths of oubliettes, as it had gone by for La Balue, crouched in his cage.[32] It went by *terribly*.

Corisande was now permitted to go outside between morning and evening. She wandered around the circle of rocks, usually without passing the limit where the men, women and children with the faces of buffaloes appeared. Her guards did not seem to see her; she did not see them much herself, for they were almost always under cover.

She wondered where the ravines hollowed out in the rock might lead. It was by that route that she dreamed of flight. She knew full well that it was chimerical—how could she deceive the vigilance of the guards with lupine senses?

She had, however, noticed the small number of warriors present in the agglomeration. Every day, the number of men

---

[32] Cardinal Jean de La Balue (1421-1491) was imprisoned in an iron cage by Louis XI, whom he had previously served as Secretary of State, for having conspired against him with the last Duc de Bourgogne, Charles le Téméraire [Charles the Bold] (1433-1477).

sent outside seemed to increase, and Corisande, whose thoughts always returned to Frédéric's escape and the Grafina, wondered whether the departure of the warriors might not be coincidental with the arrival of a rescue party.

Eventually, there was never more than a single guard. Hourv, moreover, manifested no suspicion. Corisande's escape must seem impossible to him—the captive seemed so frail by comparison with the monstrous females of the tribe.

One morning, a great agitation was manifest in the males and females alike. The last warriors disappeared outside. The women were engaged in an interminable discussion, and Corisande's guard was agitated, continually disappearing only to reappear moments later.

Two-thirds of the way through the day, a frantic clamor reverberated from the basalt blocks. The sentry, seized by a feverish agitation, set off at a run and disappeared. Corisande listened attentively. A second clamor soon followed, louder still.

The young woman put her hand on her heart, which was hammering. An obscure force impelled her, which she made no attempt to resist, and she launched herself resolutely into one of the cracks that she looked at so avidly every day. A great energy rose up within her; captivity had not weakened her at all.

The ground was abundantly studded with granite points. At first, Corisande passed between two high black walls, which only allowed her to glimpse a narrow band of sky; then she found a round enclosure, through which a thin stream of water flowed. She thought she was a prisoner, but a crack scarcely two feet wide presented itself behind a projection. She slipped into it.

Twice or three times more she thought the way was blocked, but she succeeded in passing through at an angle, and went along an exceedingly dark corridor. Finally, she found herself in an open plain dotted with marshes.

Although the place was suitable for traps, she did not stop. She was running for her life. Resolved to keep going until she was exhausted, because no direction seemed preferable to any other, she advanced at hazard, making use—to the extent she could—of vegetation and scattered stones to hide herself.

She had just crossed an isthmus between two pools when, on turning round, she saw three Carabao-Men pursuing her. Corisande was more agile than the common run of women; nevertheless, any young woman of her race would inevitably be recaptured. The pursuers, like all Carabao-Men, had more stamina than speed, but one of the three was going as fast as the fugitive; in time, he was bound to catch up with her.

Little by little, Corisande felt her strength decreasing; in spite of superhuman efforts, she was forced to slow down. Every time she looked back, she saw the man getting nearer, although his companions, by contrast, had lost ground.

It's over! she said to herself.

With a surge of desperation, she succeeded in accelerating her pace, and even gaining a little ground. That supreme effort lasted for a few minutes; then inexorable nature got the better of the young woman. Her legs became weak, her breath seemed to be splitting her sides and the beating of her heart became intolerable.

Minute by minute, the man drew closer. Soon, he was only a few meters behind. She could hear his feet hammering the ground. Then he was very close; he had only one or two strides to take to catch up with her.

She stopped, her strength giving out. She wished for death…

With a cry of triumph, the man reached out to grab her.

She closed her eyes, exhausted.

A shot rang out, followed by a wild scream, and Corisande, opening her eyes again, saw the Carabao-Man lying on the ground, writhing in the throes of death.

Voices rose up in the east. On the summit of a quadrangular rock, Corisande saw Frédéric and the Grafina, waving to her.

In the distance, the other two pursuers…

To begin with the configuration of the location had hidden Corisande completely from the sight of Frédéric and the Grafina. As, in any case, they were observing the lairs of the Marsh People rather than looking in any other direction, they had not even noticed the young woman when she finally became visible, emerging from behind a mass of vegetation. It was Rak who had called attention to her, at the very moment when she was about to be seized.

In three seconds, the Grafina shouldered her rifle and fired. The man fell just as his hand touched his prey.

Frédéric, bewildered, simultaneously proclaimed his gratitude and called out to Corisande. Evidently, she could not head for the rock without the two men who were pursuing her cutting her off.

Those men had stopped on seeing their companion fall. Then, understanding what had just happened, they became invisible. Between them and the rock there were all kinds of cover—blocks of stone, vegetation, folds in the terrain—permitting them to bar the way to the fugitive.

"I've got to go to her rescue!" Frédéric declared.

Louise de Gavres did not try to stop him. She understood that he had to do it. In fact, having rapidly studied the area, she resolved to go with him. "Rak," she said to the tracker, "you must alert our friends."

Frédéric was already climbing down the wall. While Rak disappeared into the tunnel, the Grafina started to follow the young man.

"What about me?" Karel exclaimed.

"There must be a leader here," said the young woman, imperiously, "to defend the location and await reinforcements."

Louise did not take long to catch up with Rouveyres.

Five minutes later, they were both running toward Corisande, avoiding passing close to bushes, clumps of trees or rocks favorable to ambushes.

Corisande saw them coming, but she could also see the two men who had been pursuing her creeping along a hollowed-out trail, in the dry bed of a stream that filled up in the rainy season. In order to meet up with her brother and the Grafina, the young woman had to cross the deepest part of the stream-bed, between steep banks—which would lose her sufficient time for the brutes to catch up with her. She preferred to increase the distance that separated her from them, after having made signs to her rescuers and shouted: "Two men are chasing me, invisible to you."

Although they were too far away to hear her, they understood that the gestures signaled the presence of enemies. Much speedier than Corisande, it did not take them long to get close enough to engage her in conversation.

"They're there—*there!*" Corisande shouted, breathless and exhausted, shivering with anxiety for herself and for them.

"Don't move!" shouted the Grafina, without slowing down. "You're in the open—you can't be attacked unexpectedly."

Corisande stopped. The two men were only a short distance away.

XIV. The Subterranean Skirmish

Dirk was worried. For an hour, at intervals, they had been able to see groups of Carabao-Men, at a great distance and in all directions. They only ever appeared momentarily, too far away for him to be able to risk shooting at them. Up to 500 meters, the planter's aim was almost infallible, even at a moving target—in which he surpassed the finest Swiss champions, the kings of fixed-target shooting. Beyond that range, no known marksman is the absolute master of his shot.

After making observations for some time, Dirk suspected that the Men of the Marsh were mounting a sort of siege upon the expedition. To get a better view, he climbed a dominant rock. From there, it did not take long to convince himself that the enemy was working under cover, sometimes digging in the ground, sometimes transporting blocks of stone.

"That's it all right!" the giant muttered. "They're trying to seal us in and, naturally, setting traps and laying ambushes."

Hendrik, who had accompanied his father, said: "Do you think they'll attack us, Father?"

"No, I don't think so. They'd expose themselves to excessively heavy losses, and they probably think that firearms are even more effective than they are. They're brutes…but marvelously cunning brutes. They don't want to sacrifice lives needlessly, but they're determined to bar our passage."

"They can't do that without fighting."

"They'll fight—hand to hand," his father replied, pensively. "They'll attack us when we're very close, that's clear to see—but if we can ensure that the Amdavas and the Sumatrans precede us in the attack, the plan will be largely frustrated."

"And why is that?" asked Hendrik, naively.

Dirk shrugged his shoulders, with a smile. "It's obvious that you've spent several years in Europe. It's simple, little man. If our men are ahead of us, the Carabao-Men will have to come out in the open, and then, the *Jufvrouw* and I will guarantee to put a large number of them out of the fight. I'd rather have avoided all that—I don't like bloodshed—but one has to do one's duty!" With a sigh, he concluded: "Let's go!"

Although the encampment was not under any immediate threat, Dirk gave orders to increase its safety from any surprise attack. While he was supervising the work of his men, wondering whether the Grafina, Karel and Frédéric were safe and sound, he saw Rak reappear.

He did not bother to examine the scout's face; neither joy nor anxiety ever altered its impassivity. The giant waited for Rak to speak. The latter rapidly informed him about the subterranean journey and the arrival at the summit of the Sepulcher-Rock, the appearance of Corisande, in flight and pursued, followed by the Grafina and Frédéric's sortie. The last news caused Dirk considerable consternation. In a flash, he saw all the possible perils to which it might lead. If the way back were to be barred to Louise, Corisande and Frédéric, if they were captured or killed, all the sacrifices would have been in vain.

He looked around, and wondered whether he dared leave the Amdavas and the Sumatrans to their own resources. After a minute of painful reflection, he decided. *I'll send Karel back to them*, he said to himself. *They'll obey him even better than me.*

He had, however, to warn the chiefs. "How long will it take to reach the Rock?" the planter asked Rak.

"Now that I know the way, half an hour."

"So Karel won't be able to get here within an hour. That's a long time—but after all, it's necessary…"

The chiefs listened to what Dirk thought he needed to tell them—concealing the danger run by the Grafina—and they seemed less anxious than one might have supposed. In the encampment, protected by natural obstacles and further fortified by the warriors, they believed that they would be safe— all the more so because the Carabao-Men had never yet risked a direct assault, and the reputation of the baas gave them great confidence.

They raised no objection; the chief of the Amdavas limited himself to saying: "We have put our lives in your hands."

"And I shall defend them as if they were my own life!" the tall Dutchman replied.

Hendrik had to remain in the camp, not because he could render any appreciable service—the least of the Amdavas surpassed him in a hundred ways, in terms of experience, cunning and skill—but because he represented, emblematically, his father, the Grafina and Karel.

"Quickly, now!" said the giant, after having chosen a dozen men to accompany him.

Under Rak's direction, the little troop advanced rapidly through the subterranean passage. It did not even take them half an hour to reach the Sepulcher-Rock.

Karel, who was waiting for them, drew his father to the eastern edge of the platform. The giant saw the Grafina, Frédéric and Corisande, about 1000 meters away.

"Good—that's the young Frenchwoman, isn't it?"

"Yes, Father. She's run away. Several men are pursuing her, others are barring the route. The Grafina's done her work—she shot one of them, who was about to capture the fugitive. The others, I think, have continued the pursuit while remaining under cover."

"And it was necessary to make a sortie. Good! And now, I suppose, there's a blockade!"

"Yes, the way back is barred. Two or three times I've glimpsed men slipping between the rocks or the thickets."

The planter's sagacious eyes examined the terrain. By means of signals that the distance rendered somewhat confused, the Grafina seemed to confirm what Karel had said.

"There are bare spaces—large enough for us to be able to cross them, under covering fire," muttered Dirk, "on condition that they don't launch an attack *en masse*. If the Grafina and the young man were alone, it would almost be comfortable but with the little *Jufvrouw*..." He turned to Karel. "How did they get out?" he asked.

"There's an exit at the base of this rock." He pointed to the opening. "You can get down that way."

The giant remained pensive for a moment, and then said: "Get back to the men as quickly as possible. They'll lose confidence if we leave them without a white chief for too long. They know full well that Hendrik is a stranger to life in the wilderness. Rak will guide you. Go on, Son!"

Karel did not hesitate to obey. Dirk resumed studying the location and the situation. After some time, he decided that the best route was to the north-east. There was no vegetation there, few rocks and no excavations. An entirely bare passage, 30 meters wide, led to the Sepulcher-Rock. Under the cover of Dirk's and the Grafina's rifles, an assault by a dozen men would not be very redoubtable. Once the first zone was crossed, they would soon arrive at the shelter.

What if the Carabao-Men attacked *en masse*, though? Would they dare?—or, rather, for their bravery was not in doubt, would they want to? Fear of death did not stop them, but an ancestral wisdom commanded them not to perish needlessly.

Deep down, the giant could not believe, at present, in a mass attack. Given what he had seen before leaving the encampment, he concluded that the battle would take place out there.

It was necessary to decide. Dirk tried to make the Grafina understand, by repeated signs, which route he was advising them to take. His signals were more easily understood because Louise de Gavres had identified the favorable ground for herself. She slowly got under way, while the planter said to the trail-beater: "Will you find out, Rak, whether my men can get down there?"

Rak only took two minutes to complete his mission. "The Amdavas can get down easily," he said. "It's less difficult than climbing a tree or a bamboo."

"Let's go down then," said Dirk.

Having given the men the order to follow him, he began the descent. All of them, including the Sumatran servants, imitated him without any great difficulty. Only Rak remained on the platform, in order to keep watch on the enemy from a distance.

When Dirk emerged from the Rock, the Grafina, Frédéric and Corisande had crossed the dry stream-bed and advanced by a further 200 meters. Louise was in no hurry, keeping a careful lookout and ready to fire.

"Are you strong enough to run?" she asked Corisande.

"I'm not tired out," the young woman replied. "I think I can run as far as the rock."

"It probably won't be necessary—but look over there, at that cluster of banyans and the low rocks. The passage will become narrower. There, it will doubtless be necessary to accelerate our pace. You'll help your sister, Monsieur de Rouveyres? I've seen her run as fast as most of the Carabao-Men. With your help, she will be able to go even faster."

Dirk and his men were now distributed at the base of the Sepulcher-Rock. That disposition had the advantage of showing the enemy a troop of men ready to fight, without the risk of losing contact with an impregnable refuge. The planter was counting on the prudence of the Carabao-Men to avoid a costly encounter, which would appear to them to be unnecessary if their chiefs were really preparing to prevent the return of the expedition.

Like the Grafina, he had identified the sole place where a surprise attack seemed most likely: the distance between the cluster of banyans and the rocky mass was quite short, less than 100 meters.

"It would be better," the Grafina said, "if you went 20 paces ahead of me. I can watch over you much better. Be ready to run."

There was no alarm; the passage was crossed in two minutes; henceforth, a large open space extended between the fugitives and the Sepulcher-Rock.

"We're probably safe," said the Grafina, who had caught up with Frédéric and Corisande. Further on, she added: "Now, even if we were disarmed, they couldn't overtake us before we arrive at the refuge. What's more, they'd be under our fire long enough to sustain serious losses."

The Grafina and her companions went forward rapidly. Louise de Gavres remained on her guard, however, a few paces behind the young couple, ready to fire.

They were no more than 100 meters from the Sepulcher-Rock when the ground trembled beneath the feet of Corisande and Frédéric. The young man leapt backwards, but Corisande stumbled. He tried to grab hold of her, but his hand only encountered empty air. The young woman sank downwards, and there was soon nothing to be seen but her head.

She was struggling. Frédéric hurled himself forwards to help her, and as he reached down, two powerful hands seized him by the wrists and dragged him forward.

When the Grafina reached the edge of the excavation that had been so strangely hollowed out in the ground, she saw the brother and sister disappearing together.

It would have been madness for her to follow them on her own. She hesitated for a split second, and then called out to the planter.

He had not waited for the summons. He ran forward with half a dozen Amdavas. In a moment, he had joined the Grafina.

It was one of those occasions when it is necessary to make an instantaneous choice, perhaps between life and death. Dirk and Louise looked at one another for two seconds. Their choice was made. Without further hesitation, they leapt into the hole in the ground—and the Amdavas followed them, also without any hesitation.

They found themselves in the center of a sort of natural cave, limited by near-regular walls. Light of variable brightness penetrated everywhere. In the darkest corner, they were able to make out Frédéric and several men; in the other, Corisande with only one man, who was holding her, semi-conscious, in his arms.

At the rear, they glimpsed a kind of corridor from which the men must have come. A collapse, which had occurred at the same time as the one that had buried Corisande, had blocked the passage. Dull blows and scraping sounds could be heard, which revealed the presence of individuals attempting to re-open the exit.

"Let's hurry, *Jufvrouw*," said the giant, maintaining an absolute calm. He pointed to the corridor. "We must beat them to it."

Two shots rang out and two Carabao-Men fell—but it became dangerous to fire at the others. Hourv, the Red Eagle, whose stature would have equaled Dirk's had he not had shorter legs and a narrower neck, was holding Corisande vertically against his torso. The others, five in number, retreated in the corner, maintaining Frédéric in front of them. That maneuver left no alternative but hand-to-hand combat.

"I'll take this one!" said Dirk, pointing at the Red Eagle.

"Right!" said Louise de Gavres, and, turning to the Men of the Forest, added: "Will you follow me?"

"The Amdavas are always ready for battle!" their leader replied, proudly.

Then, weapons at the ready, she advanced one step at a time, fearful of acting too abruptly, for Frédéric's sake.

Already, Dirk, armed with a kris made for his own giant hand—a kris with a heavy blade, but sharp—had arrived very close to Hourv.

The Carabao-Man's eyes gleamed in the half-light. His partly-open lips allowed a glimpse of enormous teeth. He was reluctant to let go of Corisande; he made a gesture as if to strike her with his axe; then, the love that he had conceived for her—for it was, in a physical sense, an ardent love—caused him to prefer a duel from which he believed he would emerge victorious. The most robust warriors yielded to his grip, no one wielded the axe or assegai more skillfully.

Having deposited the young woman on the ground, he hurled himself at the planter, who took several steps backwards in order to put a sufficient distance between Corisande and the combatants.

The Red Eagle's axe whirled and came down; it met empty space. Dirk riposted with a straight thrust, but his weapon only scratched the shoulder of his adversary, who had side-stepped.

A few passes followed without result; the two colossi, as agile as big cats, avoided the thrusts with a leap or a contortion. Eventually, a blow of the axe and a thrust of the kris having missed their marks, the combatants found themselves very close to one another. The Red Eagle crouched down; Dirk swayed to his right. The prospect of hand-to-hand combat tempted the Red Eagle, and he suddenly threw his arms around Dirk's body.

They had dropped their weapons. They fought like wild animals in the depths of the forest, two human giants, either of whom could have felled a buffalo. Their masses, if not their heights, were equal. The Eagle's torso was thicker, his bones more solid, his legs strongly reminiscent of stone columns; taller in stature, though, with arms as powerful as those of the great apes, Dirk was more flexible.

The two men tensed their admirable muscles frantically. Little by little, Dirk secured his grip; he mastered the force that had never been mastered; he lifted Hourv as Hercules had lifted Antaeus, and threw him down on the ground. The earth gave no new strength to the savage warrior, as it had to the fabulous monster; Hourv struggled in vain beneath the weight of the Dutchman; his throat, seized by an invincible hand, could no longer draw breath. He tried to bite and to lash out, but he was already falling into the darkness of unconsciousness...

Then Dirk seized Corisande and, having deposited her at the entrance to the grotto, rejoined Louise de Gavres.

It was just at that moment when Frédéric, hammering the face of the man who held him with his fists, succeeded in getting free. Louise, racing forward to help him, completed his deliverance. He leapt forward, grazed by the point of a spear, and found himself among his rescuers.

The Grafina and the giant had their rifles shouldered now. The Amdavas were ready to do battle.

The issue was not in doubt; before they could defend themselves, the Carabao-Men, squeezed into a corner from which they had to emerge one by one, would have succumbed to the rifle-bullets...

Seeing the most powerful of them immobile on the ground, the sentiment of a sovereign fatality overwhelmed their primitive souls. They felt that they had been condemned to death, and that any movement would only hasten the supreme moment.

The one who was bound to die first uttered a few troubled words and lowered his head resignedly.

"Let them live!" Dirk murmured. "It's impossible for me to kill defenseless men."

"Me too," said Louise. "Let's show them mercy then, although it might be a great imprudence."

The rifles were lowered. The stupefied Carabao-Men saw their enemies beat a retreat.

A few minutes later, the obstacle that had stopped the main body of the Carabao-Men crumbled. A flood of warriors surged into the cavern.

The Grafina and her companions were now too close to the Sepulcher-Rock to be overtaken.

Meanwhile, the Red Eagle began to come round. He looked at the men who were swarming around him, and murmured, with a profound sigh: "The Ancestors have abandoned us!"

XV. The Attack

It was the following day, at daybreak. The night fires were still reddening; the Grafina and Dirk were keeping watch on the places where the Men of the Marsh were hiding, on the distant plain. They had left the Sepulcher-Rock after having made the entrance almost impregnable, and had done the same with the exit that overlooked the encampment.

Not that it was necessary to fear a direct attack; the Carabao-Men had formed an idea of firearms that went beyond the redoubtable reality. Having never seen the Grafina and Dirk fire in vain, they attributed to them an almost unlimited power of destruction, in a very short time. The chiefs had resolved that there would be no combat except hand-to-hand. For that, it was necessary that the whites and their auxiliaries should initiate combats in which the Carabao-Men, remaining invisible, might have recourse to assegais, daggers and clubs.

That was what not only Dirk and the Grafina, but all the men of the expedition, had deduced. They were expecting, before they could make the return journey, a savage mêlée, in which the victory of the Carabao-Men would bring death for everyone...

With her telescope, Louise tried to obtain a glimpse of the enemy's labors. She had looked down several times from the height of one of the rocks next to which her men, Dirk's and the Amdavas were camped. "There's no doubt about it!" she said, thoughtfully. "They're linking their positions by means of trenches, which will permit them to concentrate their forces sheltered from gunfire, as we try to pass through. If we can get through their lines very quickly..."

"It's not possible to do it very quickly—we'll encounter obstacles everywhere."

At that moment, Frédéric, who had just come back from his turn to inspect the enemy positions from up above, was having their words translated. "I think it's possible to maneuver round them!" he said.

Interested, the Grafina fixed her eyes of shadow and force upon him. She communicated the young man's words to the planter, adding: "Our guest fought in the war."

Meanwhile, Frédéric continued: "The Carabao-Men's positions are much closer to us at the extremities than in the center, as necessitated by the terrain. The whole forms a kind of curved line, similar in shape to a line going from the middle of an egg-shell toward the point and coming back to the middle." So saying, the young man traced the line in the soil with a basalt pebble. "Very well! We have to feign an all-out attack on the right flank, preferably making use of the most agile of our men. I don't suppose the Carabao-Men are very subtle strategists. Their cunning is not the same kind as military cunning. If the fake attack is launched convincingly enough, especially if it's accompanied by Monsieur de Ridder, the Carabao-Men will accumulate the bulk of their forces there. It's merely a matter of calculating the moment when it's necessary to maneuver in the opposite direction—which is to say, to move the entire mass rapidly toward the left flank, from which the enemy will have withdrawn men...and where, in any case, very few defenders will remain.

"I have no need to point out that, in making that maneuver, we shall have a double advantage. Firstly, the distance to be covered between the two extremities is considerably less for us, who are inside the curved line and who can move in a straight line, than it will be for the Carabao-Men, who—if they are not to expose themselves to our fire, which they fear more than anything—will have to follow us under cover. Secondly, our men can run much more quickly than our adversaries. In brief, the left flank will be overrun before the arrival of any significant reinforcements, and the real battle, if there is a battle, will take place in the open. Your infallible rifles, aided by the fire of marksmen who are doubtless less skillful, but not negligible, and by the arrows of the Amdavas, who are excellent archers, will then give you a great advantage..."

In order to facilitate understanding, Frédéric was drawing diagrams in the soil, but from the first words, well before the end of the demonstration, the Grafina and Dirk had understood everything.

"That's very good, Monsieur," said Louise de Gavres. "Old Europe might still have something to teach its distant children."

She smiled. Frédéric, moved, no longer saw anything but the woman's charm.

"*Wel! Zeer wel!*"[33] exclaimed the planter, extending his muscular hand to the young man.

"Perhaps also," the latter continued, "it would be good to have two small wooden platforms, which would permit you to shoot over the enemy barricades. There are a few trees here." He turned to Dirk. "Besides, if they see you standing on one of those platforms, a little behind the attacking forces, they'll be

---

[33] Rosny inserts a footnote translating the Dutchman's words as "Good! Very Good!"

288

all the more convinced that you've resolved to force the blockade on the right."

"That's true too!" said Louise. "My men will be able to construct these platforms very quickly. I think a height of two or three meters should be sufficient. Thank you, Monsieur—there's a good chance your idea will save us."

"It's possible, though, that the Carabao-Men won't be taken in by the stratagem, either by virtue of suspicion or intuition."

"Yes," said the Grafina, with a laugh that rendered her strangely seductive, "but we'll be able to combine our primitive ruses with your plan."

Dirk, the Grafina and Karel summoned the Amdavas chief and the Sumatrans' leader and did not hide from them either the danger—which these men, accustomed to the adventurous life, clearly discerned for themselves—or the plan of attack, with regard to which they asked for the advice of their experience. They saw its advantages right away, and also the difficulties, proposing a few adjustments that were adopted. After a further examination of the terrain occupied by the Carabao-Men, the Sumatrans and the Amdavas set to work.

In addition to the two platforms, they constructed a small bridge of thick branches and a sort of collective shield that would permit the Sumatrans to protect themselves from assegais before engaging in hand-to-hand combat. The Amdavas knew as well as the Roman legionaries of old, and perhaps more flexibly, how to form a *testudo* with their shields.

The preparations took an entire day.

"The morale of the men seems good," said the Grafina, "except for three or four of my servants, whom we'll keep in the rear..."

"Among mine, only one is doubtful," Dirk remarked. "We'll put him in the rearguard too. As for the Amdavas..."

"I'll answer for their bravery," Karel interjected. "They're an elite race. You won't find braver warriors anywhere. If they were more numerous, they'd be the masters of the island."

"We'll attack tomorrow morning, then," concluded the big Dutchman.

The fires had just been lit. They projected their flickering light over the plain and the rocks, punctuated by shadows and phantasmal figures. Frédéric and Corisande perceived the threat of an as-yet-omnipotent nature. There were no clouds. Beyond the visible stars, they sensed other stars, their multitude suggested by the pale Milky Way. In the distance, giant frogs were croaking; a flight of bats as large as eagles emerged periodically from the shadows; predators fluttering on lacy wings, the insatiable army of insects sought its prey.

"Will there ever come a day when men cease to be wild beasts to other men?" murmured Frédéric, seduced by the beauty of the night.

He was sitting very close to Corisande. The young woman was daydreaming miserably. She felt forever profaned, and life left her no other hope than to devote herself to her brother. Someone, however, was watching her from the depths of the shadow: Karel, subject to the seduction of that pale face and those large, desolate eyes.

"I don't think that there'll ever be an end to war between men," said the Grafina, who had heard what Frédéric said. "All one can hope for are longer truces. Nature doesn't want peace."

"But men fight against nature."

"They're also part of nature! They live within it according to the mysterious law that is within them without them knowing it. They have never known what impulse it is that carries them through the centuries, and never will know, any more than a tiger knows its destiny…or those nocturnal beasts know theirs. We have never known, and never shall know, the destination of our voyage through time."

"Look how man has mastered the beasts, though…how he is taking possession of the virgin forests…how he makes the Sun and the rain on the savannah work for him."

"What's that compared to what the plants do! They're prisoners…they cannot escape from the place where they have put down roots, but do they not devour the rock, sand and clay regardless? Those virgin forests and savannahs of which you speak, what conquerors they are of that which is not alive…or seems not to be alive! And remember that, without plants, man himself would be nothing…nothing! On the day when human-kind must die, a few shocks will be sufficient. The old Earth has only to tremble momentarily and entire cities will perish. No, friend from France, man is not much more than the insects…perhaps less—for I think that the insects will survive us!"

She spoke dreamily, suddenly very feminine—and so charming that Frédéric felt a thrill of admiration. *A strange creature!* he said to himself. *No man is more redoubtable, and, in truth, no woman more seductive!*

"The Southern Cross is marking 10 p.m.," said the planter. "Let's go to sleep. Tomorrow, we'll have need of all our strength and all our skill."

"Sleep," Frédéric remarked, "is even more necessary for maintaining skill than for maintaining strength."

"Very true," agreed Louise. "Insomnia disturbs precision of movement more than anything else."

Frédéric was left alone with Corisande. "What admirable souls!" the young woman said. "No one seems to give a single thought to the fact that it's two strangers from the other side of the world for whom so many are risking their lives."

"The war showed me the extraordinary variety of our peers," Frédéric said. "If no beast can match the ferocity of millions of humans, what gentleness there is on others, what generosity, what magnificent abnegation! Nevertheless, few can compare, in the sum of their qualities, with that giant and that heroic young woman."

"I misunderstood her," murmured Corisande. "But now…" Her eyes were full of tears as she added: "Alas, what does the opinion of a poor degraded creature matter?"

"No, no!" replied Frédéric, with contained vehemence. "No, you're not degraded. No, you're not fallen from grace. In my eyes, and, I'm sure, the eyes of these brave people, you're as pure and as innocent as when we arrived on this island. It's necessary to forget, my beloved sister, as one forgets a disease after the cure…"

She shook her gleaming head; an immeasurable sadness ennobled her delicate features again; her eyes had a pathetic beauty.

The camp awoke at an early hour. The Grafina, Dirk and Karel gave their orders. Servants began by transporting the platforms to within 200 meters of the enemy positions, while others picked up the wooden bridge.

The nocturnal mist fragmented, then began to melt away. At 8 a.m., the terrain was clear; only a few slight wisps of vapor drifted above the pools and occasional clumps of trees. On the battlefield, the visibility was perfect.

"Is everything ready?" Dirk asked.

"Everything," replied Karel, the Amdavas chief and the Sumatrans' leader.

"Go!"

The bulk of the expedition headed toward the right at a modest pace, and stopped beside the platform where the Grafina was to take up a position. About a third of the men carried the bridge to the rectangular ditch observed the previous day; they stopped near the platform designed for Dirk, on which he did not hesitate to establish himself.

During the maneuver, accomplished without haste, Rak, nestling in a fissure in the flank of a rock, surveyed the enemy positions. At first, the Men of the Marsh remained invisible, observing their adversaries' singular operations, but as the Amdavas and the Sumatrans came closer, *en masse*, to the section of their line on the extreme right, the Carabao-Men removed men from the positions in the center and on the left.

The Amdavas continued to advance, with increasing slowness. When they were almost within assegai-range, they tightened their formation again. Their overlapping shields formed a wall in front of the first rank and were raised up horizontally in the following lines, so effectively that the projectiles would encounter a solid carapace in every direction.

At the same time, the Sumatrans set up their collective shield. Then, the warriors gave voice to resounding clamors, which convinced the adversaries, persuaded that the attack was imminent, to transfer even more men from the center and the left flank.

The Amdavas, were now within range and the Carabao-Men launched the first assegais, none of which pierced the carapace. The rifles held by the Grafina and the giant roared and, once again, showed themselves to be infallible.

Rak stood up on his rock and extended his arms. That was the signal. Instantaneously, the Amdavas and the Sumatrans beat a retreat and starting running toward the left.

This time, the Carabao-Men understood the mysterious maneuver; a long cry of fury rose up behind their entrenchments. They diced to flood back toward the left.

In addition to the fact that their agility was inferior to that of their antagonists, and that they were obliged to follow a rather accentuated curve, while keeping under cover to avoid the fire of the redoubtable carbines, they had no certainty as to the place where the attack would take place. Although it seemed obvious to them that it would be directed against the extreme left, the assailants had a considerable lead, which was increasing by the minute—to the extent that the Amdavas and the Sumatrans would reach the objective when the Men of the Marsh had scarcely passed the half-way point.

Their entrenchments were cursory: a few erratic blocks of stone, leaving spaces between them, plugged by branches and the trunks of young trees, were all that they had contrived. The defenders numbered scarcely more than a dozen.

They had to move quickly. The Grafina and Dirk gave the signal for the attack, which Karel transmitted to the Amdavas, who chose their own breaches and hurled themselves forward, protected by their shields. The defenders were

293

shoved side, knocked down, trampled or killed. In less than three minutes, the line was crossed. The attack had not been costly: three men wounded, only one dead.

The open plain was ahead; the Carabao-Men would either have to abandon the combat or brave the bullets, the arrows and the javelins.

The moment was critical. Thirty Carabao-Men—an advance-guard, composed almost entirely of young men—risked an attack in the open. The rifles wielded by Dirk, the Grafina, Karel, the Sumatrans and those Amdavas equipped with firearms stopped that attempt dead; half of the aggressors lay on the ground.

A formidable roar, which was an order, caused the survivors to retreat and, in a flash, become invisible.

"If they don't attack now," said Louise, "they won't attack again. We shan't stop!" She made sure that Corisande was safe, and shook Frédéric's hand, saying: "Your stratagem has saved us—thank you!"

Under that gaze of velvet and flame, he was thrilled to the core of his being.

The expedition continued on its way. The Carabao-Men remained hidden.

"Let's go! The road is definitely clear!" said the giant. "And I agree with you, *Jufvrouw*, that they'll abandon the attack. They must have concluded, rationally, that it would be too costly."

Three Amdavas and two Sumatrans were dead; there were half a dozen wounded. The Amdavas did not want to abandon the corpses any more than the wounded; they rapidly improvised primitive stretchers with branches taken from the defenses, and the expedition continued its route until the middle of the day, without catching sight of the enemy once.

"They're watching us, though," said the Grafina, while the Amdavas built a large pyre for their dead. That was their custom when they could not provide warriors with a sepulcher—a custom handed down from very ancient times.

When the pyre was ready, a sort of funeral chant went up, monotonous, somber and plaintive:

"Sons of the forest,

"Amdavas with hearts of iron

"Disdainful of the enemy and death,

"Your brothers have avenged you.

"You shall meet the ancestors,

"Who will give you valiant souls

"In forests greater than all the forests,

"On the banks of rivers greater than all the rivers...

"O Amdavas with hearts of iron

"Who have disdained the enemy and death."

The warriors placed the dead men on the pyre, piously; the chief set it alight with the aid of ancestral flints. The flames sprang up while the Amdavas uttered funereal cries, and Frédéric thought: *The Trojans, tamers of horses, the keen-eyed Achaeans, and the prehistoric Gauls did likewise.*

XVI. Through the Waters and the Woods

There were difficult days. Nevertheless, the travelers reached the river without having seen the Carabao-Men again. The rafts and canoes were still there, although they could only reckon on making use of them for two or three days; afterwards, the current would become too strong.

"I think we're now safe from surprise attacks," said Dirk, when the evening fires were lit beneath the stars.

The Amdavas and Sumatrans set about joyfully roasting meat.

"They've already forgotten everything!" said Frédéric.

"No," said Louise. "They remember; they have infallible memories—but the past leaves them with no regrets and causes them no emotion, except when they act in vengeance. Here, there's nothing to avenge: the death of each Amdava has been paid for by that of several enemies. Therefore, all is well!"

She spoke in a voice as charming as the sound of waves on crystal, with her large eyes of black fire fixed on Frédéric, and he listened tremulously.

Plunged into an immeasurable sadness, Corisande looked at them. As they drew from the perils and she ceased to tremble on Frédéric's behalf, she felt increasingly debased. Her adventure was like a corruption within her. She was horrified by her own flesh, deeming herself forever beyond the bounds of humankind, a moral leper who had no right to any of the joys reserved for other individuals. It was in vain that Frédéric, seeing her despair, said to her: "You're not being reasonable, Corisande! What sin have you committed? What honest man would dare to offer you a reproach? You must—you *must*—forget, hope, live your youth!"

She shook her head, trying to smile, but her memory retraced the irreparable days.

Meanwhile, a man fervently contemplated her beautiful sad eyes and her pale and charming cheeks. From the first time he had seen her, Karel, moved by that foreign grace, so different from the beauty of Dutch creoles, ceded to the inconceivable laws of preference. She brought him that renewal which allows certain beings to change all the aspects of our lives. In her presence, living beings and objects were subject to a metamorphosis. Neither the fire, nor the grass, nor the constellated night, nor the increasing breeze on the river was the same, because the young woman was sitting there, mysterious. Her every gesture made the young Dutchman shiver. He waited avidly for some movement of her eyelids, some flexion of her slender neck, and whenever his gaze met Corisande's afflicted gaze he was overwhelmed by a need to devote himself to her and to suffer for her.

"With God's grace," said the planter, "we have succeeded in our task; I would never have been able to console myself if we had failed."

"It was a close run thing!" said the Grafina.

I love her, Frédéric thought, anxiously, *but she would never want me. I must seem so inferior to that admirable giant and young Karel, a son of the forests and savannahs.*

The Grafina continued: "Without Monsieur de Rouveyres' stratagem, I don't know how we would have escaped..."

Frédéric was overwhelmed by a great tenderness.

The days went by. At first, the expedition went upriver, but as the banks came closer together the flow became more rapid. It was necessary to abandon the canoes and the raft. Then for long days, the forest opposed a stubborn resistance to the passage of humans. Plants and animals were in league against them—not the tigers, which scarcely counted for anything in view of the rifles, or even the arrows, nor the great trees, but the innumerable host of insects, the bushes armed with thorns, the marshy ground...

The insects, indefatigable, multitudinous, inevitable and invincible, were the true masters of the jungle. They surged over the ground, the plants and the waters, crawling, leaping or flying, troubling sleep, poisoning wakefulness, transforming halts into torments and marches into torture.

The thorny bushes and the sly lianas pierce you with hundreds of darts or strangle you like reptiles; the marshy ground gives way under foot, covering you with a stagnant and fetid mud in which disgusting creatures swarm...

The Amdavas, the Sumatrans, the giant, the Grafina and Karel cleared a passage with hatchets or knives, instinctively finding the least obstructed paths. Sometimes, the tropical forest thinned out; then the march became comfortable, and life would have been tolerable without the inexhaustible multitude of the true kings of the jungle, who will probably see the end of man.

Finally, they reached less awkward terrain. The plain was dominant, the forests became practicable. They reached the region where the catastrophe had occurred: the tumultuous river that had carried away the Carabao-Men's raft, the circle of rocks where the caravan had camped, and, on the other bank, the Red Forest, full of wild beasts.

Frédéric relived the fatal hours: the rapid dusk, the siamangs howling in the branches, the fearful beasts whose least imprudence would deliver them to the teeth of carnivores, the crocodiles sleeping on the islet, like rough tree-trunks...

"Oh, what troubles we have cost you," the young man said to Louise. "What perils you have run for us! And those poor fellows who perished..."

"It's necessary to regret nothing," she replied. "We're all accustomed to adventure. Who knows whether we might not have run as many risks staying at home, and our savage friends by remaining in their forest? Death is always ready to devour us. We have been lucky—that's all that needs to be said!"

"Evening's approaching," said Dirk, at that moment. "I propose that we camp here. Then it will be time to settle our accounts with the Amdavas."

They summoned the leaders, and Karel spoke to them.

"Chief of the Amdavas, your warriors have been braver than tigers; once more you have shown that your oaths are as solid as the rocks. The recompense we have promised you is inferior to your merits, and we also wish to give you a ransom for your dead."

"Do not pay us for our dead!" the chief replied, proudly. "Did we not depart for battle? Did those who died not know that they were risking their lives? They did not hesitate!"

"We know your pride, Amdavas. It is not payment that we are offering you; it is a gift from friends, and it would hurt us if you refused it."

"A gift from a friend warms the heart," said the chief. "We can accept."

"We promised you a rifle for each warrior, 100 cartridges and 25 guilder. In addition, we offer each of you a revolver with 100 bullets and 50 guilder. It will take us a fortnight to fulfill our promises."

The leaders' eyes sparkled with joy. "The tall whites are generous," said the chief. "The Amdavas will come whenever they are called, always ready for battle!"

"They're men, in spite of their short stature," said the planter, when they had gone. "Without them, we wouldn't have been able to do anything."

"I know what I owe them," said Frédéric, "and I won't forget—and you certainly won't oppose my repaying that small debt."

"It's us who must do that," said the Grafina. "We are responsible for our guests—but it will be done, Monsieur, as you desire."

She smiled; he admired her red lips and large eyes of black fire passionately.

The siamangs were howling frightfully on the other bank; furtive beasts were passing by; the diurnal insects were going to sleep, while their nocturnal kin were beginning to hum, and the twilight faded rapidly. As on the evening before the embarkation, Karel contemplated the pale and charming face of Corisande, while the giant fruit-bats and the moths fluttered around the red fires...

Epilogue

"Another season gone already," Frédéric murmured, as the morning Sun rose above the summits.

Dirk's domain, distributed along the large valley as far as the eye could see, extended to the foothills of the mountains. The young man examined the papers, in which human chimeras mingled with phantasmagorical realities. Beneath the formulas as dry as algebraic theorems, they assured the Rouveyres a specious territory and mineral deposits for which an agreement with the Anglo-Dutch Mining Company had just been concluded.

"A strange power!" muttered Frédéric. "Almost imponderable...but which confers as much wealth upon us as a duchy or an earldom conferred on a powerful Medieval lord. What have we done to merit that enormous privilege? The organization that assures us of it rules over us like the weather. It's necessary, according to circumstance, to resign oneself to misery or a fortune—two faces of the same fatality!"

As he completed this soliloquy, he saw Corisande approaching. She wore the tragic expression that he had seen on her face for months. Horror persisted within her like a monstrous beast.

"My dear sister," Frédéric said to her, "you don't have the right to be unhappy any longer."

"What can I do about it? If I were ill, would you reproach me for my sickness?"

"Yes, if you were to refuse the cure, and that's what you're doing. I've suffered as much as you from...the adventure—but in the end, the memory of it must be banished."

"Am I not to be reckoned dishonored?"

"No one here believes that! Certainly not the master, nor Karel, nor Hendrik...nor the Grafina either. They all feel sorry for you, yes, but for them, none of *that* matters any more. They hold you in full esteem!" After a pause he continued, almost timidly: "You've told me, Corisande, that life in this country wouldn't displease you any more than life back home. I need to be sure of that."

"You can be."

"Have you really thought about it?"

"So much that it's futile to think about it any more."

"I'm afraid of being selfish—for I, personally, love this country."

"Then I shall love it too, Frédéric. What does it matter to me? The place where you live will be the one I prefer."

"All the same, Corisande..."

"That's the way it is," she said, with a gesture of impatience. "Besides, there's nowhere I'd be better off than among these brave folk."

She sat down, and looked sadly at the conclave of mountains.

Two buffaloes were dragging an antique cart with solid wheels, laden with sugar cane. Frédéric loved the composure of those beasts, which could stand up to tigers and which men had not completely tamed. He admired their formidable hindquarters, and their muscles, almost as powerful as those of a rhinoceros.

Nature has certainly gone to as much trouble to produce them as the paltry Malay who is leading them! he thought. *They're certainly more handsome than he is—nevertheless, that frail animal is leading them!*

A horseman appeared, mounted on a bad-tempered animal, still untamed, but which he mastered nevertheless. The beast was even more handsome than the buffaloes, with a noble conformation and wild eyes, but the man, solidly planted, lithe and audacious, with the sure gestures of a conqueror, also had his beauty.

"Look," said Frédéric. "Look, Corisande..."

Corisande looked, indifferently, at Karel de Ridder, whose horse, after an attempt at rebellion, yielded to its master.

"Is it possible that you can't see anything, Corisande? If you could love that man—and I believe that he belongs to the finest human race—you would be saved...saved from your intimate enemy: yourself."

"I don't understand. Why would I be saved if I loved Karel?"

"Blind woman! By virtue of retreating into yourself, you've lost all your feminine intuition! Otherwise, you'd have seen that that man loves you as few men know how to love, with an admirable discretion and a constancy that, I feel certain, will never waver. You haven't even noticed that he's learned our language in three months...and that he speaks it as well now as his brother Hendrik."

Corisande listened, tremulously. She was a traveler lost in the darkness of a carnivorous forest, who glimpses the glimmer of dawn. Obscure hopes rose up in migratory swarms.

"Love me!" she whispered. "It's possible, then, for someone to love me?"

"Is it possible! For Karel, as for me, you have never ceased to be the purest of women, and I'm certain that your very unhappiness is a reason for him to respect you more. I've observed him, and observed him closely, while you've been living and suffering entirely within yourself. He's a soul without pettiness..."

She looked avidly at the bold rider; the impetuous beast, whose fury he was dominating, carried him away. Already, he was transfigured in the eyes of the young woman—already, because reaction has to be as rapid as the suffering has been violent. Corisande mingled images of a new life with the image of the man...

"Are you sure?" she murmured. "Are you sure you're not mistaken?"

"I'm perfectly sure. He has admitted it to me!"

She raised her eyes toward her brother, and on that hollow face, still bearing the full imprint of her long suffering, the first smile appeared.

She will get better, Frédéric said to himself. And he thought about his own adventure.

The Grafina, who had arrived that evening, was to spend a week with Dirk. She had come on horseback, only accompanied by Rak and her favorite dogs.

Frédéric did not see her until the evening meal, by the light of electric lamps powered by the nearby torrent. She had changed out of her riding costume and seemed comparable to luxuriously beautiful young women carried off by the conquistadors or the lords of the Sierra. Frédéric scarcely dared to look at her, and when she took him by the arm after the meal, he was gripped by a great anxiety.

"Aren't you weary yet of living on our island?" she said to him, in a soft contralto voice.

"I'll never be weary of it."

"Ah! You think so? It's true that you have an admirable host. Would you like to take a short walk with me in the clear night? I have more than one thing to ask you."

As they went out, she unsheathed her carbine. "A tiger has been seen prowling around Eagle Rock."

He armed himself too.

"Karel tells me," she said, "that you're on your way to becoming a great marksman."

"I wouldn't miss a horse at ten paces!" he replied, laughing.

A sparkling Moon was making its way through the constellations. Beyond the pastures and the plantations, the mountains displayed their deserted slopes in the nocturnal glow, red and pitted, eroded by the weather: the skeletal peaks, the fissures of its valleys, the gulfs through which torrents ran, the forests and pastures suspended on the ruinous slopes, the caverns and the crenellations, the colossal pillars, the extinct craters ready to resume their devastating life, the pyramids the needles, the cathedral spires, the plateaus, the glaciers and the moraines—a splendid and funereal world, where plants battled hectically, obstinate in the creation of that life which makes

303

foliage and flowers of the mineral, and flesh of the flowers and foliage...

Louise de Gavres and Frédéric drew away into the solitude, accompanied by the dog Vos. She questioned him and gave him advice, and when they went into the wilderness, she asked: "You know, don't you, that Karel is in love with Mademoiselle de Rouveyres?"

"Yes," he replied, "and she knows it, since this morning. And I think...I believe that she will be healed."

A forest extended before them, but in the foreground, the trees were sparse; the axe had made considerable inroads, with the result that the strollers found themselves in a sort of clearing, where the waters of a stream raised their naiad voices.

"Yes," he went on, in a tremulous voice, "I believe she'll be healed. Hope has entered into her, and the hope will create love."

"All is well!" said the Grafina.

"All is well," he sighed. "I've received more than I deserve!"

"There is no merit in nature," she murmured, "and there's little enough among men. Everything is given to us. Have we constructed our bodies and fashioned our minds? Our privileges and disgraces are already commenced with them!"

The dog Vos growled dully and raised his intelligent head toward his mistress.

"A powerful beast, isn't it, Vos?" she said, passing her hand over his tawny head. "If not, you would have leapt forward. Is it the tiger?"

The growling resumed, and extended, the dog's eyes staring into the Grafina's.

"It's the tiger!" She seized her carbine, immediately imitated by Frédéric. "I fear," she said, "that I haven't acted wisely in making you run this risk."

Frédéric's heart was beating with excitement, not with dread. "Ah!" he whispered. "If there's a risk, how glad I am to be running it with you."

She turned her gaze of shadow and fire toward him, keenly. "Is that true?"

"How true it is! All my being…"

A monstrous head had just appeared among the ferns, in which two phosphorus fires gleamed: the ancient ruler of the jungle!

Involuntarily, Frédéric stopped speaking. The tiger was looking at him with the gaze that it directed at prey.

"Had we not received all the gifts of the spirit," said Louise, "at this moment, without our rifles, we would be poor creatures, less than wild boars…how handsome it is!"

The tiger had taken three steps forward; now, already braced to pounce, it was watching the vertical silhouettes.

"I'd like to spare it!" Louise went on. "That would, however, cost the forest dear, and might perhaps cost our friends dear. Count up the deer, boar, tapirs, buffaloes and siamangs it must kill in a year! Count up the beautiful lives that must end to feed its own…all the creatures it devours! But it's so beautiful! If it goes away, I'll spare it."

In the silvery moonlight, the huge orange body striped with black, the massive paws, the granite head with green beacons and the dagger-like canines appeared even more magnificent than terrible.

You would have thought that it was hesitating. Perhaps it was surprised to see that these pale creatures, whose odor was reminiscent of siamangs, were not attempting to flee—but it had seen hypnotized prey more than once, and it was only fearful of some trick…not a trick of combat, but a trick of flight.

Suddenly, it rose up with a terrible bound, of some 30 feet. With a second bound, it would fall on Frédéric or Louise.

Both rifles barked twice. With a harsh cry, the sovereign beast twisted in the air and fell, almost at the feet of the young couple.

The Grafina examined it silently with the eye of a huntress.

"Your bullets hit the target!" she said. "That's very good!" Her own had drilled into the tiger's skull. "It knew nothing but force," she went on, sadly.

She shook her head, her black eyes fixing once again on Frédéric's eyes. In a soft voice, she said: "Tell me what you haven't dared to tell me."

There was no longer anything there but a beautiful human woman. Trembling, Frédéric murmured the ancient word by which we magnify the instinct that will vanquish death, until the day when all life on Earth is extinct.

Afterword

Little comment needs to be added here with regard to "Mary's Garden," although the calculatedly oblique assertion that "there are no other worlds" and the corollary remark that "all this is in contact" invite some expansion.

In Camille Flammarion's accounts of the human relationship with the stars, the souls of human beings become free after death to wander through the infinite reaches of space, no longer constrained by the limiting velocity of light, and may be reincarnated on other worlds in alien material forms, some of which belong to other "realms" than the animal and the vegetable. Rosny had no sympathy with Flammarion's Spiritualist faith, and could not believe in that sort of reincarnation, but he was attracted to the notion that the observable universe did form some kind of a whole, bound together by a "planetary physiology" operating through forces much less limited in scope and velocity than gravity and electromagnetism. If that notion, as expressed in "The Skeptical Legend" and "Mary's Garden," tends toward a vision of Unity, it was one he soon repudiated in favor of a calculated Pluralism that extrapolated the notion that "all this is in contact" in a new and unusual fashion, imagining a plenary universe comprised of many different sorts of matter, which do not normally interact with one another—and are therefore imperceptible to any conscious observers they might generate—although rare interactions, and hence perceptions, may occasionally become possible.

Accounts of such interactions are featured in "The Cataclysm" and "The Mysterious Force" (both in vol. 2), the latter featuring resultant phenomena that include a curious local "duplication" of sectors of the electromagnetic spectrum. That notion is akin to the notion of "atomic bipartition" that provides "The Givreuse Enigma" with its fundamental speculative hypothesis. One of the footnotes in the latter story points out that some such hypothesis might be used as a basis for a theory of immortality not unlike the one adopted by Spiritualists, but markedly different in its extrapolative complications by virtue of being purely materialistic. What the author did not point out is that it might also give rise to a theory of "universal reproduction," by which entire complexes of matter might undergo a kind of binary fission.

In "The Givreuse Enigma," the bipartition has to be a relatively simple and straightforward matter, in order that one person might become two in a perceptible manner, but there is no need for it to be so simple; once the hypothesis has been formed of a plenary "fourth universe" in which "emptiness" is an illusion of the senses—and Rosny had formed a version of that hypothesis long before writing "L'Enigme de Givreuse"—then the possibilities of atomic bipartition can easily be extended to the notion that such a bipartition might produce exotic matter rather than ordinary matter. If such an adjustment is made, then the "cosmic physiology" of the fourth universe may be complicated by new notions of growth and evolution. Rosny never went on to do that—although he certainly complicated the kinds of intermaterial interaction that he was prepared to envisage in "In the World of the Variants" (in vol. 2)—but there is no reason why other speculators should not.

Whether such speculations, however cleverly packaged, could ever find a place in the literary marketplace, is another matter. Rosny, at least, felt it more politic to stick to more modest projects with guaranteed reader appeal—which is what he was attempting to do, manifestly half-heartedly, in "Adventure in the Wild." I have already made some mention in the afterword to vol. 4 of the magnetic effect that its plot formula exerted on Rosny, once he had embarked on an imaginary adventure, and there is no need to add to the observations made there, but some comment on the story's ending might be appropriate, as it stands in such stark contrast to the ending of the story's obvious model, "The Boar Men" (in vol. 2). It is doubtful that Rosny had actually experienced a change of mind relative to the propriety of the earlier ending, but it ought to be noted that the ending of "The Boar Men" was atypical of his work.

Rosny was doubtless aware of the strong inclination that other male writers had to end stories of "inappropriate" love with the death of one or other of the protagonists (in contrast with love stories written by female writers, which are far more likely, in strictly statistical terms, to end "happily" in one way or another), and it was a recourse he had tended to resist. It was not simply that he had more relaxed attitudes to "propriety" than many other male writers, but that he seemed to believe that there was an innate attraction operative between people of different race or status—a notion given overt expression in "Vamireh" (in vol. 2) and extrapolated to astonishing lengths in "The Navigators of Space" (in vol. 1). Clearly this attraction can only be effective between moral near-equals, that therefore "ought not" exist with respect to such brutalized species as the Squat Men of "Hareton Ironcastle's Amazing Adventure" (in vol. 3) or the eponymous Boar Men, but the whole point of "The Boar Men" is that it might; the protagonist's decision to commit suicide is not a result of her being raped, or her being recaptured, but of her shame at having been "exalted" (i.e., having experienced orgasm) while being raped. It is not the Boar Man who horrifies her but the echo of his bestiality that he arouses in the depths of her own nature.

By the same token, the fact that Corisande, the subsidiary heroine of "Adventure in the Wild," can be considered undefiled, in spite of being raped by a Carabao Man (apparently—no such incident is explicitly described), is due to the fact that it called forth no such echo, thus becoming a mere act of violence. The situation would of course, have been complicated if she had found herself pregnant—as the Carabao Man hoped and expected—but the authorial dictatorship that masquerades as chance in worlds-within-texts spared her that. Given the improbability of Corisande's initial capture and subsequent rescue, this does not seem entirely out of place as an act of authorial generosity, but some readers may wonder what the effects might have been of the luckless abductees yielding to their instinct of miscegenation and taking on the job of beginning the evolutionary and cultural redemption of the brutal races into whose hands they had fallen. Given that "Grace" was capable of falling in love with the narrator of "The Navigators of Space," such an imaginative leap was surely not beyond the scope of Rosny's imagination—although it was certainly beyond the limits of editorial toleration pertaining to pulp fiction.

SF & FANTASY

Guy d'Armen. *Doc Ardan: The City of Gold and Lepers*
G.-J. Arnaud. *The Ice Company*
Aloysius Bertrand. *Gaspard de la Nuit*
Félix Bodin. *The Novel of the Future*
André Caroff. *The Terror of Madame Atomos*
Didier de Chousy. *Ignis*
C. I. Defontenay. *Star (Psi Cassiopeia)*
Charles Derennes. *The People of the Pole*
Harry Dickson. *The Heir of Dracula*
Sâr Dubnotal *vs. Jack the Ripper*
Alexandre Dumas. *The Return of Lord Ruthven*
J.-C. Dunyach. *The Night Orchid. The Thieves of Silence*
Henri Duvernois. *The Man Who Found Himself*
Win Scott Eckert. *Crossovers* (non-fiction; 2 vols.)
Paul Féval. *Anne of the Isles. Knightshade. Revenants. Vampire City. The Vampire Countess. The Wandering Jew's Daughter*
Paul Féval, *fils. Felifax, the Tiger-Man*
Arnould Galopin. *Doctor Omega*
V. Hugo, Foucher & Meurice. *The Hunchback of Notre-Dame*
O. Joncquel & Theo Varlet. *The Martian Epic*
Jean de La Hire. *Enter the Nyctalope. The Nyctalope on Mars. The Nyctalope vs. Lucifer*
G. Le Faure & H. de Graffigny. *The Extraordinary Adventures of a Russian Scientist Across the Solar System* (2 vols.)
Gustave Le Rouge. *The Vampires of Mars*
Jules Lermina. *Mysteryville. Panic in Paris. To-Ho and the Gold Destroyers*
Jean-Marc & Randy Lofficier. *Edgar Allan Poe on Mars. The Katrina Protocol. Pacifica. Robonocchio. Tales of the Shadowmen* (anthos.; 6 vols.) *Shadowmen* (non-fiction; 2 vols.)
Xavier Mauméjean. *The League of Heroes*
Marie Nizet. *Captain Vampire*
C. Nodier, Beraud & Toussaint-Merle. *Frankenstein*
Henri de Parville. *An Inhabitant of the Planet Mars*

Polidori, C. Nodier, E. Scribe. *Lord Ruthven the Vampire*
P.-A. Ponson du Terrail. *The Vampire and the Devil's Son*
Maurice Renard. *Doctor Lerne. A Man Among the Microbes. The Blue Peril. The Doctored Man. The Master of Light*
Albert Robida. *The Clock of the Centuries. The Adventures of Saturnin Farandoul*
J.-H. Rosny Aîné. *The Navigators of Space. The World of the Variants. The Mysterious Force. Vamireh. The Givreuse Enigma*
Brian Stableford. *The Shadow of Frankenstein. Frankenstein and the Vampire Countess. The New Faust at the Tragicomique. Sherlock Holmes & The Vampires of Eternity. The Stones of Camelot. The Wayward Muse.* (anthologist) *The Germans on Venus. News from the Moon*
Kurt Steiner. *Ortog*
Villiers de l'Isle-Adam. *The Scaffold. The Vampire Soul*
Philippe Ward. *Artahe*

MYSTERIES & THRILLERS

M. Allain & P. Souvestre. *The Daughter of Fantômas*
Anicet-Bourgeois, Lucien Dabril. *Rocambole*
A. Bisson & G. Livet. *Nick Carter vs. Fantômas*
V. Darlay & H. de Gorsse. *Lupin vs. Holmes: The Stage Play*
Paul Féval. *Gentlemen of the Night. John Devil. The Black Coats: The Companions of the Treasure. Heart of Steel. The Invisible Weapon. The Parisian Jungle. 'Salem Street*
Emile Gaboriau. *Monsieur Lecoq*
Steve Leadley. *Sherlock Holmes: The Circle of Blood*
Maurice Leblanc. *Arsène Lupin: The Blonde Phantom. The Hollow Needle. Countess Cagliostro*
Gaston Leroux. *Chéri-Bibi. The Phantom of the Opera. Rouletabille & the Mystery of the Yellow Room*
William Patrick Maynard. *The Terror of Fu Manchu*
Frank J. Morlock. *Sherlock Holmes: The Grand Horizontals*
P. de Wattyne & Y. Walter. *Sherlock Holmes vs. Fantômas*
David White. *Fantômas in America*

SCREENPLAYS

Mike Baron. *The Iron Triangle*
Emma Bull & Will Shetterly. *Nightspeeder. War for the Oaks*
Gerry Conway & Roy Thomas. *Doc Dynamo*
Steve Englehart. *Majorca*
James Hudnall. *The Devastator*
Jean-Marc & Randy Lofficier. *Royal Flush*
J.-M. & R. Lofficier & Marc Agapit. *Despair*
Andrew Paquette. *Peripheral Vision*
R. Thomas, J. Hendler & L. Sprague de Camp. *Rivers of Time*

CINEMA

Stephen R. Bissette. *Blur 1-5* (non-fiction) *Green Mountain
Cinema 1* (non-fiction)

HEXAGON COMICS

Franco Frescura & Luciano Bernasconi. *Wampus 1*
Franco Frescura & Giorgio Trevisan. *CLASH*
 Luciano Bernasconi, Jean-Marc Lofficier & Juan Roncagliolo
Berger. *Phenix 1*
Claude Legrand, Jean-Marc Lofficier & Luciano Bernasconi.
Kabur 1
Franco Oneta. *Zembla 1*
Lina Buffolente, Jean-Marc Lofficier & Jean-Jacques Dzia-
lowski. *Stangers 1: Homicron*
Danilo Grossi. *Strangers 2: Jaydee*
Claude Legrand & Luciano Bernasconi. *Strangers 3: Starlock*

ART BOOKS

Jean-Pierre Normand. *Science Fiction Illustrations*
Raven Okeefe. *Raven's L'il Critters*
Randy Lofficier & Raven OKeefe. *If Your Possum Go Daylight...*
Daniele Serra. *Illusions*